STRAIGHT
&
TRIAL RUN

Dick Francis has written over forty-one international best-sellers and is widely acclaimed as one of the world's finest thriller writers. His awards include the Crime Writers' Association's Cartier Diamond Dagger for his outstanding contribution to the crime genre, and an honorary Doctorate of Humane Letters from Tufts University of Boston. In 1996 Dick Francis was made a Mystery Writers of America Grand Master for a lifetime's achievement and in 2000 he received a CBE in the Queen's Birthday Honours list.

Dick Francis

STRAIGHT
&
TRIAL RUN

PAN BOOKS

Trial Run first published 1978 by Michael Joseph.
First published in paperback 1980 by Pan Books
in association with Michael Joseph.
Straight first published 1989 by Michael Joseph.
First published in paperback 1990 by Pan Books
in association with Michael Joseph.

This omnibus first published 2007 by Pan Books
an imprint of Pan Macmillan Ltd
Pan Macmillan, 20 New Wharf Road, London N1 9RR
Basingstoke and Oxford
Associated companies throughout the world
www.panmacmillan.com

ISBN 978-0-330-45228-1

1 3 5 7 9 8 6 4 2

A CIP catalogue record for this book is available from
the British Library.

Printed and bound in Great Britain by
Mackays of Chatham plc, Chatham, Kent

STRAIGHT

My thanks especially to

JOSEPH and DANIELLE ZERGER
of ZARLENE IMPORTS
dealers in semi-precious stones

and also to

MARY BROMILEY – ankle specialist

BARRY PARK – veterinary surgeon

JEREMY THOMPSON – doctor, pharmacologist

ANDREW HEWSON – literary agent

and as always to

MERRICK and FELIX, our sons.

All the people in this story are imaginary.
All the gadgets exist.

CHAPTER ONE

I inherited my brother's life. Inherited his desk, his business, his gadgets, his enemies, his horses and his mistress. I inherited my brother's life, and it nearly killed me.

I was thirty-four at the time and walking about on elbow crutches owing to a serious disagreement with the last fence in a steeplechase at Cheltenham. If you've never felt your ankle explode, don't try it. As usual it hadn't been the high-speed tumble that had done the damage but the half-ton of one of the other runners coming over the fence after me, his forefoot landing squarely on my boot on the baked earth of an Indian summer. The hoof mark was imprinted on the leather. The doctor who cut the boot off handed it to me as a souvenir. Medical minds have a macabre sense of humour.

Two days after this occurrence, while I was reluctantly coming to terms with the fact that I was going to miss at least six weeks of the steeplechasing season and with them possibly my last chance of making it to

1

champion again (the middle thirties being the beginning of the end for jump jockeys), I answered the telephone for about the tenth time that morning and found it was not another friend ringing to commiserate.

'Could I speak,' a female voice asked, 'to Derek Franklin?'

'I'm Derek Franklin,' I said.

'Right.' She was both brisk and hesitant, and one could understand why. 'We have you listed,' she said, 'as your brother Greville's next of kin.'

Those three words, I thought with an accelerating heart, must be among the most ominous in the language.

I said slowly, not wanting to know, 'What's happened?'

'I'm speaking from St Catherine's Hospital, Ipswich. Your brother is here, in the intensive care unit . . .'

At least he was alive, I thought numbly.

'. . . and the doctors think you should be told.'

'How is he?'

'I'm sorry I haven't seen him. This is the almoner's office. But I understand that his condition is very serious.'

'What's the matter with him?'

'He was involved in an accident,' she said. 'He has multiple injuries and is on life support.'

'I'll come,' I said.

'Yes. It might be best.'

I thanked her, not knowing exactly what for, and put

down the receiver, taking the shock physically in light-headedness and a constricted throat.

He would be all right, I told myself. Intensive care meant simply that he was being carefully looked after. He would recover, of course.

I shut out the anxiety to work prosaically instead on the practicalities of getting from Hungerford in Berkshire, where I lived, to Ipswich in Suffolk, about a hundred and fifty miles across country, with a crunched ankle. It was fortunately the left ankle, which meant I would soon be able to drive my automatic gears without trouble, but it was on that particular day at peak discomfort and even with painkillers and icepacks was hot, swollen and throbbing. I couldn't move it without holding my breath, and that was partly my own fault.

Owing to my hatred – not to say phobia – about the damaging immobility of plaster of Paris I had spent a good deal of the previous day persuading a long-suffering orthopaedic surgeon to give me the support of a plain crêpe bandage instead of imprisonment in a cast. He was himself a plate-and-screw man by preference and had grumbled as usual at my request. Such a bandage as I was demanding might be better in the end for one's muscles, but it gave no protection against knocks, as he had reminded me on other occasions, and it would be more painful, he said.

'I'll be racing much quicker with a bandage.'

'It's time you stopped breaking your bones,' he said, giving in with a shrug and a sigh and obligingly winding

3

the crêpe on tightly. 'One of these days you'll crack something serious.'

'I don't actually like breaking them.'

'At least I haven't had to pin anything this time,' he said. 'And you're mad.'

'Yes. Thanks very much.'

'Go home and rest it. Give those ligaments a chance.'

The ligaments took their chance along the back seat of my car while Brad, an unemployed welder, drove it to Ipswich. Brad, taciturn and obstinate, was unemployed by habit and choice but made a scratchy living doing odd jobs in the neighbourhood for anyone willing to endure his moods. As I much preferred his long silences to his infrequent conversation, we got along fine. He looked forty, hadn't reached thirty, and lived with his mother.

He found St Catherine's Hospital without much trouble and at the door helped me out and handed me the crutches, saying he would park and sit inside the reception area and I could take my time. He had waited for me similarly for hours the day before, expressing neither impatience nor sympathy but simply being restfully and neutrally morose.

The intensive care unit proved to be guarded by brisk nurses who looked at the crutches and said I'd come to the wrong department, but once I'd persuaded them of my identity they kitted me sympathetically with a mask and gown and let me in to see Greville.

I had vaguely expected Intensive Care to involve a

lot of bright lights and clanging bustle, but I found that it didn't, or at least not in that room in that hospital. The light was dim, the atmosphere peaceful, the noise level, once my ears adjusted to it, just above silence but lower than identification.

Greville lay alone in the room on a high bed with wires and tubes all over the place. He was naked except for a strip of sheeting lying loosely across his loins and they had shaved half the hair off his head. Other evidences of surgery marched like centipede tracks across his abdomen and down one thigh, and there were darkening bruises everywhere.

Behind his bed a bank of screens showed blank rectangular faces, as the information from the electrodes fed into other screens in a room directly outside. He didn't need, they said, an attendant constantly beside him, but they kept an eye on his reactions all the time.

He was unconscious, his face pale and calm, his head turned slightly towards the door as if expecting visitors. Decompression procedures had been performed on his skull, and that wound was covered by a large padded dressing which seemed more like a pillow to support him.

Greville Saxony Franklin, my brother. Nineteen years my senior: not expected to live. It had to be faced. To be accepted.

'Hi, guy,' I said.

It was an Americanism he himself used often, but it produced no response. I touched his hand, which was warm and relaxed, the nails, as always, clean and cared for. He had a pulse, he had circulation: his heart beat by electrical stimulus. Air went in and out of his lungs mechanically through a tube in his throat. Inside his head the synapses were shutting down. Where was his soul, I wondered: where was the intelligent, persistent, energetic spirit? Did he know that he was dying?

I didn't want just to leave him. No one should die alone. I went outside and said so.

A doctor in a green overall replied that when all the remaining brain activity had ceased, they would ask my consent before switching off the machines. I was welcome to be with my brother at this crisis point as well as before. 'But death,' he said austerely, 'will be for him an infinitesimal process, not a definitive moment.' He paused. 'There is a waiting room along the hall, with coffee and things.'

Bathos and drama, I thought: his everyday life. I crutched all the way down to the general reception area, found Brad, gave him an update and told him I might be a long time. All night, perhaps.

He waved a permissive hand. He would be around, he said, or he would leave a message at the desk. Either way, I could reach him. I nodded and went back upstairs, and found the waiting room already occupied by a very young couple engulfed in grief, whose baby was hanging on to life by threads not much stronger than Greville's.

The room itself was bright, comfortable and impersonal, and I listened to the mother's slow sobs and thought of the misery that soaked daily into those walls. Life has a way of kicking one along like a football, or so I've found. Fate had never dealt me personally a particularly easy time, but that was OK, that was normal. Most people, it seemed to me, took their turn to be football. Most survived. Some didn't.

Greville had simply been in the wrong place at the wrong time. From the scrappy information known to the hospital, I gleaned that he had been walking down Ipswich High Street when some scaffolding that was being dismantled had fallen on him from a considerable height. One of the construction workers had been killed, and a second had been taken to hospital with a broken hip.

I had been given my brother's clinical details. One metal bar had pierced his stomach, another had torn into his leg, something heavy had fallen on his head and caused brain damage with massive cerebral bleeding. It had happened late the previous afternoon, he had been deeply unconscious from the moment of the impact and he hadn't been identified until workmen dealing with the rubble in the morning had found his diary and given it to the police.

'Wallet?' I asked.

No, no wallet. Just the diary with, neatly filled in on the first page, next of kin, Derek Franklin, brother; telephone number supplied. Before that, they had no clue except the initials G.S.F. embroidered above the pocket of his torn and blood-stained shirt.

'A *silk* shirt,' a nurse added disapprovingly, as if monogrammed silk shirts were somehow immoral.

'Nothing else in his pockets?' I asked.

'A bunch of keys and a handkerchief. That was all. You'll be given them, of course, along with the diary and his watch and signet ring.'

I nodded. No need to ask when.

The afternoon stretched out, strange and unreal, a time-warped limbo. I went again to spend some time with Greville, but he lay unmoving, oblivious in his dwindling twilight, already subtly not himself. If Wordsworth were right about immortality, it was the sleep and the forgetting that were slipping away and reawakening that lay ahead, and maybe I should be glad for him, not grieve.

I thought of him as he had been, and of our lives as brothers. We had never lived together in a family unit because, by the time I was born, he was away at university, building a life of his own. By the time I was six, he had married, by the time I was ten, he'd divorced. For years he was a semi-stranger whom I met briefly at family gatherings, celebrations which grew less and less frequent as our parents aged and died, and which stopped altogether when the two sisters who bridged the gap between Greville and me both emigrated, one to Australia and one to Japan.

It wasn't until I'd reached twenty-eight myself that

after a long Christmas-and-birthday-card politeness we'd met unexpectedly on a railway platform and during the journey ahead had become friends. Not close time-sharing friends even then, but positive enough for telephoning each other sporadically and exchanging restaurant dinners and feeling good about it.

We had been brought up in different environments, Greville in the Regency London house which went with our father's job as manager of one of the great landowning estates, I in the comfortable country cottage of his retirement. Greville had been taken by our mother to museums, art galleries and the theatre: I had been given ponies.

We didn't even look much alike. Greville, like our father, was six feet tall, I three inches shorter. Greville's hair, now greying, had been light brown and straight, mine darker brown and curly. We had both inherited amber eyes and good teeth from our mother and a tendency to leanness from our father, but our faces, though both tidy enough, were quite different.

Greville best remembered our parents' vigorous years; I'd been with them through their illnesses and deaths. Our father had himself been twenty years older than our mother, and she had died first, which had seemed monstrously unfair. The old man and I had lived briefly together after that in tolerant mutual non-comprehension, though I had no doubt that he'd loved me, in his way. He had been sixty-two when I was born and he died on my eighteenth birthday, leaving me a fund for my continued education and a letter of admonitions and instructions, some of which I'd carried out.

Greville's stillness was absolute. I shifted uncomfortably on the crutches and thought of asking for a chair. I wouldn't see him smile again, I thought: not the lightening of the eyes and the gleam of teeth, the quick appreciation of the black humour of life, the awareness of his own power.

He was a magistrate, a justice of the peace, and he imported and sold semi-precious stones. Beyond these bare facts I knew few details of his day-to-day existence, as whenever we met it seemed that he was always more interested in my doings than his own. He had himself owned horses from the day he telephoned to ask my opinion: someone who owed him money had offered his racehorse to settle the debt. What did I think? I told him I'd phone back, looked up the horse, thought it was a bargain and told Greville to go right ahead if he felt like it.

'Don't see why not,' he'd said. 'Will you fix the paperwork?'

I'd said yes, of course. It wasn't hard for anyone to say yes to my brother Greville: much harder to say no.

The horse had won handsomely and given him a taste for future ownership, though he seldom went to see his horses run, which wasn't particularly unusual in an owner but always to me mystifying. He refused absolutely to own jumpers on the grounds that he might buy something that would kill me. I was too big for Flat races; he'd felt safe with those. I couldn't persuade him that I would like to ride for him and in the end I stopped trying. When Greville made up his mind he was unshakable.

Every ten minutes or so a nurse would come quietly into the room to stand for a short while beside the bed, checking that all the electrodes and tubes were still in order. She gave me brief smiles and commented once that my brother was unaware of my presence and could not be comforted by my being there.

'It's as much for me as for him,' I said.

She nodded and went away, and I stayed for a couple more hours, leaning against a wall and reflecting that it was ironic that it was he who should meet death by chance when it was I who actively risked it half the days of the year.

Strange to reflect also, looking back now to that lengthening evening, that I gave no thought to the consequences of his death. The present was vividly alive still in the silent diminishing hours, and all I saw in the future was a pretty dreary programme of form-filling and funeral arrangements, which I didn't bother to think about in any detail. I would have to telephone the sisters, I vaguely supposed, and there might be a little long-distance grief, but I knew they would say, 'You can see to it, can't you? Whatever you decide will be all right with us,' and they wouldn't come back halfway round the world to stand in mournful drizzle at the graveside of a brother they'd seen perhaps twice in ten years.

Beyond that, I considered nothing. The tie of common blood was all that truly linked Greville and me, and once it was undone there would be nothing left of him but memory. With regret I watched the pulse that flickered in his throat. When it was gone I would go back to my own life and think of him warmly sometimes, and remember this night with overall sorrow, but no more.

I went along to the waiting room for a while to rest my legs. The desperate young parents were still there, hollow-eyed and entwined, but presently a sombre nurse came to fetch them, and in the distance, shortly after, I heard the rising wail of the mother's agonized loss. I felt my own tears prickle for her, a stranger. A dead baby, a dying brother, a universal uniting misery. I grieved for Greville most intensely then because of the death of the child, and realized I had been wrong about the sorrow level. I would miss him very much.

I put my ankle up on a chair and fitfully dozed, and sometime before daybreak the same nurse with the same expression came to fetch me in my turn.

I followed her along the passage and into Greville's room. There was much more light in there this time, and more people, and the bank of monitoring screens behind the bed had been switched on. Pale greenish lines moved across them, some in regular spasms, some uncompromisingly straight.

I didn't need to be told, but they explained all the same. The straight lines were the sum of the activity in Greville's brain. None at all.

There was no private goodbye. There was no point. I was there, and that was enough. They asked for, and received, my agreement to the disconnection of the machines, and presently the pulsing lines straightened out also, and whatever had been in the quiet body was there no longer.

It took a long time to get anything done in the morning because it turned out to be Sunday.

I thought back, having lost count of time. Thursday when I broke my ankle, Friday when the scaffolding fell on Greville, Saturday when Brad drove me to Ipswich. It all seemed a cosmos away: relativity in action.

There was the possibility, it seemed, of the scaffolding constructors being liable for damages. It was suggested that I should consult a solicitor.

Plodding through the paperwork, trying to make decisions, I realized that I didn't know what Greville would want. If he'd left a will somewhere, maybe he had given instructions that I ought to carry out. Maybe no one but I, I thought with a jolt, actually knew he was dead. There had to be people I should notify, and I didn't know who.

I asked if I could have the diary the police had found in the rubble, and presently I was given not only the diary but everything else my brother had had with him: keys, watch, handkerchief, signet ring, a small amount of change, shoes, socks, jacket. The rest of his clothes, torn and drenched with blood, had been incinerated, it appeared. I was required to sign for what I was taking, putting a tick against each item.

Everything had been tipped out of the large brown plastic bag in which they had been stored. The bag said 'St Catherine's Hospital' in white on the sides. I put the shoes, socks, handkerchief and jacket back into the bag and pulled the strings tight again, then I shovelled the large bunch of keys into my own trouser pocket, along with the watch, the ring and the money, and finally consulted the diary.

On the front page he had entered his name, his London home telephone number and his office number, but no addresses. It was near the bottom, where there was a space headed 'In case of accident please notify', that he had written 'Derek Franklin, brother, next of kin.'

The diary itself was one I had sent him at Christmas: the racing diary put out by the Jockeys' Association and the Injured Jockeys' Fund. That he should have chosen to use that particular diary when he must have been given several others I found unexpectedly moving. That he had put my name in it made me wonder what he had really thought of me; whether there was much we might have been to each other, and had missed.

With regret I put the diary into my other trouser pocket. The next morning, I supposed, I would have to telephone his office with the dire news. I couldn't forewarn anyone as I didn't know the names, let alone the phone numbers, of the people who worked for him. I knew only that he had no partners, as he had said several times that the only way he could run his business was by himself. Partners too often came to blows, he said, and he would have none of it.

When all the signing was completed, I looped the strings of the plastic bag a couple of times round my wrist and took it and myself on the crutches down to the reception area, which was more or less deserted on that early Sunday morning. Brad wasn't there, nor was there any message from him at the desk, so I simply sat down and waited. I had no doubt he would come back in his own good time, glowering as usual, and eventually he did, slouching in through the door with no sign of haste.

He saw me across the acreage, came to within ten feet, and said, 'Shall I fetch the car, then?' and when I nodded, wheeled away and departed. A man of very few words, Brad. I followed slowly in his wake, the plastic bag bumping against the crutch. If I'd thought faster I would have given it to Brad to carry, but I didn't seem to be thinking fast in any way.

Outside, the October sun was bright and warm. I breathed the sweet air, took a few steps away from the door and patiently waited some more, and was totally unprepared to be savagely mugged.

I scarcely saw who did it. One moment I was upright, leaning without concentration on the crutches, the next I'd received a battering-ram shove in the back and was sprawling face forward onto the hard black surface of the entrance drive. To try to save myself, I put my left foot down instinctively and it twisted beneath me, which was excruciating and useless. I fell flat down on my stomach in a haze and I hardly cared when someone kicked one of the fallen crutches away along the ground and tugged at the bag around my wrist.

He ... it had to be a he, I thought, from the speed and strength ... thumped a foot down on my back and put his weight on it. He yanked my arm up and back roughly, and cut through the plastic with a slash that took some of my skin with it. I scarcely felt it. The messages from my ankle obliterated all else.

A voice approached saying, 'Hey! Hey!' urgently, and my attacker lifted himself off me as fast as he'd arrived and sped away.

It was Brad who had come to my rescue. On any other day there might have been people constantly coming and going, but not on Sunday morning. No one else seemed to be around to notice a thing. No one but Brad had come running.

'Friggin' hell,' Brad said from above me. 'Are you all right?'

Far from it, I thought.

He went to fetch the scattered crutch and brought it

back. 'Your hand's bleeding,' he said with disbelief. 'Don't you want to stand up?'

I wasn't too sure that I did, but it seemed the only thing to do. When I'd made it to a moderately vertical position he looked impassively at my face and gave it as his opinion that we ought to go back into the hospital. As I didn't feel like arguing, that's what we did.

I sat on the end of one of the empty rows of seats and waited for the tide of woe to recede, and when I had more command of things I went across to the desk and explained what had happened.

The woman behind the reception window was horrified.

'Someone stole your plastic bag!' she said, round-eyed. 'I mean, everyone around here knows what those bags signify, they're always used for the belongings of people who've died or come here after accidents. I mean, everyone knows they can contain wallets and jewellery and so on, but I've never heard of one being snatched. How awful! How much did you lose? You'd better report it to the police.'

The futility of it shook me with weariness. Some punk had taken a chance that the dead man's effects would be worth the risk, and the police would take notes and chalk it up among the majority of unsolved muggings. I reckoned I'd fallen into the ultra-vulnerable bracket which included little old ladies, and however much I might wince at the thought, I on my crutches had looked and been a pushover, literally.

I shuffled painfully into the washroom and ran cold water over my slowly bleeding hand, and found that the cut was more extensive than deep and could sensibly be classified as a scratch. With a sigh, I dabbed a paper towel on the scarlety oozing spots and unwound the cut-off pieces of white and brown plastic which were still wrapped tightly round my wrist, throwing them in the bin. What a bloody stupid anti-climactic postscript, I thought tiredly, to the accident that had taken my brother.

When I went outside Brad said with a certain amount of anxiety, 'You going to the police, then?' and he relaxed visibly when I shook my head and said, 'Not unless you can give them a detailed description of whoever attacked me.'

I couldn't tell from his expression whether he could or not. I thought I might ask him later, on the way home, but when I did, all that he said was, 'He had jeans on, and one of them woolly hats. And he had a knife. I didn't see his face, he sort of had his back turned my way, but the sun flashed on the knife, see? It all went down so fast. I did think you were a goner. Then he ran off with the bag. You were dead lucky, I'd say.'

I didn't feel lucky, but all things were relative.

Brad, having contributed what was for him a long speech, relapsed into his more normal silence, and I wondered what the mugger would think of the worthless haul of shoes, socks, handkerchief and jacket whose loss hadn't been realistically worth reporting. Whatever of value Greville had set out with would have been in his wallet, which had fallen to an earlier predator.

I had been wearing, was still wearing, a shirt, tie and sweater, but no jacket. A sweater was better with the crutches than a jacket. It was pointless to wonder whether the thief would have dipped into my trouser pockets if Brad hadn't shouted. Pointless to wonder if he would have put his blade through my ribs. There was no way of knowing. I did know I couldn't have stopped him, but his prize in any case would have been meagre. Apart from Greville's things I was carrying only a credit card and a few notes in a small folder, from a habit of travelling light.

I stopped thinking about it and instead, to take my mind off the ankle, wondered what Greville had been doing in Ipswich.

Wondered if, ever since Friday, anyone had been waiting for him to arrive. Wondered how he had got there. Wondered if he had parked his car somewhere there and, if so, how I would find it, considering I didn't know its number and wasn't even sure if he still had a Porsche. Someone else would know, I thought easily. His office, his local garage, a friend. It wasn't really my worry.

By the time we reached Hungerford three hours later, Brad had said, in addition, only that the car was running out of juice (which we remedied) and, half an hour from home, that if I wanted him to go on driving me during the following week, he would be willing.

'Seven-thirty tomorrow morning?' I suggested, reflecting, and he said 'Yerss' on a growl which I took to mean assent.

He drove me to my door, helped me out as before, handed me the crutches, locked the car and put the keys into my hand all without speaking.

'Thanks,' I said.

He ducked his head, not meeting my eyes, and turned and shambled off on foot towards his mother's house. I watched him go; a shy difficult man with no social skills who had possibly that morning saved my life.

CHAPTER TWO

I had for three years rented the ground floor of an old house in a turning off the main road through the ancient country town. There was a bedroom and bathroom facing the street and the sunrise, and a large all-purpose room to the rear into which the sunset flooded. Beyond that, a small stream-bordered garden which I shared with the owners of the house, an elderly couple upstairs.

Brad's mother had cooked and cleaned for them for years; Brad mended, painted and chopped when he felt like it. Soon after I'd moved in, mother and son had casually extended their services to me, which suited me well. It was all in all an easy uncluttered existence, but if home was where the heart was, I really lived out on the windy Downs and in stable yards and on the raucous racetracks where I worked.

I let myself into the quiet rooms and sat with ice-packs along a sofa, watching the sun go down on the far side of the stream and thinking I might have done better to stay in the Ipswich hospital. From the knee down my left leg was hurting abominably, and it was still getting clearer by the minute that falling had intensified Thursday's damage disastrously. My own surgeon had been going off to Wales for the weekend, but I doubted that he would have done very much except say 'I told you so', so in the end I simply took another Distalgesic and changed the icepacks and worked out the time zones in Tokyo and Sydney.

At midnight I telephoned to those cities where it was already morning and by good luck reached both of the sisters. 'Poor Greville,' they said sadly, and, 'Do whatever you think best.' 'Send some flowers for us.' 'Let us know how it goes.'

I would, I said. Poor Greville, they repeated, meaning it, and said they would love to see me in Tokyo, in Sydney, whenever. Their children, they said, were all fine. Their husbands were fine. Was I fine? Poor, poor Greville.

I put the receiver down ruefully. Families did scatter, and some scattered more than most. I knew the sisters by that time only through the photographs they sometimes sent at Christmas. They hadn't recognized my voice.

Taking things slowly in the morning, as nothing was much better, I dressed for the day in shirt, tie and sweater as before, with a shoe on the right foot, sock alone on the left, and was ready when Brad arrived five minutes early.

'We're going to London,' I said. 'Here's a map with the place marked. Do you think you can find it?'

'Got a tongue in my head,' he said, peering at the maze of roads. 'Reckon so.'

'Give it a go, then.'

He nodded, helped me inch onto the back seat, and drove seventy miles through the heavy morning traffic in silence. Then, by dint of shouting at street vendors via the driver's window, he zig-zagged across Holborn, took a couple of wrong turns, righted himself, and drew up with a jerk in a busy street round the corner from Hatton Garden.

'That's it,' he said, pointing. 'Number fifty-six. That office block.'

'Brilliant.'

He helped me out, gave me the crutches, and came with me to hold open the heavy glass entrance door. Inside, behind a desk, was a man in a peaked cap personifying security who asked me forbiddingly what floor I wanted.

'Saxony Franklin,' I said.

'Name?' he asked, consulting a list.

'Franklin.'

'Your name, I mean.'

I explained who I was. He raised his eyebrows, picked up a telephone, pressed a button and said, 'A Mr Franklin is on his way up.'

Brad asked where he could park the car and was told

23

there was a yard round the back. He would wait for me, he said. No hurry. No problem.

The office building, which was modern, had been built rubbing shoulders to the sixth floor with Victorian curlicued neighbours, soaring free to the tenth with a severe lot of glass.

Saxony Franklin was on the eighth floor, it appeared. I went up in a smooth lift and elbowed my way through some heavy double doors into a lobby furnished with a reception desk, several armchairs for waiting in and two policemen.

Behind the policemen was a middle-aged woman who looked definitely flustered.

I thought immediately that news of Greville's death had already arrived and that I probably hadn't needed to come, but it seemed the Force was there for a different reason entirely.

The flustered lady gave me a blank stare and said, 'That's not Mr Franklin. The guard said Mr Franklin was on his way up.'

I allayed the police suspicions a little by saying again that I was Greville Franklin's brother.

'Oh,' said the woman. 'Yes, he does have a brother.'

They all swept their gaze over my comparative immobility.

'Mr Franklin isn't here yet,' the woman told me.

'Er . . .' I said, 'what's going on?'

They all looked disinclined to explain. I said to her, 'I'm afraid I don't know your name.'

24

'Adams,' she said distractedly. 'Annette Adams. I'm your brother's personal assistant.'

'I'm sorry,' I said slowly, 'but my brother won't be coming at all today. He was involved in an accident.'

Annette Adams heard the bad news in my voice. She put a hand over her heart in the classic gesture as if to hold it still in her chest and with anxiety said, 'What sort of accident? A car crash? Is he hurt?'

She saw the answer clearly in my expression and with her free hand felt for one of the armchairs, buckling into it with shock.

'He died in hospital yesterday morning,' I said to her and to the policemen, 'after some scaffolding fell on him last Friday. I was with him in the hospital.'

One of the policemen pointed at my dangling foot. 'You were injured at the same time, sir?'

'No. This was different. I didn't see his accident. I meant, I was there when he died. The hospital sent for me.'

The two policemen consulted each other's eyes and decided after all to say why they were there.

'These offices were broken into during the weekend, sir. Mrs Adams here discovered it when she arrived early for work, and she called us in.'

'What does it matter? It doesn't matter now,' the lady said, growing paler.

'There's a good deal of mess,' the policeman went on, 'and Mrs Adams doesn't know what's been stolen. We were waiting for your brother to tell us.'

'Oh dear, oh dear,' said Annette, gulping.

'Is there anyone else here?' I asked her. 'Someone who could get you a cup of tea?' Before you faint, I thought, but didn't say it.

She nodded a fraction, glancing at a door behind the desk, and I swung over there and tried to open it. It wouldn't open: the knob wouldn't turn.

'It's electronic,' Annette said weakly. 'You have to put in the right numbers . . .' She flopped her head back against the chair and said she couldn't remember what today's number was; it was changed often. She and the policemen had come through it, it seemed, and let it swing shut behind them.

One of the policemen came over and pounded on the door with his fist, shouting 'Police' very positively which had the desired effect like a reflex. Without finesse he told the much younger woman who stood there framed in the doorway that her boss was dead and that Mrs Adams was about to pass out and was needing some strong hot sweet tea, love, like five minutes ago.

Wild-eyed, the young woman retreated to spread more consternation behind the scenes and the policeman nullified the firm's defences by wedging the electronic door open, using the chair from behind the reception desk.

I took in a few more details of the surroundings, beyond my first impression of grey. On the light greenish-grey of the carpet stood the armchairs in charcoal and the desk in matt black unpainted and unpolished wood. The walls, palest grey, were hung with a series of framed geological maps, the frames black and narrow and uniform in size. The propped-open door, and another similar door to one side, still closed, were painted the same colour as the walls. The total effect, lit by recessed spotlights in the ceiling, looked both straightforward and immensely sophisticated, a true representation of my brother.

Mrs Annette Adams, still flaccid from too many unpleasant surprises on a Monday morning, wore a cream shirt, a charcoal grey skirt and a string of knobbly pearls. She was dark haired, in her late forties, perhaps, and from the starkness in her eyes, just beginning to realize, I guessed, that the upheaval of the present would be permanent.

The younger woman returned effectively with a scarlet steaming mug and Annette Adams sipped from it obediently for a while, listening to the policemen telling me that the intruder had not come in this way up the front lift, which was for visitors, but up another lift at the rear of the building which was used by the staff of all floors of offices, and for freight. That lift went down into a rear lobby which, in its turn, led out to the yard where cars and vans were parked: where Brad was presumably waiting at that moment.

The intruder had apparently ridden to the tenth floor, climbed some service stairs to the roof, and by some means had come down outside the building to the eighth floor, where he had smashed a window to let himself in.

'What sort of means?' I asked.

'We don't know, sir. Whatever it was, he took it with him. Maybe a rope.' He shrugged. 'We've had only a quick preliminary look around up there. We wanted to know what's been stolen before we ... er ... See, we don't want to waste our time for nothing.'

I nodded. Like Greville's stolen shoes, I thought.

'This whole area round Hatton Garden is packed with the jewel trade. We get break-ins, or attempted break-ins, all the time.'

The other policeman said, 'This place here is loaded with stones, of course, but the vault's still shut and Mrs Adams says nothing seems to be missing from the other stock-rooms. Only Mr Franklin has a key to the vault which is where their more valuable faceted stones are kept.'

Mr Franklin had no keys at all. Mr Franklin's keys were in my own pocket. There was no harm, I supposed, in producing them.

The sight of what must have been a familiar bunch brought tears to Annette Adams's eyes. She put down the mug, searched around for a tissue and cried, 'He really is dead, then,' as if she hadn't thoroughly believed it before.

When she'd recovered a little I asked her to point out the vault key, which proved to be the longest and slenderest of the lot, and shortly afterwards we were all walking through the propped-open door and down a central corridor with spacious offices opening to either side. Faces showing shock looked out at our passing. We stopped at an ordinary-looking door which might have been mistaken for a cupboard and certainly looked nothing like a vault.

'That's it,' Annette Adams insisted, nodding; so I slid the narrow key into the small ordinary keyhole, and found that it turned unexpectedly anti-clockwise. The thick and heavy door swung inwards to the right under pressure and a light came on automatically, shining in what did indeed seem exactly like a large walk-in cupboard, with rows of white cardboard boxes on several plain white-painted shelves stretching away along the left-hand wall.

Everyone looked in silence. Nothing seemed to have been disturbed.

'Who knows what should be in the boxes?' I asked, and got the expected answer: my brother.

I took a step into the vault and took the lid off one of the nearest boxes which bore a sticky label saying $MgAl_2O_4$, Burma. Inside the box there were about a dozen glossy white envelopes, each taking up the whole width. I lifted one out to open it.

'Be careful!' Annette Adams exclaimed, fearful of my clumsiness as I balanced on the crutches. 'The packets unfold.'

I handed to her the one I held, and she unfolded it carefully on the palm of her hand. Inside, cushioned by white tissue, lay two large red translucent stones, cut and polished, oblong in shape, almost pulsing with intense colour under the lights.

'Are they rubies?' I asked, impressed.

Annette Adams smiled indulgently. 'No, they're spinel. Very fine specimens. We rarely deal in rubies.'

'Are there any diamonds in here?' one of the policemen asked.

'No, we don't deal in diamonds. Almost never.'

I asked her to look into some of the other boxes, which she did, first carefully folding the two red stones into their packet and restoring them to their right place. We watched her stretch and bend, tipping up random lids on several shelves to take out a white packet here and there for inspection, but there were clearly no dismaying surprises, and at the end she shook her head and said that nothing at all was missing, as far as she could see.

'The real value of these stones is in quantity,' she said. 'Each individual stone isn't worth a fortune. We sell stones in tens and hundreds . . .' Her voice trailed off into a sort of forlornness. 'I don't know what to do,' she said, 'about the orders.'

The policemen weren't affected by the problem. If nothing was missing, they had other burglaries to look into, and they would put in a report, but goodbye for now, or words to that effect.

When they'd gone, Annette Adams and I stood in the passage and looked at each other.

'What do I do?' she said. 'Are we still in business?'

I didn't like to tell her that I hadn't the foggiest notion. I said, 'Did Greville have an office?'

'That's where most of the mess is,' she said, turning away and retracing her steps to a large corner room near the entrance lobby. 'In here.'

I followed her and saw what she meant about mess. The contents of every wide-open drawer seemed to be out on the floor, most of it paper. Pictures had been removed from the walls and dropped. One filing cabinet lay on its side like a fallen soldier. The desk top was a shambles.

'The police said the burglar was looking behind the pictures for a safe. But there isn't one . . . just the vault.' She sighed unhappily. 'It's all so pointless.'

I looked around. 'How many people work here altogether?' I said.

'Six of us. And Mr Franklin, of course.' She swallowed. 'Oh dear.'

'Mm,' I agreed. 'Is there anywhere I can meet everyone?'

She nodded mutely and led the way into another large office where three of the others were already gathered, wide-eyed and rudderless. Another two came when called; four women and two men, all worried and uncertain and looking to me for decisions.

Greville, I perceived, hadn't chosen potential leaders to work around him. Annette Adams herself was no aggressive waiting-in-the-wings manager but a true

31

second-in-command, skilled at carrying out orders, incapable of initiating them. Not so good, all things considered.

I introduced myself and described what had happened to Greville.

They had liked him, I was glad to see. There were tears on his behalf. I said that I needed their help because there were people I ought to notify about his death, like his solicitor and his accountant, for instance, and his closest friends, and I didn't know who they were. I would like, I said, to make a list, and sat beside one of the desks, arming myself with paper and pen.

Annette said she would fetch Greville's address book from his office but after a while returned in frustration: in all the mess she couldn't find it.

'There must be other records,' I said. 'What about that computer?' I pointed across the room. 'Do you have addresses on that?'

The girl who had brought the tea brightened a good deal and informed me that this was the stock control room, and the computer in question was programmed to record 'stock in, stock out', statements, invoices and accounts. But, she said encouragingly, in her other domain across the corridor there was another computer which she used for letters. She was out of the door by the end of the sentence and Annette remarked that June was a whirlwind always.

June, blonde, long-legged, flat-chested, came back with a fast print-out of Greville's ten most frequent correspondents (ignoring customers) which included not only the lawyers and the accountants but also the bank, a stockbroker and an insurance company.

'Terrific,' I said. 'And could one of you get through to the big credit card companies, and see if Greville was a customer of theirs and say his cards have been stolen, and he's dead.' Annette agreed mournfully that she would do it at once.

I then asked if any of them knew the make and number of Greville's car. They all did. It seemed they saw it every day in the yard. He came to work in a ten-year-old Rover 3500 without radio or cassette player because the Porsche he'd owned before had been broken into twice and finally stolen altogether.

'The old car's still bursting with gadgets, though,' the younger of the two men said, 'but he keeps them all locked in the boot.'

Greville had always been a sucker for gadgets, full of enthusiasm for the latest fidgety way of performing an ordinary task. He'd told me more about those toys of his, when we'd met, than ever about his own human relationships.

'Why did you ask about his car?' the young man said. He had rows of badges attached to a black leather jacket and orange spiky hair set with gel. A need to prove he existed, I supposed.

'It may be outside his front door,' I said. 'Or it may be parked somewhere in Ipswich.'

'Yeah,' he said thoughtfully. 'See what you mean.'

The telephone rang on the desk beside me, and Annette after a moment's hesitation came and picked up the receiver. She listened with a worried expression and then, covering the mouthpiece, asked me, 'What shall I do? It's a customer who wants to give an order.'

'Have you got what he wants?' I asked.

'Yes, we're sure to have.'

'Then say it's OK.'

'But do I tell him about Mr Franklin?'

'No,' I said instinctively, 'just take the order.'

She seemed glad of the direction and wrote down the list, and when she'd disconnected I suggested to them all that for that day at least they should take and send out orders in the normal way, and just say if asked that Mr Franklin was out of the office and couldn't be reached. We wouldn't start telling people he was dead until after I'd talked to his lawyers, accountants, bank and the rest, and found out our legal position. They were relieved and agreed without demur, and the older man asked if I would soon get the broken window fixed, as it was in the packing and despatch room, where he worked.

With a feeling of being sucked feet first into quicksand I said I would try. I felt I didn't belong in that place or in those people's lives, and all I knew about the jewellery business was where to find two red stones in a box marked $MgA1_2O_4$, Burma.

At the fourth try among the Yellow Pages I got a promise of instant action on the window and after that, with office procedure beginning to tick over again all around me, I put a call through to the lawyers.

They were grave, they were sympathetic, they were at my service. I asked if by any chance Greville had made a will, as specifically I wanted to know if he had left any instructions about cremation or burial, and if he hadn't, did they know of anyone I should consult, or should I make whatever arrangements I thought best.

There was a certain amount of clearing of throats and a promise to look up files and call back, and they kept their word almost immediately, to my surprise.

My brother had indeed left a will: they had drawn it up for him themselves three years earlier. They couldn't swear it was his *last* will, but it was the only one they had. They had consulted it. Greville, they said, pedantically, had expressed no preference as to the disposal of his remains.

'Shall I just . . . go ahead, then?'

'Certainly,' they said. 'You are in fact named as your brother's sole executor. It is your duty to make the decisions.'

Hell, I thought, and I asked for a list of the beneficiaries so that I could notify them of the death and invite them to the funeral.

After a pause they said they didn't normally give out that information on the telephone. Could I not come to their office? It was just across the City, at Temple.

'I've broken an ankle,' I said, apologetically. 'It takes me all my time to cross the room.'

Dear, dear, they said. They consulted among themselves in guarded whispers and finally said they supposed there was no harm in my knowing. Greville's will was extremely simple; he had left everything he possessed to Derek Saxony Franklin, his brother. To my good self, in fact.

'What?' I said stupidly. 'He can't have.'

He had written his will in a hurry, they said, because he had been flying off to a dangerous country to buy stones. He had been persuaded by the lawyers not to go intestate, and he had given in to them, and as far as they knew, that was the only will he had ever made.

'He can't have meant it to be his last,' I said blankly.

Perhaps not, they agreed: few men in good health expected to die at fifty-three. They then discussed probate procedures discreetly and asked for my instructions, and I felt the quicksands rising above my knees.

'Is it legal,' I asked, 'for this business to go on running, for the time being?'

They saw no impediment in law. Subject to probate, and in the absence of any later will, the business would be mine. If I wanted to sell it in due course, it would be in my own interest to keep it running. As my brother's executor it would also be my duty to do my best for the estate. An interesting situation, they said with humour.

Not wholeheartedly appreciating the subtlety, I asked how long probate would take.

Always difficult to forecast, was the answer. Anything between six months or two years, depending on the complexity of Greville's affairs.

'Two years!'

More probably six months, they murmured soothingly. The speed would depend on the accountants and the Inland Revenue, who could seldom be hurried. It was in the lap of the gods.

I mentioned that there might be work to do over claiming damages for the accident. Happy to see to it, they said, and promised to contact the Ipswich police. Meanwhile, good luck.

I put the receiver down in sinking dismay. This business, like any other, might run on its own impetus for two weeks, maybe even for four, but after that . . . After that I would be back on horses, trying to get fit again to race.

I would have to get a manager, I thought vaguely, and had no idea where to start looking. Annette Adams with furrows of anxiety across her forehead asked if it would be all right to begin clearing up Mr Franklin's office, and I said yes, and thought that her lack of drive could sink the ship.

Please would someone, I asked the world in general, mind going down to the yard and telling the man in my car that I wouldn't be leaving for two or three hours; and June with her bright face whisked out of the door again and soon returned to relate that my man would lock the car, go on foot for lunch, and be back in good time to wait for me.

'Did he say all that?' I asked curiously.

June laughed. 'Actually he said, "Right. Bite to eat," and off he stomped.'

She asked if I would like her to bring me a sandwich when she went out for her own lunch and, surprised and grateful, I accepted.

'Your foot hurts, doesn't it?' she said judiciously.

'Mm.'

'You should put it up on a chair.'

She fetched one without ado and placed it in front of me, watching with a motherly air of approval as I lifted my leg into place. She must have been all of twenty, I thought.

A telephone rang beside the computer on the far side of the room and she went to answer it.

'Yes, sir, we have everything in stock. Yes, sir, what size and how many? A hundred twelve-by-ten milli-metre ovals . . . yes . . . yes . . . yes.'

She tapped the lengthy order rapidly straight on to the computer, not writing in longhand as Annette had done.

'Yes, sir, they will go off today. Usual terms, sir, of course.' She put the phone down, printed a copy of the order and laid it in a shallow wire tray. A fax machine simultaneously clicked on and whined away and switched off with little shrieks, and she tore off the emergent sheet and tapped its information also into the computer, making a print-out and putting it into the tray.

'Do you fill all the orders the day they come in?' I asked.

'Oh, sure, if we can. Within twenty-four hours without fail. Mr Franklin says speed is the essence of good business. I've known him stay here all evening by himself packing parcels when we're swamped.'

She remembered with a rush that he would never come back. It did take a bit of getting used to. Tears welled in her uncontrollably as they had earlier, and she stared at me through them, which made her blue eyes look huge.

'You couldn't help liking him,' she said. 'Working with him, I mean.'

I felt almost jealous that she'd known Greville better than I had; yet I could have known him better if I'd tried. Regret stabbed in again, a needle of grief.

Annette came to announce that Mr Franklin's room was at least partially clear so I transferred myself into there to make more phone calls in comparative privacy. I sat in Greville's black leather swivelling chunk of luxury and put my foot on the typist's chair June carried in after me, and I surveyed the opulent carpet, deep armchairs and framed maps as in the lobby, and smoothed a hand over the grainy black expanse of the oversized desk, and felt like a jockey, not a tycoon.

Annette had picked up from the floor and assembled at one end of the desk some of the army of gadgets, most of them matt black and small, as if miniaturization were part of the attraction. Easily identifiable at a glance were battery-operated things like pencil sharpener, hand-held copier, printing calculator, dictionary-thesaurus, but most needed investigation. I stretched out a hand to the nearest and found that it was a casing with a dial face, plus a head like a microphone on a lead.

'What's this?' I asked Annette who was picking up a stack of paper from the far reaches of the floor. 'Some sort of meter?'

She flashed a look at it. 'A Geiger counter,' she said matter-of-factly, as if everyone kept a Geiger counter routinely among their pens and pencils.

I flipped the switch from off to on, but apart from a couple of ticks, nothing happened.

Annette paused, sitting back on her heels as she knelt among the remaining clutter.

'A lot of stones change colour for the better under gamma radiation,' she said. 'They're not radioactive afterwards, but Mr Franklin was once accidentally sent a batch of topaz from Brazil that had been irradiated in a nuclear reactor and the stones were bordering on dangerous. A hundred of them. There was a terrible lot of trouble because, apart from being unsaleable, they had come in without a radioactivity import licence, or something like that, but it wasn't Mr Franklin's fault, of course. But he got the Geiger counter then.' She paused. 'He had an amazing flair for stones, you know. He just felt there was something wrong with that topaz.

Such a beautiful deep blue they'd made it, when it must have been almost colourless to begin with. So he sent a few of them to a lab for testing.' She paused again. 'He'd just been reading about some old diamonds that had been exposed to radium and turned green, and were as radioactive as anything . . .'

Her face crumpled and she blinked her eyes rapidly, turning away from me and looking down to the floor so that I shouldn't see her distress. She made a great fuss among the papers and finally, with a sniff or two, said indistinctly, 'Here's his desk diary,' and then, more slowly, 'That's odd.'

'What's odd?'

'October's missing.'

She stood up and brought me the desk diary, which proved to be a largish appointments calendar showing a week at a glance. The month on current display was November, with a few of the daily spaces filled in but most of them empty. I flipped back the page and came next to September.

'I expect October's still on the floor, torn off,' I said.

She shook her head doubtfully, and in fact couldn't find it.

'Has the address book turned up?' I asked.

'No.' She was puzzled. 'It hasn't.'

'Is anything else missing?'

'I'm not really sure.'

It seemed bizarre that anyone should risk breaking in via the roof simply to steal an address book and some pages from a desk diary. Something else had to be missing.

The Yellow-Pages glaziers arrived at that point, putting a stop to my speculation. I went along with them to the packing room and saw the efficient hole that had been smashed in the six-by-four-foot window. All the glass that must have been scattered over every surface had been collected and swept into a pile of dagger-sharp glittering triangles, and a chill breeze ruffled papers in clipboards.

'You don't break glass this quality by tapping it with a fingernail,' one of the workmen said knowledgeably, picking up a piece. 'They must have swung a weight against it, like a wrecking ball.'

CHAPTER THREE

While the workmen measured the window frame, I watched the oldest of Greville's employees take transparent bags of beads from one cardboard box, insert them into bubble-plastic sleeves and stack them in another brown cardboard box. When all was transferred he put a list of contents on top, crossed the flaps and stuck the whole box around with wide reinforced tape.

'Where do the beads come from?' I asked.

'Taiwan, I dare say,' he said briefly, fixing a large address label on the top.

'No . . . I meant, where do you keep them here?'

He looked at me in pitying astonishment, a white-haired grandfatherly figure in storemen's brown overalls. 'In the stock-rooms, of course.'

'Of course.'

'Down the hall,' he said.

I went back to Greville's office and in the interests of good public relations asked Annette if she would show me the stock-rooms. Her heavyish face lightened with

43

pleasure and she led the way to the far end of the corridor.

'In here,' she said with obvious pride, passing through a central doorway into a small inner lobby, 'there are four rooms.' She pointed through open doorways. 'In there, mineral cabochons, oval and round; in there, beads; in there, oddities, and in there, organics.'

'What are organics?' I asked.

She beckoned me forward into the room in question, and I walked into a windowless space lined from floor to shoulder height with column after column of narrow grey metal drawers, each presenting a face to the world of about the size of a side of a shoebox. Each drawer, above a handle, bore a label identifying what it contained.

'Organics are things that grow,' Annette said patiently, and I reflected I should have worked that out for myself. 'Coral, for instance.' She pulled open a nearby drawer which proved to extend lengthily backwards, and showed me the contents: clear plastic bags, each packed with many strings of bright red twiglets. 'Italian,' she said. 'The best coral comes from the Mediterranean.' She closed that drawer, walked a few paces, pulled open another. 'Abalone, from abalone shells.' Another: 'Ivory. We still have a little, but we can't sell it now.' Another: 'Mother of pearl. We sell tons of it.' 'Pink mussel.' 'Freshwater pearls.' Finally, 'Imitation pearls. Cultured pearls are in the vault.'

Everything, it seemed, came in dozens of shapes and

sizes. Annette smiled at my bemused expression and invited me into the room next door.

Floor to shoulder height metal drawers, as before, not only lining the walls this time but filling the centre space with aisles, as in a supermarket.

'Cabochons, for setting into rings, and so on,' Annette said. 'They're in alphabetical order.'

Amethyst to turquoise via garnet, jade, lapis lazuli and onyx, with dozens of others I'd only half heard of. 'Semi-precious,' Annette said briefly. 'All genuine stones. Mr Franklin doesn't touch glass or plastic.' She stopped abruptly. Let five seconds lengthen. 'He didn't touch them,' she said lamely.

His presence was there strongly, I felt. It was almost as if he would walk through the door, all energy, saying 'Hello, Derek, what brings you here?' and if he seemed alive to me, who had seen him dead, how much more physical he must still be to Annette and June.

And to Lily too, I supposed. Lily was in the third stock-room pushing a brown cardboard box around on a thing like a tea-trolley, collecting bags of strings of beads and checking them against a list. With her centre-parted hair drawn back into a slide at her neck, with her small pale mouth and rounded cheeks, Lily looked like a Charlotte Brontë governess and dressed as if immolation were her personal choice. The sort to love the master in painful silence, I thought, and wondered what she'd felt for Greville.

Whatever it was, she wasn't letting it show. She raised

downcast eyes briefly to my face and at Annette's prompting told me she was putting together a consignment of rhodonite, jasper, aventurine and tiger eye, for one of the largest firms of jewellery manufacturers.

'We import the stones,' Annette said. 'We're wholesalers. We sell to about three thousand jewellers, maybe more. Some are big businesses. Many are small ones. We're at the top of the semi-precious trade. Highly regarded.' She swallowed. 'People trust us.'

Greville, I knew, had travelled the world to buy the stones. When we'd met he'd often been on the point of departing for Arizona or Hong Kong or had just returned from Israel, but he'd never told me more than the destinations. I at last understood what he'd been doing, and realized he couldn't easily be replaced.

Depressed, I went back to his office and telephoned to his accountant and his bank.

They were shocked and they were helpful, impressively so. The bank manager said I would need to call on him in the morning, but Saxony Franklin, as a limited company, could go straight on functioning. I could take over without trouble. All he would want was confirmation from my brother's lawyers that his will was as I said.

'Thank you very much,' I said, slightly surprised, and he told me warmly he was glad to be of service. Greville's affairs, I thought with a smile, must be amazingly healthy.

To the insurance company, also, my brother's death

seemed scarcely a hiccup. A limited company's insurance went marching steadily on, it seemed: it was the company that was insured, not my brother. I said I would like to claim for a smashed window. No problem. They would send a form.

After that I telephoned to the Ipswich undertakers who had been engaged to remove Greville's body from the hospital, and arranged that he should be cremated. They said they had 'a slot' at two o'clock on Friday: would that do? 'Yes,' I said, sighing. 'I'll be there.' They gave me the address of the crematorium in a hushed obsequious voice, and I wondered what it must be like to do business always with the bereaved. Happier by far to sell glittering baubles to the living or to ride jump-racing horses at thirty miles an hour, win, lose or break your bones.

I made yet another phone call, this time to the ortho-paedic surgeon, and as usual came up against the barrier of his receptionist. He wasn't in his own private consulting rooms, she announced, but at the hospital.

I said, 'Could you ask him to leave me a prescription somewhere, because I've fallen on my ankle and twisted it, and I'm running out of Distalgesic.'

'Hold on,' she said, and I held until she returned. 'I've spoken to him,' she said. 'He'll be back here later. He says can you be here at five?'

I said gratefully that I could, and reckoned that I'd have to leave soon after two-thirty to be sure of making it. I told Annette, and asked what they did about locking up.

'Mr Franklin usually gets here first and leaves last.' She stopped, confused. 'I mean . . .'

'I know,' I said. 'It's all right. I think of him in the present tense too. So go on.'

'Well, the double front doors bolt on the inside. Then the door from the lobby to the offices has an electronic bolt, as you know. So does the door from the corridor to the stock-rooms. So does the rear door, where we all come in and out. Mr Franklin changes . . . changed . . . the numbers at least every week. And there's another electronic lock, of course, on the door from the lobby to the showroom, and from the corridor into the showroom . . .' She paused. 'It does seem a lot, I know, but the electronic locks are very simple, really. You only have to remember three digits. Last Friday they were five, three, two. They're easy to work. Mr Franklin installed them so that we shouldn't have too many keys lying around. He and I both have a key, though, that will unlock all the electronic locks manually, if we need to.'

'So you've remembered the numbers?' I asked.

'Oh, yes. It was just, this morning, with everything . . . they went out of my head.'

'And the vault,' I said. 'Does that have any electronics?'

'No, but it has an intricate locking system in that heavy door, though it looks so simple from the outside. Mr Franklin always locks . . . locked . . . the vault before he left. When he went away on long trips, he made the key available to me.'

I wondered fleetingly about the awkward phrase, but didn't pursue it. I asked her instead about the show-room, which I hadn't seen and, again with pride, she went into the corridor, programmed a shining brass doorknob with the open sesame numbers, and ushered me into a windowed room that looked much like a shop, with glass-topped display counters and the firm's overall ambience of wealth.

Annette switched on powerful lights and the place came to life. She moved contentedly behind the counters, pointing out to me the contents now bright with illumination.

'In here are examples of everything we stock, except not all the sizes, of course, and not the faceted stones in the vault. We don't really use the showroom a great deal, only for new customers mostly, but I like being in here. I love the stones. They're fascinating. Mr Franklin says stones are the only things the human race takes from the earth and makes more beautiful.' She lifted a face heavy with loss. 'What will happen without him?'

'I don't know yet,' I said, 'but in the short term we fill the orders and despatch them, and order more stock from where you usually get it. We keep to all the old routines and practices. OK?'

She nodded, relieved at least for the present.

'Except,' I added, 'that it will be you who arrives first and leaves last, if you don't mind.'

'That's all right. I always do when Mr Franklin's away.'

We stared briefly at each other, not putting words to the obvious, then she switched off the showroom lights almost as if it were a symbolic act, and as we left pulled the self-locking door shut behind us.

Back in Greville's office I wrote down for her my own address and telephone number and said that if she felt insecure, or wanted to talk, I would be at home all evening.

'I'll come back here tomorrow morning, after I've seen the bank manager,' I said. 'Will you be all right until then?'

She nodded shakily. 'What do we call you? We can't call you Mr Franklin, it wouldn't seem right.'

'How about Derek?'

'Oh no.' She was instinctively against it. 'Would you mind, say . . . Mr Derek?'

'If you prefer it.' It sounded quaintly old-fashioned to me, but she was happy with it and said she would tell the others.

'About the others,' I said, 'sort everyone out for me, with their jobs. There's you, June, Lily . . .'

'June works the computers and the stock control,' she said. 'Lily fills the orders. Tina, she's a general assistant, she helps Lily and does some of the secretarial work. So does June. So do I, actually. We all do what's needed, really. There are few hard and fast divisions.

Except that Alfie doesn't do much except pack up the orders. It takes him all his time.'

'And that younger guy with the spiky orange halo?'

'Jason? Don't worry about the hair, he's harmless. He's our muscles. The stones are very heavy in bulk, you know. Jason shifts boxes, fills the stock-rooms, does odd jobs and hoovers the carpets. He helps Alfie sometimes, or Lily, if we're busy. Like I said, we all do anything, whatever's needed. Mr Franklin has never let anyone mark out a territory.'

'His words?'

'Yes, of course.'

Collective responsibility, I thought. I bowed to my brother's wisdom. If it worked, it worked. And from the look of everything in the place, it did indeed work, and I wouldn't disturb it.

I closed and locked the vault door with Greville's key and asked Annette which of his large bunch overrode the electronic locks. That one, she said, pointing, separating it.

'What are all the others, do you know?'

She looked blank. 'I've no idea.'

Car, house, whatever. I supposed I might eventually sort them out. I gave her what I hoped was a reassuring smile, sketched a goodbye to some of the others and rode down in the service lift to find Brad out in the yard.

'Swindon,' I said. 'The medical centre where we were on Friday. Would you mind?'

'Course not.' Positively radiant, I thought.

It was an eighty-mile journey, ten miles beyond home. Brad managed it without further communication and I spent the time thinking of all the things I hadn't yet done, like seeing to Greville's house and stopping delivery of his daily paper, wherever it might come from, and telling the post office to divert his letters . . . To hell with it, I thought wearily, why did the damned man have to die?

The orthopod X-rayed and unwrapped my ankle and tut-tutted. From toes to shin it looked hard, black and swollen, the skin almost shiny from the stretching.

'I advised you to rest it,' he said, a touch crossly.

'My brother died . . .' and I explained about the mugging, and also about having to see to Greville's affairs.

He listened carefully, a strong sensible man with prematurely white hair. I didn't know a jockey who didn't trust him. He understood our needs and our imperatives, because he treated a good many of us who lived in or near the training centre of Lambourn.

'As I told you the other day,' he said when I'd finished, 'you've fractured the lower end of the fibula, and where the tibia and fibula should be joined, they've sprung apart. Today, they are further apart. They're now providing no support at all for the talus, the heel bone. You've now completely ripped the lateral ligament which normally binds the ankle together. The whole

52

joint is insecure and coming apart inside, like a mortise joint in a piece of furniture when the glue's given way.'

'So how long will it take?' I asked.

He smiled briefly. 'In a crêpe bandage it will hurt for about another ten days, and after that you can walk on it. You could be back on a horse in three weeks from now, if you don't mind the stirrup hurting you, which it will. About another three weeks after that, the ankle might be strong enough for racing.'

'Good,' I said, relieved. 'Not much worse than before, then.'

'It's worse, but it won't take much longer to mend.'

'Fine.'

He looked down at the depressing sight. 'If you're going to be doing all this travelling about, you'd be much more comfortable in a rigid cast. You could put your weight on it in a couple of days. You'd have almost no pain.'

'And wear it for six weeks? And get atrophied muscles?'

'Atrophy is a strong word.' He knew all the same that jump jockeys needed strong leg muscles above all else, and the way to keep them strong was to keep them moving. Inside plaster they couldn't move at all and weakened rapidly. If movement cost a few twinges, it was worth it.

'Delta-cast is lightweight,' he said persuasively. 'It's a polymer, not like the old plaster of Paris. It's porous, so air circulates, and you don't get skin problems. It's good.

And I could make you a cast with a zip in it so you could take it off for physiotherapy.'

'How long before I was racing?'

'Nine or ten weeks.'

I didn't say anything for a moment or two and he looked up fast, his eyes bright and quizzical.

'A cast, then?' he said.

'No.'

He smiled and picked up a roll of crêpe bandage. 'Don't fall on it again in the next month, or you'll be back to square one.'

'I'll try not to.'

He bandaged it all tight again from just below the knee down to my toes and back, and gave me another prescription for Distalgesic. 'No more than eight tablets in twenty-four hours and not with alcohol.' He said it every time.

'Right.'

He considered me thoughtfully for a moment and then rose and went over to a cabinet where he kept packets and bottles of drugs. He came back tucking a small plastic bag into an envelope which he held out to me.

'I'm giving you something known as DF 1–1–8s. Rather appropriate, as they're your own initials! I've given you three of them. They are serious painkillers, and I don't want you to use them unless something like yesterday happens again.'

'OK,' I said, putting the envelope in my pocket. 'Thanks.'

'If you take one, you won't feel a thing.' He smiled. 'If you take two at once, you'll be spaced out, high as a kite. If you take all three at once, you'll be unconscious. So be warned.' He paused. 'They are a last resort.'

'I won't forget,' I said, 'and I truly am grateful.'

Brad drove to a chemist's, took my prescription in, waited for it to be dispensed, and finished the ten miles home, parking outside my door.

'Same time tomorrow morning?' I asked. 'Back to London.'

'Yerss.'

'I'd be in trouble without you,' I said, climbing out with his help. He gave me a brief haunted glance and handed me the crutches. 'You drive great,' I said.

He was embarrassed, but also pleased. Nowhere near a smile, of course, but a definite twitch in the cheeks. He turned away, ducking my gaze, and set off doggedly towards his mother.

I let myself into the house and regretted the embargo on a large scotch. Instead, with June's lunchtime sandwich a distant memory, I refuelled with sardines on toast and ice-cream after, which more or less reflected my habitual laziness about cooking.

Then, aligned with icepacks along the sofa, I

telephoned the man in Newmarket who trained Greville's two racehorses.

He picked up the receiver as if he'd been waiting for it to ring.

'Yes?' he said. 'What are they offering?'

'I've no idea,' I said. 'Is that Nicholas Loder?'

'What? Who are you?' He was brusque and impatient, then took a second look at things and with more honey said, 'I beg your pardon, I was expecting someone else. I'm Loder, yes, who am I talking to?'

'Greville Franklin's brother.'

'Oh yes?'

It meant nothing to him immediately. I pictured him as I knew him, more by sight than face to face, a big light-haired man in his forties with enormous presence and self-esteem to match. Undoubtedly a good-to-great trainer, but in television interviews occasionally overbearing and condescending to the interviewer, as I'd heard he could be also to his owners. Greville kept his horses with him because the original horse he'd taken as a bad debt had been in that stable. Nicholas Loder had bought Greville all his subsequent horses and done notably well with them, and Greville had assured me that he got on well with the man by telephone, and that he was perfectly friendly.

The last time I'd spoken to Greville myself on the telephone he'd been talking of buying another two-year-old, saying that Loder would get him one at the October sales, perhaps.

I explained to Loder that Greville had died and after the first sympathetic exclamations of dismay he reacted as I would have expected, not as if missing a close friend but on a practical business level.

'It won't affect the running of his horses,' he said. 'They're owned in any case by the Saxony Franklin company, not by Greville himself. I can run the horses still in the company name. I have the company's Authority to Act. There should be no problem.'

'I'm afraid there may be,' I began.

'No, no. Dozen Roses runs on Saturday at York. In with a great chance. I informed Greville of it only a few days ago. He always wanted to know when they were running, though he never went to see them.'

'The problem is,' I said, 'about my being his brother. He has left the Saxony Franklin company to me.'

The size of the problem suddenly revealed itself to him forcibly. 'You're not his brother *Derek* Franklin? That brother? The jockey?'

'Yes. So ... could you find out from Weatherby's whether the horses can still run while the estate is subject to probate?'

'My God,' he said weakly.

Professional jockeys, as we both knew well, were not allowed to own runners in races. They could own other horses such as brood mares, foals, stallions, hacks, hunters, show-jumpers, anything in horseshoes; they could even own racehorses, but they couldn't run them.'

'Can you find out?' I asked again.

'I will.' He sounded exasperated. 'Dozen Roses should trot up on Saturday.'

Dozen Roses was currently the better of Greville's two horses whose fortunes I followed regularly in the newspapers and on television. A triple winner as a three-year-old, he had been disappointing at four, but in the current year, as a five-year-old, he had regained all his old form and had scored three times in the past few weeks. A 'trot-up' on Saturday was a reasonable expectation.

Loder said, 'If Weatherby's give the thumbs down to the horse running, will you sell it? I'll find a buyer by Saturday, among my owners.'

I listened to the urgency in his voice and wondered whether Dozen Roses was more than just another trot-up, of which season by season he had many. He sounded a lot more fussed than seemed normal.

'I don't know whether I can sell before probate,' I said. 'You'd better find that out, too.'

'But if you can, will you?'

'I don't know,' I said, puzzled. 'Let's wait and see, first.'

'You won't be able to hang on to him, you know,' he said, forcefully. 'He's got another season in him. He's still worth a good bit. But unless you do something like turn in your licence, you won't be able to run him, and he's not worth turning in your licence for. It's not as if he were favourite for the Derby.'

'I'll decide during the week.'

'But you're not thinking of turning in your licence, are you?' He sounded almost alarmed. 'Didn't I read in the paper that you're on the injured list but hope to be back racing well before Christmas?'

'You did read that, yes.'

'Well, then.' The relief was as indefinable as the alarm, but came clear down the wires. I didn't understand any of it. He shouldn't have been so worried.

'Perhaps Saxony Franklin could lease the horse to someone,' I said.

'Oh. Ah. To me?' He sounded as if it were the perfect solution.

'I don't know,' I said cautiously. 'We'll have to find out.'

I realized that I didn't totally trust him, and it wasn't a doubt I'd have felt before the phone call. He was one of the top five Flat race trainers in the country, automatically held to be reliable because of his rock-solid success.

'When Greville came to see his horses,' I asked, 'did he ever bring anyone with him? I'm trying to reach people he knew, to tell them of his death.'

'He never came here to see his horses. I hardly knew him personally myself, except on the telephone.'

'Well, his funeral is on Friday at Ipswich,' I said. 'What if I called in at Newmarket that day, as I'll be over your way, to see you and the horses and complete any paperwork that's necessary?'

'No,' he said instantly. Then, softening it, 'I always

discourage owners from visiting. They disrupt the stable routine. I can't make any exceptions. If I need you to sign anything I'll arrange it another way.'

'All right,' I agreed mildly, not crowding him into corners. 'I'll wait to hear from you about what Weatherby's decide.'

He said he would get in touch and abruptly disconnected, leaving me thinking that on the subject of his behaviour I didn't know the questions let alone the answers.

Perhaps I had been imagining things: but I knew I hadn't. One could often hear more nuances in someone's voice on the telephone than one could face to face. When people were relaxed, the lower vibrations of their voices came over the wires undisturbed; under stress, the lower vibrations disappeared because the vocal cords involuntarily tightened. After Loder had discovered I would be inheriting Dozen Roses, there had been no lower vibrations at all.

Shelving the enigma I pondered the persisting difficulty of informing Greville's friends. They had to exist, no one lived in a vacuum; but if it had been the other way round, I supposed that Greville would have had the same trouble. He hadn't known my friends either. Our worlds had scarcely touched except briefly when we met, and then we had talked a bit about horses, a bit about gadgets, a bit about the world in general and any interesting current events.

He'd lived alone, as I did. He'd told me nothing about any love life. He'd said merely, 'Bad luck' when three years earlier I'd remarked that my live-in girlfriend had gone to live-in somewhere else. It didn't matter, I said. It had been a mutual agreement, a natural ending. I'd asked him once about his long-ago divorced wife. 'She remarried. Haven't seen her since,' was all he'd said.

If it had been I that had died, I thought, he would have told the world I worked in: he'd have told, perhaps, the trainer I mostly rode for and maybe the racing papers. So I should tell his world: tell the semi-precious stone fraternity. Annette could do it, regardless of the absence of Greville's address book, because of June's computer. The computer made more and more nonsense of the break-in. I came back to the same conviction: something else had been stolen, and I didn't know what.

I remembered at about that point that I did have Greville's pocket diary, even if his desk diary had lost October, so I went and fetched it from the bedroom where I'd left it the night before. I thought I might find friends' names and phone numbers in the addresses section at the back, but he had been frugal in that department as everywhere in the slim brown book. I turned the pages, which were mostly unused, seeing only short entries like 'R arrives from Brazil' and 'B in Paris' and 'Buy citrine for P'.

In March I was brought up short. Because it was a racing diary, the race-meetings to be held on each day of the year were listed under the day's date. I came to Thursday 16 March which listed 'Cheltenham'. The word Cheltenham had been ringed with a ball-point pen, and Greville had written 'Gold Cup' in the day's space; and then, with a different pen, he had added the words 'Derek won it!!'

It brought me to sudden tears. I couldn't help it.

I longed for him to be alive so I could get to know him better. I wept for the lost opportunities, the time wasted. I longed to know the brother who had cared what I did, who had noted in his almost empty diary that I'd won one of the top races of the year.

CHAPTER FOUR

There were only three telephone numbers in the addresses section at the back, all identified merely by initials. One, NL, was Nicholas Loder's. I tried the other two, which were London numbers, and got no reply.

Scattered through the rest of the diary were three more numbers. Two of them proved to be restaurants in full evening flood, and I wrote down their names, recognizing one of them as the place I'd last dined with Greville, two or three months back. On 25 July, presumably, as that was the date on which he'd written the number. It had been an Indian restaurant, I remembered, and we had eaten ultra-hot curry.

Sighing, I turned the pages and tried a number occurring on 2 September, about five weeks earlier. It wasn't a London number, but I didn't recognize the code. I listened to the bell ringing continuously at the other end and had resigned myself to another blank when someone lifted the distant receiver and in a low breathy voice said, 'Hello?'

'Hello,' I replied. 'I'm ringing on behalf of Greville Franklin.'

'Who?'

'Greville Franklin.' I spoke the words slowly and clearly.

'Just a moment.'

There was a long uninformative silence and then someone else clattered on sharp heels up to the receiver and decisively spoke, her voice high and angry.

'How dare you!' she said. 'Don't ever do this again. I will not have your name spoken in this house.'

She put the receiver down with a crash before I could utter a word, and I sat bemusedly looking at my own telephone and feeling as if I'd swallowed a wasp.

Whoever she was, I thought wryly, she wouldn't want to send flowers to the funeral, though she might have been gladdened by the death. I wondered what on earth Greville could have done to raise such a storm, but that was the trouble, I didn't know him well enough to make a good guess.

Thankful on the whole that there weren't any more numbers to be tried I looked again at what few entries he had made, more out of curiosity than looking for helpful facts.

He had noted the days on which his horses had run, again only with initials. DR, Dozen Roses, appeared most, each time with a number following, like 300 at 8s, which I took to mean the amounts he'd wagered at what odds. Below the numbers he had put each time another number inside a circle which, when I compared them with the form book, were revealed as the placings of the horse at the finish. Its last three appearances, all with 5 in the circle, seemed to have netted Greville respectively 500 at 14s, 500 at 5s, 1000 at 6/4. The trot-up scheduled for Saturday, I thought, would be likely to be at odds-on.

Greville's second horse, Gemstones appearing simply as G, had run six times, winning only once but profitably: 500 at 100/6.

All in all, I thought, a moderate betting pattern for an owner. He had made, I calculated, a useful profit overall, more than most owners achieved. With his prize money in addition to offset both the training fees and the capital cost of buying the horses in the first place, I guessed that he had come out comfortably ahead, and it was in the business sense, I supposed, that owning horses had chiefly pleased him.

I flicked casually forward to the end of the book and in the last few pages headed 'NOTES' came across a lot of doodling and then a list of numbers.

The doodling was the sort one does while listening on the telephone, a lot of boxes and zig-zags, haphazard and criss-crossed with lines of shading. On the page facing, there was an equation: $CZ=C \times 1.7$. I supposed it had been of sparkling clarity to Greville, but of no use to me.

Overleaf I found the sort of numbers list I kept in my own diary: passport, bank account, national insurance.

After those, in small capital letters further down the page, was the single word DEREK. Another jolt, seeing it again in his writing.

I wondered briefly whether, from its placing, Greville had used my name as some sort of mnemonic, or whether it was just another doodle: there was no way of telling. With a sigh I riffled back through the pages and came to something I'd looked at before, a lightly-pencilled entry for the day before his death. Second time around, it meant just as little.

Koningin Beatrix? he had written. Just the two words and the question mark. I wondered idly if it were the name of a horse, if he'd been considering buying it; my mind tended to work that way. Then I thought that perhaps he'd written the last name first, such as Smith, Jane, and that maybe he'd been going to Ipswich to meet a Beatrix Koningin.

I returned to the horse theory and got through to the trainer I rode for, Milo Shandy, who enquired breezily about the ankle and said would I please waste no time in coming back.

'I could ride out in a couple of weeks,' I said.

'At least that's something, I suppose. Get some massage.'

The mere thought of it was painful. I said I would, not meaning it, and asked about Koningin Beatrix, spelling it out.

'Don't know of any horse called that, but I can find out for you in the morning. I'll ask Weatherby's if the name's available, and if they say yes, it means there isn't a horse called that registered for racing.'

'Thanks a lot.'

'Think nothing of it. I heard your brother died. Bad luck.'

'Yes . . . How did you know?'

'Nicholas Loder rang me just now, explaining your dilemma and wanting me to persuade you to lease him Dozen Roses.'

'But that's crazy. His ringing you, I mean.'

He chuckled. 'I told him so. I told him I could bend you like a block of teak. He didn't seem to take it in. Anyway, I don't think leasing would solve anything. Jockeys aren't allowed to own racing horses, period. If you lease a horse, you still own it.'

'I'm sure you're right.'

'Put your shirt on it.'

'Loder bets, doesn't he?' I asked. 'In large amounts?'

'So I've heard.'

'He said Dozen Roses would trot up at York on Saturday.'

'In that case, do you want me to put a bit on for you?'

Besides not being allowed to run horses in races, jockeys also were banned from betting, but there were always ways round that, like helpful friends.

'I don't think so, not this time,' I said, 'but thanks anyway.'

'You won't mind if I do?'

'Be my guest. If Weatherby's let it run, that is.'

'A nice little puzzle,' he said appreciatively. 'Come over soon for a drink. Come for evening stables.'

I would, I said.

'Take care.'

I put down the phone, smiling at his easy farewell colloquialism. Jump jockeys were paid not to take care, on the whole. Not too much care.

Milo would be horrified if I obeyed him.

In the morning, Brad drove me to Saxony Franklin's bank to see the manager who was young and bright and spoke with deliberate slowness, as if waiting for his clients' intelligence to catch up. Was there something about crutches, I wondered, that intensified the habit? It took him five minutes to suspect that I wasn't a moron. After that he told me Greville had borrowed a sizeable chunk of the bank's money, and he would be looking to me to repay it. 'One point five million United States dollars in cash, as a matter of fact.'

'One point five million dollars,' I repeated, trying not to show that he had punched most of the breath out of me. '*What for?*'

'For buying diamonds. Diamonds from the DTC of the CSO are, of course, normally paid for in cash, in dollars.'

Bank managers around Hatton Garden, it seemed, saw nothing extraordinary in such an exercise.

'He doesn't . . . didn't deal in diamonds,' I protested.

'He had decided to expand and, of course, we made the funds available. Your brother dealt with us for many years and as you'll know was a careful and conscientious businessman. A valued client. We have several times advanced him money for expansion and each time we have been repaid without difficulty. Punctiliously, in fact.' He cleared his throat. 'The present loan, taken out three months ago, is due for repayment progressively over a period of five years, and of course as the loan was made to the company, not to your brother personally, the terms of the loan will be unchanged by his death.'

'Yes,' I said.

'I understood from what you said yesterday that you propose to run the business yourself?' He seemed happy enough where I might have expected a shade of anxiety. So why no anxiety? What wasn't I grasping?

'Do you hold security for the loan?' I asked.

'An agreement. We lent the money against the stock of Saxony Franklin.'

'All the stones?'

'As many as would satisfy the debt. But our best security has always been your brother's integrity and his business ability.'

I said, 'I'm not a gemmologist. I'll probably sell the business after probate.'

He nodded comfortably. 'That might be the best course. We would expect the Saxony Franklin loan to be repaid on schedule, but we would welcome a dialogue with the purchasers.'

He produced papers for me to sign and asked for extra specimen signatures so that I could put my name to Saxony Franklin cheques. He didn't ask what experience I'd had in running a business. Instead, he wished me luck.

I rose to my crutches and shook his hand, thinking of the things I hadn't said.

I hadn't told him I was a jockey, which might have caused a panic in Hatton Garden. And I hadn't told him that, if Greville had bought one and a half million dollars' worth of diamonds, I didn't know where they were.

'Diamonds?' Annette said. 'No. I told you. We never deal in diamonds.'

'The bank manager believes that Greville bought some recently. From something called the DTC of the CSO.'

'The Central Selling Organization? That's De Beers. The DTC is their diamond trading company. No, no.' She looked anxiously at my face. 'He can't have done. He never said anything about it.'

'Well, has the stock-buying here increased over the past three months?'

'It usually does,' she said, nodding. 'The business always grows. Mr Franklin comes back from world trips with new stones all the time. Beautiful stones. He can't resist them. He sells most of the special ones to a jewel-

70

lery designer who has several boutiques in places like Knightsbridge and Bond Street. Gorgeous costume jewellery, but with real stones. Many of his pieces are one-offs, designed for a single stone. He has a great name. People prize some of his pieces like Fabergé's.'

'Who is he?'

'Prospero Jenks,' she said, expecting my awe at least.

I hadn't heard of him, but I nodded all the same.

'Does he set the stones with diamonds?' I asked.

'Yes, sometimes. But he doesn't buy those from Saxony Franklin.'

We were in Greville's office, I sitting in his swivel chair behind the vast expanse of desk, Annette sorting yesterday's roughly heaped higgledy-piggledy papers back into the drawers and files that had earlier contained them.

'You don't think Greville would ever have kept diamonds in this actual office, do you?' I asked.

'Certainly not.' The idea shocked her. 'He was always very careful about security.'

'So no one who broke in here would expect to find anything valuable lying about?'

She paused with a sheaf of papers in one hand, her brow wrinkling.

'It's odd, isn't it? They wouldn't expect to find anything valuable lying about in an office if they knew anything about the jewellery trade. And if they didn't know anything about the jewellery trade, why pick this office?'

The same old unanswerable question.

June with her incongruous motherliness brought in the typist's chair again for me to put my foot on. I thanked her and asked if her stock control computer kept day-to-day tabs on the number and value of all the polished pebbles in the place.

'Goodness, yes,' she said with amusement. 'Dates and amounts in, dates and amounts out. Prices in, prices out, profit margin, VAT, tax, you name it, the computer will tell you what we've got, what it's worth, what sells slowly, what sells fast, what's been hanging around here wasting space for two years or more, which isn't much.'

'The stones in the vault as well?'

'Sure.'

'But no diamonds?'

'No, we don't deal in them.' She gave me a bright incurious smile and swiftly departed, saying over her shoulder that the Christmas rush was still going strong and they'd been bombarded by fax orders overnight.

'Who reorders what you sell?' I asked Annette.

'I do for ordinary stock. June tells me what we need. Mr Franklin himself ordered the faceted stones and anything unusual.'

She went on sorting the papers, basically unconcerned because her responsibility ended on her way home. She was wearing that day the charcoal skirt of the day before but topped with a black sweater, perhaps out of respect for Greville. Solid in body, but not large, she had good legs in black tights and a settled, well-groomed, middle-aged air. I couldn't imagine her being as buoyant as June even in her youth.

I asked her if she could lay her hands on the company's insurance policy and she said as it happened she had just refiled it. I read its terms with misgivings and then telephoned the insurance company. Had my brother, I asked, recently increased the insurance? Had he increased it to cover diamonds to the value of one point five million dollars? He had not. It had been discussed only. My brother had said the premium asked was too high, and he had decided against it. The voice explained that the premium had been high because the stones would be often in transit, which made them vulnerable. He didn't know if Mr Franklin had gone ahead with buying the diamonds. It had been an enquiry only, he thought, three or four months ago. I thanked him numbly and put down the receiver.

The telephone rang again immediately and as Annette seemed to be waiting for me to do so, I answered it.

'Hello?' I said.

A male voice said, 'Is that Mr Franklin? I want to speak to Mr Franklin, please.'

'Er . . . could I help? I'm his brother.'

'Perhaps you can,' he said. 'This is the clerk of the West London Magistrates Court. Your brother was due here twenty minutes ago and it is unlike him to be late. Could you tell me when to expect him?'

'Just a minute.' I put my hand over the mouthpiece

and told Annette what I'd just heard. Her eyes widened and she showed signs of horrified memory.

'It's his day for the Bench! Alternate Tuesdays. I'd clean forgotten.'

I returned to the phone and explained the situation.

'Oh. Oh. How dreadfully upsetting.' He did indeed sound upset, but also a shade impatient. 'It really would have been more helpful if you could have alerted me in advance. It's very short notice to have to find a replacement.'

'Yes,' I agreed, 'but this office was broken into during the weekend. My brother's appointments diary was stolen, and in fact we cannot alert anybody not to expect him.'

'How extremely inconvenient.' It didn't seem an inappropriate statement to him. I thought Greville might find it inconvenient to be dead. Maybe it wasn't the best time for black humour.

'If my brother had personal friends among the magistrates,' I said, 'I would be happy for them to get in touch with me here. If you wouldn't mind telling them.'

'I'll do that, certainly.' He hesitated. 'Mr Franklin sits on the licensing committee. Do you want me to inform the chairman?'

'Yes, please. Tell anyone you can.'

He said goodbye with all the cares of the world on his shoulders and I sighed to Annette that we had better begin telling everyone else as soon as possible, but the trade was to expect business as usual.

'What about the papers?' she asked. 'Shall we put it in *The Times* and so on?'

'Good idea. Can you do it?'

She said she could, but in fact showed me the paragraph she'd written before phoning the papers. 'Suddenly, as the result of an accident, Greville Saxony Franklin JP, son of . . .' She'd left a space after 'son of' which I filled in for her: 'the late Lt. Col. and Mrs Miles Franklin'. I changed 'brother of Derek' to 'brother of Susan, Miranda and Derek', and I added a few final words, 'Cremation, Ipswich, Friday'.

'Have you any idea,' I asked Annette, 'what he could have been doing in Ipswich?'

She shook her head. 'I've never heard him mention the place. But then he didn't ever tell me very much that wasn't business.' She paused. 'He wasn't exactly secretive, but he never chatted about his private life.' She hesitated. 'He never talked about you.'

I thought of all the times he'd been good company and told me virtually nothing, and I understood very well what she meant.

'He used to say that the best security was a still tongue,' she said. 'He asked us not to talk too much about our jobs to total strangers, and we all know it's safer not to, even though we don't have precious stones here. All the people in the trade are security mad and the diamantaires can be paranoid.'

'What,' I said, 'are diamantaires?'

'Not what, who,' she said. 'They're dealers in rough

diamonds. They get the stones cut and polished and sell them to manufacturing jewellers. Mr Franklin always said diamonds were a world of their own, quite separate from other gemstones. There was a ridiculous boom and a terrible crash in world diamond prices during the eighties and a lot of the diamantaires lost fortunes and went bankrupt and Mr Franklin was often saying that they must have been mad to over-extend the way they had.' She paused. 'You couldn't help but know what was happening all round us in this area, where every second business is in gemstones. No one in the pubs and restaurants talked of much else. So you see, I'm sure the bank manager must be wrong. Mr Franklin would never buy diamonds.'

If he hadn't bought diamonds, I thought, what the hell had he done with one point five million dollars in cash?

Bought diamonds. He had to have done. Either that or the money was still lying around somewhere, undoubtedly carefully hidden. Either the money or diamonds to the value were lying around uninsured, and if my semi-secretive ultra-security-conscious brother had left a treasure-island map with X marking the precious spot, I hadn't yet found it. Much more likely, I feared, that the knowledge had died under the scaffolding. If it had, the firm would be forfeited to the bank, the last thing Greville would have wanted.

If it had, a major part of the inheritance he'd left me had vanished like morning mist.

He should have stuck to his old beliefs, I thought gloomily, and let diamonds strictly alone.

The telephone on the desk rang again and this time Annette answered it, as she was beside it.

'Saxony Franklin, can I help you?' she said, and listened. 'No, I'm very sorry, you won't be able to talk to Mr Franklin personally ... Could I have your name, please?' She listened. 'Well, Mrs Williams, we must most unhappily inform you that Mr Franklin died as a result of an accident over the weekend. We are however continuing in business. Can I help you at all?'

She listened for a moment or two in increasing puzzlement, then said, 'Are you there? Mrs Williams, can you hear me?' But it seemed as though there was no reply, and in a while she put the receiver down, frowning. 'Whoever it was hung up.'

'Do I gather you don't know Mrs Williams?'

'No, I don't.' She hesitated. 'But I think she rang yesterday, too. I think I told her yesterday that Mr Franklin wasn't expected in the office all day, like I told everyone. I didn't ask for her name yesterday. But she has a voice you don't forget.'

'Why not?'

'Cut glass,' she said succinctly. 'Like Mr Franklin, but more so. Like you too, a bit.'

I was amused. She herself spoke what I thought of as unaccented English, though I supposed any way of speaking sounded like an accent to someone else. I wondered briefly about the cut-glass Mrs Williams who had received the news of the accident in silence and hadn't asked where, or how, or when.

Annette went off to her own office to get through to the newspapers and I picked Greville's diary out of my trouser pocket and tried the numbers that had been unreachable the night before. The two at the back of the book turned out to be first his bookmaker and second his barber, both of whom sounded sorry to be losing his custom, though the bookmaker less so because of Greville's habit of winning.

My ankle heavily ached; the result, I dared say, of general depression as much as aggrieved bones and muscle. Depression because whatever decisions I'd made to that point had been merely common sense, but there would come a stage ahead when I could make awful mistakes through ignorance. I'd never before handled finances bigger than my own bank balance and the only business I knew anything about was the training of racehorses, and that only from observation, not from hands-on experience. I knew what I was doing around horses: I could tell the spinel from the ruby. In Greville's world, I could be taken for a ride and never know it. I could lose badly before I'd learned even the elementary rules of the game.

Greville's great black desk stretched away to each side of me, the wide knee-hole flanked to right and left by twin stacks of drawers, four stacks in all. Most of them now contained what they had before the break-in, and I began desultorily to investigate the nearest on the left, looking vaguely for anything that would prompt me as to what I'd overlooked or hadn't known was necessary to be done.

I first found not tasks but the toys: the small black gadgets now tidied away into serried ranks. The Geiger counter was there, also the hand-held copier and a variety of calculators, and I picked out a small black contraption about the size of a paperback book and, turning it over curiously, couldn't think what it could be used for.

'That's an electric measurer,' June said, coming breezily into the office with her hands full of paper. 'Want to see how it works?'

I nodded and she put it flat on its back on the desk. 'It'll tell you how far it is from the desk to the ceiling,' she said, pressing knobs. 'There you are, seven feet five and a half inches. In metres,' she pressed another knob, 'two metres twenty-six centimetres.'

'I don't really need to know how far it is to the ceiling,' I said.

She laughed. 'If you hold it flat against a wall, it measures how far it is to the opposite wall. Does it in a flash, as you saw. You don't need to mess around with tape measures. Mr Franklin got it when he was redesigning the stock-rooms. And he worked out how much carpet we'd need, and how much paint for the walls. This gadget tells you all that.'

'You like computers, don't you?' I said.

'Love them. All shapes, all sizes.' She peered into the

79

open drawer. 'Mr Franklin was always buying the tiny ones.' She picked out a small grey leather slip-cover the size of a pack of cards and slid the contents onto her palm. 'This little dilly is a travel guide. It tells you things like phone numbers for taxis, airlines, tourist information, the weather, embassies, American Express.' She demonstrated, pushing buttons happily. 'It's an American gadget, it even tells you the TV channels and radio frequencies for about a hundred cities in the US, including Tucson, Arizona, where they hold the biggest gem fair every February. It helps you with fifty other cities round the world, places like Tel Aviv and Hong Kong and Taipei where Mr Greville was always going.'

She put the travel guide down and picked up something else. 'This little round number is a sort of telescope, but it also tells you how far you are away from things. It's for golfers. It tells you how far you are away from the flag on the green, Mr Franklin said, so that you know which club to use.'

'How often did he play golf?' I said, looking through the less than four-inch-long telescope and seeing inside a scale marked GREEN on the lowest line with diminishing numbers above, from 200 yards at the bottom to 40 yards at the top. 'He never talked about it much.'

'He sometimes played at weekends, I think,' June said doubtfully. 'You line up the word GREEN with the actual green, and then the flag stick is always eight feet high. I think, so wherever the top of the stick is on the scale, that's how far away you are. He said it was a good gadget for amateurs like him. He said never to be ashamed of landing in life's bunkers if you'd tried your best shot.' She blinked a bit. 'He always used to show these things to me when he bought them. He knew I liked them too.' She fished for a tissue and without apology wiped her eyes.

'Where did he get them all from?' I asked.

'Mail order catalogues, mostly.'

I was faintly surprised. Mail order and Greville didn't seem to go together, somehow, but I was wrong about that, as I promptly found out.

'Would you like to see our own new catalogue?' June asked, and was out of the door and back again before I could remember if I'd ever seen an old one and decide I hadn't. 'Fresh from the printers,' she said. 'I was just unpacking them.'

I turned the glossy pages of the 50-page booklet, seeing in faithful colours all the polished goodies I'd met in the stock-rooms and also a great many of lesser breeding. Amulets, heart shapes, hoops and butterflies: there seemed to be no end to the possibilities of adornment. When I murmured derogatorily that they were a load of junk, June came fast and strongly to their defence, a mother-hen whose chickens had been snubbed.

'Not everyone can afford diamonds,' she said sharply, 'and, anyway, these things are pretty and we sell them in thousands, and they wind up in hundreds of High Street shops and department stores and I often see people buying the odd shapes we've had through here. People do like them, even if they're not your taste.'

'Sorry,' I said.

Some of her fire subsided. 'I suppose I shouldn't speak to you like that,' she said uncertainly, 'but you're not Mr Franklin . . .' She stopped with a frown.

'It's OK,' I said. 'I am, but I'm not. I know what you mean.'

'Alfie says,' she said slowly, 'that there's a steeple-chase jockey called Derek Franklin.' She looked at my foot as if with new understanding. 'Champion jockey one year, he said. Always in the top ten. Is that . . . you?'

I said neutrally, 'Yes.'

'I *had* to ask you,' she said. 'The others didn't want to.'

'Why not?'

'Annette didn't think you could be a jockey. You're too tall. She said Mr Franklin never said anything about you being one. All she knew was that he had a brother he saw a few times a year. She said she was going to ignore what Alfie thought, because it was most unlikely.' She paused. 'Alfie mentioned it yesterday, after you'd gone. Then he said . . . they all said . . . they didn't see how a jockey could run a business of this sort. If you were one, that is. They didn't want it to be true, so they didn't want to ask.'

'You tell Alfie and the others that if the jockey doesn't run the business their jobs will be down the tubes and they'll be out in the cold before the week's over.'

Her blue eyes widened. 'You sound just like Mr Franklin!'

'And you don't need to mention my profession to the customers, in case I get the same vote of no confidence I've got from the staff.'

Her lips shaped the word 'Wow' but she didn't quite say it. She disappeared fast from the room and presently returned, followed by all the others who were only too clearly in a renewed state of anxiety.

Not one of them a leader. What a pity.

I said, 'You all look as if the ship's been wrecked and the lifeboat's leaking. Well, we've lost the captain, and I agree we're in trouble. My job is with horses and not in an office. But, like I said yesterday, this business is going to stay open and thrive. One way or another, I'll see that it does. So if you'll all go on working normally and keep the customers happy, you'll be doing yourselves a favour because if we get through safely you'll all be due for a bonus. I'm not my brother, but I'm not a fool either, and I'm a pretty fast learner. So just let's get on with the orders, and, er, cheer up.'

Lily, the Charlotte Brontë lookalike, said meekly, 'We don't really doubt your ability . . .'

'Of course we do,' interrupted Jason. He stared at me with half a snigger, with a suggestion of curling lip. 'Give us a tip for the three-thirty, then.'

I listened to the street-smart bravado which went with the spiky orange hair. He thought me easy game.

I said, 'When you are personally able to ride the winner of any three-thirty, you'll be entitled to your jeer. Until then, work or leave, it's up to you.'

There was a resounding silence. Alfie almost smiled. Jason looked merely sullen. Annette took a deep breath, and June's eyes were shining with laughter.

They all drifted away still wordless and I couldn't tell to what extent they'd been reassured, if at all. I listened to the echo of my own voice saying I wasn't a fool, and wondering ruefully if it were true: but until the diamonds were found or I'd lost all hope of finding them, I thought it more essential than ever that Saxony Franklin Ltd should stay shakily afloat. All hands, I thought, to the pumps.

June came back and said tentatively, 'The pep talk seems to be working.'

'Good.'

'Alfie gave Jason a proper ticking off, and Jason's staying.'

'Right.'

'What can I do to help?'

I looked at her thin alert face with its fair eyelashes and blonde-to-invisible eyebrows and realized that without her the save-the-firm enterprise would be a non-starter. She, more than her computer, was at the heart of things. She more than Annette, I thought.

'How long have you worked here?' I asked.

'Three years. Since I left school. Don't ask if I like the job, I love it. What can I do?'

'Look up in your computer's memory any reference to diamonds,' I said.

She was briefly impatient. 'I told you, we don't deal in diamonds.'

'All the same, would you?'

She shrugged and was gone. I got to my feet – foot – and followed her, and watched while she expertly tapped her keys.

'Nothing at all under diamonds,' she said finally. 'Nothing. I told you.'

'Yes.' I thought about the boxes in the vault with the mineral information on the labels. 'Do you happen to know the chemical formula for diamonds?'

'Yes, I do,' she said instantly. 'It's C. Diamonds are pure carbon.'

'Could you try again, then, under C?'

She tried. There was no file for C.

'Did my brother know how to use this computer?' I asked.

'He knew how to work all computers. Given five minutes or so to read the instructions.'

I pondered, staring at the blank unhelpful screen.

'Are there,' I asked eventually, 'any secret files in this?'

She stared. 'We never use secret files.'

'But you could do?'

'Of course. Yes. But we don't need to.'

'If,' I said, 'there were any secret files, would you know that they were there?'

She nodded briefly. 'I wouldn't know, but I could find out.'

'How?' I asked. 'I mean, please would you?'

'What am I looking for? I don't understand.'

'Diamonds.'

'But I told you, we don't . . .'

'I know,' I said, 'but my brother said he was going to buy diamonds and I need to know if he did. If there's any chance he made a private entry on this computer some day when he was first or last in this office, I need to find it.'

She shook her head but tapped away obligingly, bringing what she called menus to the screen. It seemed a fairly lengthy business but finally, frowning, she found something that gave her pause. Then her concentration increased abruptly until the screen was showing the word 'Password?' as before.

'I don't understand,' she said. 'We gave this computer a general password which is Saxony, though we almost never use it. But you can put in any password you like on any particular document to supersede Saxony. This entry was made only a month ago. The date is on the menu. But whoever made it didn't use Saxony as the password. So the password could be anything, literally any word in the world.'

I said, 'By document you mean file?'

'Yes, file. Every entry has a document name, like, say,

"oriental cultured pearls". If I load "oriental cultured pearls" onto the screen I can review our whole stock. I do it all the time. But this document with an unknown password is listed under pearl in the singular, not pearls in the plural, and I don't understand it. I didn't put it there.' She glanced at me. 'At any rate, it doesn't say diamonds.'

'Have another try to guess the password.'

She tried Franklin and Greville without result. 'It could be *anything*,' she said helplessly.

'Try Dozen Roses.'

'Why Dozen Roses?' She thought it extraordinary.

'Greville owned a horse – a racehorse – with that name.'

'Really? He never said. He was so nice, and awfully private.'

'He owned another horse called Gemstones.'

With visible doubt she tried 'Dozen Roses' and then 'Gemstones'. Nothing happened except another insistent demand for the password.

'Try "diamonds", then,' I said.

She tried 'diamonds'. Nothing changed.

'You knew him,' I said. 'Why would he enter something under "pearl"?'

'No idea.' She sat hunched over the keys, drumming her fingers on her mouth. 'Pearl. Pearl. Why pearl?'

'What is a pearl?' I said. 'Does it have a formula?'

'Oh.' She suddenly sat up straight. 'It's a birthstone.'

She typed in 'birthstone', and nothing happened.

Then she blushed slightly.

'It's one of the birthstones for the month of June,' she said. 'I could try it, anyway.'

She typed 'June', and the screen flashed and gave up its secrets.

CHAPTER FIVE

We hadn't found the diamonds.

The screen said:

June, if you are reading this, come straight into my office for a rise. You are worth your weight in your birthstone, but I'm only offering to increase your salary by twenty per cent. Regards, Greville Franklin.

'Oh!' She sat transfixed. 'So that's what he meant.'

'Explain,' I said.

'One morning . . .' She stopped, her mouth screwing up in an effort not to cry. It took her a while to be able to continue, then she said, 'One morning he told me he'd invented a little puzzle for me and he would give me six months to solve it. After six months it would self-destruct. He was smiling so much.' She swallowed. 'I asked him what sort of puzzle and he wouldn't tell me. He just said he hoped I would find it.'

'Did you look?' I asked.

'Of course I did. I looked everywhere in the office, though I didn't know what I was looking for. I even looked for a new document in the computer, but I just never gave a thought to its being filed as a secret, and my eyes just slid over the word "pearl", as I see it so often. Silly of me. Stupid.'

I said, 'I don't think you're stupid, and I'll honour my brother's promise.'

She gave me a swift look of pleasure but shook her head a little and said, 'I didn't find it. I'd never have solved it except for you.' She hesitated. 'How about ten per cent?'

'Twenty,' I said firmly. 'I'm going to need your help and your knowledge, and if Annette is Personal Assistant, as it says on the door of her office, you can be Deputy Personal Assistant, with the new salary to go with the job.'

She turned a deeper shade of rose and busied herself with making a print-out of Greville's instruction, which she folded and put in her handbag.

'I'll leave the secret in the computer,' she said with misty fondness. 'No one else will ever find it.' She pressed a few buttons and the screen went blank, and I wondered how many times in private she would call up the magic words that Greville had left her.

I wondered if they would really self-destruct: if one could programme something on a computer to erase itself on a given date. I didn't see why not, but I thought

Greville might have given her strong clues before the six months were out.

I asked her if she would print out first a list of everything currently in the vault and then as many things as she thought would help me understand the business better, like the volume and value of a day's, a week's, a month's sales; like which items were most popular, and which least.

'I can tell you that what's very popular just now is black onyx. Fifty years ago they say it was all amber, now no one buys it. Jewellery goes in and out of fashion like everything else.' She began tapping keys. 'Give me a little while and I'll print you a crash course.'

'Thanks.' I smiled, and waited while the printer spat out a gargantuan mouthful of glittering facets. Then I took the list in search of Annette, who was alone in the stock-rooms, and asked her to give me a quick canter round the vault.

'There aren't any diamonds there,' she said positively.

'I'd better learn what is.'

'You don't seem like a jockey,' she said.

'How many do you know?'

She stared. 'None, except you.'

'On the whole,' I said mildly, 'jockeys are like anyone else. Would you feel I was better able to manage here if I were, say, a piano tuner? Or an actor? Or a clergyman?'

She said faintly, 'No.'

91

'OK, then. We're stuck with a jockey. Twist of fate. Do your best for the poor fellow.'

She involuntarily smiled a genuine smile which lightened her heavy face miraculously. 'All right.' She paused. 'You're really like Mr Franklin in some ways. The way you say things. Deal with honour, he said, and sleep at night.'

'You all remember what he said, don't you?'

'Of course.'

He would have been glad, I supposed, to have left so positive a legacy. So many precepts. So much wisdom. But so few signposts to his personal life. No visible signpost to the diamonds.

In the vault Annette showed me that, besides its chemical formula, each label bore a number: if I looked at that number on the list June had printed, I would see the formula again, but also the normal names of the stones, with colours, shapes and sizes and country of origin.

'Why did he label them like this?' I asked. 'It just makes it difficult to find things.'

'I believe that was his purpose,' she answered. 'I told you, he was very security conscious. We had a secretary working here once who managed to steal a lot of our most valuable turquoise out of the vault. The labels read "turquoise" then, which made it easy, but now they don't.'

'What do they say?'

She smiled and pointed to a row of boxes. I looked

at the labels and read $CuAl_6(PO_4)_4(OH)_8 \cdot 4\text{--}5(H_2O)$ on each of them.

'Enough to put anyone off for life,' I said.

'Exactly. That's the point. Mr Franklin could read formulas as easily as words, and I've got used to them myself now. No one but he and I handle these stones in here. We pack them into boxes ourselves and seal them before they go to Alfie for despatch.' She looked along the rows of labels and did her best to educate me. 'We sell these stones at so much per carat. A carat weighs two hundred milligrams, which means five carats to a gram, a hundred and forty-two carats to an ounce and five thousand carats to the kilo.'

'Stop right there,' I begged.

'You said you learned fast.'

'Give me a day or two.'

She nodded and said if I didn't need her any more she had better get on with the ledgers.

Ledgers, I thought, wilting internally. I hadn't even started on those. I thought of the joy with which I'd left Lancaster University with a degree in Independent Studies, swearing never again to pore dutifully over books and heading straight (against my father's written wishes) to the steeplechase stable where I'd been spending truant days as an amateur. It was true that at college I'd learned fast, because I'd had to, and learned all night often enough, keeping faith with at least the first half of my father's letter. He'd hoped I would grow out of the lure he knew I felt for race-riding, but it was all I'd ever wanted and I couldn't have settled to anything else. There was no long-term future in it, he'd written, besides a complete lack of financial security along with a constant risk of disablement. I ask you to be sensible, he'd said, to think it through and decide against.

Fat chance.

I sighed for the simplicity of the certainty I'd felt in those days, yet, given a second beginning, I wouldn't have lived any differently. I had been deeply fulfilled in racing and grown old in spirit only because of the way life worked in general. Disappointments, injustices, small betrayals, they were everyone's lot. I no longer expected everything to go right, but enough had gone right to leave me at least in a balance of content.

With no feeling that the world owed me anything, I applied myself to the present boring task of opening every packet in every box in the quest for little bits of pure carbon. It wasn't that I expected to find the diamonds there: it was just that it would be so stupid not to look, in case they were.

I worked methodically, putting the boxes one at a time on the wide shelf which ran along the right-hand wall, unfolding the stiff white papers with the soft inner linings and looking at hundreds of thousands of peridots, chrysoberyls, garnets and aquamarines until my head spun. I stopped in fact when I'd done only a third of the stock because apart from the airlessness of the vault it was physically tiring standing on one leg all the time, and the crutches got in the way as much as they helped. I refolded the last of the $XY_3Z_6[(O,OH,F)_4(BO_3)_3Si_6O_{18}]$ (tourmaline) and gave it best.

'What did you learn?' Annette asked when I reappeared in Greville's office. She was in there, replacing yet more papers in their proper files, a task apparently nearing completion.

'Enough to look at jewellery differently,' I said.

She smiled. 'When I read magazines I don't look at the clothes, I look at the jewellery.'

I could see that she would. I thought that I might also, despite myself, from then on. I might even develop an affinity with black onyx cufflinks.

It was by that time four o'clock in the afternoon of what seemed a very long day. I looked up the racing programme in Greville's diary, decided that Nicholas Loder might well have passed over going to Redcar, Warwick and Folkestone, and dialled his number. His secretary answered, and yes, Mr Loder was at home, and yes, he would speak to me.

He came on the line with almost none of the previous evening's agitation, bass resonances positively throbbing down the wire.

'I've been talking to Weatherby's and the Jockey Club,' he said easily, 'and there's fortunately no problem. They agree that before probate the horses belong to Saxony Franklin Limited and not to you, and they will not bar them from racing in that name.'

'Good,' I said, and was faintly surprised.

'They say of course that there has to be at least one registered agent appointed by the company to be responsible for the horses, such appointment to be sealed with the company's seal and registered at Weatherby's. Your brother appointed both himself and myself as registered agents, and although he has died I remain a registered agent as before and can act for the company on my own.'

'Ah,' I said.

'Which being so,' Loder said happily, 'Dozen Roses runs at York as planned.'

'And trots up?'

He chuckled. 'Let's hope so.'

That chuckle, I thought, was the ultimate in confidence.

'I'd be grateful if you could let Saxony Franklin know whenever the horses are due to run in the future,' I said.

'I used to speak to your brother personally at his home number. I can hardly do that with you, as you don't own the horses.'

'No,' I agreed. 'I meant, please will you tell the company? I'll give you the number. And would you ask for Mrs Annette Adams? She was Greville's second-in-command.'

He could hardly say he wouldn't, so I read out the number and he repeated it as he wrote it down.

'Don't forget though that there's only a month left of the Flat season,' he said. 'They'll probably run only once more each. Two at the very most. Then I'll sell them for you, that would be best. No problem. Leave it to me.'

He was right, logically, but I still illogically disliked his haste.

'As executor, I'd have to approve any sale,' I said, hoping I was right. 'In advance.'

'Yes, yes, of course.' Reassuring heartiness. 'Your injury,' he said, 'what exactly is it?'

'Busted ankle.'

'Ah. Bad luck. Getting on well, I hope?' The sympathy sounded more like relief to me than anything else, and again I couldn't think why.

'Getting on,' I said.

'Good, good. Goodbye then. The York race should be on the television on Saturday. I expect you'll watch it?'

'I expect so.'

'Fine.' He put down the receiver in great good humour and left me wondering what I'd missed.

Greville's telephone rang again immediately, and it was Brad to tell me that he had returned from his day's visit to an obscure aunt in Walthamstow and was downstairs in the front hall: all he actually said was, 'I'm back.'

'Great. I won't be long.'

I got a click in reply. End of conversation.

I did mean to leave almost at once but there were two more phone calls in fairly quick succession. The first was from a man introducing himself as Elliot Trelawney, a colleague of Greville's from the West London Magistrates Court. He was extremely sorry, he said, to hear about his death, and he truly sounded it. A positive voice, used to attention: a touch of plummy accent.

'Also,' he said, 'I'd like to talk to you about some projects Greville and I were working on. I'd like to have his notes.'

I said rather blankly, 'What projects? What notes?'

'I could explain better face to face,' he said. 'Could I ask you to meet me? Say tomorrow, early evening, over a drink? You know that pub just round the corner from Greville's house? The Rook and Castle? There. He and I often met there. Five-thirty, six, either of those suit you?'

'Five-thirty,' I said obligingly.

'How shall I know you?'

'By my crutches.'

It silenced him momentarily. I let him off embarrassment.

'They're temporary,' I said.

'Er, fine, then. Until tomorrow.'

He cut himself off, and I asked Annette if she knew him, Elliot Trelawney? She shook her head. She couldn't honestly say she knew anyone outside the office who was known to Greville personally. Unless you counted Prospero Jenks, she said doubtfully. And even then, she herself had never really met him, only talked to him frequently on the telephone.

'Prospero Jenks . . . alias Fabergé?'

'That's the one.'

I thought a bit. 'Would you mind phoning him now?' I said. 'Tell him about Greville and ask if I can go to see him to discuss the future. Just say I'm Greville's brother, nothing else.'

She grinned. 'No horses? Pas de gee-gees?'

Annette, I thought in amusement, was definitely loosening up.

'No horses,' I agreed.

She made the call but without results. Prospero Jenks wouldn't be reachable until morning. She would try then, she said.

I levered myself upright and said I'd see her tomorrow. She nodded, taking it for granted that I would be there. The quicksands were winning, I thought. I was less and less able to get out.

Going down the passage I stopped to look in on Alfie whose day's work stood in columns of loaded cardboard boxes waiting to be entrusted to the post.

'How many do you send out every day?' I asked, gesturing to them.

He looked up briefly from stretching sticky tape round yet another parcel. 'About twenty, twenty-five regular, but more from August to Christmas.' He cut off the tape expertly and stuck an address label deftly on the box top. 'Twenty-eight so far today.'

'Do you bet, Alfie?' I asked. 'Read the racing papers?'

He glanced at me with a mixture of defensiveness

and defiance, neither of which feeling was necessary. 'I *knew* you was him,' he said. 'The others said you couldn't be.'

'You know Dozen Roses too?'

A tinge of craftiness took over in his expression. 'Started winning again, didn't he? I missed him the first time, but yes, I've had a little tickle since.'

'He runs on Saturday at York, but he'll be odds-on,' I said.

'Will he win, though? Will they be trying with him? I wouldn't put my shirt on that.'

'Nicholas Loder says he'll trot up.'

He knew who Nicholas Loder was: didn't need to ask. With cynicism, he put his just-finished box on some sturdy scales and wrote the result on the cardboard with a thick black pen. He must have been well into his sixties, I thought, with deep lines from his nose to the corners of his mouth and pale sagging skin everywhere from which most of the elasticity had vanished. His hands, with the veins of age beginning to show dark blue, were nimble and strong however, and he bent to pick up another heavy box with a supple back. A tough old customer, I thought, and essentially more in touch with street awareness than the exaggerated Jason.

'Mr Franklin's horses run in and out,' he said pointedly. 'And as a jock you'd know about that.'

Before I could decide whether or not he was intentionally insulting me, Annette came hurrying down the passage calling my name.

'Derek . . . Oh there you are. Still here, good. There's another phone call for you.' She about-turned and went back towards Greville's office, and I followed her, noticing with interest that she'd dropped the Mister from my name. Yesterday's unthinkable was today's natural, now that I was established as a jockey, which was OK as far as it went, as long as it didn't go too far.

I picked up the receiver which was lying on the black desk and said, 'Hello? Derek Franklin speaking.'

A familiar voice said, 'Thank God for that. I've been trying your Hungerford number all day. Then I remembered about your brother . . .' He spoke loudly, driven by urgency.

Milo Shandy, the trainer I'd ridden most for during the past three seasons: a perpetual optimist in the face of world evidence of corruption, greed and lies.

'I've a crisis on my hands,' he bellowed, 'and can you come over? Will you pull out all stops to come over first thing in the morning?'

'Er, what for?'

'You know the Ostermeyers? They've flown over from Pittsburgh for some affair in London and they phoned me and I told them Datepalm is for sale. And you know that if they buy him I can keep him here, otherwise I'll lose him because he'll have to go to auction. And they want you here when they see him work on the Downs and they can only manage first lot tomorrow, and they think the sun twinkles out of your backside, so for God's sake *come*.'

Interpreting the agitation was easy. Datepalm was the horse on which I'd won the Gold Cup: a seven-year-old gelding still near the beginning of what with luck would be a notable jumping career. Its owner had recently dropped the bombshell of telling Milo she was leaving England to marry an Australian, and if he could sell Datepalm to one of his other owners for the astronomical figure she named, she wouldn't send it to public auction and out of his yard.

Milo had been in a panic most of the time since then because none of his other owners had so far thought the horse worth the price, his Gold Cup success having been judged lucky in the absence through coughing of a couple of more established stars. Both Milo and I thought Datepalm better than his press, and I had as strong a motive as Milo for wanting him to stay in the stable.

'Calm down,' I assured him. 'I'll be there.'

He let out a lot of breath in a rush. 'Tell the Ostermeyers he's a really good horse.'

'He is,' I said, 'and I will.'

'Thanks, Derek.' His voice dropped to normal decibels. 'Oh, and by the way, there's no horse called Koningin Beatrix, and not likely to be. Weatherby's say Koningin Beatrix means Queen Beatrix, as in Queen Beatrix of the Netherlands, and they frown on people naming racehorses after royal persons.'

'Oh,' I said. 'Well, thanks for finding out.'

'Any time. See you in the morning. For God's sake

don't be late. You know the Ostermeyers get up before larks.'

'What I need,' I said to Annette, putting down the receiver, 'is an appointments book, so as not to forget where I've said I'll be.'

She began looking in the drawerful of gadgets.

'Mr Franklin had an electric memory thing he used to put appointments in. You could use that for now.' She sorted through the black collection, but without result. 'Stay here a minute,' she said, closing the drawer, 'while I ask June if she knows where it is.'

She went away busily and I thought about how to convince the Ostermeyers, who could afford anything they set their hearts on, that Datepalm would bring them glory if not necessarily repay their bucks. They had had steeplechasers with Milo from time to time, but not for almost a year at the moment. I'd do a great deal, I thought, to persuade them it was time to come back.

An alarm like a digital watch alarm sounded faintly, muffled, and to begin with I paid it no attention, but as it persisted I opened the gadget drawer to investigate and, of course, as I did so it immediately stopped. Shrugging, I closed the drawer again, and Annette came back bearing a sheet of paper but no gadget.

'June doesn't know where the Wizard is, so I'll make out a rough calendar on plain paper.'

'What's the Wizard?' I asked.

'The calculator. Baby computer. June says it does everything but boil eggs.'

'Why do you call it the Wizard?' I asked.

'It has that name on it. It's about the size of a paper-back book and it was Mr Franklin's favourite object. He took it everywhere.' She frowned. 'Maybe it's in his car, wherever that is.'

The car. Another problem. 'I'll find the car,' I said, with more confidence than I felt. Somehow or other I would have to find the car. 'Maybe the Wizard was stolen out of this office in the break-in,' I said.

She stared at me with widely opening eyes. 'The thief would have to have known what it was. It folds up flat. You can't see any buttons.'

'All the gadgets were out on the floor, weren't they?'

'Yes.' It troubled her. 'Why the address book? Why the engagements for October? Why the Wizard?'

Because of diamonds, I thought instinctively, but couldn't rationalize it. Someone had perhaps been look-ing, as I was, for the treasure map marked X. Perhaps they'd known it existed. Perhaps they'd found it.

'I'll get here a couple of hours later tomorrow,' I said to Annette. 'And I must leave by five to meet Elliot Trelawney at five-thirty. So if you reach Prospero Jenks, ask him if I could go to see him in between. Or failing that, any time Thursday. Write off Friday because of the funeral.'

Greville died only the day before yesterday, I thought. It already seemed half a lifetime.

Annette said, 'Yes, Mr Franklin,' and bit her lip in dismay.

I half smiled at her. 'Call me Derek. Just plain Derek. And invest it with whatever you feel.'

'It's confusing,' she said weakly, 'from minute to minute.'

'Yes, I know.'

With a certain relief I rode down in the service lift and swung across to Brad in the car. He hopped out of the front seat and shovelled me into the back, tucking the crutches in beside me and waiting while I lifted my leg along the padded leather and wedged myself into the corner for the most comfortable angle of ride.

'Home?' he said.

'No. Like I told you on the way up, we'll stop in Kensington for a while, if you don't mind.'

He gave the tiniest of nods. I'd provided him in the morning with a detailed large-scale map of West London, asking him to work out how to get to the road where Greville had lived, and I hoped to hell he had done it, because I was feeling more drained than I cared to admit and not ready to ride in irritating traffic-clogged circles.

'Look out for a pub called The Rook and Castle, would you?' I asked, as we neared the area. 'Tomorrow at five-thirty I have to meet someone there.'

Brad nodded and with the unerring instinct of the beer drinker quickly found it, merely pointing vigorously to tell me.

'Great,' I said, and he acknowledged that with a wiggle of the shoulders.

He drew up so confidently outside Greville's address that I wondered if he had reconnoitred earlier in the day, except that his aunt lived theoretically in the opposite direction. In any case, he handed me the crutches, opened the gate of the small front garden and said loquaciously, 'I'll wait in the car.'

'I might be an hour or more. Would you mind having a quick recce up and down this street and those nearby to see if you can find an old Rover with this number?' I gave him a card with it on. 'My brother's car,' I said.

He gave me a brief nod and turned away, and I looked up at the tall townhouse that Greville had moved into about three months previously, and which I'd never visited. It was creamy-grey, gracefully proportioned, with balustraded steps leading up to the black front door, and businesslike but decorative metal grilles showing behind the glass in every window from semi-basement to roof.

I crossed the grassy front garden and went up the steps, and found there were three locks on the front door. Cursing slightly I yanked out Greville's half-ton of keys and by trial and error found the way into his fortress.

Late afternoon sun slanted yellowly into a long main drawing room which was on the left of the entrance hall, throwing the pattern of the grilles in shadows on the greyish-brown carpet. The walls, pale salmon, were adorned with vivid paintings of stained-glass cathedral windows, and the fabric covering sofa and armchairs was of a large broken herringbone pattern in dark brown and white, confusing to the eye. I reflected rue-fully that I didn't know whether it all represented Greville's own taste or whether he'd taken it over from the past owner. I knew only his taste in clothes, food, gadgets and horses. Not very much. Not enough.

The drawing room was dustless and tidy; unlived in. I returned to the front hall from where stairs led up and down, but before tackling those I went through a door at the rear which opened into a much smaller room filled with a homely clutter of books, newspapers, maga-zines, black leather chairs, clocks, chrysanthemums in pots, a tray of booze and framed medieval brass rub-bings on deep green walls. This was all Greville, I thought. This was home.

I left it for the moment and hopped down the stairs to the semi-basement, where there was a bedroom, unused, a small bathroom and decorator-style dining room looking out through grilles to a rear garden, with a narrow spotless kitchen alongside.

Fixed to the fridge by a magnetic strawberry was a note.

Dear Mr Franklin,
    I didn't know you'd be away this weekend. I brought in the papers, they're in the back room. You didn't leave your laundry out, so I haven't taken it. Thanks for the money. I'll be back next Tuesday as usual.
    Mrs P

I looked around for a pencil, found a ball-point, pulled the note from its clip and wrote on the back, asking Mrs P to call the following number (Saxony Franklin's) and speak to Derek or Annette. I didn't sign it, but put it back under the strawberry where I supposed it would stay for another week, a sorry message in waiting.

I looked in the fridge which contained little but milk, butter, grapes, a pork pie and two bottles of champagne.

Diamonds in the ice cubes? I didn't think he would have put them anywhere so chancy: besides, he was security conscious, not paranoid.

I hauled myself upstairs to the hall again and then went on up to the next floor where there was a bedroom and bathroom suite in self-conscious black and white. Greville had slept there: the built-in cupboards and drawers held his clothes, the bathroom closet his privacy. He had been sparing in his possessions, leaving a single row of shoes, several white shirts on hangers, six assorted suits and a rack of silk ties. The drawers were tidy with sweaters, sports shirts, underclothes, socks. Our mother, I thought with a smile, would have been proud of him. She'd tried hard and unsuccessfully to instil tidiness into both of us as children, and it looked as if we'd both got better with age.

There was little else to see. The drawer in the bedside table revealed indigestion tablets, a torch and a paperback, John D. MacDonald. No gadgets and no treasure maps.

With a sigh I went into the only other room on that floor and found it unfurnished and papered with garish metallic silvery roses which had been half ripped off at one point. So much for the decorator.

There was another flight of stairs going upwards, but I didn't climb them. There would only be, by the looks of things, unused rooms to find there, and I thought I would go and look later when stairs weren't such a sweat. Anything deeply interesting in that house seemed likely to be found in the small back sitting room, so it was to there that I returned.

I sat for a while in the chair that was clearly Greville's favourite, from where he could see the television and the view over the garden. Places that people had left for ever should be seen through their eyes, I thought. His presence was strong in that room, and in me.

Beside his chair there was a small antique table with, on its polished top, a telephone and an answering machine. A red light for messages received was shining on the machine, so after a while I pressed a button marked 'rewind', followed by another marked 'play'.

A woman's voice spoke without preamble.

'Darling, where are you? Do ring me.'

There was a series of between-message clicks, then the same voice again, this time packed with anxiety.

'Darling, please please ring. I'm very worried. Where are you, darling? *Please* ring. I love you.'

Again the clicks, but no more messages.

Poor lady, I thought. Grief and tears waiting in the wings.

I got up and explored the room more fully, pausing by two drawers in a table beside the window. They contained two small black unidentified gadgets which baffled me and which I stowed in my pockets, and also a slotted tray containing a rather nice collection of small bears, polished and carved from shaded pink, brown and charcoal stone. I laid the tray on top of the table beside some chrysanthemums and came next to a box made of greenish stone, also polished and which, true to Greville's habit, was firmly locked. Thinking perhaps that one of the keys fitted it I brought out the bunch again and began to try the smallest.

I was facing the window with my back to the room, balancing on one foot and leaning a thigh against the table, my arms out of the crutches, intent on what I was doing and disastrously unheeding. The first I knew of anyone else in the house was a muffled exclamation behind me, and I turned to see a dark-haired woman coming through the doorway, her wild glance rigidly fixed on the green stone box. Without pause she came fast towards me, pulling out of a pocket a black object like a long fat cigar.

I opened my mouth to speak but she brought her hand round in a strong swinging arc, and in that travel

the short black cylinder more than doubled its length
into a thick silvery flexible stick which crashed with
shattering force against my left upper arm, enough to
stop a heavyweight in round one.

CHAPTER SIX

My fingers went numb and dropped the box. I swayed
and spun on the force of the impact and overbalanced,
toppling, thinking sharply that I mustn't this time put
my foot on the ground. I dropped the bunch of keys and
grabbed at the back of an upright black leather chair
with my right hand to save myself, but it turned over
under my weight and came down on top of me onto the
carpet in a tangle of chair legs, table legs and crutches,
the green box underneath and digging into my back.

In a spitting fury I tried to orientate myself and
finally got enough breath for one single choice, charm-
ing and heartfelt word.

'*Bitch.*'

She gave me a baleful glare and picked up the telephone, pressing three fast buttons.

'Police,' she said, and in as short a time as it took the
emergency service to connect her, 'Police, I want to
report a burglary. I've caught a burglar.'

'I'm Greville's brother,' I said thickly, from the floor.

For a moment it didn't seem to reach her. I said again, more loudly, 'I'm Greville's brother.'

'What?' she said vaguely.

'For Christ's sake, are you deaf? I'm not a burglar, I'm Greville Franklin's brother.' I gingerly sat up into an L-shape and found no strength anywhere.

She put the phone down. 'Why didn't you say so?' she demanded.

'What chance did you give me? And who the hell are you, walking into my brother's house and belting people?'

She held at the ready the fearsome thing she'd hit me with, looking as if she thought I'd attack her in my turn, which I certainly felt like. In the last six days I'd been crunched by a horse, a mugger and a woman. All I needed was a toddler to amble up with a coup de grâce. I pressed the fingers of my right hand on my forehead and the palm against my mouth and considered the blackness of life in general.

'What's the matter with you?' she said after a pause.

I slid the hand away and drawled, 'Absolutely bloody nothing.'

'I only tapped you,' she said with criticism.

'Shall I give you a hefty clip with that thing so you can feel what it's like?'

'You're angry.' She sounded surprised.

'Dead right.'

I struggled up off the floor, straightened the fallen chair and sat on it. 'Who are you?' I repeated. But I knew who she was: the woman on the answering machine. The same voice. The cut-crystal accent. Darling, where are you? I love you.

'Did you ring his office?' I said. 'Are you Mrs Williams?'

She seemed to tremble and crumple inwardly and she walked past me to the window to stare out into the garden.

'Is he really dead?' she said.

'Yes.'

She was forty, I thought. Perhaps more. Nearly my height. In no way tiny or delicate. A woman of decision and power, sorely troubled.

She wore a leather-belted raincoat, though it hadn't rained for weeks, and plain black businesslike court shoes. Her hair, thick and dark, was combed smoothly back from her forehead to curl under on her collar, a cool groomed look achieved only by expert cutting. There was no visible jewellery, little remaining lipstick, no trace of scent.

'How?' she said eventually.

I had a strong impulse to deny her the information, to punish her for her precipitous attack, to hurt her and get even. But there was no point in it, and I knew I would end up with more shame than satisfaction, so after a struggle I explained briefly about the scaffolding.

'Friday afternoon,' I said. 'He was unconscious at once. He died early on Sunday.'

She turned her head slowly to look at me directly. 'Are you Derek?' she said.

'Yes.'

'I'm Clarissa Williams.'

Neither of us made any attempt to shake hands. It would have been incongruous, I thought.

'I came to fetch some things of mine,' she said. 'I didn't expect anyone to be here.'

It was an apology of sorts, I supposed: and if I had indeed been a burglar she would have saved the bric-à-brac.

'What things?' I asked.

She hesitated, but in the end said, 'A few letters, that's all.' Her gaze strayed to the answering machine and there was a definite tightening of muscles round her eyes.

'I played the messages,' I said.

'Oh God.'

'Why should it worry you?'

She had her reasons, it seemed, but she wasn't going to tell me what they were: or not then, at any rate.

'I want to wipe them off,' she said. 'It was one of the purposes of coming.'

She glanced at me, but I couldn't think of any urgent reason why she shouldn't, so I didn't say anything. Tentatively, as if asking my forbearance every step of the way, she walked jerkily to the machine, rewound the tape and pressed the record button, recording silence over what had gone before. After a while she rewound

the tape again and played it, and there were no desperate appeals any more.

'Did anyone else hear . . .?'

'I don't think so. Not unless the cleaner was in the
habit of listening. She came today, I think.'

'Oh God.'

'You left no name.' Why the hell was I reassuring her,
I wondered. I still had no strength in my fingers. I could
still feel that awful blow like a shudder.

'Do you want a drink?' she said abruptly. 'I've had a
dreadful day.' She went over to the tray of bottles and
poured vodka into a heavy tumbler. 'What do you
want?'

'Water,' I said. 'Make it a double.'

She tightened her mouth and put down the vodka
bottle with a clink. 'Soda or tonic?' she asked starchily.

'Soda.'

She poured soda into a glass for me and tonic into
her own, diluting the spirit by not very much. Ice was
downstairs in the kitchen. No one mentioned it.

I noticed she'd left her lethal weapon lying harmlessly beside the answering machine. Presumably I no
longer represented any threat. As if avoiding personal
contact, she set my soda water formally on the table
beside me between the little stone bears and the chrysanthemums and drank deeply from her own glass.
Better than tranquillizers, I thought. Alcohol loosened
the stress, calmed the mental pain. The world's first
anaesthetic. I could have done with some myself.

'Where are your letters?' I asked.

She switched on a table light. The on-creeping dusk in the garden deepened abruptly towards night and I wished she would hurry up because I wanted to go home.

She looked at a bookcase which covered a good deal of one wall.

'In there, I think. In a book.'

'Do start looking, then. It could take all night.'

'You don't need to wait.'

'I think I will,' I said.

'Don't you trust me?' she demanded.

'No.'

She stared at me hard. 'Why not?'

I didn't say that because of the diamonds I didn't trust anyone. I didn't know who I could safely ask to look out for them, or who would search to steal them, if they knew they might be found.

'I don't know you,' I said neutrally.

'But I . . .' She stopped and shrugged. 'I suppose I don't know you either.' She went over to the bookshelves. 'Some of these books are hollow,' she said.

Oh Greville, I thought. How would I ever find anything he had hidden? I liked straight paths. He'd had a mind like a labyrinth.

She began pulling out books from the lower shelves and opening the front covers. Not methodically book by book along any row but always, it seemed to me, those with predominantly blue spines. After a while, on her knees, she found a hollow one which she laid open on the floor with careful sarcasm, so that I could see she wasn't concealing anything.

The interior of the book was in effect a blue velvet box with a close-fitting lid that could be pulled out by a tab. When she pulled the lid out, the shallow blue velvet-lined space beneath was revealed as being entirely empty.

Shrugging, she replaced the lid and closed the book, which immediately looked like any other book, and returned it to the shelves: and a few seconds later found another hollow one, this time with red velvet interiors. Inside this one lay an envelope.

She looked at it without touching it, and then at me. 'It's not my letters,' she said. 'Not my writing paper.'

I said, 'Greville made a will leaving everything he possessed to me.'

She didn't seem to find it extraordinary, although I did: he had done it that way for simplicity when he was in a hurry, and he would certainly have changed it, given time.

'You'd better see what's in here, then,' she said calmly, and she picked the envelope out and stretched across to hand it to me.

The envelope, which hadn't been stuck down, contained a single ornate key, about four inches long, the top flattened and pierced like metal lace, the business end narrow with small but intricate teeth. I laid it on my palm and showed it to her, asking her if she knew what it unlocked.

She shook her head. 'I haven't seen it before.' She paused. 'He was a man of secrets,' she said.

I listened to the wistfulness in her voice. She might be strongly controlled at that moment, but she hadn't been before Annette told her Greville was dead. There had been raw panicky emotion on the tape. Annette had simply confirmed her frightful fears and put what I imagined was a false calmness in place of escalating despair. A man of secrets . . . Greville had apparently not opened his mind to her much more than he had to me.

I put the key back in its envelope and handed it across.

'It had better stay in the book for now,' I said, 'until I find a keyhole it fits.'

She put the key in the book and returned it to the shelves, and shortly afterwards found her letters. They were fastened not with romantic ribbons but held together by a prosaic rubber band; not a great many of them by the look of things but carefully kept.

She stared at me from her knees. 'I don't want you to read them,' she said. 'Whatever Greville left you, they're mine, not yours.'

I wondered why she needed so urgently to remove all traces of herself from the house. Out of curiosity I'd have read the letters with interest if I'd found them myself, but I could hardly demand now to see her love letters . . . if they were love letters.

'Show me just a short page,' I said.

She looked bitter. 'You really don't trust me, do you? I'd like to know why.'

'Someone broke into Greville's office over the weekend,' I said, 'and I'm not quite sure what they were looking for.'

'Not my letters,' she said positively.

'Show me just a page,' I said, 'so I know they're what you say.'

I thought she would refuse altogether, but after a moment's thought she slid the rubber band off the letters and fingered through them, finally, with all expression repressed, handing me one small sheet.

It said:

. . . and until next Monday my life will be a desert.
What am I to do? After your touch I shrink from
him. It's dreadful. I am running out of headaches.
I adore you.

C.

I handed the page back in silence, embarrassed at having intruded.

'Take them,' I said.

She blinked a few times, snapped the rubber band back round the small collection, and put them into a plain black leather handbag which lay beside her on the carpet.

I felt down onto the floor, collected the crutches and stood up, concentrating on at least holding the hand support of the left one, even if not putting much weight on it. Clarissa Williams watched me go over towards Greville's chair with a touch of awkwardness.

'Look,' she said, 'I didn't realize . . . I mean, when I came in here and saw you stealing things I thought you were stealing things . . . I didn't notice the crutches.'

I supposed that was the truth. Bona fide burglars didn't go around peg-legged, and I'd laid the supports aside at the time she'd come storming in. She'd been too fired up to ask questions: propelled no doubt by grief, anxiety and fear of the intruder. None of which lessened my contrary feeling that she damned well *ought* to have asked questions before waging war.

I wondered how she would have explained her presence to the police, if they had arrived, when she was urgent to remove all traces of herself from the house. Perhaps she would have realized her mistake and simply departed, leaving the incapacitated burglar on the floor.

I went over to the telephone table and picked up the brutal little man-tamer. The heavy handle, a black cigar-shaped cylinder, knurled for a good grip, was under an inch in diameter and about seven inches long. Protruding beyond that was a short length of solidly thick chromium-plated closely-coiled spring, with a similar but narrower spring extending beyond that, the whole tipped with a black metal knob, fifteen or sixteen inches overall. A kick as hard as a horse.

'What is this?' I said, holding it, feeling its weight.

'Greville gave it to me. He said the streets aren't safe. He wanted me to carry it always ready. He said all women should carry them because of muggers and rapists ... as a magistrate he heard so much about women being attacked ... he said one blow would render the toughest man helpless and give me time to escape.'

I hadn't much difficulty in believing it. I bent the black knob to one side and watched the close heavy spring flex and straighten fast when I let it go. She got to her feet and said, 'I'm sorry. I've never used it before, not in anger. Greville showed me how ... he just said to swing as hard as I could so that the springs would shoot out and do the maximum damage.'

My dear brother, I thought. Thank you very much.

'Does it go back into its shell?' I asked.

She nodded. 'Twist the bigger spring clockwise ... it'll come loose and slide into the casing.' I did that, but the smaller spring with the black knob still stuck out. 'You have to give the knob a bang against something, then it will slide in.'

I banged the knob against the wall, and like a meek lamb the narrower spring slid smoothly into the wider, and the end of the knob became the harmless-looking end of yet another gadget.

'What makes it work?' I asked, but she didn't know.

I found that the end opposite the knob unscrewed if one tried, so I unscrewed it about twenty turns until the inch-long piece came off, and I discovered that the whole end section was a very strong magnet.

Simple, I thought. Ordinarily the magnet held the heavy springs inside the cylinder. Make a strong flicking arc, in effect throw the springs out, and the magnet couldn't hold them, but let them go, letting loose the full whipping strength of the thing.

I screwed back the cap, held the cylinder, swung it hard. The springs shot out, flexible, shining, horrific.

Wordlessly, I closed the thing up again and offered it to her.

'It's called a kiyoga,' she said.

I didn't care what it was called. I didn't care if I never saw it again. She put it familiarly into her raincoat pocket, every woman's ultimate reply to footpads, maniacs and assorted misogynists.

She looked unhappily and uncertainly at my face. 'I suppose I can't ask you to forget I came here?' she said.

'It would be impossible.'

'Could you just . . . not speak of it?'

If I'd met her in another way I suppose I might have liked her. She had generous eyes that would have looked better smiling, and an air of basic good humour which persisted despite her jumbling emotions.

With an effort she said, 'Please.'

'Don't beg,' I said sharply. It made me uncomfortable and it didn't suit her.

She swallowed. 'Greville told me about you. I guess . . . I'll have to trust to his judgement.'

She felt in the opposite pocket to the one with the kiyoga and brought out a plain keyring with three keys on it.

'You'd better have these,' she said. 'I won't be using them any more.' She put them down by the answering machine and in her eyes I saw the shininess of sudden tears.

'He died in Ipswich,' I said. 'He'll be cremated there on Friday afternoon. Two o'clock.'

She nodded speechlessly in acknowledgement, not looking at me, and went past me, through the doorway and down the hall and out of the front door, closing it with a quiet finality behind her.

With a sigh, I looked round the room. The book-box that had contained her letters still lay open on the floor and I bent down, picked it up, and restored it to the shelves. I wondered just how many books were hollow. Tomorrow evening, I thought, after Elliot Trelawney, I would come and look.

Meanwhile I picked up the fallen green stone box and put it on the table by the chrysanthemums, reflecting that the ornate key in the red-lined book-box was far too large to fit its tiny lock. Greville's bunch of keys was down on the carpet also. I returned to what I'd been doing before being so violently interrupted, but found that the smallest of the bunch was still too big for the green stone.

A whole load of no progress, I thought moodily.

I drank the soda water, which had lost its fizz.

I rubbed my arm, which didn't make it much better.

I wondered what judgement Greville had passed on me, that could be trusted.

There was a polished cupboard that I hadn't investigated underneath the television set and, not expecting much, I bent down and pulled one of the doors open by its brass ring handle. The other door opened of its own accord and the contents of the cupboard slid outwards as a unit; a video machine on top with, on two shelves below, rows of black boxes holding recording tapes. There were small uniform labels on the boxes bearing, not formulas this time, but dates.

I pulled one of the boxes out at random and was stunned to see the larger label stuck to its front: 'Race Video Club', it said in heavy print, and underneath, in typing, 'July 7th, Sandown Park, Dozen Roses.'

The Race Video Club, as I knew well, sold tapes of races to owners, trainers and anyone else interested. Greville, I thought in growing amazement as I looked further, must have given them a standing order: every race his horses had run in for the past two years, I judged, was there on his shelves to be watched.

He'd told me once, when I asked why he didn't go to see his runners, that he saw them enough on television;

and I'd thought he meant on the ordinary scheduled programmes, live from the racetracks in the afternoons.

The front doorbell rang, jarring and unexpected. I went along and looked through a small peephole and found Brad standing on the doorstep, blinking and blinded by two spotlights shining on his face. The lights came from above the door and lit up the whole path and the gate. I opened the door as he shielded his eyes with his arm.

'Hello,' I said. 'Are you all right?'

'Turn the lights off. Can't see.'

I looked for a switch beside the front door, found several, and by pressing them all upwards indiscriminately, put out the blaze.

'Came to see you were OK,' Brad explained. 'Those lights just went on.'

Of their own accord, I realized. Another manifestation of Greville's security, no doubt. Anyone who came up the path after dark would get illuminated for his pains.

'Sorry I've been so long,' I said. 'Now you're here, would you carry a few things?'

He nodded as if he'd let out enough words already to last the evening, and followed me silently, when I beckoned him, towards the small sitting room.

'I'm taking that green stone box and as many of those video tapes as you can carry, starting from that end,' I said, and he obligingly picked up about ten recent tapes, balancing the box on top.

I found a hall light, switched that on, and turned off the lamp in the sitting room. It promptly turned itself on again, unasked.

'Cor,' Brad said.

I thought that maybe it was time to leave before I tripped any other alarms wired direct after dark to the local constabulary. I closed the sitting-room door and we went along the hall to the outer world. Before leaving I pressed all the switches beside the front door downwards, and maybe I turned more on than I'd turned off: the spotlights didn't go on, but a dog started barking noisily behind us.

'Strewth,' Brad said, whirling round and clutching the video tapes to his chest as if they would defend him.

There was no dog. There was a loudspeaker like a bull horn on a low hall table emitting the deep-throated growls and barks of a determined Alsatian.

'Bleeding hell,' Brad said.

'Let's go,' I said in amusement, and he could hardly wait.

The barking stopped of its own accord as we stepped out into the air. I pulled the door shut, and we set off to go down the steps and along the path, and we'd gone barely three paces when the spotlights blazed on again.

'Keep going,' I said to Brad. 'I daresay they'll turn themselves off in time.'

It was fine by him. He'd parked the car round the corner, and I spent the swift journey to Hungerford wondering about Clarissa Williams; her life, love and adultery.

During the evening I failed both to open the green stone box and to understand the gadgets.

Shaking the box gave me no impression of contents and I supposed it could well be empty. A cigarette box, I thought, though I couldn't remember ever seeing Greville smoking. Perhaps a box to hold twin packs of cards. Perhaps a box for jewellery. Its tiny keyhole remained impervious to probes from nail scissors, suitcase keys and a piece of wire, and in the end I surrendered and laid it aside.

Neither of the gadgets opened or shut. One was a small black cylindrical object about the size of a thumb with one end narrowly ridged, like a coin. Turning the ridged end a quarter-turn clockwise, its full extent of travel, produced a thin faint high-pitched whine which proved to be the unexciting sum of the thing's activity. Shrugging, I switched the whine off again and stood the small tube upright on the green box.

The second gadget didn't even produce a whine. It was a flat black plastic container about the size of a pack of cards with a single square red button placed centrally on the front. I pressed the button: no results. A round chromiumed knob set into one of the sides of the cover revealed itself on further inspection as the end of a telescopic aerial. I pulled it out as far as it would go,

about ten inches, and was rewarded with what I pre-
sumed was a small transmitter which transmitted I
didn't know what to I didn't know where.

Sighing, I pushed the aerial back into its socket and
added the transmitter to the top of the green box,
and after that I fed Greville's tapes one by one into my
video machine and watched the races.

Alfie's comment about in-and-out running had
interested me more than I would have wanted him to
know. Dozen Roses, from my own reading of the results,
had had a long doldrum period followed by a burst
of success, suggestive of the classic 'cheating' pattern of
running a horse to lose and go on losing until he was low
in the handicap and unbacked, then setting him off to
win at long odds in a race below his latent abilities and
wheeling away the winnings in a barrow.

All trainers did that in a mild way sometimes, whatever the rules might say about always running flat out.
Young and inexperienced horses could be ruined by
being pressed too hard too soon: one had to give them a
chance to enjoy themselves, to let their racing instinct
develop fully.

That said, there was a point beyond which no modern
trainer dared go. In the bad old days before universal
camera coverage, it had been harder to prove a horse
hadn't been trying: many jockeys had been artists at
waving their whips while hauling on the reins. Under
the eagle lenses and fierce discipline of the current
scene, even natural and unforeseen fluctuations in a

horse's form could find the trainer yanked in before the Stewards for an explanation, and if the trainer couldn't explain why his short-priced favourite had turned leaden footed it could cost him a depressing fine.

. No trainer, however industrious, was safe from suspicion, yet I'd never read or heard of Nicholas Loder getting himself into that sort of trouble. Maybe Alfie, I thought dryly, knew something the Stewards didn't. Maybe Alfie could tell me why Loder had all but panicked when he'd feared Dozen Roses might not run on Saturday next.

Brad had picked up the six most recent outings of Dozen Roses, interspersed by four of Gemstones's. I played all six of Dozen Roses's first, starting with the earliest, back in May, checking the details with what Greville had written in his diary.

On the screen there were shots of the runners walking round the parade ring and going down to the start, with Greville's pink and orange colours bright and easy to see. The May race was a ten-furlong handicap for three-year-olds and upwards, run at Newmarket on a Friday. Eighteen runners. Dozen Roses ridden by a second-string jockey because Loder's chief retained jockey was riding the stable's other runner which started favourite.

Down at the start there was some sort of fracas involving Dozen Roses. I rewound the tape and played it through in slow motion and couldn't help laughing.

Dozen Roses, his mind far from racing, had been showing unseemly interest in a mare.

I remembered Greville saying once that he thought it
a shame and unfair to curb a colt's enthusiasm: no horse
of his would ever be gelded. I remembered him vividly,
leaning across a small table and saying it over a glass of
brandy with a gleam in which I'd seen his own enjoyment of sex. So many glimpses of him in my mind, I
thought. Too few, also. I couldn't really believe I would
never eat with him again, whatever my senses said.

Trainers didn't normally run mares that had come
into season, but sometimes one couldn't tell early on.
Horses knew, though. Dozen Roses had been aroused.
The mare was loaded into the stalls in a hurry and
Dozen Roses had been walked around until the last
minute to cool his ardour. After that, he had run without sparkle and finished mid-field, the mare to the rear
of him trailing in last. Loder's other runner, the favourite, had won by a length.

Too bad, I thought, smiling, and watched Dozen
Roses's next attempt three weeks later.

No distracting attractions this time. The horse had
behaved quietly, sleepily almost, and had turned in the
sort of moderate performance which set owners wondering if the game was worth it. The next race was much
the same, and if I'd been Greville I would have decided
it was time to sell.

Greville, it seemed, had had more faith. After seven
weeks' rest Dozen Roses had gone bouncing down to

the start, raced full of zest and zoomed over the finishing line in front, netting 14/1 for anyone ignorant enough to have backed him. Like Greville, of course.

Watching the sequence of tapes I did indeed wonder why the Stewards hadn't made a fuss, but Greville hadn't mentioned anything except his pleasure in the horse's return to his three-year-old form.

Dozen Roses had next produced two further copybook performances of stamina and determination, which brought us up to date. I rewound and removed the last tape and could see why Loder thought it would be another trot-up on Saturday.

Gemstones's tapes weren't as interesting. Despite his name he wasn't of much value, and the one race he'd won looked more like a fluke than constructive engineering. I would sell them both, I decided, as Loder wanted.

CHAPTER SEVEN

Brad came early on Wednesday and drove me to Lambourn. The ankle was sore in spite of Distalgesics but less of a constant drag that morning and I could have driven the car myself if I'd put my mind to it. Having Brad around, I reflected on the way, was a luxury I was all too easily getting used to.

Clarissa Williams's attentions had worn off completely except for a little stiffness and a blackening bruise like a bar midway between shoulder and elbow. That didn't matter. For much of the year I had bruises somewhere or other, result of the law of averages operating in steeplechasing. Falls occurred about once every fourteen races, sometimes oftener, and while a few of the jockeys had bodies that hardly seemed to bruise at all, mine always did. On the other hand I healed everywhere fast, bones, skin and optimism.

Milo Shandy, striding about in his stable yard as if incapable of standing still, came over to my car as it rolled to a stop and yanked open the driver's door. The words he was about to say didn't come out as he stared first at Brad, then at me on the back seat, and what he eventually said was, 'A chauffeur, by God. Coddling yourself, aren't you?'

Brad got out of the car, gave Milo a neanderthal look and handed me the crutches as usual.

Milo, dark, short and squarely built, watched the proceedings with disgust.

'I want you to ride Datepalm,' he said.

'Well, I can't.'

'The Ostermeyers will want it. I told them you'd be here.'

'Gerry rides Datepalm perfectly well,' I said, Gerry being the lad who rode the horse at exercise as a matter of course most days of the week.

'Gerry isn't you.'

'He's better than me with a groggy ankle.'

Milo glared. 'Do you want to keep the horse here or don't you?'

I did.

Milo and I spent a fair amount of time arguing at the best of times. He was pugnacious by nature, mercurial by temperament, full of instant opinions that could be reversed the next day, didactic, dynamic and outspoken. He believed absolutely in his own judgement and was sure that everything would turn out all right in the end. He was moderately tactful to the owners, hard on his work-force and full of swearwords for his horses, which he produced as winners by the dozen.

I'd been outraged by the way he'd often spoken to

me when I first started to ride for him three years earlier, but one day I lost my temper and yelled back at him, and he burst out laughing and told me we would get along just fine, which in fact we did, though seldom on the surface.

I knew people thought ours an unlikely alliance, I neat and quiet, he restless and flamboyant, but in fact I liked the way he trained horses and they seemed to run well for him, and we had both prospered.

The Ostermeyers arrived at that point and they too had a chauffeur, which Milo took for granted. The bullishness at once disappeared from his manner to be replaced by the jocular charm that had owners regularly mesmerized, that morning being no exception. The Ostermeyers responded immediately, she with a roguish wiggle of the hips, he with a big handshake and a wide smile.

They were not so delighted about my crutches.

'Oh dear,' Martha Ostermeyer exclaimed in dismay. 'What have you done? Don't say you can't ride Datepalm. We only came, you know, because dear Milo said you'd be here to ride it.'

'He'll ride it,' Milo said before I had a chance of answering, and Martha Ostermeyer clapped her small gloved hands with relief.

'If we're going to buy him,' she said, smiling, 'we want to see him with his real jockey up, not some exercise rider.'

Harley Ostermeyer nodded in agreement, benignly.

Not really my week, I thought.

The Ostermeyers were all sweetness and light while people were pleasing them, and I'd never had any trouble liking them, but I'd also seen Harley Ostermeyer's underlying streak of ruthless viciousness once in a racecourse car-park where he'd verbally reduced to rubble an attendant who had allowed someone to park behind him, closing him in. He had had to wait half an hour. The attendant had looked genuinely scared. 'Goodnight, Derek,' he'd croaked as I went past, and Ostermeyer had whirled round and cooled his temper fifty per cent, inviting my sympathy in his trouble. Harley Ostermeyer liked to be thought a good guy, most of the time. He was the boss, as I understood it, of a giant supermarket chain. Martha Ostermeyer was also rich, a fourth-generation multi-millionaire in banking. I'd ridden for them often in the past years and been well rewarded, because generosity was one of their pleasures.

Milo drove them and me up to the Downs where Datepalm and the other horses were already circling, having walked up earlier. The day was bright and chilly, the Downs rolling away to the horizon, the sky clear, the horses' coats glossy in the sun. A perfect day for buying a champion chaser.

Milo sent three other horses down to the bottom of the gallop to work fast so that the Ostermeyers would know where to look and what to expect when Datepalm came up and passed them. They stood out on the grass, looking where Milo pointed, intent and happy.

Milo had brought a spare helmet with us in the big-wheeled vehicle that rolled over the mud and ruts on the Downs, and with an inward sigh I put it on. The enterprise was stupid really, as my leg wasn't strong enough and if anything wild happened to upset Date-palm, he might get loose and injure himself and we'd lose him surely one way or another.

On the other hand, I'd ridden races now and then with cracked bones, not just exercise gallops, and I knew one jockey who in the past had broken three bones in his foot and won races with it, sitting with it in an ice bucket in the changing room betweentimes and literally hopping out to the parade ring, supported by friends. The authorities had later brought in strict medical rules to stop that sort of thing as being unfair to the betting public, but one could still get away with it sometimes.

Milo saw me slide out of the vehicle with the helmet on and came over happily and said, 'I knew you would.'

'Mm,' I said. 'When you give me a leg up, put both hands round my knee and be careful, because if you twist my foot there'll be no sale.'

'You're such a wimp,' he said.

Nevertheless, he was circumspect and I landed in the saddle with little trouble. I was wearing jeans, and that morning for the first time I'd managed to get a shoe on, or rather one of the wide soft black leather moccasins I used as bedroom slippers. Milo threaded the stirrup over the moccasin with unexpected gentleness and I wondered if he were having last-minute doubts about the wisdom of all this.

One look at the Ostermeyers' faces dispelled both his doubts and mine. They were beaming at Datepalm already with proprietary pride.

Certainly he looked good. He filled the eye, as they say. A bay with black points, excellent head, short sturdy legs with plenty of bone. The Ostermeyers always preferred handsome animals, perhaps because they were handsome themselves, and Datepalm was well-mannered besides, which made him a peach of a ride.

He and I and two others from the rest of the string set off at a walk towards the far end of the gallop but were presently trotting, which I achieved by standing in the stirrups with all my weight on my right foot while cursing Milo imaginatively for the sensations in my left. Datepalm, who knew how horses should be ridden, which was not lopsided like this, did a good deal of head and tail shaking but otherwise seemed willing to trust me. He and I knew each other well as I'd ridden him in all his races for the past three years. Horses had no direct way of expressing recognition, but occasionally he would turn his head to look at me when he heard my voice, and I also thought he might know me by scent as he would put his muzzle against my neck sometimes and make small whiffling movements of his nostrils. In any case we did have a definite rapport and that morning it stood us in good stead.

At the far end the two lads and I sorted out our three horses ready to set off at a working gallop back towards Milo and the Ostermeyers, a pace fast enough to be interesting but not flat out like racing.

There wasn't much finesse in riding a gallop to please customers, one simply saw to it that one was on their side of the accompanying horses, to give them a clear view of the merchandise, and that one finished in front to persuade them that that's what would happen in future.

Walking him around to get in position I chatted quietly as I often did to Datepalm, because in common with many racehorses he was always reassured by a calm human voice, sensing from one's tone that all was well. Maybe horses heard the lower resonances: one never knew.

'Just go up there like a pro,' I told him, 'because I don't want to lose you, you old bugger. I want us to win the National one day, so shine, boy. Dazzle. Do your bloody best.'

I shook up the reins as we got the horses going, and in fact Datepalm put up one of his smoothest perform-ances, staying with his companions for most of the jour-ney, lengthening his stride when I gave him the signal, coming away alone and then sweeping collectedly past the Ostermeyers with fluid power; and if the jockey found it an acutely stabbing discomfort all the way, it was a fair price for the result. Even before I'd pulled up, the Ostermeyers had bought the horse and shaken hands on the deal.

'Subject to a veterinarian's report, of course,' Harley was saying as I walked Datepalm back to join them. 'Otherwise, he's superb.'

Milo's smile looked as if it would split his face. He held the reins while Martha excitedly patted the new acquisition, and went on holding them while I took my feet out of the stirrups and lowered myself very carefully to the ground, hopping a couple of steps to where the crutches lay on the grass.

'What did you do to your foot?' Martha asked unworriedly.

'Wrenched it,' I said, slipping the arm cuffs on with relief. 'Very boring.'

She smiled, nodded and patted my arm. 'Milo said it was nothing much.'

Milo gave me a gruesome look, handed Datepalm back to his lad, Gerry, and helped the Ostermeyers into the big-wheeled vehicle for the drive home. We bumped down the tracks and I took off the helmet and ran my fingers through my hair, reflecting that although I wouldn't care to ride gallops like that every day of the week, I would do it again for as good an outcome.

We all went into Milo's house for breakfast, a ritual there as in many other racing stables, and over coffee, toast and scrambled eggs Milo and the Ostermeyers planned Datepalm's future programme, including all the top races with of course another crack at the Gold Cup.

'What about the Grand National?' Martha said, her eyes like stars.

'Well, now, we'll have to see,' Milo said, but his dreams too were as visible as searchlights. First thing on our return, he'd telephoned to Datepalm's former owner and got confirmation that she agreed to the sale and was pleased by it, and since then one had almost needed to pull him down from the ceiling with a string like a helium-filled balloon. My own feelings weren't actually much lower. Datepalm really was a horse to build dreams on.

After the food and a dozen repetitions of the horse's virtues, Milo told the Ostermeyers about my inheriting Dozen Roses and about the probate saga, which seemed to fascinate them. Martha sat up straighter and exclaimed, 'Did you say York?'

Milo nodded.

'Do you mean this Saturday? Why, Harley and I are going to York races on Saturday, aren't we, Harley?'

Harley agreed that they were. 'Our dear friends Lord and Lady Knightwood have asked us to lunch.'

Martha said, 'Why don't we give Derek a ride up there to see his horse run? What do you say, Harley?'

'Be glad to have you along,' Harley said to me genuinely. 'Don't give us no for an answer.'

I looked at their kind insistent faces and said lamely, 'I thought of going by train, if I went at all.'

'No, no,' Martha said. 'Come to London by train and we'll go up together. Do say you will.'

Milo was looking at me anxiously: pleasing the Ostermeyers was still an absolute priority. I said I'd be glad to accept their kindness and Martha, mixing gratification with sudden alarm, said she hoped the inheritance wouldn't persuade me to stop riding races.

'No,' I said.

'That's positive enough.' Harley was pleased. 'You're part of the package, fella. You and Datepalm together.'

Brad and I went on to London, and I was very glad to have him drive.

'Office?' he asked, and I said, 'Yes,' and we travelled there in silent harmony.

He'd told me the evening before that Greville's car wasn't parked anywhere near Greville's house: or rather he'd handed me back the piece of paper with the car's number on it and said, 'Couldn't find it.' I thought I'd better get on to the police and other towers-away in Ipswich, and I'd better start learning the company's finances and Greville's as well, and I had two-thirds of the vault still to check and I could feel the suction of the quicksands inexorably.

I took the two baffling little gadgets from Greville's sitting room upstairs to Greville's office and showed them to June.

'That one,' she said immediately, pointing to the

thumb-sized tube with the whine, 'is a device to discourage mosquitoes. Mr Franklin said it's the noise of a male mosquito, and it frightens the blood-sucking females away.' She laughed. 'He said every man should have one.'

She picked up the other gadget and frowned at it, pressing the red button with no results.

'It has an aerial,' I said.

'Oh yes.' She pulled it out to its full extent. 'I think . . .' She paused. 'He used to have a transmitter which started his car from a distance, so he could warm the engine up in cold weather before he left his house, but the receiver bit got stolen with his Porsche. Then he bought the old Rover, and he said a car-starter wouldn't work on it because it only worked with direct transmission or fuel injection, or something, which the Rover doesn't have.'

'So this is the car-starter?'

'Well . . . no. This one doesn't do so much. The car-starter had buttons that would also switch on the headlights so that you could see where your car was, if you'd left it in a dark car-park.' She pushed the aerial down again. 'I think this one only switches the lights on, or makes the car whistle, if I remember right. He was awfully pleased with it when he got it, but I haven't seen it for ages. He had so many gadgets, he couldn't take them all in his pockets and I think he'd got a bit tired of carrying them about. He used to leave them in his desk, mostly.'

'You just earned your twenty per cent all over again,' I said.

'What?'

'Let's just check that the batteries work,' I said.

She opened the battery compartment and discovered it was empty. As if it were routine, she then pulled open a drawer in one of the other tiers of the desk and revealed a large open box containing packet after packet of new batteries in every possible size. She pulled out a packet, opened it and fed the necessary power packs into the slots, and although pressing the red button still provided no visible results, I was pretty confident we were in business.

June said suddenly, 'You're going to take this to Ipswich, aren't you? To find his car? Isn't that what you mean?'

I nodded. 'Let's hope it works.'

'Oh, it must.'

'It's quite a big town, and the car could be anywhere.'

'Yes,' she said, 'but it must be *somewhere*. I'm sure you'll find it.'

'Mm.' I looked at her bright, intelligent face. 'June,' I said slowly, 'don't tell anyone else about this gadget.'

'Why ever not?'

'Because,' I said, 'someone broke into this office looking for something and we don't know if they found it. If they didn't, and it is by any chance in the car, I don't want anyone to realize that the car is still lost.' I paused. 'I'd much rather you said nothing.'

'Not even to Annette?'

'Not to anyone.'

'But that means you think . . . you think . . .'

'I don't really think anything. It's just for security.'

Security was all right with her. She looked less troubled and agreed to keep quiet about the car-finder; and I hadn't needed to tell her about the mugger who had knocked me down to steal Greville's bag of clothes, which to me, in hindsight, was looking less and less a random hit and more and more a shot at a target.

Someone must have known Greville was dying, I thought. Someone who had organized or executed a mugging. I hadn't the faintest idea who could have done either, but it did seem to me possible that one of Greville's staff might have unwittingly chattered within earshot of receptive ears. Yet what could they have said? Greville hadn't told any of them he was buying diamonds. And why hadn't he? Secretive as he was, gems were his business.

The useless thoughts squirrelled around and got me nowhere. The gloomiest of them was that someone could have gone looking for Greville's car at any time since the scaffolding fell, and although I might find the engine and the wheels, the essential cupboard would be bare.

Annette came into the office carrying a fistful of papers which she said had come in the morning post and needed to be dealt with – by me, her manner inferred.

'Sit down, then,' I said, 'and tell me what they all mean.'

There were letters from insurance people, fund raisers, dissatisfied customers, gemmology forecasters, and a cable from a supplier in Hong Kong saying he didn't have enough African 12 mm amethyst AA quality round beads to fill our order and would we take Brazilian amethyst to make it up.

'What's the difference?' I asked. 'Does it matter?'

Annette developed worry lines over my ignorance. 'The best amethyst is found in Africa,' she said. 'Then it goes to Hong Kong or Taiwan for cutting and polishing into beads, then comes here. The amethyst from Brazil isn't such a good deep colour. Do you want me to order the Brazilian amethyst or wait until he has more of the African?'

'What do you think?' I said.

'Mr Franklin always decided.'

She looked at me anxiously. It's hopeless, I thought. The simplest decision was impossible without knowledge.

'Would the customers take the Brazilian instead?' I asked.

'Some would, some wouldn't. It's much cheaper. We sell a lot of the Brazilian anyway, in all sizes.'

'Well,' I said, 'if we run out of the African beads, offer the customers Brazilian. Or offer a different size of African. Cable the Chinese supplier to send just the

African AA 12 mm he's got now and the rest as soon as he can.'

She looked relieved. 'That's what I'd have said.'

Then why didn't you, I thought, but it was no use being angry. If she gave me bad advice I'd probably blame her for it: it was safer from her viewpoint, I supposed, not to stick her neck out.

'Incidentally,' she said, 'I did reach Prospero Jenks. He said he'd be in his Knightsbridge shop at two-thirty today, if you wanted to see him.'

'Great.'

She smiled. 'I didn't mention horses.'

I smiled back. 'Fine.'

She took the letters off to her own office to answer them, and I went from department to department on a round trip to the vault, watching everyone at work, all of them capable, willing and beginning to settle obligingly into the change of regime, keeping their inner reservations to themselves. I asked if one of them would go down and tell Brad I'd need him at two, not before: June went and returned like a boomerang.

I unlocked the vault and started on topaz: thousands of brilliant translucent slippery stones in a rainbow of colours, some bigger than acorns, some like peas.

No diamonds.

After that, every imaginable shape and size of garnet which could be yellow and green, I found, as well as red, and boxes of citrine.

Two and a half hours of unfolding and folding glossy white packets, and no diamonds.

June swirled in and out at one point with a long order for faceted stones which she handed to me without comment, and I remembered that only Greville and Annette packed orders from the vault. I went in search of Annette and asked if I might watch while she worked down the list, found what was needed from twenty or more boxes and assembled the total on the shelf. She was quick and sure, knowing exactly where to find everything. It was quite easy, she said, reassuring me. I would soon get the hang of it. God help me, I thought.

At two, after another of June's sandwich lunches, I went down to the car and gave Prospero Jenks's address to Brad. 'It's a shop somewhere near Harrods,' I said, climbing in.

He nodded, drove through the traffic, found the shop.

'Great,' I said. 'Now this time you'll have to answer the car phone whether you like it or not, because there's nowhere here to park.'

He shook his head. He'd resisted the suggestion several times before.

'Yes,' I said. 'It's very easy. I'll switch it on for you now. When it rings pick it up and press this button, SND, and you'll be able to hear me. OK? I'll ring when I'm ready to leave, then you just come back here and pick me up.'

He looked at the telephone as if it were contaminated.

It was a totally portable phone, not a fixture in the car, and it didn't receive calls unless one switched it on, which I quite often forgot to do and sometimes didn't do on purpose. I put the phone ready on the passenger seat beside him, to make it easy, and hoped for the best.

Prospero Jenks's shop window glittered with the sort of intense lighting that makes jewellery sparkle, but the lettering of his name over the window was neat and plain, as if ostentation there would have been superfluous.

I looked at the window with a curiosity I would never have felt a week earlier and found it filled not with conventional displays of rings and wristwatches but with joyous toys: model cars, aeroplanes, skiing figures, racing yachts, pheasants and horses, all gold and enamel and shining with gems. Almost every passer-by, I noticed, paused to look.

Pushing awkwardly through the heavy glass front door I stepped into a deep-carpeted area with chairs at the ready before every counter. Apart from the plushness, it was basically an ordinary shop, not very big, quiet in decor, all the excitement in the baubles.

There was no one but me in there and I swung over to one of the counters to see what was on display. Rings, I found, but not simple little circles. These were huge, often asymmetric, all colourful eyecatchers supreme.

'Can I help you?' a voice said.

A neutral man, middle-aged, in a black suit, coming from a doorway at the rear.

'My name's Franklin,' I said. 'Came to see Prospero Jenks.'

'A minute.'

He retreated, returned with a half-smile and invited me through the doorway to the privacies beyond. Shielded from customers' view by a screening partition lay a much longer space which doubled as office and workroom and contained a fearsome-looking safe and several tiers of little drawers like the ones in Saxony Franklin. On one wall a large framed sign read: 'NEVER TURN YOUR BACK TO CUSTOMERS. ALWAYS WATCH THEIR HANDS.' A fine statement of no trust, I thought in amusement.

Sitting on a stool by a workbench, a jeweller's lens screwed into one eye, was a hunched man in pale pink and white striped shirtsleeves, fiddling intently with a small gold object fixed into a vice. Patience and expert workmanship were much on view, all of it calm and painstaking.

He removed the lens with a sigh and rose to his feet, turning to inspect me from crown to crutches to toecaps with growing surprise. Whatever he'd been expecting, I was not it.

The feeling, I supposed, was mutual. He was maybe fifty but looked younger in a Peter Pan sort of way; a boyish face with intense bright blue eyes and a lot of lines developing across the forehead. Fairish hair, no beard, no moustache, no personal display. I had expected someone fancier, more extravagant, temperamental.

'Grev's brother?' he said. 'What a turn-up. There I was, thinking you'd be his age, his height.' He narrowed his eyes. 'He never said he had a brother. How do I know you're legit?'

'His assistant, Annette Adams, made the appointment.'

'Yes, so she did. Fair enough. Told me Grev was dead, long live the King. Said his brother was running the shop, life would go on. But I'll tell you, unless you know as much as Grev, I'm in trouble.'

'I came to talk to you about that.'

'It don't look like tidings of great joy,' he said, watching me judiciously. 'Want a seat?' He pointed at an office chair for me and took his place on the stool. His voice was a long way from cut-glass. More like East End London tidied up for West; the sort that came from nowhere with no privileges and made it to the top from sheer undeniable talent. He had the confident manner of long success, a creative spirit who was also a tradesman, an original artist without airs.

'I'm just learning the business,' I said cautiously. 'I'll do what I can.'

'Grev was a genius,' he said explosively. 'No one like him with stones. He'd bring me oddities, one-offs from all over the world, and I've made pieces . . .' He stopped and spread his arms out. 'They're in palaces,' he said,

'and museums and mansions in Palm Beach. Well, I'm
in business. I sell them to wherever the money's coming
from. I've got my pride, but it's in the pieces. They're
good, I'm expensive, it works a treat.'

'Do you make everything you sell?' I asked.

He laughed. 'No, not myself personally, I couldn't. I
design everything, don't get me wrong, but I have a
workshop making them. I just make the special pieces
myself, the unique ones. In between, I invent for the
general market. Grev said he had some decent spinel,
have you still got it?'

'Er,' I said, 'red?'

'Red,' he affirmed. 'Three, four or five carats. I'll take
all you've got.'

'We'll send it tomorrow.'

'By messenger,' he said. 'Not post.'

'All right.'

'And a slab of rock crystal like the Eiger. Grev
showed me a photo. I've got a commission for a
fantasy . . . Send the crystal too.'

'All right,' I said again, and hid my doubts. I hadn't
seen any slab of rock crystal. Annette would know, I
thought.

He said casually, 'What about the diamonds?'

I let the breath out and into my lungs with conscious
control.

'What about them?' I said.

'Grev was getting me some. He'd got them, in fact.

He told me. He'd sent a batch off to be cut. Are they back yet?'

'Not yet,' I said, hoping I wasn't croaking. 'Are those the diamonds he bought a couple of months ago from the Central Selling Organization that you're talking about?'

'Sure. He bought a share in a sight from a sight-holder. I asked him to. I'm still running the big chunky rings and necklaces I made my name in, but I'm setting some of them now with bigger diamonds, making more profit per item since the market will stand it, and I wanted Grev to get them because I trust him. Trust is like gold dust in this business, even though diamonds weren't his thing really. You wouldn't want to buy two-to three-carat stones from just anyone, even if they're not D or E flawless, right?'

'Er, right.'

'So he bought the share of the sight and he's having them cut in Antwerp as I require them, as I expect you know.'

I nodded. I did know, but only since he'd just told me.

'I'm going to make stars of some of them to shine from the rock crystal...' He broke off, gave a self-deprecating shrug of the shoulders, and said, 'And I'm making a mobile, with diamonds on gold trembler wires that move in the lightest air. It's to hang by a window and flash fire in the sunlight.' Again the self-deprecation, this time in a smile. 'Diamonds are ravishing in sunlight, they're at their best in it, and all the social snobs in this city scream that it's so frightfully vulgar, darling, to wear diamond earrings or bracelets in the daytime. It makes me sick, to be honest. Such a waste.'

I had never thought about diamonds in sunlight before, though I suppose I would in future. Vistas opened could never be closed, as maybe Greville would have said.

'I haven't caught up with everything yet,' I said, which was the understatement of the century. 'Have any of the diamonds been delivered to you so far?'

He shook his head. 'I haven't been in a hurry for them before.'

'And . . . er . . . how many are involved?'

'About a hundred. Like I said, not the very best colour in the accepted way of things but they can look warmer with gold sometimes if they're not ultra blue-white. I work with gold mostly. I like the feel.'

'How much,' I said slowly, doing sums, 'will your rock crystal fantasy sell for?'

'Trade secret. But then, I guess you're trade. It's commissioned, I've got a contract for a quarter of a million if they like it. If they don't like it, I get it back, sell it somewhere else, dismantle it, whatever. In the worst event I'd lose nothing but my time in making it, but don't you worry, they'll like it.'

His certainty was absolute, built on experience.

I said, 'Do you happen to know the name of the Antwerp cutter Greville sent the diamonds to? I mean, it's bound to be on file in the office, but if I know who to look for . . .' I paused. 'I could try to hurry him up for you, if you like.'

'I'd like you to, but I don't know who Grev knew there, exactly.'

I shrugged. 'I'll look it up, then.'

Exactly where was I going to look it up, I wondered? Not in the missing address book, for sure.

'Do you know the name of the sightholder?' I asked.

'Nope.'

'There's a ton of paper in the office,' I said in explanation. 'I'm going through it as fast as I can.'

'Grev never said a word he didn't have to,' Jenks said unexpectedly. 'I'd talk, he listened. We got on fine. He understood what I do better than anybody.'

The sadness of his voice was my brother's universal accolade, I thought. He'd been liked. He'd been trusted. He would be missed.

I stood up and said, 'Thank you, Mr Jenks.'

'Call me Pross,' he said easily. 'Everyone does.'

'My name's Derek.'

'Right,' he said, smiling. 'Now I'll keep on dealing with you, I won't say I won't, but I'm going to have to find me another traveller like Grev, with an eye like his . . . He's been supplying me ever since I started on my own, he gave me credit when the banks wouldn't, he had faith in what I could do . . . Near the beginning he brought me two rare sticks of watermelon tourmaline that were each over two inches long and were half pink, half green mixed all the way up and transparent with the light shining through them and changing while you watched. It would have been a sin to cut them for jewellery. I mounted them in gold and platinum to hang and twist in sunlight.' He smiled his deprecating smile. 'I like gemstones to have life. I didn't have to pay Grev for that tourmaline ever. It made my name for me, the piece was reviewed in the papers and won prizes, and he said the trade we'd do together would be his reward.' He clicked his mouth. 'I do go on a bit.'

'I like to hear it,' I said. I looked down the room to his workbench and said, 'Where did you learn all this? How does one start?'

'I started in metalwork classes at the local comprehensive,' he said frankly. 'Then I stuck bits of glass in gold-plated wire to give to my mum. Then her friends wanted some. So when I left school I took some of those things to show to a jewellery manufacturer and asked for a job. Costume jewellery, they made. I was soon designing for them, and I never looked back.'

CHAPTER EIGHT

I borrowed Prospero's telephone to get Brad, but although I could hear the ringing tone in the car, he didn't answer. Cursing slightly, I asked Pross for a second call and got through to Annette.

'Please keep on trying this number,' I said, giving it to her. 'When Brad answers, tell him I'm ready to go.'

'Are you coming back here?' she asked.

I looked at my watch. It wasn't worth going back as I had to return to Kensington by five-thirty. I said no, I wasn't.

'Well, there are one or two things . . .'

'I can't really tie this phone up,' I said. 'I'll go to my brother's house and ring you from there. Just keep trying Brad.'

I thanked Pross again for the calls. Any time, he said vaguely. He was sitting again in front of his vice, thinking and tinkering, producing his marvels.

There were customers in the shop being attended to by the black-suited salesman. He glanced up very briefly in acknowledgement as I went through and

157

immediately returned to watching the customers' hands. A business without trust; much worse than racing. But then, it was probably impossible to slip a racehorse into a pocket when the trainer wasn't looking.

I stood on the pavement and wondered pessimistically how long it would take Brad to answer the telephone but in the event he surprised me by arriving within a very few minutes. When I opened the car door, the phone was ringing.

'Why don't you answer it?' I asked, wriggling my way into the seat.

'Forgot which button.'

'But you came,' I said.

'Yerss.'

I picked up the phone myself and talked to Annette. 'Brad apparently reckoned that if the phone rang it meant I was ready, so he saw no need to answer it.'

Brad gave a silent nod.

'So now we're setting off to Kensington.' I paused. 'Annette, what's a sightholder, and what's a sight?'

'You're back to diamonds again!'

'Yes. Do you know?'

'Of course I do. A sightholder is someone who is permitted to buy rough diamonds from the CSO. There aren't so many sightholders, only about a hundred and fifty world-wide, I think. They sell the diamonds then to other people. A sight is what they call the sales CSO hold every five weeks, and a sight-box is a packet of stones they sell, though that's often called a sight too.'

'Is a sightholder the same as a diamantaire?' I asked.

'All sightholders are diamantaires, but all diamant-aires are not sightholders. Diamantaires buy from the sightholders, or share in a sight, or buy somewhere else, not from De Beers.'

Ask a simple question, I thought.

Annette said, 'A consignment of cultured pearls has come from Japan. Where shall I put them?'

'Um ... Do you mean where because the vault is locked?'

'Yes.'

'Where did you put things when my brother was travelling?'

She said doubtfully, 'He always said to put them in the stock-room under "miscellaneous beads".'

'Put them in there, then.'

'But the drawer is full with some things that came last week. I wouldn't want the responsibility of putting the pearls anywhere Mr Franklin hadn't approved.' I couldn't believe she needed direction over the simplest thing, but apparently she did. 'The pearls are valuable,' she said. 'Mr Franklin would never leave them out in plain view.'

'Aren't there any empty drawers?'

'Well, I ...'

'Find an empty drawer or a nearby empty drawer and put them there. We'll see to them properly in the morning.'

'Yes, all right.'

She seemed happy with it and said everything else could wait until I came back. I switched off the telephone feeling absolutely swamped by the prospect she'd opened up: if Greville hid precious things under 'miscellaneous beads', where else might he not have hidden them? Would I find a hundred diamonds stuffed in at the back of rhodocrosite or jasper, if I looked?

The vault alone was taking too long. The four big stock-rooms promised a nightmare.

Brad miraculously found a parking space right outside Greville's house, which seemed obscurely to disappoint him.

'Twenty past five,' he said, 'for the pub?'

'If you wouldn't mind. And ... er ... would you just stand there now while I take a look-see?' I had grown cautious, I found.

He ducked his head in assent and watched me manoeuvre the few steps up to the front door. No floodlights came on and no dog barked, presumably because it was daylight. I opened the three locks and pushed the door.

The house was still. No movements of air. I propped the door open with a bronze horse clearly lying around for the purpose and went down the passage to the small sitting room.

No intruders. No mess. No amazons waving riot sticks, no wrecking balls trying to get past the grilles on the windows. If anyone had attempted to penetrate Greville's fortress, they hadn't succeeded.

I returned to the front door. Brad was still standing beside the car, looking towards the house. I gave him a thumbs-up sign, and he climbed into the driver's seat while I closed the heavy door, and in the little sitting room, started taking all of the books off the shelves methodically, riffling the pages and putting each back where I found it.

There were ten hollow books altogether, mostly with titles like *Tales of the Outback* and *With a Mule in Patagonia*. Four were empty, including the one which had held Clarissa Williams's letters. One held the big ornate key. One held an expensive-looking gold watch, the hands pointing to the correct time.

The watch Greville had been wearing in Ipswich was one of those affairs with more knobs than instructions. It lay now beside my bed in Hungerford emitting bleeps at odd intervals and telling me which way was north. The slim gold elegance in the hollow box was for a different mood, a different man; and when I turned it over on my palm I found the inscription on the back: G my love C.

She couldn't have known it was there, I thought. She hadn't looked for it. She'd looked only for the letters, and by chance had come to them first. I put the watch back into the box and back on the shelf. There was no way I could return it to her, and perhaps she wouldn't want it, not with that inscription.

Two of the remaining boxes contained large keys, again unspecified, and one contained a folded instruction leaflet detailing how to set a safe in a concrete nest. The last revealed two very small plastic cases containing baby recording tapes, each adorned with the printed legend 'microcassette'. The cassette cases were all of two inches long by one and a half wide, the featherweight tapes inside a fraction smaller.

I tossed one in my hand indecisively. Nowhere among Greville's tidy belongings had I so far found a microcassette player, which didn't mean I wouldn't in time. Sufficient to the day, I thought in the end, and left the tiny tapes in the book.

With the scintillating titles and their secrets all back on the shelves I stared at them gloomily. Not a diamond in the lot.

Instructions for concrete nests were all very well, but where was the safe? Tapes were OK, but where was the player? Keys were fine, but where were the keyholes? The most frustrating thing about it was that Greville hadn't meant to leave such puzzles. For him, the answers were part of his fabric.

I'd noticed on my way in and out of the house that mail was accumulating in the wire container fixed inside the letter-box on the front door, so to fill in the time before I was due at the pub I took the letters along to the sitting room and began opening the envelopes.

It seemed all wrong. I kept telling myself it was necessary but I still felt as if I were trespassing on ground Greville had surrounded with keep-out fences. There were bills, requests from charities, a bank statement for his private account, a gemmology magazine and two invitations. No letters from sightholders, diamantaires or cutters in Antwerp. I put the letters into the gemmology magazine's large envelope and added to them some similar unfinished business that I'd found in the drawer under the telephone, and reflected ruefully, putting it all ready to take to Hungerford, that I loathed paperwork at the best of times. My own had a habit of mounting up into increasingly urgent heaps. Perhaps having to do Greville's would teach me some sense.

Brad whisked us round to The Rook and Castle at five-thirty and pointed to the phone to let me know how I could call him when I'd finished, and I saw from his twitch of a smile that he found it a satisfactory amusement.

The Rook and Castle was old fashioned inside as well as out, an oasis of drinking peace without a juke-box. There was a lot of dark wood and tiffany lampshades and small tables with beer mats. A clientele of mostly business-suited men was beginning to trickle in and I paused inside the door both to get accustomed to the comparative darkness and to give anyone who was interested a plain view of the crutches.

The interest level being nil, I judged Elliot Trelawney to be absent. I went over to the bar, ordered some Perrier and swallowed a Distalgesic, as it was time. The morning's gallop had done no good to the ankle department but it wasn't to be regretted.

A bulky man of about fifty came into the place as if

familiar with his surroundings and looked purposefully around, sharpening his gaze on the crutches and coming without hesitation to the bar.

'Mr Franklin?'

I shook his offered hand.

'What are you drinking?' he said briskly, eyeing my glass.

'Perrier. That's temporary also.'

He smiled swiftly, showing white teeth. 'You won't mind if I have a double Glenlivet? Greville and I drank many of them together here. I'm going to miss him abominably. Tell me what happened.'

I told him. He listened intently, but at the end he said merely, 'You look very uncomfortable propped against that stool. Why don't we move to a table?' And without more ado he picked up my glass along with the one the bartender had fixed for him, and carried them over to two wooden armchairs under a multicoloured lampshade by the wall.

'That's better,' he said, taking a sip and eyeing me over the glass. 'So you're the brother he talked about. You're Derek.'

'I'm Derek. His only brother, actually. I didn't know he talked about me.'

'Oh, yes. Now and then.'

Elliot Trelawney was big, almost bald, with half-moon glasses and a face that was fleshy but healthy looking. He had thin lips but laugh lines around his eyes, and I'd have said on a snap judgement that he was a realist with a sense of humour.

'He was proud of you,' he said.

'Proud?' I was surprised.

He glimmered. 'We often played golf together on Saturday mornings and sometimes he would be wanting to finish before the two o'clock race at Sandown or somewhere, and it would be because you were riding and it was on the box. He liked to watch you. He liked you to win.'

'He never told me,' I said regretfully.

'He wouldn't, would he? I watched with him a couple of times and all he said after you'd won was, "That's all right then." '

'And when I lost?'

'When you lost?' He smiled. 'Nothing at all. Once you had a crashing fall and he said he'd be glad on the whole when you retired, as race-riding was so dangerous. Ironic, isn't it?'

'Yes.'

'By God, I'll miss him.' His voice was deep. 'We were friends for twenty years.'

I envied him. I wanted intolerably what it was too late to have, and the more I listened to people remembering Greville the worse it got.

'Are you a magistrate?' I asked.

He nodded. 'We often sat together. Greville introduced me to it, but I've never had quite his gift. He seemed to know the truth of things by instinct. He said goodness was visible, therefore in its absence one sought for answers.'

'What sort of cases did . . . do you try?'

'All sorts.' He smiled again briefly. 'Shoplifters. Vagrants. Possession of drugs. TV licence fee evaders. Sex offenders . . . that's prostitution, rape, sex with minors, kerb crawlers. Greville always seemed to know infallibly when those were lying.'

'Go on,' I said, when he stopped. 'Anything else?'

'Well, there are a lot of diplomats in West London, in all the embassies. You'd be astonished what they get away with by claiming diplomatic immunity. Greville hated diplomatic immunity, but we have to grant it. Then we have a lot of small businessmen who "forget" to pay the road tax on the company vehicles, and there are TDAs by the hundred – that's Taking and Driving Away cars. Other motoring offences, speeding and so on, are dealt with separately, like domestic offences and juveniles. And then occasionally we get the preliminary hearings in a murder case, but of course we have to refer those to the Crown Court.'

'Does it all ever depress you?' I said.

He took a sip and considered me. 'It makes you sad,' he said eventually. 'We see as much inadequacy and stupidity as downright villainy. Some of it makes you laugh. I wouldn't say it's depressing, but one learns to see the world from underneath, so to speak. To see the dirt and the delusions, to see through the offenders' eyes and understand their weird logic. But one's disillusion is sporadic because we don't have a bench every day. Twice a month, in Greville's and my cases, plus a little committee work. And that's what I really want from you: the notes Greville was making on the licensing of a new-style gambling club. He said he'd learned disturbing allegations against one of the organizers and he was going to advise turning down the application at the next committee meeting even though it was a project we'd formerly looked on favourably.'

'I'm afraid,' I said, 'that I haven't so far found any notes like that.'

'Damn . . . Where would he have put them?'

'I don't know. I'll look for them, though.' No harm in keeping an eye open for notes while I searched for C.

Elliot Trelawney reached into an inner jacket pocket and brought out two flat black objects, one a notebook, the other a folded black case a bit like a cigarette case.

'These were Greville's,' he said. 'I brought them for you.' He put them on the small table and moved them towards me with plump and deliberate fingers. 'He lent me that one,' he pointed, 'and the notebook he left on the table after a committee meeting last week.'

'Thank you,' I said. I picked up the folded case and opened it and found inside a miniature electronic chess set, the sort that challenged a player to beat it. I looked up. Trelawney's expression, unguarded, was intensely sorrowful. 'Would you like it?' I said. 'I know it's not much, but would you like to keep it?'

'If you mean it.'

I nodded and he put the chess set back in his pocket. 'Greville and I used to play ... *dammit* ...' he finished explosively. 'Why should such a futile thing happen?'

No answer was possible. I regretfully picked up the black notebook and opened it at random.

'The bad scorn the good,' I read aloud, 'and the crooked despise the straight.'

'The thoughts of Chairman Mao,' Trelawney said dryly, recovering himself. 'I used to tease him ... he said it was a habit he'd had from university when he'd learned to clarify his thoughts by writing them down. When I knew he was dead I read that notebook from cover to cover. I've copied down some of the things in it, I hope you won't mind.' He smiled. 'You'll find parts of it especially interesting.'

'About his horses?'

'Those too.'

I stowed the notebook in a trouser pocket which was already pretty full and brought out from there the racing diary, struck by a thought. I explained what the diary was, showing it to Trelawney.

'I phoned that number,' I said, turning pages and pointing, 'and mentioned Greville's name, and a woman told me in no uncertain terms never to telephone again as she wouldn't have the name Greville Franklin spoken in her house.'

Elliot Trelawney blinked. 'Greville? Doesn't sound like Greville.'

'I didn't think so, either. So would it have had something to do with one of your cases? Someone he found guilty of something?'

'Hah. Perhaps.' He considered. 'I could probably find out whose number it is, if you like. Strange he would have had it in his diary, though. Do you want to follow it up?'

'It just seemed so odd,' I said.

'Quite right.' He unclipped a gold pencil from another inner pocket and in a slim notebook of black leather with gold corners wrote down the number.

'Do you make enemies much, because of the court?' I asked.

He looked up and shrugged. 'We get cursed now and then. Screamed at, one might say. But usually not. Mostly they plead guilty because it's so obvious they are. The only real enemy Greville might have had is the gambling club organizer who's not going to get his licence. A drugs baron is what Greville called him. A man suspected of murder but not tried through lack of evidence. He might have had very hard feelings.' He hesitated. 'When I heard Greville was dead, I even wondered about Vaccaro. But it seems clear the scaffolding was a sheer accident ... wasn't it?'

'Yes, it was. The scaffolding broke high up. One man working on it fell three storeys to his death. Pieces just rained down on Greville. A minute earlier, a minute later ...' I sighed. 'Is Vaccaro the gambling-licence man?'

'He is. He appeared before the committee and

seemed perfectly straightforward. Subject to screening, we said. And then someone contacted Greville and uncovered the muck. But we don't ourselves have any details, so we need his notes.'

'I'll look for them,' I promised again. I turned more pages in the diary. 'Does Koningin Beatrix mean anything to you?' I showed him the entry. 'Or CZ = C × 1.7?'

C, I thought, looking at it again, stood for diamond.

'Nothing,' Elliot Trelawney said. 'But as you know, Greville could be as obscure as he was clear-headed. And these were private notes to himself, after all. Same as his notebook. It was never for public consumption.'

I nodded and put away the diary and paid for Elliot Trelawney's repeat Glenlivet but felt waterlogged myself. He stayed for a while, seeming to be glad to talk about Greville, as I was content to listen. We parted eventually on friendly terms, he giving me his card with his phone number for when I found Greville's notes.

If, I silently thought. If I find them.

When he'd gone I used the pub's telephone to ring the car, and after five unanswered brr-brrs disconnected and went outside, and Brad with almost a grin reappeared to pick me up.

'Home,' I said, and he said, 'Yerss,' and that was that.

On the way I read bits of Greville's notebook, pausing often to digest the passing thoughts which had clearly been chiefly prompted by the flotsam drifting through the West London Magistrates Court.

'Goodness is sickening to the evil,' he wrote, 'as evil is sickening to the good. Both the evil and the good may be complacent.'

'In all income groups you find your average regulation slob who sniggers at anarchy but calls the police indignantly to his burglarized home, who is actively anti-authority until he needs to be saved from someone with a gun.'

'The palm outstretched for a hand-out can turn in a flash into a cursing fist. A nation's palm, a nation's fist.'

'Crime to many is not crime but simply a way of life. If laws are inconvenient, ignore them, they don't apply to you.'

'Infinite sadness is not to trust an old friend.'

'Historically, more people have died of religion than cancer.'

'I hate rapists. I imagine being anally assaulted myself, and the anger overwhelms me. It's essential to make my judgement cold.'

Further on I came unexpectedly to what Elliot Trelawney must have meant.

Greville had written, 'Derek came to dinner very stiff with broken ribs. I asked him how he managed to live with all those injuries. "Forget the pain and get on with the party," he said. So we drank fizz.'

I stopped reading and stared out at the autumn countryside which was darkening now, lights going on. I remembered that evening very well, up to a point. Greville had been good fun. I'd got pretty high on the cocktail of champagne and painkillers and I hadn't felt a thing until I'd woken in the morning. I'd driven myself seventy miles home and forgotten it, which frightening fact was roughly why I was currently and obediently sticking to water.

It was almost too dark to read more, but I flicked over one more page and came to what amounted to a prayer, so private and impassioned that I felt my mouth go dry. Alone on the page were three brief lines:

> May I deal with honour.
> May I act with courage.
> May I achieve humility.

I felt as if I shouldn't have read it; knew he hadn't meant it to be read. May I achieve humility . . . that prayer was for saints.

When we reached my house I told Brad I would go to London the next day by train, and he looked devastated.

'I'll drive you for nowt,' he said, hoarsely.

'It isn't the money.' I was surprised by the strength of his feelings. 'I just thought you'd be tired of all the waiting about.'

He shook his head vigorously, his eyes positively pleading.

'All right, then,' I said. 'London tomorrow, Ipswich on Friday. OK?'

'Yerss,' he said with obvious relief.

'And I'll pay you, of course.'

He looked at me dumbly for a moment, then ducked his head into the car to fetch the big brown envelope from Greville's house, and he waited while I unlocked my door and made sure that there were no unwelcome visitors lurking.

Everything was quiet, everything orderly. Brad nodded at my all-clear, gave me the envelope and loped off into the night more tongue-tied than ever. I'd never wondered very much about his thoughts during all the silent hours; had never tried, I supposed, to understand him. I wasn't sure that I wanted to. It was restful the way things were.

I ate a microwaved chicken pie from the freezer and made an unenthusiastic start on Greville's letters, paying his bills for him, closing his accounts, declining his invitations, saying sorry, sorry, very sorry.

After that, in spite of good resolutions, I did not attack my own backlog but read right through Greville's notebook looking for diamonds. Maybe there were some solid gold nuggets, maybe some pearls of wisdom, but no helpful instructions like turn right at the fourth apple tree, walk five paces and dig.

I did however find the answer to one small mystery, which I read with wry amusement.

The green soapstone box pleases me as an exercise in misdirection and deviousness. The keyhole has no key because it has no lock. It's impossible to unlock men's minds with keys, but guile and pressure will do it, as with the box.

Even with the plain instruction to be guileful and devious it took me ages to find the secret. I tried pressing each of the two hinges, pressing the lock, twisting, pressing everything again with the box upside down. The green stone stayed stubbornly shut.

Misdirection, I thought. If the keyhole wasn't a lock, maybe the hinges weren't hinges. Maybe the lid wasn't a lid. Maybe the whole thing was solid.

I tried the box upside down again, put my thumbs on its bottom surface with firm pressure and tried to push it out endways, like a slide. Nothing happened. I reversed it and pushed the other way and as if with a sigh for the length of my stupidity the bottom of the box slid out reluctantly to halfway, and stopped.

It was beautifully made, I thought. When it was shut one couldn't see the bottom edges weren't solid stone, so closely did they fit. I looked with great curiosity to see what Greville had hidden in his ingenious hiding place, not really expecting diamonds, and brought out two well-worn chamois leather pouches with drawstrings, the sort jewellers use, with the name of the jeweller indistinctly stamped on the front.

Both of the pouches were empty, to my great disappointment. I stuffed them back into the hole and shut the box, and it sat on the table beside the telephone all evening, an enigma solved but useless.

It wasn't until I'd decided to go to bed that some switch or other clicked in my brain and a word half-seen became suddenly a conscious thought. Van Ekeren, stamped in gold. Perhaps the jeweller's name stamped on the chamois pouches was worth another look.

I opened the box and pulled the pouches out again and in the rubbed and faded lettering read the full name and address.

> Jacob van Ekeren
> Pelikanstraat 70
> Antwerp

There had to be, I thought, about ten thousand jewellers in Antwerp. The pouches were far from new, certainly not only a few weeks old. All the same . . . better find out.

I took one and left one, closing the box again, and in the morning bore the crumpled trophy to London and through international telephone enquiries found Jacob van Ekeren's number.

The voice that answered from Antwerp spoke either Dutch or Flemish, so I tried in French, *'Je veux parler avec Monsieur Jacob van Ekeren, s'il vous plaît.'*

'Ne quittez pas.'

I held on as instructed until another voice spoke, this time in French, of which I knew far too little.

'*Monsieur van Ekeren n'est pas ici maintenant, monsieur.*'

'*Parlez vous anglais?*' I asked. 'I'm speaking from England.'

'*Attendez.*'

I waited again and was rewarded with an extremely English voice asking if he could help.

I explained that I was speaking from Saxony Franklin Ltd, gemstone importers in London.

'How can I help you?' He was courteous and non-committal.

'Do you,' I said baldly, 'cut and polish rough diamonds?'

'Yes, of course,' he answered. 'But before we do business with any new client we need introductions and references.'

'Um,' I said. 'Wouldn't Saxony Franklin Ltd be a client of yours already? Or Greville Saxony Franklin, maybe? Or just Greville Franklin? It's really important.'

'May I have your name?'

'Derek Franklin. Greville's brother.'

'One moment.' He returned after a while and said he would call me back shortly with an answer.

'Thank you very much,' I said.

'*Pas du tout.*' Bilingual besides.

I put down the phone and asked both Annette and June, who were busily moving around, if they could find

Jacob van Ekeren anywhere in Greville's files. 'See if you can find any mention of Antwerp in the computer,' I added to June.

'Diamonds again!'

'Yup. The van Ekeren address is 70 Pelikanstraat.'

Annette wrinkled her brow. 'That's the Belgian equivalent of Hatton Garden,' she said.

It disrupted their normal work and they weren't keen, but Annette was very soon able to say she had no record of any Jacob van Ekeren, but the files were kept in the office for only six years, and any contact before that would be in storage in the basement. June whisked in to confirm that she couldn't find van Ekeren or Pelikanstraat or Antwerp in the computer.

It wasn't exactly surprising. If Greville had wanted his diamond transaction to be common knowledge in the office he would have conducted it out in the open. Very odd, I thought, that he hadn't. If it had been anyone but Greville one would have suspected him of something underhand, but as far as I knew he always had dealt with honour, as he'd prayed.

The telephone rang and Annette answered it. 'Saxony Franklin, can I help you?' She listened. 'Derek Franklin? Yes, just a moment.' She handed me the receiver and I found it was the return of the smooth French–English voice from Belgium. I knew as well as he did that he had spent the time between the two calls getting our number from international enquiries so that he could check back and be sure I was who I'd said. Merely prudent. I'd have done the same.

'Mr Jacob van Ekeren has retired,' he said. 'I am his nephew Hans. I can tell you now after our researches that we have done no business with your firm within the past six or seven years, but I can't speak for the time before that, when my uncle was in charge.'

'I see,' I said. 'Could you, er, ask your uncle?'

'I will if you like,' he said civilly. 'I did telephone his house, but I understand that he and my aunt will be away from home until Monday, and their maid doesn't seem to know where they went.' He paused. 'Could I ask what all this is about?'

I explained that my brother had died suddenly, leaving a good deal of unfinished business which I was trying to sort out. 'I came across the name and address of your firm. I'm following up everything I can.'

'Ah,' he said sympathetically. 'I will certainly ask my uncle on Monday, and let you know.'

'I'm most grateful.'

'Not at all.'

The uncle, I thought morosely, was a dead-end.

I went along and opened the vault, telling Annette that Prospero Jenks wanted all the spinel. 'And he says we have a piece of rock crystal like the Eiger.'

'The what?'

'Sharp mountain. Like Mont Blanc.'

'Oh.' She moved down the rows of boxes and chose a heavy one from near the bottom at the far end. 'This is it,' she said, humping it on to the shelf and opening the lid. 'Beautiful.'

The Eiger, filling the box, was lying on its side and had a knobbly base so that it wouldn't stand up, but I supposed one could see in the lucent faces and angled planes that, studded with diamond stars and given the Jenks's sunlight treatment, it could make the basis of a fantasy worthy of the name.

'Do we have a price for it?' I asked.

'Double what it cost,' she said cheerfully. 'Plus VAT, plus packing and transport.'

'He wants everything sent by messenger.'

She nodded. 'He always does. Jason takes them in a taxi. Leave it to me, I'll see to it.'

'And we'd better put the pearls away that came yesterday.'

'Oh, yes.'

She went off to fetch them and I moved down to where I'd given up the day before, feeling certain that the search was futile but committed to it all the same. Annette returned with the pearls, which were at least in plastic bags on strings, not in the awkward open envelopes, so while she counted and stored the new intake, I checked my way through the old.

Boxes of pearls, all sizes. No diamonds.

'Does CZ mean anything to you?' I asked Annette idly.

'CZ is cubic zirconia,' she said promptly. 'We sell a fair amount of it.'

'Isn't that, um, imitation diamond?'

'It's a manufactured crystal very like diamond,' she said, 'but about ten thousand times cheaper. If it's in a ring, you can't tell the difference.'

'Can't anyone?' I asked. 'They must do.'

'Mr Franklin said that most high-street jewellers can't at a glance. The best way to tell the difference, he said, is to take the stones out of their setting and weigh them.'

'*Weigh* them?'

'Yes. Cubic zirconia's much heavier than diamond, so one carat of cubic zirconia is smaller than a one-carat diamond.'

'CZ equals C times one point seven,' I said slowly.

'That's right,' she said, surprised. 'How did you know?'

CHAPTER NINE

From noon on, when I closed the last box-lid unproductively on the softly changing colours of rainbow opal from Oregon, I sat in Greville's office reading June's print-out of a crash course in business studies, beginning to see the pattern of a cash flow that ended on the side of the angels. Annette, who as a matter of routine had been banking the receipts daily, produced a sheaf of cheques for me to sign, which I did, feeling that it was the wrong name on the line, and she brought the day's post for decisions, which I strugglingly made.

Several people in the jewellery business telephoned in response to the notices of Greville's death which had appeared in the papers that morning. Annette, reassuring them that the show would go on, sounded more confident than she looked. 'They all say Ipswich is too far, but they'll be there in spirit,' she reported.

At four there was a phone call from Elliot Trelawney, who said he'd cracked the number of the lady who didn't want Greville's name spoken in her house.

'It's sad, really,' he said with a chuckle. 'I suppose I

181

shouldn't laugh. That lady can't and won't forgive Greville because he sent her upper-crust daughter to jail for three months for selling cocaine to a friend. The mother was in court, I remember her, and she talked to the press afterwards. She couldn't believe that selling cocaine to a friend was an offence. Drug peddlers were despicable, of course, but that wasn't the same as selling to a friend.'

'If a law is inconvenient, ignore it, it doesn't apply to you.'

'What?'

'Something Greville wrote in his notebook.'

'Oh yes. It seems Greville got the mother's phone number to suggest ways of rehabilitation for the daughter, but mother wouldn't listen. Look,' he hesitated. 'Keep in touch now and then, would you? Have a drink in The Rook and Castle occasionally?'

'All right.'

'And let me know as soon as you find those notes.'

'Sure,' I said.

'We want to stop Vaccaro, you know.'

'I'll look everywhere,' I promised.

When I put the phone down I asked Annette.

'Notes about his cases?' she said. 'Oh no, he never brought those to the office.'

Like he never bought diamonds, I thought dryly. And there wasn't a trace of them in the spreadsheets or the ledgers.

The small insistent alarm went off again, muffled

inside the desk. Twenty past four, my watch said. I reached over and pulled open the drawer and the alarm stopped, as it had before.

'Looking for something?' June said, breezing in.

'Something with an alarm like a digital watch.'

'It's bound to be the world clock,' she said. 'Mr Franklin used to set it to remind himself to phone suppliers in Tokyo, and so on.'

I reflected that as I wouldn't know what to say to suppliers in Tokyo I hardly needed the alarm.

'Do you want me to send a fax to Tokyo to say the pearls arrived OK?' she said.

'Do you usually?'

She nodded. 'They worry.'

'Then please do.'

When she'd gone Jason with his orange hair appeared through the doorway and without any trace of insolence told me he'd taken the stuff to Prospero Jenks and brought back a cheque, which he'd given to Annette.

'Thank you,' I said neutrally.

He gave me an unreadable glance, said, 'Annette said to tell you,' and took himself off. An amazing improvement, I thought.

I stayed behind that evening after they'd all left and went slowly round Greville's domain looking for hiding places that were guileful and devious and full of misdirection.

It was impossible to search the hundreds of shallow

drawers in the stock-rooms and I concluded he wouldn't have used them because Lily or any of the others might easily have found what they weren't meant to. That was the trouble with the whole place, I decided in the end. Greville's own policy of not encouraging private territories had extended also to himself, as all of his staff seemed to pop in and out of his office familiarly whenever the need arose.

Hovering always was the uncomfortable thought that if any pointer to the diamonds' whereabouts had been left by Greville in his office, it could have vanished with the break-in artist, leaving nothing for me to find; and indeed I found nothing of any use. After a fruitless hour I locked everything that locked and went down to the yard to find Brad and go home.

The day of Greville's funeral dawned cold and clear and we were heading east when the sun came up. The run to Ipswich taking three hours altogether, we came into the town with generous time to search for Greville's car.

Enquiries from the police had been negative. They hadn't towed, clamped or ticketed any ancient Rover. They hadn't spotted its number in any public road or car-park, but that wasn't conclusive, they'd assured me. Finding the car had no priority with them as it hadn't been stolen but they would let me know if, if.

I explained the car-finder to Brad en route, producing a street map to go with it.

'Apparently when you press this red button the car's lights switch on and a whistle blows,' I said. 'So you drive and I'll press, OK?'

He nodded, seeming amused, and we began to search in this slightly bizarre fashion, starting in the town centre near to where Greville had died and very slowly rolling up and down the streets, first to the north, then to the south, checking them off on the map. In many of the residential streets there were cars parked nose to tail outside houses, but nowhere did we get a whistle. There were public car-parks and shop car-parks and the station car-park, but nowhere did we turn lights on. Rover 3500s in any case were sparse: when we saw one we stopped to look at the plates, even if the paint wasn't grey, but none of them was Greville's.

Disappointment settled heavily. I'd seriously intended to find that car. As lunchtime dragged towards two o'clock I began to believe that I shouldn't have left it so long, that I should have started looking as soon as Greville died. But last Sunday, I thought, I hadn't been in any shape to, and anyway it wasn't until Tuesday that I knew there was anything valuable to look for. Even now I was sure that he wouldn't have left the diamonds themselves vulnerable, but some reason for being in Ipswich at all . . . given luck, why not?

The crematorium was set in a garden with neatly planted rose trees: Brad dropped me at the door and drove away to find some food. I was met by two blacksuited men, both with suitable expressions, who introduced themselves as the undertaker I'd engaged and one of the crematorium's officials. A lot of flowers had arrived, they said, and which did I want on the coffin.

In some bemusement I let them show me where the flowers were, which was in a long covered cloister beside the building, where one or two weeping groups were looking at wreaths of their own.

'These are Mr Franklin's,' the official said, indicating two long rows of bright bouquets blazing with colourful life in that place of death.

'All of these?' I said, astonished.

'They've been arriving all morning. Which do you want inside, on the coffin?'

There were cards on the bunches, I saw.

'I sent some from myself and our sisters,' I said doubtfully. 'The card has Susan, Miranda and Derek on it. I'll have that.'

The official and the undertaker took pity on the crutches and helped me find the right flowers; and I came first not to the card I was looking for but to another that shortened my breath.

'I will think of you every day at four-twenty. Love, C.'

The flowers that went with it were velvety red roses arranged with ferns in a dark green bowl. Twelve sweet-smelling blooms. Dozen Roses, I thought. Heavens above.

'I've found them,' the undertaker called, picking up a large display of pink and bronze chrysanthemums. 'Here you are.'

'Great. Well, we'll have these roses as well, and this wreath next to them, which is from the staff in his office. Is that all right?'

It appeared to be. Annette and June had decided on all-white flowers after agonizing and phoning from the office, and they'd made me promise to notice and tell them that they were pretty. We had decided that all the staff should stay behind and keep the office open as trade was so heavy, though I'd thought from her downcast expression that June would have liked to have made the journey.

I asked the official where all the other flowers had come from: from businesses, he said, and he would collect all the cards afterwards and give them to me.

I supposed for the first time that perhaps I should have taken Greville back to London to be seen off by colleagues and friends, but during the very quiet half-hour that followed had no single regret. The clergyman engaged by the undertakers asked if I wanted the whole service read as I appeared to be the only mourner, and I said yes, go ahead, it was fitting.

His voice droned a bit. I half listened and half watched the way the sunshine fell onto the flowers on the coffin from the high windows along one wall and thought mostly not of Greville as he'd been alive but what he had become to me during the past week.

His life had settled on my shoulders like a mantle. Through Monday, Tuesday, Wednesday and Thursday I'd learned enough of his business never to forget it.

People who'd relied on him had transferred their reliance onto me, including in a way his friend Elliot Trelawney who wanted me as a Greville substitute to drink with. Clarissa Williams had sent her flowers knowing I would see them, wanting me to be aware of her, as if I weren't already. Nicholas Loder aimed to manipulate me for his own stable's ends. Prospero Jenks would soon be pressing hard for the diamonds for his fantasy, and the bank loan hung like a thundercloud in my mind.

Greville, lying cold in the coffin, hadn't meant any of it to happen.

A man of honour, I thought. I mentally repeated his own prayer for him, as it seemed a good time for it. May I deal with honour. May I act with courage. May I achieve humility. I didn't know if he'd managed that last one; I knew that I couldn't.

The clergyman droned to a halt. The official removed the three lots of flowers from the coffin to put them on the floor and, with a whirring and creaking of machinery that sounded loud in the silence, the coffin slid away forward, out of sight, heading for fire.

Goodbye, pal, I said silently. Goodbye, except that you are with me now more than ever before.

I went outside into the cold fresh air and thanked everyone and paid them and arranged for all of the flowers to go to St Catherine's Hospital, which seemed to be no problem. The official gave me the severed cards and asked what I wanted to do with my brother's ashes, and I had a ridiculous urge to laugh, which I saw from his hushed face would be wildly inappropriate. The business of ashes had always seemed to me an embarrassment.

He waited patiently for a decision. 'If you have any tall red rose trees,' I said finally, 'I daresay that would do, if you plant one along there with the others. Put the ashes there.'

I paid for the rose tree and thanked him again, and waited for a while for Brad to return, which he did looking smug and sporting a definite grin.

'I found it,' he said.

'What?' I was still thinking of Greville.

'Your brother's wheels.'

'You didn't!'

He nodded, highly pleased with himself.

'Where?'

He wouldn't say. He waited for me to sit and drove off in triumph into the centre of town, drawing up barely three hundred yards from where the scaffolding had fallen. Then, with his normal economy, he pointed to the forecourt of a used car sales business where under strips of fluttering pennants rows of offerings stood with large white prices painted on their windscreens.

'One of those?' I asked in disbelief.

Brad gurgled; no other word for the delight in his throat. 'Round the back,' he said.

He drove into the forecourt, then along behind the cars, and turned a corner, and we found ourselves outside the wide-open doors of a garage advertising repairs, oil changes, MOT tests and Ladies and Gents. Brad held the car-finder out of his open window and pressed the red button, and somewhere in the shadowy depths of the garage a pair of headlights began flashing on and off and a piercing whistle shrieked.

A cross-looking mechanic in oily overalls came hurrying out. He told me he was the foreman in charge and he'd be glad to see the back of the Rover 3500, and I owed him a week's parking besides the cleaning of the sparking plugs of the V.8 engine, plus a surcharge for inconvenience.

'What inconvenience?'

'Taking up space for a week when it was meant to be for an hour, and having that whistle blast my eardrums three times today.'

'Three times?' I said, surprised.

'Once this morning, twice this afternoon. This man came here earlier, you know. He said he'd bring the Rover's new owner.'

Brad gave me a bright glance. The car-finder had done its best for us early on in the morning, it seemed: it was our own eyes and ears that had missed it, out of sight as the car had been.

I asked the foreman to make out a bill and, getting out of my own car, swung over to Greville's. The Rover's doors would open, I found, but the boot was locked.

'Here,' said the foreman, coming over with the

account and the ignition keys. 'The boot won't open. Some sort of fancy lock. Custom made. It's been a bloody nuisance.'

I mollifyingly gave him a credit card in settlement and he took it off to his cubby-hole of an office.

I looked at the Rover. 'Can you drive that?' I asked Brad.

'Yerss,' he said gloomily.

I smiled and pulled Greville's keys out of my pocket to see if any of them would unlock the boot; and one did, to my relief, though not a key one would normally have associated with cars. More like the keys to a safe, I thought; and the lock revealed was intricate and steel. Its installation was typically Greville, ultra security-conscious after his experiences with the Porsche.

The treasure so well guarded included an expensive-looking set of golf clubs, with a trolley and a new box of golf balls, a large brown envelope, an overnight bag with pyjamas, clean shirt, toothbrush and a scarlet can of shaving cream, a portable telephone like my own, a personal computer, a portable fax machine, an opened carton of spare fax paper, a polished wooden box containing a beautiful set of brass scales with featherlight weights, an anti-thief device for locking onto the steering wheel, a huge torch, and a heavy complicated-looking orange metal contraption that I recognized from Greville's enthusiastic description as a device for sliding under flat tyres so that one could drive to a garage on it instead of changing a wheel by the roadside.

'Cor,' Brad said, looking at the haul, and the foreman too, returning with the paperwork, was brought to an understanding of the need for the defences.

I shut the boot and locked it again, which seemed a very Greville-like thing to do, and took a quick look round inside the body of the car, seeing the sort of minor clutter which defies the tidiest habit: matchbooks, time-clock parking slips, blue sunglasses, and a cellophane packet of tissues. In the door pocket on the driver's side, jammed in untidily, a map.

I picked it out. It was a road map of East Anglia, the route from London to Ipswich drawn heavily in black with, written down one side, the numbers of the roads to be followed. The marked route, I saw with interest, didn't stop at Ipswich but went on beyond, to Harwich.

Harwich, on the North Sea, was a ferry port. Harwich to the Hook of Holland; the route of one of the historic crossings, like Dover to Calais, Folkestone to Ostend. I didn't know if the Harwich ferries still ran, and I thought that if Greville had been going to Holland he would certainly have gone by air. All the same he had, presumably, been going to Harwich.

I said abruptly to the foreman, who was showing impatience for our departure, 'Is there a travel agent near here?'

'Three doors along,' he said, pointing, 'and you can't park here while you go there.'

I gave him a tip big enough to change his mind, and left Brad keeping watch over the cars while I peg-legged along the street. Right on schedule the travel agents came up, and I went in to enquire about ferries for the Hook of Holland.

'Sure,' said an obliging girl. 'They run every day and every night. Sealink operate them. When do you want to go?'

'I don't know, exactly.'

She thought me feeble. 'Well, the *St Nicholas* goes over to Holland every morning, and the *Koningin Beatrix* every night.'

I must have looked as stunned as I felt. I closed my open mouth.

'What's the matter?' she said.

'Nothing at all. Thank you very much.'

She shrugged as if the lunacies of the travelling public were past comprehension, and I shunted back to the garage with my chunk of new knowledge which had solved one little conundrum but posed another, such as what was Greville doing with Queen Beatrix, not a horse but a boat.

Brad drove the Rover to London and I drove my own car, the pace throughout enough to make a snail weep. Whatever the Ipswich garage had done to Greville's plugs hadn't cured any trouble, the V.8 running more like a V.4 or even a V.1½ as far as I could see. Brad stopped fairly soon after we'd left the town and, cursing, cleaned the plugs again himself, but to no avail.

'Needs new ones,' he said.

I used the time to search thoroughly through the golf bag, the box of golf balls, the overnight bag and all the gadgets.

No diamonds.

We set off again, the Rover going precariously slowly in very low gear up hills, with me staying on its tail in case it petered out altogether. I didn't much mind the slow progress except that resting my left foot on the floor sent frequent jabs up my leg and eventually reawoke the overall ache in the ankle, but in comparison with the ride home from Ipswich five days earlier it was chickenfeed. I still mended fast, I thought gratefully. By Tuesday at the latest I'd be walking. Well, limping, maybe, like Greville's car.

There was no joy in reflecting, as I did, that if the sparking plugs had been efficient he wouldn't have stopped to have them fixed and he wouldn't have been walking along a street in Ipswich at the wrong moment. If one could foresee the future, accidents wouldn't happen. 'If only' were wretched words.

We reached Greville's road eventually and found two spaces to park, though not outside the house. I'd told Brad in the morning that I would sleep in London that night to be handy for going to York with the Ostermeyers the next day. I'd planned originally that if we found the Rover he would take it on the orbital route direct to Hungerford and I would drive into London and go on home from there after I got back from York. The plugs having changed that plan near Ipswich, it was now Brad who would go to Hungerford in my car, and I would finish the journey by train. Greville's car, ruin that it was, could decorate the street.

We transferred all the gear from Greville's boot into the back of my car, or rather Brad did the transferring while I mostly watched. Then, Brad carrying the big brown envelope from the Rover and my own overnight grip, we went up the path to the house in the dark and set off the lights and the barking. No one in the houses around paid any attention. I undid the three locks and went in cautiously but, as before, once I'd switched the dog off the house was quiet and deserted. Brad, declining food and drink, went home to his mum, and I, sitting in Greville's chair, opened the big brown envelope and read all about Vaccaro who had been a very bad boy indeed.

Most of the envelope's contents were a copy of Vaccaro's detailed application, but on an attached sheet in abbreviated prose Greville had hand-written:

Ramón Vaccaro, wanted for drug-running, Florida, USA.

Suspected of several murders, victims mostly pilots, wanting out from flying drug crates. Vaccaro leaves no mouths alive to chatter. My info from scared-to-death pilot's widow. She won't come to the committee meeting but gave enough insider details for me to believe her.

Vaccaro seduced private pilots with a big pay-off, then when they'd done one run to Colombia and got away with it, they'd be hooked and do it again and again until they finally got rich enough to have cold feet. Then the poor sods would die from being shot on their own doorsteps from passing cars, no sounds because of silencers, no witnesses and no clues. But all were pilots owning their own small planes, too many for coincidence. Widow says her husband scared stiff but left it too late. She's remarried, lives in London, always wanted revenge, couldn't believe it was the same man when she saw local newspaper snippet, Vaccaro's Family Gaming, with his photo. Family! She went to Town Hall anonymously, they put her on to me.

We don't have to find Vaccaro guilty. We just don't give him a gaming licence. Widow says not to let him know who turned his application down, he's dangerous and vengeful, but how can he silence a whole committee? The Florida police might like to know his whereabouts. Extradition?

I telephoned Elliot Trelawney at his weekend home, told him I'd found the red-hot notes and read them to him, which brought forth a whistle and a groan.

'But Vaccaro didn't kill Greville,' I said.

'No.' He sighed. 'How did the funeral go?'

'Fine. Thank you for your flowers.'

'Just sorry I couldn't get there – but on a working day, and so far . . .'

'It was fine,' I said again, and it had been. I'd been relieved, on the whole, to be alone.

'Would you mind,' he said, diffidently, 'if I arranged a memorial service for him? Sometime soon. Within a month?'

'Go right ahead,' I said warmly. 'A great idea.'

He hoped I would send the Vaccaro notes by messenger on Monday to the Magistrates Court, and he asked if I played golf.

In the morning, after a dream-filled night in Greville's black and white bed, I took a taxi to the Ostermeyers' hotel, meeting them in the foyer as arranged on the telephone the evening before.

They were in very good form, Martha resplendent in a red wool tailored dress with a mink jacket, Harley with a new English-looking hat over his easy grin, binoculars and racing paper ready. Both of them seemed determined to enjoy whatever the day brought forth and Harley's occasional ill-humour was far out of sight.

The driver, a different one from Wednesday, brought a huge super-comfortable Daimler to the front door exactly on time, and with all auspices pointing to felicity, the Ostermeyers arranged themselves on the rear seat, I sitting in front of them beside the chauffeur.

The chauffeur, who announced his name as Simms,

kindly stowed my crutches in the boot and said it was no trouble at all, sir, when I thanked him. The crutches themselves seemed to be the only tiny cloud on Martha's horizon, bringing a brief frown to the proceedings.

'Is that foot still bothering you? Milo said it was nothing to worry about.'

'No, it isn't, and it's much better,' I said truthfully.

'Oh, good. Just as long as it doesn't stop you riding Datepalm.'

'Of course not,' I assured her.

'We're so pleased to have him. He's just darling.'

I made some nice noises about Datepalm, which wasn't very difficult, as we nosed through the traffic to go north on the M1.

Harley said, 'Milo says Datepalm might go for the Charisma 'Chase at Kempton next Saturday. What do you think?'

'A good race for him,' I said calmly. I would kill Milo, I thought. A dicey gallop was one thing, but no medic on earth was going to sign my card in one week to say I was fit; and I wouldn't be, because half a ton of horse over jumps at thirty-plus miles an hour was no puffball matter.

'Milo might prefer to save him for the Mackeson at Cheltenham next month,' I said judiciously, sowing the idea. 'Or of course for the Hennessy Cognac Gold Cup two weeks later.' I'd definitely be fit for the Hennessy, six weeks ahead. The Mackeson, at four weeks, was a toss-up.

'Then there's that big race the day after Christmas,' Martha sighed happily. 'It's all so exciting. Harley promises we can come back to see him run.'

They talked about horses for another half hour and then asked if I knew anything about a Dick Turpin.

'Oh, sure.'

'Some guy said he was riding to York. I didn't understand any part of it.'

I laughed. 'It happened a couple of centuries ago. Dick Turpin was a highwayman, a real villain, who rode his mare Black Bess north to escape the law. They caught him in York and flung him in gaol and for a fortnight he held a sort of riotous court in his cell, making jokes and drinking with all the notables of the city who came to see the famous thief in his chains. Then they took him out and hanged him on a piece of land called the Knavesmire, which is now the racecourse.'

'Oh, my,' Martha said, ghoulishly diverted. 'How perfectly grisly.'

In time we left the M1 and travelled north-east to the difficult old A1, and I thought that no one in their senses would drive from London to York when they could go by train. The Ostermeyers, of course, weren't doing the driving.

Harley said as we neared the city, 'You're expected at lunch with us, Derek.'

Expected, in Ostermeyer speech, meant invited. I protested mildly that it wasn't so.

'It sure is. I talked with Lord Knightwood yesterday

evening, told him we'd have you with us. He said right away to have you join us for lunch. They're giving their name to one of the races, it'll be a big party.'

'Which race?' I asked with curiosity. Knightwood wasn't a name I knew.

'Here it is.' Harley rustled the racing newspaper. 'The University of York Trophy. Lord Knightwood is the University's top man, president or governor, some kind of figurehead. A Yorkshire VIP. Anyway, you're expected.'

I thanked him. There wasn't much else to do, though a sponsor's lunch on top of no exercise could give me weight problems if I wasn't careful. However, I could almost hear Milo's agitated voice in my ear: 'Whatever the Ostermeyers want, for Christ's sake give it to them.'

'There's also the York Minster Cup,' Harley said, reading his paper, 'and the Civic Pride Challenge. Your horse Dozen Roses is in the York Castle Champions.'

'My brother's horse,' I said.

Harley chuckled. 'We won't forget.'

Simms dropped us neatly at the Club entrance. One could get addicted to chauffeurs, I thought, accepting the crutches gravely offered. No parking problems. Someone to drive one home on crunch days. But no spontaneity, no real privacy ... No thanks, not even long-term Brad.

Back the first horse you see, they say. Or the first jockey. Or the first trainer.

The first trainer we saw was Nicholas Loder. He

looked truly furious and, I thought in surprise, alarmed when I came face to face with him after he'd watched our emergence from the Daimler.

'What are you doing here?' he demanded brusquely. 'You've no business here.'

'Do you know Mr and Mrs Ostermeyer?' I asked politely, introducing them. 'They've just bought Date-palm. I'm their guest today.'

He glared; there wasn't any other word for it. He had been waiting for a man, perhaps one of his owners, to collect a Club badge from the allotted window and, the transaction achieved, the two of them marched off into the racecourse without another word.

'Well!' Martha said, outraged. 'If Milo ever behaved like that we'd whisk our horses out of his yard before he could say goodbye.'

'It isn't my horse,' I pointed out. 'Not yet.'

'When it is, what will you do?'

'The same as you, I think, though I didn't mean to.'

'Good,' Martha said emphatically.

I didn't really understand Loder's attitude or reaction. If he wanted a favour from me, which was that I'd let him sell Dozen Roses and Gemstones to others of his owners either for the commission or to keep them in his yard, he should at least have shown an echo of Milo's feelings for the Ostermeyers.

If Dozen Roses had been cleared by the authorities to run, why was Loder scared that I was there to watch it?

Crazy, I thought. The only thing I'd wholly learned was that Loder's ability to dissimulate was underdeveloped for a leading trainer.

Harley Ostermeyer said the York University's lunch was to be held at one end of the Club members' dining room in the grandstand, so I showed the way there, reflecting that it was lucky I'd decided on a decent suit for that day, not just a sweater. I might have been a last-minute addition to the party but I was happy not to look it.

There was already a small crowd of people, glasses in hand, chatting away inside a temporary white-lattice-fenced area, a long buffet set out behind them with tables and chairs to sit at for eating.

'There are the Knightwoods,' said the Ostermeyers, clucking contentedly, and I found myself being introduced presently to a tall white-haired kindly-looking man who had benevolence shining from every perhaps seventy-year-old wrinkle. He shook my hand amicably as a friend of the Ostermeyers with whom, it seemed, he had dined on a reciprocal visit to Harley's alma mater, the University of Pennsylvania. Harley was endowing a Chair there. Harley was a VIP in Pittsburgh, Pennsylvania.

I made the right faces and listened to the way the world went round, and said I thought it was great of the city of York to support its industry on the turf.

'Have you met my wife?' Lord Knightwood said vaguely. 'My dear,' he touched the arm of a woman with her back to us, 'you remember Harley and Martha Ostermeyer? And this is their friend Derek Franklin that I told you about.'

She turned to the Ostermeyers smiling and greeting them readily, and she held out a hand for me to shake, saying, 'How do you do. So glad you could come.'

'How do you do, Lady Knightwood,' I said politely. She gave me a very small smile, in command of herself.

Clarissa Williams was Lord Knightwood's wife.

CHAPTER TEN

She had known I would be there, it was clear, and if she hadn't wanted me to find out who she was she could have developed a strategic illness in plenty of time.

She was saying graciously, 'Didn't I see you on television winning the Gold Cup?' and I thought of her speed with that frightful kiyoga and the tumult of her feelings on Tuesday, four days ago. She seemed to have no fear that I would give her away, and indeed, what could I say? Lord Knightwood, my brother was your wife's lover? Just the right sort of thing to get the happy party off to a good start.

The said Lord was introducing the Ostermeyers to a professor of physics who with twinkles said that as he was the only true aficionado of horse-racing among the teaching academics he had been pressed into service to carry the flag, although there were about fifty undergraduates out on the course ready to bet their socks off in the cause.

'Derek has a degree,' Martha said brightly, making conversation.

The professorial eyeballs swivelled my way speculatively. 'What university?'

'Lancaster,' I said dryly, which raised a laugh. Lancaster and York had fought battles of the red and white roses for many a long year.

'And subject?'

'Independent Studies.'

His desultory attention sharpened abruptly.

'What are Independent Studies?' Harley asked, seeing his interest.

'The student designs his own course and invents his own final subject,' the professor said. 'Lancaster is the only university offering such a course and they let only about eight students a year do it. It's not for the weak-willed or the feeble-minded.'

The Knightwoods and the Ostermeyers listened in silence and I felt embarrassed. I had been young then, I thought.

'What did you choose as your subject?' asked the professor, intent now on an answer. 'Horses, in some way?'

I shook my head. 'No. . . er. . . "Roots and Results of War".'

'My dear chap,' Lord Knightwood said heartily, 'sit next to the professor at lunch.' He moved away benignly, taking his wife and the Ostermeyers with him, and the professor, left behind, asked what I fancied for the races.

Clarissa, by accident or design, remained out of

talking distance throughout the meal and I didn't try to approach her. The party broke up during and after the first race, although everyone was invited to return for tea, and I spent most of the afternoon, as I'd spent so many others, watching horses stretch and surge and run as their individual natures dictated. The will to win was born and bred in them all, but some cared more than others: it was those with the implacable impulse to lead a wild herd who fought hardest and oftenest won. Sports writers tended to call it courage but it went deeper than that, right down into the gene pool, into instinct, into the primordial soup on the same evolutionary level as the belligerence so easily aroused in Homo sapiens, that was the taproot of water.

I was no stranger to the thought that I sought battle on the turf because, though the instinct to fight and conquer ran strong, I was averse to guns. Sublimation, the pundits would no doubt call it. Datepalm and I both, on the same primitive plane, wanted to win.

'What are you thinking?' someone asked at my shoulder.

I would have known her voice anywhere, I thought. I turned to see her half-calm half-anxious expression, the Lady Knightwood social poise explicit in the smooth hair, the patrician bones and the tailoring of her clothes, the passionate woman merely a hint in the eyes.

'Thinking about horses,' I said.

'I suppose you're wondering why I came today, after I learned last night that you'd not only be at the races,

206

which I expected you might be anyway because of Dozen Roses, but actually be coming to our lunch ...' She stopped, sounding uncertain.

'I'm not Greville,' I said. 'Don't think of me as Greville.'

Her eyelids flickered. 'You're too damned perceptive.' She did a bit of introspection. 'Yes, all right, I wanted to be near you. It's a sort of comfort.'

We were standing by the rails of the parade ring watching the runners for the next race walk round, led by their lads. It was the race before the University Trophy, two races before that of Dozen Roses, a period without urgency for either of us. There were crowd noises all around and the clip-clop of horses walking by, and we could speak quietly as in an oasis of private space without being overheard.

'Are you still angry with me for hitting you?' she said a shade bitterly, as I'd made no comment after her last remark.

I half smiled. 'No.'

'I did think you were a burglar.'

'And what would you have explained to the police, if they'd come?'

She said ruefully, 'I hope I would have come to my senses and done a bunk before they got there.' She sighed. 'Greville said if I ever had to use the kiyoga in earnest to escape at once and not worry what I'd done to my attacker, but he never thought of a burglar in his own house.'

'I'm surprised he gave you a weapon like that,' I said mildly. 'Aren't they illegal? And him a magistrate.'

'I'm a magistrate too,' she said unexpectedly. 'That's how we originally met, at a magistrates' conference. I've not enquired into the legality of kiyogas. If I were prosecuted for carrying and using an offensive weapon, well, that would be much preferable to being a victim of the appalling assaults that come before us every week.'

'Where did he get it?' I asked curiously.

'America.'

'Do you have it with you here?'

She nodded and touched her handbag. 'It's second nature, now.'

She must have been thirty years younger than her husband, I thought inconsequentially, and I knew what she felt about him. I didn't know whether or not I liked her, but I did recognize there was a weird sort of intimacy between us and that I didn't resent it.

The jockeys came out and stood around the owners in little groups. Nicholas Loder was there with the man he'd come in with, a thickset powerful-looking man in a dark suit, the pink cardboard Club badge fluttering from his lapel.

'Dozen Roses,' I said, watching Loder talking to the owner and his jockey, 'was he named for you?'

'Oh, God,' she said, disconcerted. 'How ever . . .?'

I said, 'I put your roses on the coffin for the service.'

'Oh . . .' she murmured with difficulty, her throat closing, her mouth twisting, 'I . . . can't . . .'

'Tell me how York University came to be putting its name to a race.' I made it sound conversational, to give her composure time.

She swallowed, fighting for control, steadying her breathing. 'I'm sorry. It's just that I can't even mourn for him except inside; can't let it show to anyone except you, and it sweeps over me, I can't help it.' She paused and answered my unimportant question. 'The Clerk of the Course wanted to involve the city. Some of the bigwigs of the University were against joining in, but Henry persuaded them. He and I have always come here to meetings now and then. We both like it, for a day out with friends.'

'Your husband doesn't actually lecture at the University, does he?'

'Oh, no, he's just a figurehead. He's chairman of a fair number of things in York. A public figure here.'

Vulnerable to scandal, I thought: as she was herself, and Greville also. She and he must have been unwaveringly discreet.

'How long since you first met Greville?' I asked noncommittally.

'Four years.' She paused. 'Four marvellous years. Not enough.'

The jockeys swung up onto the horses and moved away to go out onto the course. Nicholas Loder and his owner, busily talking, went off to the stands.

'May I watch the race with you?' Clarissa said. 'Do you mind?'

'I was going to watch from the grass.' I glanced down apologetically at the crutches. 'It's easier.'

'I don't mind the grass.'

So we stood side by side on the grass in front of the grandstand and she said, 'Whenever we could be together, he bought twelve red roses. It just . . . well . . .' She stopped, swallowing again hard.

'Mm,' I said. I thought of the ashes and the red rose tree and decided to tell her about that another time. It had been for him, anyway, not for her.

Nicholas Loder's two-year-old won the sprint at a convincing clip and I caught a glimpse of the owner afterwards looking heavily satisfied but unsmiling. Hardly a jolly character, I thought.

Clarissa went off to join her husband for the University race and after that, during their speeches and presentations, I went in search of Dozen Roses who was being led round in the pre-parade ring before being taken into a box or a stall to have his saddle put on.

Dozen Roses looked docile to dozy, I thought. An unremarkable bay, he had none of the looks or presence of Datepalm, nor the chaser's alert interest in his surroundings. He was a good performer, of that there was no question, but he didn't at that moment give an impression of going to be a 'trot-up' within half an hour, and he was vaguely not what I'd expected. Was this the colt that on the video tapes had won his last three races full of verve? Was this the young buck who had tried to mount a filly at the starting gate at Newmarket?

No, I saw with a sense of shock, he was not. I peered under his belly more closely, as it was sometimes difficult to tell, but there seemed to be no doubt that he had lost the essential tackle; that he had in fact been gelded.

I was stunned, and I didn't know whether to laugh or be furious. It explained so much: the loss of form when he had his mind on procreation rather than racing, and the return to speed once the temptation was removed. It explained why the Stewards hadn't called Loder in to justify the difference in running: horses very often did better after the operation.

I unfolded my racecard at Dozen Roses's race, and there, sure enough, against his name stood not c for colt or h for horse, but g for gelding.

Nicholas Loder's voice, vibrating with fury, spoke from not far behind me, 'That horse is not your horse. Keep away from him.'

I turned. Loder was advancing fast with Dozen Roses's saddle over his arm and full-blown rage in his face. The heavily unjoyful owner, still for some reason in tow, was watching the proceedings with puzzlement.

'Mine or not, I'm entitled to look at him,' I said. 'And look at him I darned well have, and either he is not Dozen Roses or you have gelded him against my brother's express wishes.'

His mouth opened and snapped shut.

'What's the matter, Nick?' the owner said. 'Who is this?'

Loder failed to introduce us. Instead he said to me

vehemently, 'You can't do anything about it. I have an Authority to Act. I am the registered agent for this horse and what I decide is none of your business.'

'My brother refused to have any of his horses gelded. You knew it well. You disobeyed him because you were sure he wouldn't find out, as he never went to the races.'

He glared at me. He was aware that if I lodged a formal complaint he would be in a good deal of trouble, and I thought he was certainly afraid that as my brother's executor I could and quite likely would do just that. Even if I only talked about it to others, it could do him damage: it was the sort of titbit the hungry racing press would pounce on for a giggle, and the owners of all the princely colts in his prestigious stable would get cold feet that the same might happen to their own property without their knowledge or consent.

He had understood all that, I thought, in the moment I'd told him on the telephone that it was I who would be inheriting Dozen Roses. He'd known that if I ever saw the horse I would realize at once what had been done. No wonder he'd lost his lower resonances.

'Greville was a fool,' he said angrily. 'The horse has done much better since he was cut.'

'That's true,' I agreed, 'but it's not the point.'

'How much do you want, then?' he demanded roughly.

My own turn, I thought, to gape like a fish. I said feebly, 'It's not a matter of money.'

'Everything is,' he declared. 'Name your price and get out of my way.'

I glanced at the attendant owner who looked more phlegmatic than riveted, but might remember and repeat this conversation, and I said merely, 'We'll discuss it later, OK?' and hitched myself away from them without aggression.

Behind me the owner was saying, 'What was that all about, Nick?' and I heard Loder reply, 'Nothing, Rollo. Don't worry about it,' and when I looked back a few seconds later I saw both of them stalking off towards the saddling boxes followed by Dozen Roses in the grasp of his lad.

Despite Nicholas Loder's anxious rage, or maybe because of it, I came down on the side of amusement. I would myself have had the horse gelded several months before the trainer had done it out of no doubt unbearable frustration: Greville had been pigheaded on the subject from both misplaced sympathy and not knowing enough about horses. I thought I would make peace with Loder that evening on the telephone, whatever the outcome of the race, as I certainly didn't want a fight on my hands for so rocky a cause. Talk about the roots of war, I thought wryly: there had been sillier reasons for bloody strife in history than the castration of a thoroughbred.

At York some of the saddling boxes were open to public view, some were furnished with doors. Nicholas

Loder seemed to favour the privacy and took Dozen Roses inside away from my eyes.

Harley and Martha Ostermeyer, coming to see the horses saddle, were full of beaming anticipation. They had backed the winner of the University Trophy and had wagered all the proceeds on my, that was to say, my *brother*'s horse.

'You won't get much return,' I warned them. 'It's favourite.'

'We know that, dear,' Martha said happily, looking around. 'Where is he? Which one?'

'He's inside that box,' I pointed, 'being saddled.'

'Harley and I have had a marvellous idea,' she said sweetly, her eyes sparkling.

'Now, Martha,' Harley said. He sounded faintly alarmed as if Martha's marvellous ideas weren't always the best possible news.

'We went you to dine with us when we get back to London,' she finished.

Harley relaxed, relieved. 'Yes. Hope you can.' He clearly meant that this particular marvellous idea was passable, even welcome. 'London at weekends is a graveyard.'

With a twitching of an inward grin I accepted my role as graveyard alleviator and, in the general good cause of cementing Ostermeyer–Shandy–Franklin relations, said I would be very pleased to stay to dinner. Martha and Harley expressed such gratification as to make me wonder whether when they were alone they bored each other to silence.

Dozen Roses emerged from his box with his saddle on and was led along towards the parade ring. He walked well, I thought, his good straight hocks encouraging lengthy strides, and he also seemed to have woken up a good deal, now that the excitement was at hand.

In the horse's wake hurried Nicholas Loder and his friend Rollo, and it was because they were crowding him, I thought, that Dozen Roses swung round on his leading rein and pulled backwards from his lad, and in straightening up again hit the Rollo man a hefty buffet with his rump and knocked him to his knees.

Martha with instinctive kindness rushed forward to help him, but he floundered to his feet with a curse that made her blink. All the same she bent and picked up a thing like a blue rubber ball which had fallen out of his jacket and held it towards him, saying, 'You dropped this, I think.'

He ungraciously snatched it from her, gave her an unnecessarily fierce stare as if she'd frightened the horse into knocking him over, which she certainly hadn't, and hurried into the parade ring after Nicholas Loder. He, looking back and seeing me still there, reacted with another show of fury.

'What perfectly horrid people,' Martha said, making a face. 'Did you hear what that man said? Disgusting! Fancy saying it aloud!'

Dear Martha, I thought, that word was everyday

coinage on racecourses. The nicest people used it: it made no one a villain. She was brushing dust off her gloves fastidiously as if getting rid of contamination and I half expected her to go up to Rollo and in the tradition of the indomitable American female to tell him to wash his mouth out with soap.

Harley had meanwhile picked something else up off the grass and was looking at it helplessly. 'He dropped this too,' he said. 'I think.'

Martha peered at his hands and took the object out of them.

'Oh, yes,' she said with recognition, 'that's the other half of the baster. You'd better have it, Derek, then you can give it back to that obnoxious friend of your trainer, if you want to.'

I frowned at what she'd given me, which was a rigid plastic tube, semi-transparent, about an inch in diameter, nine inches long, open at one end and narrowing to half the width at the other.

'A baster,' Martha said again. 'For basting meat when it's roasting. You know them, don't you? You press the bulb thing and release it to suck up the juices which you then squirt over the meat.'

I nodded. I knew what a baster was.

'What an extraordinary thing to take to the races,' Martha said wonderingly.

'Mm,' I agreed. 'He seems an odd sort of man altogether.' I tucked the plastic tube into an inside jacket pocket, from which its nozzle end protruded a couple of inches, and we went first to see Dozen Roses joined with his jockey in the parade ring and then up onto the stands to watch him race.

The jockey was Loder's chief stable jockey, as able as any, as honest as most. The stable money was definitely on the horse, I thought, watching the forecast odds on the information board change from 2/1 on to 5/2 on. When a gambling stable didn't put its money up front, the whisper went round and the price eased dramatically. The whisper where it mattered that day had to be saying that Loder was in earnest about the 'trot-up', and Alfie's base imputation would have to wait for another occasion.

Perhaps as a result of his year-by-year successes, Loder's stable always, it was well-known in the racing world, attracted as owners serious gamblers whose satisfaction was more in winning money than in winning races: and that wasn't the truism it seemed, because in steeplechasing the owners tended to want to win the races more than the money. Steeplechasing owners only occasionally made a profit overall and realistically expected to have to pay for their pleasure.

Wondering if the Rollo man was one of the big Loder gamblers, I flicked back the pages of the racecard and looked up his name beside the horse of his that had won the sprint. Owner, Mr T. Rollway, the card read. Rollo for short to his friends. Never heard of him, I thought, and wondered if Greville had.

Dozen Roses cantered down to the start with at least

as much energy and enthusiasm as any of the seven other runners and was fed into the stalls without fuss. He'd been striding out well, I thought, and taking a good hold of the bit. An old hand at the game by now, of course, as I was also, I thought dryly.

I'd ridden in several Flat races in my teens as an amateur, learning that the hardest and most surprising thing about the unrelenting Flat race crouch over the withers was the way it cramped one's lungs and affected one's breathing. The first few times I'd almost fallen off at the finish from lack of oxygen. A long time ago, I thought, watching the gates fly open in the distance and the colours spill out, long ago when I was young and it all lay ahead.

If I could find Greville's diamonds, I thought, I would in due course be able to buy a good big yard in Lambourn and start training free of a mortgage and on a decent scale, providing of course I could get owners to send me horses, and I had no longer any doubt that one of these years, when my body packed up mending fast, as everyone's did in the end, I would be content with the new life, even though the consuming passion I still felt for race-riding couldn't be replaced by anything tamer.

Dozen Roses was running with the pack, all seven bunched after the first three furlongs, flying along the far side of the track at more than cruising speed but with acceleration still in reserve.

If I didn't find Greville's diamonds, I thought, I

would just scrape together whatever I could and borrow the rest, and still buy a place and set my hand to the future. But not yet, not yet.

Dozen Roses and the others swung left-handed into the long bend round the far end of the track, the bunch coming apart as the curve element hit them. Turning into the straight five furlongs from the winning post Dozen Roses was in fourth place and making not much progress. I wanted him quite suddenly to win and was surprised by the strength of the feeling; I wanted him to win for Greville, who wouldn't care anyway, and perhaps also for Clarissa, who would. Sentimental fool, I told myself. Anyway, when the crowd started yelling home their fancy I yelled for mine also, and I'd never done that before as far as I could remember.

There was not going to be a trot-up, whatever Nicholas Loder might have thought. Dozen Roses was visibly struggling as he took second place at a searing speed a furlong from home and he wouldn't have got the race at all if the horse half a length in front, equally extended and equally exhausted, hadn't veered from a straight line at the last moment and bumped into him.

'Oh dear,' Martha exclaimed sadly, as the two horses passed the winning post. 'Second. Oh well, never mind.'

'He'll get the race on an objection,' I said. 'Which I suppose is better than nothing. Your winnings are safe.'

'Are you sure?'

'Certain,' I said, and almost immediately the loud-speakers were announcing 'Stewards' enquiry'.

More slowly than I would have liked to be able to manage, the three of us descended to the area outside the weighing room where the horse that was not my horse stood in the place for the unsaddling of the second, a net rug over his back and steam flowing from his sweating skin. He was moving about restlessly, as horses often do after an all-out effort, and his lad was holding tight to the reins, trying to calm him.

'He ran a great race,' I said to Martha, and she said, 'Did he, dear?'

'He didn't give up. That's really what matters.'

Of Nicholas Loder there was no sign: probably inside the Stewards' room putting forward his complaint. The Stewards would show themselves the views from the side camera and the head-on camera, and at any moment now . . .

'Result of Stewards' enquiry,' said the loudspeakers. 'Placing of first and second reversed.' Hardly justice, but inevitable: the faster horse had lost. Nicholas Loder came out of the weighing room and saw me standing with the Ostermeyers, but before I could utter even the first conciliatory words like, 'Well done,' he'd given me a sick look and hurried off in the opposite direction. No Rollo in his shadow, I noticed.

Martha, Harley and I returned to the luncheon room for the University's tea where the Knightwoods were being gracious hosts and Clarissa, at the sight of me, developed renewed trouble with the tear glands. I left the Ostermeyers taking cups and saucers from a wait-ress and drifted across to her side.

'So silly,' she said crossly, blinking hard as she offered me a sandwich. 'But wasn't he great?'

'He was.'

'I wish . . .' She stopped. I wished it too. No need at all to put it into words. But Greville never went to the races.

'I go to London fairly often,' she said. 'May I phone you when I'm there?'

'Yes, if you like.' I wrote my home number on my racecard and handed it to her. 'I live in Berkshire,' I said, 'not in Greville's house.'

She met my eyes, hers full of confusion.

'I'm not Greville,' I said.

'My dear chap,' said her husband boomingly, coming to a halt beside us, 'delighted your horse finally won. Though, of course, not technically your horse, what?'

'No, sir.'

He was shrewd enough, I thought, looking at the intelligent eyes amid the bonhomie. Not easy to fool. I wondered fleetingly if he'd ever suspected his wife had a lover, even if he hadn't known who. I thought that if he had known who, he wouldn't have asked me to lunch.

He chuckled. 'The professor says you tipped him three winners.'

'A miracle.'

'He's very impressed.' He looked at me benignly. 'Join us at any time, my dear chap.' It was the sort of vague invitation, not meant to be accepted, that was a mild seal of approval, in its way.

'Thank you,' I said, and he nodded, knowing he'd been understood.

Martha Ostermeyer gushed up to say how marvellous the whole day had been, and gradually from then on, as such things always do, the University party evaporated.

I shook Clarissa's outstretched hand in farewell, and also her husband's who stood beside her. They looked good together, and settled, a fine couple on the surface.

'We'll see you again,' she said to me, and I wondered if it were only I who could hear her smothered desperation.

'Yes,' I said positively. 'Of course.'

'My dear chap,' her husband said. 'Any time.'

Harley, Martha and I left the racecourse and climbed into the Daimler, Simms following Brad's routine of stowing the crutches.

Martha said reproachfully, 'Your ankle's broken, not twisted. One of the guests told us. I said you'd ridden a gallop for us on Wednesday and they couldn't believe it.'

'It's practically mended,' I said weakly.

'But you won't be able to ride Datepalm in that race next Saturday, will you?'

'Not really. No.'

She sighed. 'You're very naughty. We'll simply have to wait until you're ready.'

I gave her a fast smile of intense gratitude. There weren't many owners who would have dreamed of waiting. No trainer would; they couldn't afford to. Milo was currently putting up one of my arch-rivals on the horses I usually rode, and I just hoped I would get all of them back once I was fit. That was the main trouble with injuries, not the injury itself but losing one's mounts to other jockeys. Permanently, sometimes, if they won.

'And now,' Martha said as we set off south towards London, 'I have had another simply marvellous idea, and Harley agrees with me.'

I glanced back to Harley who was sitting behind Simms. He was nodding indulgently. No anxiety this time.

'We think,' she said happily, 'that we'll buy Dozen Roses and send him to Milo to train for jumping. That is,' she laughed, 'if your brother's executor will sell him to us.'

'Martha!' I was dumbstruck and used her first name without thinking, though I'd called her Mrs Ostermeyer before, when I'd called her anything.

'There,' she said, gratified at my reaction, 'I told you it was a marvellous idea. What do you say?'

'My brother's executor is speechless.'

'But you will sell him?'

'I certainly will.'

'Then let's use the car phone to call Milo and tell him.' She was full of high good spirits and in no mood for waiting, but when she reached Milo he apparently

223

didn't immediately catch fire. She handed the phone to me with a frown, saying, 'He wants to talk to you.'

'Milo,' I said, 'what's the trouble?'

'That horse is an entire. They don't jump well.'

'He's a gelding,' I assured him.

'You told me your brother wouldn't ever have it done.'

'Nicholas Loder did it without permission.'

'You're kidding!'

'No,' I said. 'Anyway the horse got the race today on a Stewards' enquiry but he ran gamely, and he's fit.'

'Has he ever jumped?'

'I shouldn't think so. But I'll teach him.'

'All right then. Put me back to Martha.'

'Don't go away when she's finished. I want another word.'

I handed the phone to Martha who listened and spoke with a return to enthusiasm, and eventually I talked to Milo again.

'Why,' I asked, 'would one of Nicholas Loder's owners carry a baster about at the races?'

'A what?'

'Baster. Thing that's really for cooking. You've got one. You use it as a nebuliser.'

'Simple and effective.'

He used it, I reflected, on the rare occasions when it was the best way to give some sort of medication to a horse. One dissolved or diluted the medicine in water and filled the rubber bulb of the baster with it. Then one fitted the tube onto that, slid the tube up the horse's nostril, and squeezed the bulb sharply. The liquid came out in a vigorous spray straight onto the mucous membranes and from there passed immediately into the bloodstream. One could puff out dry powder with the same result. It was the fastest way of getting some drugs to act.

'At the races?' Milo was saying. 'An owner?'

'That's right. His horse won the five-furlong sprint.'

'He'd have to be mad. They dope-test two horses in every race, as you know. Nearly always the winner, and another at random. No owner is going to pump drugs into his horse at the races.'

'I don't know that he did. He had a baster with him, that's all.'

'Did you tell the Stewards?'

'No, I didn't. Nicholas Loder was with his owner and he would have exploded as he was angry with me already for spotting Dozen Roses's alteration.'

Milo laughed. 'So that was what all the heat was about this past week?'

'You've got it.'

'Will you kick up a storm?'

'Probably not.'

'You're too soft,' he said, 'and oh yes, I almost forgot. There was a phone message for you. Wait a tick. I wrote it down.' He went away for a bit and returned. 'Here you are. Something about your brother's diamonds.' He sounded doubtful. 'Is that right?'

'Yes. What about them?'

He must have heard the urgency in my voice because he said, 'It's nothing much. Just that someone had been trying to ring you last night and all day today, but I said you'd slept in London and gone to York.'

'Who was it?'

'He didn't say. Just said that he had some info for you. Then he hummed and hahed and said if I talked to you would I tell you he would telephone your brother's house, in case you went there, at about ten tonight, or later. Or it might have been a she. Difficult to tell. One of those middle-range voices. I said I didn't know if you would be speaking to me, but I'd tell you if I could.'

'Well, thanks.'

'I'm not a message service,' he said testily. 'Why don't you switch on your answer phone like everyone else?'

'I do sometimes.'

'Not enough.'

I switched off the phone with a smile and wondered who'd been trying to reach me. It had to be someone who knew Greville had bought diamonds. It might even be Annette, I thought: her voice had a mid-range quality.

I would have liked to have gone to Greville's house as soon as we got back to London, but I couldn't exactly renege on the dinner after Martha's truly marvellous idea, so the three of us ate together as planned and I tried to please them as much as they'd pleased me.

Martha announced yet another marvellous idea during dinner. She and Harley would get Simms or another of the car firm's chauffeurs to drive us all down to Lambourn the next day to take Milo out to lunch, so that they could see Datepalm again before they went back to the States on Tuesday. They could drop me at my house afterwards, and then go on to visit a castle in Dorset they'd missed last time around. Harley looked resigned. It was Martha, I saw, who always made the decisions, which was maybe why the repressed side of him needed to lash out sometimes at car-park attendants who boxed him in.

Milo, again on the telephone, told me he'd do practically anything to please the Ostermeyers, definitely including Sunday lunch. He also said that my informant had rung again and he had told him/her that I'd got the message.

'Thanks,' I said.

'See you tomorrow.'

I thanked the Ostermeyers inadequately for everything and went to Greville's house by taxi. I did think of asking the taxi driver to stay, like Brad, until I'd reconnoitred, but the house was quiet and dark behind the impregnable grilles, and I thought the taxi driver would think me a fool or a coward or both, so I paid him off and, fishing out the keys, opened the gate in the hedge and went up the path until the lights blazed on and the dog started barking.

Everyone can make mistakes.

CHAPTER ELEVEN

I didn't get as far as the steps up to the front door. A dark figure, dimly glimpsed in the floodlight's glare, came launching itself at me from behind in a cannonball rugger tackle and when I reached the ground something very hard hit my head.

I had no sensation of blacking out or of time passing. One moment I was awake, and the next moment I was awake also, or so it seemed, but I knew in a dim way that there had been an interval.

I didn't know where I was except that I was lying face down on grass. I'd woken up concussed on grass several times in my life, but never before in the dark. They couldn't have all gone home from the races, I thought, and left me alone out on the course all night.

The memory of where I was drifted back quietly. In Greville's front garden. Alive. Hooray for small mercies.

I knew from experience that the best way to deal with being knocked out was not to hurry. On the other hand, this time I hadn't come off a horse, not on

Greville's pocket handkerchief turf. There might be urgent reasons for getting up quickly, if I could think of them.

I remembered a lot of things in a rush and groaned slightly, rolling up onto my knees, wincing and groping about for the crutches. I felt stupid and went on behaving stupidly, acting on fifty per cent brainpower. Looking back afterwards, I thought that what I ought to have done was slither silently away through the gate to go to any neighbouring house and call the police. What I actually did was to start towards Greville's front door, and of course the lights flashed on again and the dog started barking and I stood rooted to the spot expecting another attack, swaying unsteadily on the crutches, absolutely dim and pathetic.

The door was ajar, I saw, with lights on in the hall, and while I stood dithering it was pulled wide open from inside and the cannonball figure shot out.

The cannonball was a motor-cycle helmet, shiny and black, its transparent visor pulled down over the face. Behind the visor the face also seemed to be black, but a black balaclava, I thought, not black skin. There was an impression of jeans, denim jacket, gloves, black running shoes, all moving fast. He turned his head a fraction and must have seen me standing there insecurely, but he didn't stop to give me another unbalancing shove. He vaulted the gate and set off at a run down the street and I simply stood where I was in the garden waiting for my head to clear a bit more and start working.

When that happened to some extent, I went up the short flight of steps and in through the front door. The keys, I found, were still in the lowest of the locks; the small bunch of three keys that Clarissa had had, which I'd been using instead of Greville's larger bunch as they were easier. I'd made things simple for the intruder, I thought, by having them ready in my hand.

With a spurt of alarm I felt my trouser pocket to find if Greville's main bunch had been stolen, but to my relief they were still there, clinking.

I switched off the floodlights and the dog and in the sudden silence closed the front door. Greville's small sitting room, when I reached it, looked like the path of a hurricane. I surveyed the mess in fury rather than horror and picked the tumbled phone off the floor to call the police. A burglary, I said. The burglar had gone.

Then I sat in Greville's chair with my head in my hands and said '*Shit*' aloud with heartfelt rage and gingerly felt the sore bump swelling on my scalp. A bloody pushover, I thought. Like last Sunday. Too like last Sunday to be a coincidence. The cannonball had known both times that I wouldn't be able to stand upright against a sudden unexpected rush. I supposed I should be grateful he hadn't smashed my head in altogether this time while he had the chance. No knife, this time, either.

After a bit I looked wearily round the room. The pictures were off the walls, most of the glass smashed. The drawers had been yanked out of the tables and the tables themselves overturned. The little pink and brown stone bears lay scattered on the floor, the chrysanthemum plant and its dirt were trampled into the carpet, the chrysanthemum pot itself was embedded in the smashed screen of the television, the video recorder had been torn from from its unit and dropped, the video cassettes of the races lay pulled out in yards of ruined tape. The violence of it all angered me as much as my own sense of failure in letting it happen.

Many of the books were out of the bookshelves, but I saw with grim satisfaction that none of them lay open. Even if none of the hollow books had contained diamonds, at least the burglar hadn't known the books were hollow. A poor consolation, I thought.

The police arrived eventually, one in uniform, one not. I went along the hall when they rang the doorbell, checked through the peep-hole and let them in, explaining who I was and why I was there. They were both of about my own age and they'd seen a great many break-ins.

Looking without emotion at Greville's wrecked room, they produced notebooks and took down an account of the assault in the garden. (Did I want a doctor for the bump? No, I didn't.) They knew of this house, they said. The new owner, my brother, had installed all the window grilles and had them wired on a direct alarm to the police station so that if anyone tried to enter that way they would be nicked. Police specialists had given their advice over the defences and had considered the house as secure as was possible, up to now: but shouldn't there have been active floodlights and a dog alarm? They'd worked well, I said, but before they came I'd turned them off.

'Well, sir,' they said, not caring much, 'what's been stolen?'

I didn't know. Nothing large, I said, because the burglar had had both hands free, when he vaulted the gate.

Small enough to go in a pocket, they wrote.

What about the rest of the house? Was it in the same state?

I said I hadn't looked yet. Crutches. Bang on head. That sort of thing. They asked about the crutches. Broken ankle, I said. Paining me, perhaps? Just a bit.

I went with them on a tour of the house and found the tornado had blown through all of it. The long drawing room on the ground floor was missing all the pictures from the walls and all the drawers from chests and tables.

'Looking for a safe,' one of the policemen said, turning over a ruined picture. 'Did your brother have one here, do you know?'

'I haven't seen one,' I said.

They nodded and we went upstairs. The black and white bedroom had been ransacked in the same fashion and the bathroom also. Clothes were scattered everywhere. In the bathroom, aspirins and other pills were scattered on the floor. A toothpaste tube had been squeezed flat by a shoe. A can of shaving cream lay in the wash basin, with some of the contents squirted out in loops on the mirror. They commented that as there was no graffiti and no excrement smeared over everything, I had got off lightly.

'Looking for something small,' the non-uniformed man said. 'Your brother was a gem merchant, wasn't he?'

'Yes.'

'Have you found any jewels here yourself?'

'No, I haven't.'

They looked into the empty bedroom on that floor, still empty, and went up the stairs to look round above, but coming down reported nothing to see but space. It's one big attic room, they explained, when I said I hadn't been up there. Might have been a studio once, perhaps.

We all descended to the semi-basement where the mess in the kitchen was indescribable. Every packet of cereal had been poured out, sugar and flour had been emptied and apparently sieved in a strainer. The fridge's door hung open with the contents gutted. All liquids had been poured down the sinks, the cartons and bottles either standing empty or smashed by the draining boards. The ice cubes I'd wondered about were missing, presumably melted. Half of the floor of carpet tiles had been pulled up from the concrete beneath.

The policemen went phlegmatically round looking at things but touching little, leaving a few footprints in the floury dust.

I said uncertainly, 'How long was I unconscious? If he did all this . . .'

'Twenty minutes, I'd say,' one said, and the other nodded. 'He was working fast, you can see. He was probably longest down here. I'd say he was pulling up these tiles looking for a floor safe when you set the alarms off again. I'd reckon he panicked then, he'd been here long enough. And also, if it's any use to you, I'd guess that if he was looking for anything particular, he didn't find it.'

'Good news, is that?' asked the other, shrewdly, watching me.

'Yes, of course.' I explained about the Saxony Franklin office being broken into the previous weekend. 'We weren't sure what had been stolen, apart from an address book. In view of this,' I gestured to the shambles, 'probably nothing was.'

'Reasonable assumption,' one said.

'When you come back here another time in the dark,' the other advised, 'shine a good big torch all around the garden before you come through the gate. Sounds as if he was waiting there for you, hiding in the shadow of the hedge, out of range of the body-heat detecting mechanism of the lights.'

'Thank you,' I said.

'And switch all the alarms on again, when we leave.'

'Yes.'

'And draw all the curtains. Burglars sometimes wait about outside, if they haven't found what they're after,

234

hoping that the householders, when they come home, will go straight to the valuables to check if they're there. Then they come rampaging back to steal them.'

'I'll draw the curtains,' I said.

They looked around in the garden on the way out and found half a brick lying on the grass near where I'd woken up. They showed it to me. Robbery with violence, that made it.

'If you catch the robber,' I said.

They shrugged. They were unlikely to, as things stood. I thanked them for coming and they said they'd be putting in a report, which I could refer to for insurance purposes when I made a claim. Then they retreated to the police car doubled-parked outside the gate and presently drove away, and I shut the front door, switched on the alarms, and felt depressed and stupid and without energy, none of which states was normal.

The policemen had left lights on behind them everywhere. I went slowly down the stairs to the kitchen meaning merely to turn them off, but when I got there I stood for a while contemplating the mess and the reason for it.

Whoever had come had come because the diamonds were still somewhere to be found. I supposed I should be grateful at least for that information; and I was also inclined to believe the policeman who said the burglar hadn't found what he was looking for. But could I find it, if I looked harder?

I hadn't particularly noticed on my first trip downstairs that the kitchen's red carpet was in fact carpet tiles, washable squares that were silent and warmer underfoot than conventional tiles. I'd been brought up on such flooring in our parents' house.

The big tiles, lying flat and fitting snugly, weren't stuck to the hard surface beneath, and the intruder had had no trouble in pulling them up. The intruder hadn't been certain there was a safe, I thought, or he wouldn't have sieved the sugar. And if he'd been successful and found a safe, what then? He hadn't given himself time to do anything about it. He hadn't killed me. Hadn't tied me. Must have known I would wake up.

All it added up to, I thought, was a frantic and rather unintelligent search, which didn't make the bump on my head or my again knocked-about ankle any less sore. Mincing machines had no brains either. Nor, I thought dispiritedly, had the mince.

I drew the curtains as advised and bent down and pulled up another of the red tiles, thinking about Greville's security complex. It would be just like him to build a safe into the solid base of the house and cover it with something deceptive. Setting a safe in concrete, as the pamphlet had said. People tended to think of safes as being built into walls: floors were less obvious and more secure, but far less convenient. I pulled up a few more tiles, doubting my conclusions, doubting my sanity.

The same sort of feeling as in the vaults kept me

going. I didn't expect to find anything but it would be stupid not to make sure, just in case. This time it took half an hour, not three days, and in the end the whole area was up except for a piece under a serving table on wheels. Under that carpet square, when I'd moved the table, I found a flat circular piece of silvery metal flush with the hard base floor, with a recessed ring in it for lifting.

Amazed and suddenly unbearably hopeful I knelt and pulled the ring up and tugged, and the flat piece of metal came away and off like the lid of a biscuit-tin, revealing another layer of metal beneath: an extremely solid-looking circular metal plate the size of a dinner plate in which there was a single keyhole and another handle for lifting.

I pulled the second handle. As well try to pull up the house by its roots. I tried all of Greville's bunch of keys in the keyhole but none of them came near to fitting.

Even Greville, I thought, must have kept the key reasonably handy, but the prospect of searching anew for anything at all filled me with weariness. Greville's affairs were a maze with more blind alleys than Hampton Court.

There were keys in the hollow books, I remembered. Might as well start with those. I shifted upstairs and dug out *With a Mule in Patagonia* and the others, rediscovering the two businesslike keys and also the decorative one which looked too flamboyant for sensible use. True to Greville's mind, however, it was that one whose wards slid easily into the keyhole of the safe and under pressure turned the mechanism inside.

Even then the circular lid wouldn't pull out. Seesawing between hope and frustration I found that, if one turned instead of pulling, the whole top of the safe went round like a wheel until it came against stops; and at that point it finally gave up the struggle and came up loose in my grasp.

The space below was big enough to hold a case of champagne but to my acute disappointment it contained no nest-egg, only a clutch of business-like brown envelopes. Sighing deeply I took out the top two and found the first contained the freehold deeds of the house and the second the paperwork involved in raising a mortgage to buy it. I read the latter with resignation. Greville's house belonged in essence to a finance company, not to me.

Another of the envelopes contained a copy of his will, which was as simple as the lawyers had said, and in another there was his birth certificate and our parents' birth and marriage certificates. Another yielded an endowment insurance policy taken out long ago to provide him with an income at sixty-five: but inflation had eaten away its worth and he had apparently not bothered to increase it. Instead, I realized, remembering what I'd learned of his company's finances, he had ploughed back his profits into expanding his business which would itself ride on the tide of inflation and provide him with a munificent income when he retired and sold.

A good plan, I thought, until he'd knocked the props out by throwing one point five million dollars to the winds. Only he hadn't, of course. He'd had a sensible plan for a sober profit. Deal with honour . . . He'd made a good income, lived a comfortable life and run his racehorses, but he had stacked away no great personal fortune. His wealth, whichever way one looked at it, was in the stones.

Hell and damnation, I thought. If I couldn't find the damned diamonds I'd be failing him as much as myself. He would long for me to find them, but where the bloody *hell* had he put them?

I stuffed most of the envelopes back into their private basement, keeping out only the insurance policy, and replaced the heavy circular lid. Turned it, turned the key, replaced the upper piece of metal and laid a carpet tile on top. Fireproof the hiding place undoubtedly was, and thiefproof it had proved, and I couldn't imagine why Greville hadn't used it for jewels.

Feeling defeated, I climbed at length to the bedroom where I found my own overnight bag had, along with everything else, been tipped up and emptied. It hardly seemed to matter. I picked up my sleeping shorts and changed into them and went into the bathroom. The mirror was still half covered with shaving cream and by the time I'd wiped that off with a face cloth and swallowed a Distalgesic and brushed my teeth and swept a lot of the crunching underfoot junk to one side with a towel, I had used up that day's ration of stamina pretty thoroughly.

Even then, though it was long past midnight. I couldn't sleep. Bangs on the head were odd, I thought. There had been one time when I'd dozed for a week afterwards, going to sleep in mid-sentence as often as not. Another time I'd apparently walked and talked rationally to a doctor but hadn't any recollection of it half an hour later. This time, in Greville's bed, I felt shivery and unsettled, and thought that that had probably as much to do with being attacked as concussed.

I lay still and let the hours pass, thinking of bad and good and of why things happened, and by morning felt calm and much better. Sitting on the lid of the loo in the bathroom I unwrapped the crêpe bandage and by hopping and holding on to things took a long, luxurious and much needed shower, washing my hair, letting the dust and debris and the mental tensions of the week run away in the soft bombardment of water. After that, loin-clothed in a bath towel, I sat on the black and white bed and more closely surveyed the ankle scenery.

It was better than six days earlier, one could confidently say that. On the other hand, it was still black, still fairly swollen and still sore to the touch. Still vulnerable to knocks. I flexed my calf and foot muscles several times: the bones and ligaments still violently protested, but none of it could be helped. To stay strong, the muscles had to move, and that was that. I kneaded the calf muscle a bit to give it some encouragement and thought about borrowing an apparatus called Electrovet which Milo had tucked away somewhere, which he used on his horses' legs to give their muscles electrical stimuli to bring down swelling and get them fit again. What worked on horses should work on me, I reckoned.

Eventually I wound the bandage on again, not as neatly as the surgeon, but I hoped as effectively. Then I dressed, borrowing one of Greville's clean white shirts and, down in the forlorn little sitting room, telephoned to Nicholas Loder.

He didn't sound pleased to hear my voice.

'Well done with Dozen Roses,' I said.

He grunted.

'To solve the question of who owns him,' I continued, 'I've found a buyer for him.'

'Now look here!' he began angrily. 'I—'

'Yes, I know,' I interrupted, 'you'd ideally like to sell him to one of your own owners and keep him in your yard, and I do sympathize with that, but Mr and Mrs Ostermeyer, the people I was with yesterday at York, they've told me they would like the horse themselves.'

'I strongly protest,' he said.

'They want to send him to Milo Shandy to be trained for jumping.'

'You owe it to me to leave him here,' he said obstinately. 'Four wins in a row . . . it's downright dishonourable to take him away.'

'He's suitable for jumping, now that he's been

241

gelded.' I said it without threat, but he knew he was in an awkward position. He'd had no right to geld the horse. In addition, there was in fact nothing to stop Greville's executor selling the horse to whomever he pleased, as Milo had discovered for me, and which Nicholas Loder had no doubt discovered for himself, and in the racing world in general the sale to the Ostermeyers would make exquisite sense as I would get to ride the horse even if I couldn't own him.

Into Loder's continued silence I said, 'If you find a buyer for Gemstones, though, I'll give my approval.'

'He's not as good.'

'No, but not useless. No doubt you'd take a commission, I wouldn't object to that.'

He grunted again, which I took to mean assent, but he also said grittily, 'Don't expect any favours from me, ever.'

'I've done one for you,' I pointed out, 'in not lodging a complaint. Anyway, I'm lunching with the Ostermeyers at Milo's today and we'll do the paperwork of the sale. So Milo should be sending a box to collect Dozen Roses sometime this week. No doubt he'll fix a day with you.'

'Rot you,' he said.

'I don't want to quarrel.'

'You're having a damn good try.' He slammed down his receiver and left me feeling perplexed as much as anything else by his constant rudeness. All trainers lost horses regularly when owners sold them and, as he'd said himself, it wasn't as if Dozen Roses were a Derby hope. Nicholas Loder's stable held far better prospects than a five-year-old gelding, prolific winner though he might be.

Shrugging, I picked up my overnight bag and felt vaguely guilty at turning my back on so much chaos in the house. I'd done minimum tidying upstairs, hanging up Greville's suits and shirts and so on, and I'd left my own suit and some other things with them because it seemed I might spend more nights there, but the rest was physically difficult and would have to wait for the anonymous Mrs P, poor woman, who was going to get an atrocious shock.

I went by taxi to the Ostermeyers' hotel and again found them in champagne spirits, and it was again Simms, fortyish, with a moustache, who turned up as chauffeur. When I commented on his working Sunday as well as Saturday he smiled faintly and said he was glad of the opportunity to earn extra; Monday to Friday he developed films in the dark.

'Films?' Martha asked. 'Do you mean movies?'

'Family snapshots, madam, in a one-hour photo shop.'

'Oh.' Martha sounded as if she couldn't envisage such a life. 'How interesting.'

'Not very, madam,' Simms said resignedly, and set off smoothly into the sparse Sunday traffic. He asked me for directions as we neared Lambourn and we arrived without delay at Milo's door, where Milo himself greeted me with the news that Nicholas Loder wanted me to phone him at once.

'It sounded to me,' Milo said, 'like a great deal of agitation pretending to be casual.'

'I don't understand him.'

'He doesn't want me to have Dozen Roses, for some reason.'

'Oh, but,' Martha said to him anxiously, overhearing, 'you are going to, aren't you?'

'Of course, yes, don't worry. Derek, get it over with while we go and look at Datepalm.' He bore the Ostermeyers away, dazzling them with twinkling charm, and I went into his kitchen and phoned Nicholas Loder, wondering why I was bothering.

'Look,' he said, sounding persuasive. 'I've an owner who's very interested in Dozen Roses. He says he'll top whatever your Ostermeyers are offering. What do you say?'

I didn't answer immediately, and he said forcefully, 'You'll make a good clear profit that way. There's no guarantee the horse will be able to jump. You can't ask a high price for him, because of that. My owner will top their offer and add a cash bonus for you personally. Name your figure.'

'Um,' I said slowly, 'this owner wouldn't be yourself, would it?'

He said sharply, 'No, certainly not.'

'The horse that ran at York yesterday,' I said even more slowly, 'does he fit Dozen Roses's passport?'

244

'That's slanderous!'

'It's a question.'

'The answer is yes. The horse is Dozen Roses. Is that good enough for you?'

'Yes.'

'Well, then,' he sounded relieved, 'name your figure.'

I hadn't yet discussed any figure at all with Martha and Harley and I'd been going to ask a bloodstock agent friend for a snap valuation. I said as much to Nicholas Loder who, sounding exasperated, repeated that his owner would offer more, plus a tax-free sweetener for myself.

I had every firm intention of selling Dozen Roses to the Ostermeyers and no so-called sweetener that I could think of would have persuaded me otherwise.

'Please tell your owner I'm sorry,' I said, 'but the Ostermeyers have bought Datepalm, as I told you, and I am obligated to them, and loyalty to them comes first. I'm sure you'll find your owner another horse as good as Dozen Roses.'

'What if he offered double what you'd take from the Ostermeyers?'

'It's not a matter of money.'

'Everyone can be bought,' he said.

'Well, no. I'm sorry, but no.'

'Think it over,' he said, and slammed the receiver down again. I wondered in amusement how often he broke them. But he hadn't in fact been amusing, and the situation as a whole held no joy. I was going to have to meet him on racecourses for ever once I was a trainer myself, and I had no appetite for chronic feuds.

I went out into the yard where, seeing me, Milo broke away from the Ostermeyers who were feasting their eyes as Datepalm was being led round on the gravel to delight them.

'What did Loder want?' Milo demanded, coming towards me.

'He offered double whatever I was asking the Ostermeyers to pay for Dozen Roses.'

Milo stared. 'Double! Without knowing what it was?'

'That's right.'

'What are you going to do?'

'What do you think?' I asked.

'If you've accepted, I'll flatten you.'

I laughed. Too many people that past week had flattened me and no doubt Milo could do it with the best.

'Well?' he said belligerently.

'I told him to stuff it.'

'Good.'

'Mm, perhaps. But you'd better arrange to fetch the horse here at once. Like tomorrow morning, as we don't want him having a nasty accident and ending up at the knackers, do you think?'

'Christ!' He was appalled. 'He wouldn't! Not Nicholas Loder.'

'One wouldn't think so. But no harm in removing the temptation.'

'No.' He looked at me attentively. 'Are you all right?' he asked suddenly. 'You don't look too well.'

I told him briefly about being knocked out in Greville's garden. 'Those phone calls you took,' I said, 'were designed to make sure I turned up in the right place at the right time. So I walked straight into an ambush and, if you want to know, I feel a fool.'

'Derek!' He was dumbfounded, but also of course practical. 'It's not going to delay your getting back on a horse?'

'No, don't worry.'

'Did you tell the Ostermeyers?'

'No, don't bother them. They don't like me being unfit.'

He nodded in complete understanding. To Martha, and to Harley to a lesser but still considerable extent, it seemed that proprietorship in the jockey was as important as in the horse. I'd met that feeling a few times before and never undervalued it: they were the best owners to ride for, even if often the most demanding. The quasi-love relationship could however turn to dust and damaging rejection if one ever put them second, which was why I would never jeopardize my place on Datepalm for a profit on Dozen Roses. It was hard to explain to more rational people, but I rode races, as every jump jockey did, from a different impetus than making money, though the money was nice enough and thoroughly earned besides.

When Martha and Harley at length ran out of questions and admiration of Datepalm we all returned to the house, where over drinks in Milo's comfortable sitting room we telephoned to the bloodstock agent for an opinion and then agreed on a price which was less than he'd suggested. Milo beamed. Martha clapped her hands together with pleasure. Harley drew out his chequebook and wrote in it carefully, 'Saxony Franklin Ltd.'

'Subject to a vet's certificate,' I said.

'Oh yes, dear,' Martha agreed, smiling. 'As if you would ever sell us a lemon.'

Milo produced the 'Change of Ownership' forms which Martha and Harley and I all signed, and Milo said he would register the new arrangements with Weatherby's in the morning.

'Is Dozen Roses ours, now?' Martha asked, shiny-eyed.

'Indeed he is,' Milo said, 'subject to his being alive and in good condition when he arrives here. If he isn't the sale is void and he still belongs to Saxony Franklin.'

I wondered briefly if he were insured. Didn't want to find out the hard way.

With business concluded, Milo drove us all out to lunch at a nearby restaurant which as usual was crammed with Lambourn people: Martha and Harley held splendid court as the new owners of Gold Cup winner Datepalm and were pink with gratification over the compliments to their purchase. I watched their stimulated faces, hers rounded and still pretty under the blonde-rinsed grey hair, his heavily handsome, the square jaw showing the beginning of jowls. Both now looking sixty, they still displayed enthusiasms and enjoyments that were almost childlike in their simplicity, which did no harm in the weary old world.

Milo drove us back to rejoin the Daimler and Simms, who'd eaten his lunch in a village pub, and Martha in farewell gave Milo a kiss with flirtation but also real affection. Milo had bound the Ostermeyers to his stable with hoops of charm and all we needed now was for the two horses to carry on winning.

Milo said 'Thanks' to me briefly as we got into the car, but in truth I wanted what he wanted, and securing the Ostermeyers had been a joint venture. We drove out of the yard with Martha waving and then settling back into her seat with murmurs and soft remarks of pleasure.

I told Simms the way to Hungerford so that he could drop me off there, and the big car purred along with Sunday afternoon somnolence.

Martha said something I didn't quite catch and I turned my face back between the headrests, looking towards her and asking her to say it again. I saw a flash of raw horror begin on Harley's face, and then with a crash and a bang the car rocketed out of control across the road towards a wall and there was blood and shredded glass everywhere and we careered off the wall back onto the road and into the path of a fifty-seater touring coach which had been behind us and was now bearing down on us like a runaway cliff.

CHAPTER TWELVE

In a split second before the front of the bus hit the side of the car where I was sitting, in the freeze-frame awareness of the tons of bright metal thundering inexorably towards us, I totally believed I would be mangled to pulp within a breath.

There was no time for regrets or anger or any other emotion. The bus plunged into the Daimler and turned it again forwards and both vehicles screeched along the road together, monstrously joined wheel to wheel, the white front wing of the coach buried deep in the black Daimler's engine, the noise and buffeting too much for thinking, the speed of everything truly terrifying and the nearness of death an inevitability merely postponed.

Inertia dragged the two vehicles towards a halt, but they were blocking the whole width of the road. Towards us, round the bend, came a family car travelling too fast to stop in the space available. The driver in a frenzy braked so hard that his rear end swung round and hit the front of the Daimler broadside with a sickening jolt and a crunching bang and behind us, somewhere, another car ran into the back of the bus.

About that time I stopped being clear about the sequence of events. Against all catastrophe probability, I was still alive and that seemed enough. After the first stunned moments of silence when the tearing of metal had stopped, there were voices shouting everywhere, and people screaming and a sharp petrifying smell of raw petrol.

The whole thing was going to burn, I thought. Explode. Fireballs coming. Greville had burned two days ago. Greville had at least been dead at the time. Talk about delirious. I had half a car in my lap and in my head the warmed-up leftovers of yesterday's concussion.

The heat of the dead engine filled the cracked-open body of the car, forewarning of worse. There would be oil dripping out of it. There were electrical circuits . . . sparks . . . there was dread and despair and a vision of hell.

I couldn't escape. The glass had gone from the window beside me and from the windscreen, and what might have been part of the frame of the door had bent somehow across my chest, pinning me deep against the seat. What had been the fascia and the glove compartment seemed to be digging into my waist. What had been ample room for a dicky ankle was now as constricting as any cast. The car seemed to have wrapped itself around me in an iron-maiden embrace and the only parts free to move at all were my head and the arm nearest Simms. There was intense pressure rather than active agony, but what I felt most was fear.

Almost automatically, as if logic had gone on working on its own, I stretched as far as I could, got my fingers on the keys, twisted and pulled them out of the ignition. At least, no more sparks. At most, I was breathing.

Martha, too, was alive, her thoughts probably as abysmal as my own. I could hear her whimpering behind me, a small moaning without words. Simms and Harley were silent; and it was Simms's blood that had spurted over everything, scarlet and sticky. I could smell it under the smell of petrol; it was on my arm and face and clothes and in my hair.

The side of the car where I sat was jammed tight against the bus. People came in time to the opposite side and tried to open the doors, but they were immovably buckled. Dazed people emerged from the family car in front, the children weeping. People from the coach spread along the roadside, all of them elderly, most of them, it seemed to me, with their mouths open. I wanted to tell them all to keep away, to go further to safety, far from what was going to be a conflagration at any second, but I didn't seem to be able to shout, and the croak I achieved got no further than six inches.

Behind me Martha stopped moaning. I thought wretchedly that she was dying, but it seemed to be the opposite. In a quavery small voice she said, 'Derek?'

'Yes.' Another croak.

'I'm frightened.'

So was I, by God. I said futilely, hoarsely, 'Don't worry.'

She scarcely listened. She was saying 'Harley? Harley, honey?' in alarm and awakening anguish. 'Oh, get us out, please, someone get us out.'

I turned my head as far as I could and looked back sideways at Harley. He was cold to the world but his eyes were closed, which was a hopeful sign on the whole.

Simms's eyes were half open and would never blink again. Simms, poor man, had developed his last one-hour photo. Simms wouldn't feel any flames.

'Oh God, honey. Honey, wake up.' Her voice cracked, high with rising panic. 'Derek, get us out of here, can't you smell the gas?'

'People will come,' I said, knowing it was of little comfort. Comfort seemed impossible, out of reach.

People and comfort came, however, in the shape of a works foreman-type of man, used to getting things done. He peered through the window beside Harley and was presently yelling to Martha that he was going to break the rear window to get her out and she should cover her face in case of flying glass.

Martha hid her face against Harley's chest, calling to him and weeping, and the rear window gave way to determination and a metal bar.

'Come on, Missis,' encouraged the best of British

workmen. 'Climb up on the seat, we'll have you out of there in no time.'

'My husband . . .' she wailed.

'Him too. No trouble. Come on, now.'

It appeared that strong arms hauled Martha out bodily. Almost at once her rescuer was himself inside the car, lifting the still unconscious Harley far enough to be raised by other hands outside. Then he put his head forward near to mine, and took a look at me and Simms.

'Christ,' he said.

He was smallish, with a moustache and bright brown eyes.

'Can you slide out of there?' he asked.

'No.'

He tried to pull me, but we could both see it was hopeless.

'They'll have to cut you out,' he said, and I nodded. He wrinkled his nose. 'The smell of petrol's very strong in here. Much worse than outside.'

'It's vapour,' I said. 'It ignites.'

He knew that, but it hadn't seemed to worry him until then.

'Clear all those people further away,' I said. I raised perhaps a twitch of a smile. 'Ask them not to smoke.'

He gave me a sick look and retreated through the rear window, and soon I saw him outside delivering a warning which must have been the quickest crowd control measure on record.

Perhaps because with more of the glass missing there

was a through current of air, the smell of petrol did begin to abate, but there was still, I imagined, a severed fuel line somewhere beneath me, with freshly-released vapour continually seeping through the cracks. How much liquid bonfire, I wondered numbly, did a Daimler's tank hold?

There were a great many more cars now ahead in the road, all stopped, their occupants out and crash-gazing. No doubt to the rear it would be the same thing. Sunday afternoon entertainment at its worst.

Simms and I sat on in our silent immobility and I thought of the old joke about worrying, that there was no point in it. If one worried that things would get bad and they didn't, there was no point in worrying. If they got bad and one worried they would get worse, and they didn't, there was no point in worrying. If they got worse and one worried that one might die, and one didn't, there was no point in worrying, and if one died one could no longer worry, so why worry?

For worry read fear, I thought; but the theory didn't work. I went straight on being scared silly.

It was odd, I thought, that for all the risks I took, I very seldom felt any fear of death. I thought about physical pain, as indeed one often had to in a trade like mine, and remembered things I'd endured, and I didn't know why the imagined pain of burning should fill me with a terror hard to control. I swallowed and felt lonely, and hoped that if it came it would be over quickly.

There were sirens at length in the distance and the best sight in the world, as far as I was concerned, was the red fire-engine which slowly forced its way forward, scattering spectator cars to either side of the road. There was room, just, for three cars abreast; a wall on one side of the road, a row of trees on the other. Behind the fire-engine I could see the flashing blue light of a police car and beyond that another flashing light which might betoken an ambulance.

Figures in authority uniforms appeared from the vehicles, the best being in flameproof suits lugging a hose. They stopped in front of the Daimler, seeing the bus wedged into one side of it and the family car on the other and one of them shouted to me through the space where the windscreen should have been.

'There's petrol running from these vehicles,' he said. 'Can't you get out?'

What a damn silly question, I thought. I said, 'No.'

'We're going to spray the road underneath you. Shut your eyes and hold something over your mouth and nose.'

I nodded and did as I was bid, managing to shield my face inside the neck of my jersey. I listened to the long whooshing of the spray and thought no sound could be sweeter. Incineration faded progressively from near certainty to diminishing probability to unlikely outcome, and the release from fear was almost as hard to manage as the fear itself. I wiped blood and sweat off my face and felt shaky.

After a while some of the firemen brought up metal-cutting gear and more or less tore out of its frame the buckled door next to where Harley had been sitting. Into this new entrance edged a policeman who took a preliminary look at Simms and me and then perched on the rear seat where he could see my head. I turned it as far as I could towards him, seeing a serious face under the peaked cap: about my own age, I judged, and full of strain.

'A doctor's coming,' he said, offering crumbs. 'He'll deal with your wounds.'

'I don't think I'm bleeding,' I said. 'It's Simms's blood that's on me.'

'Ah.' He drew out a notebook and consulted it. 'Did you see what caused this . . . all this?'

'No,' I said, thinking it faintly surprising that he should be asking at this point. 'I was looking back at Mr and Mrs Ostermeyer, who were sitting where you are now. The car just seemed to go out of control.' I thought back, remembering. 'I think Harley . . . Mr Ostermeyer . . . may have seen something. For a second he looked horrified . . . then we hit the wall and rebounded into the path of the bus.'

He nodded, making a note.

'Mr Ostermeyer is now conscious,' he said, sounding carefully noncommittal. 'He says you were shot.'

'We were *what*?'

'Shot. Not all of you. You, personally.'

'No.' I must have sounded as bewildered as I felt. 'Of course not.'

'Mr and Mrs Ostermeyer are very distressed but he is quite clear he saw a gun. He says the chauffeur had just pulled out to pass a car that had been in front of you for some way, and the driver of that car had the window down and was pointing a gun out of it. He says the gun was pointing at you, and you were shot. Twice at least, he says. He saw the spurts of flame.'

I looked from the policeman to Simms, and at the chauffeur's blood over everything and at the solidly scarlet congealed mess below his jaw.

'No,' I protested, not wanting to believe it. 'It can't be right.'

'Mrs Ostermeyer is intensely worried that you are sitting here bleeding to death.'

'I feel squeezed, not punctured.'

'Can you feel your feet?'

I moved my toes, one foot after another. There wasn't the slightest doubt, particularly about the left.

'Good,' he said. 'Well, sir, we are treating this from now on as a possible murder enquiry, and apart from that I'm afraid the firemen say it may be some time before they can get you loose. They need more gear. Can you be patient?' He didn't wait for a reply, and went on, 'As I said, a doctor is here and will come to you, but if you aren't in urgent need of him there are two other people back there in a very bad way, and I hope you can be patient about that also.'

I nodded slightly. I could be patient for hours if I wasn't going to burn.

'Why,' I asked, 'would anyone shoot at us?'

'Have you no idea?'

'None at all.'

'Unfortunately,' he said, 'there isn't always an understandable reason.'

I met his eyes. 'I live in Hungerford,' I said.

'Yes, sir, so I've been told.' He nodded and slithered out of the car, and left me thinking about the time in Hungerford when a berserk man had gunned down many innocent people, including some in cars, and turned the quiet country town into a place of horror. No one who lived in Hungerford would ever discount the possibility of being randomly slaughtered.

The bullet that had torn into Simms would have gone through my own neck or head, I thought, if I hadn't turned round to talk to Martha. I'd put my head between the headrests, the better to see her. I tried to sort out what had happened next, but I hadn't seen Simms hit. I'd heard only the bang and crash of the window breaking and felt the hot spray of the blood that had fountained out of his smashed main artery in the time it had taken him to die. He had been dead, I thought, before anyone had started screaming: the jet of blood had stopped by then.

The steering wheel was now rammed hard against his chest with the instrument panel slanting down across his knees, higher my end than his. The edge of it pressed uncomfortably into my stomach, and I could see that if it had travelled back another six inches, it would have cut me in half.

A good many people arrived looking official with measuring tapes and cameras, taking photographs of Simms particularly and consulting in low tones. A police surgeon solemnly put a stethoscope to Simms's chest and declared him dead, and without bothering with the stethoscope declared me alive.

How bad was the compression, he wanted to know. Uncomfortable, I said.

'I know you, don't I?' he said, considering me. 'Aren't you one of the local jockeys? The jumping boys?'

'Mm.'

'Then you know enough about being injured to give me an assessment of your state.'

I said that my toes, fingers and lungs were OK and that I had cramp in my legs, the trapped arm was aching and the instrument panel was inhibiting the digestion of a good Sunday lunch.

'Do you want an injection?' he asked, listening.

'Not unless it gets worse.'

He nodded, allowed himself a small smile and wriggled his way out onto the road. It struck me that there was much less leg-room for the back seat than there had been when we set out. A miracle Martha's and Harley's legs hadn't been broken. Three of us, I thought, had been incredibly lucky.

Simms and I went on sitting quietly side by side for what seemed several more ages but finally the extra gear to free us appeared in the form of winches, cranes and an acetylene torch, which I hoped they would use around me with discretion.

Large mechanics scratched their heads over the problems. They couldn't get to me from my side of the car because it was tight against the bus. They decided that if they tried to cut through the support under the front seats and pull them backwards they might upset the tricky equilibrium of the engine and instead of freeing my trapped legs bring the whole weight of the front of the car down to crush them. I was against the idea, and said so.

In the end, working from inside the car in fireproof suits and with thick foam pumped all around, using a well-sheltered but still scorching hot acetylene flame, which roared and threw terrifying sparks around like matches, they cut away most of the driver's side, and after that, because he couldn't feel or protest, they forcefully pulled Simms's stiffening body out and laid it on a stretcher. I wondered greyly if he had a wife, who wouldn't know yet.

With Simms gone, the mechanics began fixing chains and operating jacks and I sat and waited without bothering them with questions. From time to time they said, 'You all right, mate?' and I answered 'Yes,' and was grateful to them.

After a while they fastened chains and a winch to the

family car still impacted broadside on the Daimler's wing and with inching care began to pull it away. There was almost instantly a fearful shudder through the Daimler's crushed body and also through mine, and the pulling stopped immediately. A little more head-scratching went on, and one of them explained to me that their crane couldn't get a good enough stabilizing purchase on the Daimler because the family car was in the way, and they would have to try something else. Was I all right? Yes, I said.

One of them began calling me Derek. 'Seen you in Hungerford, haven't I,' he said, 'and on the telly?' He told the others, who made jolly remarks like, 'Don't worry, we'll have you out in time for the three-thirty tomorrow. Sure to.' One of them seriously told me that it sometimes did take hours to free people because of the dangers of getting it wrong. Lucky, he said, that it was a Daimler I was in, with its tank-like strength. In anything less I would have been history.

They decided to rethink the rear approach. They wouldn't disturb the seat anchorages from their pushed-back position: the seats were off their runners, they said, and had dug into the floor. Also the recliner-mechanism had jammed and broken. However they were going to cut off the back of Simms's seat to give themselves more room to work. They were then going to extract the padding and springs from under my bottom and see if they could get rid of the back of my seat also, and draw me out backwards so that they wouldn't have to manoeuvre me out sideways past the steering column, which they didn't want to remove as it was the anchor for one of the chief stabilizing chains. Did I understand? Yes, I did.

They more or less followed this plan, although they had to dismantle the back of my seat before the cushion, the lowering effect of having the first spring removed from under me having jammed me even tighter against the fascia and made breathing difficult. They yanked padding out from behind me to relieve that, and then with a hacksaw took the back of the seat off near the roots; and, finally, with one of them supporting my shoulders, another pulled out handfuls of springs and other seat innards, the bear-hug pressure on my abdomen and arm and legs lessened and went away, and I had only blessed pins and needles instead.

Even then the big car was loath to let me go. With my top half free the two men began to pull me backwards, and I grunted and stiffened, and they stopped at once.

'What's the matter?' one asked anxiously.

'Well, nothing. Pull again.'

In truth, the pulling hurt the left ankle but I'd sat there long enough. It was at least an old, recognizable pain, nothing threateningly new. Reassured, my rescuers hooked their arms under my armpits and used a bit of strength, and at last extracted me from the car's crushing embrace like a breeched calf from a cow.

Relief was an inadequate word. They gave me a minute's rest on the back seat, and sat each side of me, all three of us breathing deeply.

'Thanks,' I said briefly.

'Think nothing of it.'

I guessed they knew the depths of my gratitude, as I knew the thought and care they'd expended. Thanks, think nothing of it: it was enough.

One by one we edged out onto the road, and I was astonished to find that after all that time there was still a small crowd standing around waiting: policemen, firemen, mechanics, ambulance men and assorted civilians, many with cameras. There was a small cheer and applause as I stood up free, and I smiled and moved my head in a gesture of both embarrassment and thanksgiving.

I was offered a stretcher but said I'd much rather have the crutches that might still be in the boot, and that caused a bit of general consternation, but someone brought them out unharmed, about the only thing still unbent in the whole mess. I stood for a bit with their support simply looking at all the intertwined wreckage; at the bus and the family car and above all at the Daimler's buckled-up roof, at its sheared-off bonnet, its dislodged engine awry at a tilted angle, its gleaming black paintwork now unrecognizable scrap, its former shape mangled and compressed like a stamped-on toy. I thought it incredible that I'd sat where I'd sat and lived. I reckoned that I'd used up a lifetime's luck.

The Ostermeyers had been taken to Swindon Hospital and treated for shock, bruises and concussion. From there, recovering a little, they had telephoned Milo and told him what had happened and he, reacting I guessed with spontaneous generosity but also with strong business sense, had told them they must stay with him for the night and he would collect them. All three were on the point of leaving when I in my turn arrived.

There was a predictable amount of fussing from Martha over my rescue, but she herself looked as exhausted as I felt and she was pliably content to be supported on Harley's arm on their way to the door.

Milo, coming back a step, said, 'Come as well, if you like. There's always a bed.'

'Thanks, I'll let you know.'

He stared at me. 'Is it true Simms was shot?'

'Mm.'

'It could have been you.'

'Nearly was.'

'The police took statements here from Martha and Harley, it seems.' He paused, looking towards them as they reached the door. 'I'll have to go. How's the ankle?'

'Be back racing as scheduled.'

'Good.'

He bustled off and I went through the paperwork

routines, but there was nothing wrong with me that a small application of time wouldn't fix and I got myself discharged pretty fast as a patient and was invited instead to give a more detailed statement to the police. I couldn't add much more than I'd told them in the first place, but some of their questions were in the end disturbing.

Could we have been shot at for any purpose?

I knew of no purpose.

How long had the car driven by the man with the gun been in front of us?

I couldn't remember: hadn't noticed.

Could anyone have known we would be on that road at that time? I stared at the policeman. Anyone, perhaps, who had been in the restaurant for lunch. Anyone there could have followed us from there to Milo's house, perhaps, and waited for us to leave, and passed us, allowing us then to pass again. But why ever should they?

Who else might know?

Perhaps the car company who employed Simms.

Who else?

Milo Shandy, and he'd have been as likely to shoot himself as the Ostermeyers.

Mr Ostermeyer said the gun was pointing at you, sir.

With all due respect to Mr Ostermeyer, he was looking through the car and both cars were moving, and at different speeds presumably, and I didn't think one could be certain.

Could I think of any reason why anyone should want to kill me?

Me, personally? No . . . I couldn't.

They pounced on the hesitation I could hear in my own voice, and I told them I'd been attacked and knocked out the previous evening. I explained about Greville's death. I told them he had been dealing in precious stones as he was a gem merchant and I thought my attacker had been trying to find and steal part of the stock. But I had no idea why the would-be thief should want to shoot me today when he could easily have bashed my head in yesterday.

They wrote it down without comment. Had I any idea who had attacked me the previous evening?

No, I hadn't.

They didn't say they didn't believe me, but something in their manner gave me the impression they thought anyone attacked twice in two days had to know who was after him.

I would have liked very much to be able to tell them. It had just occurred to me, if not to them, that there might be more to come.

I'd better find out soon, I thought.

I'd better not find out too late.

CHAPTER THIRTEEN

I didn't go to Milo's house nor to my own bed, but stayed in an anonymous hotel in Swindon where unknown enemies wouldn't find me.

The urge simply to go home was strong, as if one could retreat to safety into one's den, but I thought I would probably be alarmed and wakeful all night there, when what I most wanted was sleep. All in all it had been a rough ten days, and however easily my body usually shook off bumps and bangs, the accumulation was making an insistent demand for rest.

RICE, I thought wryly, RICE being the acronym of the best way to treat sports injuries: rest, ice, compression, elevation. I rarely seemed to be managing all of them at the same time, though all, in one way or another, separately. With elevation in place, I phoned Milo from the hotel to say I wouldn't be coming and asked how Martha and Harley were doing.

'They're quavery. It must have been some crash. Martha keeps crying. It seems a car ran into the back of the bus and two people in the car were terribly injured.

269

She saw them, and it's upsetting her almost as much as knowing Simms was shot. Can't you come and comfort her?'

'You and Harley can do it better.'

'She thought you were dying too. She's badly shocked. You'd better come.'

'They gave her a sedative at the hospital, didn't they?'

'Yes,' he agreed grudgingly. 'Harley too.'

'Look . . . persuade them to sleep. I'll come in the morning and pick them up and take them back to their hotel in London. Will that do?'

He said unwillingly that he supposed so.

'Say goodnight to them from me,' I said. 'Tell them I think they're terrific.'

'Do you?' He sounded surprised.

'It does no harm to say it.'

'Cynic.'

'Seriously,' I said, 'they'll feel better if you tell them.'

'All right then. See you at breakfast.'

I put down the receiver and on reflection a few minutes later got through to Brad.

'Cor,' he said, 'you were in that crash.'

'How did you hear about it?' I asked, surprised.

'Down the pub. Talk of Hungerford. Another madman. It's shook everyone up. My mum won't go out.'

It had shaken his tongue loose, I thought in amusement. 'Have you still got my car?' I said.

'Yerss.' He sounded anxious. 'You said keep it here.'

'Yes. I meant keep it there.'

'I walked down your house earlier. There weren't no one there then.'

'I'm not there now,' I said. 'Do you still want to go on driving?'

'Yerss.' Very positive. 'Now?'

'In the morning.' I said I would meet him at eight outside the hotel near the railway station at Swindon, and we would be going to London. 'OK?'

'Yerss,' he said, signing off, and it sounded like a cat purring over the resumption of milk.

Smiling and yawning, a jaw-cracking combination, I ran a bath, took off my clothes and the bandage and lay gratefully in hot water, letting it soak away the fatigue along with Simms's blood. Then, my overnight bag having survived unharmed along with the crutches, I scrubbed my teeth, put on sleeping shorts, rewrapped the ankle, hung a 'Do not disturb' card outside my door and was in bed by nine and slept and dreamed of crashes and fire and hovering unidentified threats.

Brad came on the dot in the morning and we went first to my place in a necessary quest for clean clothes. His mum, Brad agreed, would wash the things I'd worn in the crash.

My rooms were still quiet and unransacked and no

dangers lurked outside in daylight. I changed uneventfully and repacked the travelling bag and we drove in good order to Lambourn, I sitting beside Brad and thinking I could have done the driving myself, except that I found his presence reassuring and I'd come to grief on both of the days he hadn't been with me.

'If a car passes us and sits in front of us,' I said, 'don't pass it. Fall right back and turn up a side road.'

'Why?'

I told him that the police thought we'd been caught in a deliberate moving ambush. Neither the Ostermeyers nor I, I pointed out, would be happy to repeat the experience, and Brad wouldn't be wanting to double for Simms. He grinned, an unnerving sight, and gave me to understand with a nod that he would follow the instruction.

The usual road to Lambourn turned out to be still blocked off, and I wondered briefly, as we detoured, whether it was because of the murder enquiry or simply technical difficulties in disentangling the omelette.

Martha and Harley were still shaking over breakfast, the coffee cups trembling against their lips. Milo with relief shifted the burden of their reliance smartly from himself to me, telling them that now Derek was here, they'd be safe. I wasn't so sure about that, particularly if both Harley and the police were right about me personally being yesterday's target. Neither Martha nor Harley seemed to suffer such qualms and gave me the instant status of surrogate son/nephew, the one to be naturally leaned on, psychologically if not physically, for succour and support.

I looked at them with affection. Martha had retained enough spirit to put on lipstick. Harley was making light of a sticking plaster on his temple. They couldn't help their nervous systems' reaction to mental trauma, and I hoped it wouldn't be long before their habitual preference for enjoyment resurfaced.

'The only good thing about yesterday,' Martha said with a sigh, 'was buying Dozen Roses. Milo says he's already sent a van for him.'

I'd forgotten about Dozen Roses. Nicholas Loder and his tizzies seemed a long way off and unimportant. I said I was glad they were glad, and that in about a week or so, when he'd settled down in his new quarters, I would start teaching him to jump.

'I'm sure he'll be brilliant,' Martha said bravely, trying hard to make normal conversation. 'Won't he?'

'Some horses take to it better than others,' I said neutrally. 'Like humans.'

'I'll believe he'll be brilliant.'

Averagely good, I thought, would be good enough for me: but most racehorses could jump if started patiently over low obstacles like logs.

Milo offered fresh coffee and more toast, but they were ready to leave and in a short while we were on the road to London. No one passed us and slowed, no one ambushed or shot us, and Brad drew up with a flourish outside their hotel, at least the equal of Simms.

Martha with a shine of tears kissed my cheek in goodbye, and I hers: Harley gruffly shook my hand. They would come back soon, they said, but they were sure glad to be going home tomorrow. I watched them go shakily into the hotel and thought uncomplicated thoughts, like hoping Datepalm would cover himself with glory for them, and Dozen Roses also, once he could jump.

'Office?' I suggested to Brad, and he nodded, and made the now familiar turns towards the environs of Hatton Garden.

Little in Saxony Franklin appeared to have changed. It seemed extraordinary that it was only a week since I'd walked in there for the first time, so familiar did it feel on going back. The staff said, 'Good morning, Derek,' as if they'd been used to me for years, and Annette said there were letters left over from Friday which needed decisions.

'How was the funeral?' she asked sadly, laying out papers on the desk.

A thousand light years ago, I thought. 'Quiet,' I said.

'Good. Your flowers were good. They were on top of his coffin.'

She looked pleased and said she would tell the others, and received the news that there would be a memorial service with obvious satisfaction. 'It didn't seem right, not being at his funeral, not on Friday. We had a minute's silence here at two o'clock. I suppose you'll think us silly.'

'Far from it.' I was moved and let her see it. She smiled sweetly in her heavy way and went off to relay to the others and leave me floundering in the old treacle of deciding things on a basis of no knowledge.

June whisked in looking happy with a pink glow on both cheeks and told me we were low in blue lace agate chips and snowflake obsidian and amazonite beads.

'Order some more, same as before.'

'Yes, right.'

She turned and was on her way out again when I called her back and asked her if there was an alarm clock among all the gadgets. I pulled open the deep drawer and pointed downwards.

'An alarm clock?' She was doubtful and peered at the assorted black objects. 'Telescopes, dictionaries, Geiger counter, calculators, spy juice . . .'

'What's spy juice?' I asked, intrigued.

'Oh, this.' She reached in and extracted an aerosol can. 'That's just my name for it. You squirt this stuff on anyone's envelopes and it makes the paper transparent so you can read the private letters inside.' She looked at my face and laughed. 'Banks have got round it by printing patterns all over the insides of their envelopes. If you spray their envelopes, all you see is the pattern.'

'Whatever did Greville use it for?'

'Someone gave it to him, I think. He didn't use it much, just to check if it was worth opening things that looked like advertisements.'

She put a plain sheet of paper over one of the letters

lying on the desk and squirted a little liquid over it. The plain paper immediately became transparent so that one could read the letter through it, and then slowly went opaque again as it dried.

'Sneaky,' she said, 'isn't it?'

'Very.'

She was about to replace the can in the drawer but I said to put it on top of the desk, and I brought out all the other gadgets and stood them around in plain sight. None of them, as far as I could see, had an alarm function.

'You mentioned something about a world clock,' I said, 'but there isn't one here.'

'I've a clock with an alarm in my room,' she said helpfully. 'Would you like me to bring that?'

'Um, yes, perhaps. Could you set it to four-fifteen?'

'Sure, anything you like.'

She vanished and returned fiddling with a tiny thing like a black credit card which turned out to be a highly versatile timepiece.

'There you are,' she said. 'Four-fifteen – pm, I suppose you mean.' She put the clock on the desk.

'This afternoon, yes. There's an alarm somewhere here that goes off every day at four-twenty. I thought I might find it.'

Her eyes widened. 'Oh, but that's Mr Franklin's watch.'

'Which one?' I asked.

'He only ever wore one. It's a computer itself, a calendar and a compass.'

That watch, I reflected, was beside my bed in Hungerford.

'I think,' I said, 'that he may have had more than one alarm set to four-twenty.'

The fair eyebrows lifted. 'I did sometimes wonder why,' she said. 'I mean, why four-twenty? If he was in the stock-room and his watch alarm went off he would stop doing whatever it was for a few moments. I sort of asked him once, but he didn't really answer, he said it was a convenient time for communication, or something like that. I didn't understand what he meant, but that was all right, he didn't mean me to.'

She spoke without resentment and with regret. I thought that Greville must have enjoyed having June around him as much as I did. All that bright intelligence and unspoiled good humour and common sense. He'd liked her enough to make puzzles for her and let her share his toys.

'What's this one?' I asked, picking up a small grey contraption with black ear sponges on a headband with a cord like a walkabout cassette player, but with no provision for cassettes in what might have been a holder.

'That's a sound-enhancer. It's for deaf people, really, but Mr Franklin took it away from someone who was using it to listen to a private conversation he was having with another gem merchant. In Tucson, it was. He said he was so furious at the time that he just snatched the amplifier and headphones off the man who was listening and walked away with them uttering threats about commercial espionage, and he said the man hadn't even tried to get them back.' She paused. 'Put the earphones on. You can hear everything everyone's saying anywhere in the office. It's pretty powerful. Uncanny, really.'

I put on the ultra-light earphones and pressed the ON switch on the cigarette-packet-sized amplifier and sure enough I could straightaway hear Annette across the hallway talking to Lily about remembering to ask Derek for time off for the dentist.

I removed the earphones and looked at June.

'What did you hear?' she asked. 'Secrets?'

'Not that time, no.'

'Scary, though?'

'As you say.'

The sound quality was in fact excellent, astonishingly sensitive for so small a microphone and amplifier. Some of Greville's toys, I thought, were decidedly unfriendly.

'Mr Franklin was telling me that there's a voice transformer that you can fix on the telephone that can change the pitch of your voice and make a woman sound like a man. He said he thought it was excellent for women living alone so that they wouldn't be bothered by obscene phone calls and no one would think they were alone and vulnerable.'

I smiled. 'It might disconcert a bona fide boyfriend innocently ringing up.'

'Well, you'd have to warn them,' she agreed. 'Mr Franklin was very keen on women taking precautions.'

'Mm,' I said wryly.

'He said the jungle came into his court.'

'Did you get a voice changer?' I asked.

'No. We were only talking about it just before . . .' She stopped. 'Well . . . anyway, do you want a sandwich for lunch?'

'Yes, please.'

She nodded and was gone. I sighed and tried to apply myself to the tricky letters and was relieved at the interruption when the telephone rang.

It was Elliot Trelawney on the line, asking if I would messenger round the Vaccaro notes at once if I wouldn't mind as they had a committee meeting that afternoon.

'Vaccaro notes,' I repeated. I'd clean forgotten about them. I couldn't remember, for a moment, where they were.

'You said you would send them this morning,' Trelawney said with a tinge of civilized reproach. 'Do you remember?'

'Yes.' I did, vaguely.

Where the hell were they? Oh yes, in Greville's sitting room. Somewhere in all that mess. Somewhere there, unless the thief had taken them.

I apologized. I didn't actually say I'd come near to being killed twice since I'd last spoken to him and it was playing tricks with my concentration. I said things had cropped up. I was truly sorry. I would try to get them to the court by . . . when?

'The committee meets at two and Vaccaro is first on the agenda,' he said.

'The notes are still in Greville's house,' I replied, 'but I'll get them to you.'

'Awfully good of you.' He was affable again. 'It's frightfully important we turn this application down.'

'Yes, I know.'

Vaccaro, I thought uncomfortably, replacing the receiver, was alleged to have had his wanting-out cocaine-smuggling pilots murdered by shots from moving cars.

I stared into space. There was no reason on earth for Vaccaro to shoot me, even supposing he knew I existed. I wasn't Greville, and I had no power to stand in the way of his plans. All I had, or probably had, were the notes on his transgressions, and how could he know that? And how could he know I would be in a car between Lambourn and Hungerford on Sunday afternoon? And couldn't the notes be gathered again by someone else besides Greville, even if they were now lost?

I shook myself out of the horrors and went down to the yard to see if Brad was sitting in the car, which he was, reading a magazine about fishing.

Fishing? 'I didn't know you fished,' I said.

'I don't.'

End of conversation.

Laughing inwardly I invited him to go on the journey. I gave him the simple keyring of three keys and explained about the upheaval he would find. I described the Vaccaro notes in and out of their envelope and wrote down Elliot Trelawney's name and the address of the court.

'Can you do it?' I asked, a shade doubtfully.

'Yerss.' He seemed to be slighted by my tone and took the paper with the address with brusqueness.

'Sorry,' I said.

He nodded without looking at me and started the car, and by the time I'd reached the rear entrance to the offices he was driving out of the yard.

Upstairs, Annette said there had just been a phone call from Antwerp and she had written down the number for me to ring back.

Antwerp.

With an effort I thought back to Thursday's distant conversations. What was it I should remember about Antwerp?

Van Ekeren. Jacob. His nephew, Hans.

I got through to the Belgian town and was rewarded with the smooth bilingual voice telling me that he had been able now to speak to his uncle on my behalf.

'You're very kind,' I said.

'I'm not sure that we will be of much help. My uncle says he knew your brother for a long time, but not very well. However, about six months ago your brother

281

telephoned my uncle for advice about a sightholder.' He paused. 'It seems your brother was considering buying diamonds and trusted my uncle's judgement.'

'Ah,' I said hopefully. 'Did your uncle recommend anyone?'

'Your brother suggested three or four possible names. My uncle said they were all trustworthy. He told your brother to go ahead with any of them.'

I sighed. 'Does he possibly remember who they were?'

Hans said, 'He knows one of them was Guy Servi here in Antwerp, because we ourselves do business with him often. He can't remember the others. He doesn't know which one your brother decided on, or if he did business at all.'

'Well, thank you, anyway.'

'My uncle wishes to express his condolences.'

'Very kind.'

He disconnected with politeness, having dictated to me carefully the name, address and telephone number of Guy Servi, the one sightholder Greville had asked about that his uncle remembered.

I dialled the number immediately and again went through the rigmarole of being handed from voice to voice until I reached someone who had both the language and the information.

Mr Greville Saxony Franklin, now deceased, had been my brother? They would consult their files and call me back.

I waited without much patience while they went through whatever security checks they considered necessary but finally, after a long hour, they came back on the line.

What was my problem, they wanted to know.

'My problem is that our offices were ransacked and a lot of paperwork is missing. I've taken over since Greville's death, and I'm trying to sort out his affairs. Could you please tell me if it was your firm who bought diamonds for him?'

'Yes,' the voice said matter-of-factly. 'We did.'

Wow, I thought. I quietened my breath and I tried not to sound eager.

'Could you, er, give me the details?' I asked.

'Certainly. Your brother wanted colour H diamonds of approximately three carats each. We bought a normal sight-box of mixed diamonds at the July sight at the CSO in London and from it and from our stocks chose one hundred colour H stones, total weight three hundred and twenty carats, which we delivered to your brother.'

'He . . . er . . . paid for them in advance didn't he?'

'Certainly. One point five million United States dollars in cash. You don't need to worry about that.'

'Thank you,' I said, suppressing irony. 'Um, when you delivered them, did you send any sort of, er, packing note?'

It seemed he found the plebeian words 'packing note' faintly shocking.

'We sent the diamonds by personal messenger,' he said austerely. 'Our man took them to your brother at his private residence in London. As is our custom, your brother inspected the merchandise in our messenger's presence and weighed it, and when he was satisfied he signed a release certificate. He would have the carbon copy of that release. There was no other – uh – packing note.'

'Unfortunately I can't find the carbon copy.'

'I assure you, sir . . .'

'I don't doubt it,' I said hastily. 'It's just that the tax people have a habit of wanting documentation.'

'Ah.' His hurt feelings subsided. 'Yes, of course.'

I thought a bit and asked, 'When you delivered the stones to him, were they rough or faceted?'

'Rough, of course. He was going to get them cut and polished over a few months, as he needed them, I believe, but it was more convenient for us and for him to buy them all at once.'

'You don't happen to know who he was getting to polish them?'

'I understood they were to be cut for one special client who had his own requirements, but no, he didn't say who would be cutting them.'

I sighed. 'Well, thank you anyway.'

'We'll be happy to send you copies of the paperwork of the transaction, if it would be of any use?'

'Yes, please,' I said. 'It would be most helpful.'

'We'll put them in the post this afternoon.'

I put the receiver down slowly. I might now know where the diamonds had come *from* but was no nearer knowing where they'd gone *to*. I began to hope that they were safely sitting somewhere with a cutter who would kindly write to tell me they were ready for delivery. Not an impossible dream, really. But if Greville had sent them to a cutter, why was there no record?

Perhaps there had been a record, now stolen. But if the record had been stolen the thief would know the diamonds were with a cutter, and there would be no point in searching Greville's house. Unprofitable thoughts, chasing their own tails.

I straightened my neck and back and eased a few of the muscles which had developed small aches since the crash.

June came in and said, 'You look fair knackered,' and then put her hand to her mouth in horror and said, 'I'd never have said that to Mr Franklin.'

'I'm not him.'

'No, but . . . you're the boss.'

'Then think of someone who could supply a list of cutters and polishers of diamonds, particularly those specializing in unusual requirements, starting with Antwerp. What we want is a sort of Yellow Pages directory. After Antwerp, New York, Tel Aviv and Bombay, isn't that right? Aren't those the four main centres?' I'd been reading his books.

'But we don't deal—'

'Don't say it,' I said. 'We do. Greville bought some

for Prospero Jenks who wants them cut to suit his sculptures or fantasy pieces, or whatever one calls them.'

'Oh.' She looked first blank and then interested. 'Yes, all right, I'm sure I can do that. Do you want me to do it now?'

'Yes, please.'

She went as far as the door and looked back with a smile. 'You still look fair . . .'

'Mm. Go and get on with it.'

I watched her back view disappear. Grey skirt, white shirt. Blonde hair held back with combs behind the ears. Long legs. Flat shoes. Exit June.

The day wore on. I assembled three orders in the vault by myself and got Annette to check they were all right, which it seemed they were. I made a slow tour of the whole place, calling in to see Alfie pack his parcels, watching Lily with her squashed governess air move endlessly from drawer to little drawer collecting orders, seeing Jason manhandle heavy boxes of newly arrived stock, stopping for a moment beside strong-looking Tina, whom I knew least, as she checked the new intake against the packing list and sorted it into trays.

None of them paid me great attention. I was already wallpaper. Alfie made no more innuendoes about Dozen Roses and Jason, though giving me a dark sideways look, again kept his cracks to himself. Lily said, 'Yes, Derek,' meekly, Annette looked anxious, June was busy. I returned to Greville's office and made another effort with the letters.

By four o'clock, in between her normal work with the stock movements on the computer, June had received answers to her 'feelers', as she described them, in the shape of a long list of Antwerp cutters and a shorter one so far for New York. Tel Aviv was 'coming' but had language difficulties and she had nothing for Bombay, though she didn't think Mr Franklin would have sent anything to Bombay because with Antwerp so close there was no point. She put the lists down and departed.

At the rate all the cautious diamond-dealers worked, I thought, picking up the roll call, it would take a week just to get yes or no answers from the Antwerp list. Maybe it would be worth trying. I was down to straws. One of the letters was from the bank, reminding me that interest on the loan was now due.

June's tiny alarm clock suddenly began bleeping. All the other mute gadgets on top of the desk remained unmoved. June returned through my doorway at high speed and paid them vivid attention.

'Five minutes to go,' I said calmingly. 'Is every single gadget in sight?'

She checked all the drawers swiftly and peered into filing cabinets, leaving everything wide open, as I asked.

'Can't find any more,' she said. 'Why does it matter?'

'I don't know,' I said. 'I try everything.'

She stared. I smiled lopsidedly.

'Greville left me a puzzle too,' I said. 'I try to solve it, though I don't know where to look.'

'Oh.' It made a sort of sense to her, even without more explanation. 'Like my rise?'

I nodded. 'Something like that.' But not so positive, I thought. Not so certain. He had at least assured her that the solution was there to find.

The minutes ticked away and at four-twenty by June's clock the little alarm duly sounded. Very distant, not at all loud. Insistent. June looked rather wildly at the assembled gadgets and put her ear down to them.

'I will think of you every day at four-twenty.'

Clarissa had written it on her card at the funeral. Greville had apparently done it every day in the office. It had been their own private language, a long way from diamonds. I acknowledged with regret that I would learn nothing from whatever he'd used to jog his awareness of loving and being loved.

The muffled alarm stopped. June raised her head, frowning.

'It wasn't any of these,' she said.

'No. It was still inside the desk.'

'But it can't have been.' She was mystified. 'I've taken everything out.'

'There must be another drawer.'

She shook her head, but it was the only reasonable explanation.

'Ask Annette,' I suggested.

Annette, consulted, said with a worried frown that she knew nothing at all about another drawer. The three of us looked at the uninformative three-inch-deep slab of black grainy wood that formed the enormous top surface. There was no way it could be a drawer, but there wasn't any other possibility.

I thought back to the green stone box. To the keyhole that wasn't a keyhole, to the sliding base.

To the astonishment of Annette and June I lowered myself to the floor and looked upwards at the desk from under the knee-hole part. The wood from there looked just as solid, but in the centre, three inches in from the front, there was what looked like a sliding switch. With satisfaction I regained the black leather chair and felt under the desk top for the switch. It moved away from one under pressure, I found. I pressed it, and absolutely nothing happened.

Something had to have happened, I reasoned. The switch wasn't there for nothing. Nothing about Greville was for nothing. I pressed it back hard again and tried to raise, slide or otherwise move anything else I could reach. Nothing happened. I banged my fist with frustration down on the desk top, and a section of the front edge of the solid-looking slab fell off in my lap.

Annette and June gasped. The piece that had come off was like a strip of veneer furnished with metal clips for fastening it in place. Behind it was more wood, but this time with a keyhole in it. Watched breathlessly by Annette and June, I brought out Greville's bunch of keys and tried those that looked the right size: and one of them turned obligingly with hardly a click. I pulled the key, still in the hole, towards me, and like silk a wide shallow drawer slid out.

We all looked at the contents. Passport. Little flat black gadgets, four or five of them.

No diamonds.

June was delighted. 'That's the Wizard,' she said.

CHAPTER FOURTEEN

'Which is the Wizard?' I asked.

'That one.'

She pointed at a black rectangle a good deal smaller than a paperback, and when I picked it up and turned it over, sure enough, it had WIZARD written on it in gold. I handed it to June who opened it like a book, laying it flat on the desk. The right-hand panel was covered with buttons and looked like an ultra-versatile calculator. The left-hand side had a small screen at the top and a touch panel at the bottom with headings like 'expense record', 'time accounting', 'reports' and 'reference'.

'It does everything,' June said. 'It's a diary, a phone directory, a memo pad, an appointments calendar, an accounts keeper . . . a world clock.'

'And does it have an alarm system set to four-twenty?'

She switched the thing on, pressed three keys and showed me the screen. Daily alarm, it announced. 4.20 pm, set.

'Fair enough.'

For Annette the excitement seemed to be over. There were things she needed to see to, she said, and went away. June suggested she should tidy away all the gadgets and close all the doors, and while she did that I investigated further the contents of the one drawer we left open.

I frowned a bit over the passport. I'd assumed that in going to Harwich, Greville had meant to catch the ferry. The *Koningin Beatrix* sailed every night . . .

If one looked at it the other way round, the *Koningin Beatrix* must sail from Holland to Harwich every day. If he hadn't taken the passport with him, perhaps he'd been going to *meet* the *Koningin Beatrix*, not leave on her.

Meet *who*?

I looked at his photograph which, like all passport photographs, wasn't very good but good enough to bring him vividly into the office; his office, where I sat in his chair.

June looked over my shoulder and said, 'Oh,' in a small voice. 'I do miss him, you know.'

'Yes.'

I put the passport with regret back into the drawer and took out a flat square object hardly larger than the Wizard, that had a narrow curl of paper coming out of it.

'That's the printer,' June said.

'A printer? So small?'

'It'll print everything stored in the Wizard.'

292

She plugged the printer's short cord into a slot in the side of the Wizard and dexterously pressed a few keys. With a whirr the tiny machine went into action and began printing out a strip of half the telephone directory, or so it seemed.

'Lovely, isn't it?' June said, pressing another button to stop it. 'When he was away on trips, Mr Franklin would enter all his expenses on here and we would print them out when he got home, or sometimes transfer them from the Wizard to our main computer through an interface . . . oh, dear.' She smothered the uprush of emotion and with an attempt at controlling her voice said, 'He would note down in there a lot of things he wanted to remember when he got home. Things like who had offered him unusual stones. Then he'd tell Prospero Jenks, and quite often I'd be writing to the addresses to have the stones sent.'

I looked at the small black electronic marvel. So much information quiescent in its circuits.

'Is there an instruction manual?' I asked.

'Of course. All the instruction manuals for everything are in this drawer.' She opened one on the outer right-hand stack. 'So are the warranty cards, and everything.' She sorted through a rank of booklets. 'Here you are. One for the Wizard, one for the printer, one for the expenses organizer.'

'I'll borrow them,' I said.

'They're yours now,' she replied blankly. 'Aren't they?'

'I can't get used to it any more than you can.'

I laid the manuals on top of the desk next to the Wizard and the printer and took a third black object out of the secret drawer.

This one needed no explanation. This was the micro-cassette recorder that went with the tiny tapes I'd found in the hollowed-out books.

'That's voice activated,' June said, looking at it. 'It will sit quietly around doing nothing for hours, then when anyone speaks it will record what's said. Mr Franklin used it sometimes for dictating letters or notes because it let him say a bit, think a bit, and say a bit more, without using up masses of tape. I used to listen to the tapes and type straight onto the word processor.'

Worth her weight in pearls, Greville had judged. I wouldn't quarrel with that.

I put the microcassette player beside the other things and brought out the last two gadgets. One was a tiny Minolta camera which June said Greville used quite often for pictures of unusual stones for Prospero Jenks, and the last was a grey thing one could hold in one's hand that had an on/off switch but no obvious purpose.

'That's to frighten dogs away,' June said with a smile. 'Mr Franklin didn't like dogs, but I think he was ashamed of not liking them, because at first he didn't want to tell me what that was, when I asked him.'

I hadn't known Greville didn't like dogs. I fiercely wanted him back, if only to tease him about it. The real trouble with death was what it left unsaid: and knowing that that thought was a more or less universal regret made it no less sharp.

I put the dog frightener back beside the passport and also the baby camera, which had no film in it. Then I closed and locked the shallow drawer and fitted the piece of veneer back in place, pushing it home with a click. The vast top again looked wholly solid, and I wondered if Greville had bought that desk simply because of the drawer's existence, or whether he'd had the whole piece especially made.

'You'd never know that drawer was there,' June said. 'I wonder how many fortunes have been lost by people getting rid of hiding places they didn't suspect?'

'I read a story about that once. Something about money stuffed in an old armchair that was left to someone.' I couldn't remember the details: but Greville had left me more than an old armchair, and more than one place to look, and I too could get rid of the treasure from not suspecting the right hiding place, if there were one at all to find.

Meanwhile there was the problem of staying healthy while I searched. There was the worse problem of sorting out ways of taking the war to the enemy, if I could identify the enemy in the first place.

I asked June if she could find something I could carry the Wizard and the other things in and she was back in a flash with a soft plastic bag with handles. It reminded me fleetingly of the bag I'd had snatched at Ipswich but this time, I thought, when I carried the booty to the car,

I would take with me an invincible bodyguard, a long-legged flat-chested twenty-one-year-old blonde half in love with my brother.

The telephone rang. I picked up the receiver and said, 'Saxony Franklin' out of newly acquired habit.

'Derek? Is that you?'

'Yes, Milo, it is.'

'I'm not satisfied with this horse.' He sounded aggressive, which wasn't unusual, and also apologetic, which was.

'Which horse?' I asked.

'Dozen Roses, of course. What else?'

'Oh.'

'What do you mean, oh? You knew damn well I was fetching it today. The damn thing's half asleep. I'm getting the vet round at once and I'll want urine and blood tests. The damn thing looks doped.'

'Maybe they gave him a tranquillizer for the journey.'

'They've no right to, you know that. If they have, I'll have Nicholas Loder's head on a platter, like you should, if you had any sense. The man does what he damn well likes. Anyway, if the horse doesn't pass my vet he's going straight back, Ostermeyers or no Ostermeyers. It's not fair on them if I accept shoddy goods.'

'Um,' I said calmingly, 'perhaps Nicholas Loder wants you to do just that.'

'What? What do you mean?'

'Wants you to send him straight back.'

'Oh.'

'And,' I said, 'Dozen Roses was the property of Saxony Franklin Ltd, not Nicholas Loder, and if you think it's fair to the Ostermeyers to void the sale, so be it, but my brother's executor will direct you to send the horse anywhere else but back to Loder.'

There was a silence. Then he said with a smothered laugh, 'You always were a bright tricky bastard.'

'Thanks.'

'But get down here, will you? Take a look at him. Talk to the vet. How soon can you get here?'

'Couple of hours. Maybe more.'

'No, come on, Derek.'

'It's a long way to Tipperary,' I said. 'It never gets any nearer.'

'You're delirious.'

'I shouldn't wonder.'

'Soon as you can, then,' he said. 'See you.'

I put down the receiver with an inward groan. I did not want to go belting down to Lambourn to a crisis, however easily resolved. I wanted to let my aches unwind.

I telephoned the car and heard the ringing tone, but Brad, wherever he was, didn't answer. Then, as the first step towards leaving, I went along and locked the vault. Alfie in the packing room was stretching his back, his day's load finished. Lily, standing idle, gave me a repressed look from under her lashes. Jason goosed Tina in the doorway to the stock-rooms, which she didn't seem to mind. There was a feeling of afternoon ending, of abeyance in the offing, of corporate activity drifting to suspense. Like the last race on an October card.

Saying goodnights and collecting the plastic bag I went down to the yard and found Brad there waiting.

'Did you find those papers OK?' I asked him, climbing in beside him after storing the crutches on the back seat.

'Yerss,' he said.

'And delivered them?'

'Yerss.'

'Thanks. Great. How long have you been back?'

He shrugged. I left it. It wasn't important.

'Lambourn,' I said, as we turned out of the yard. 'But on the way, back to my brother's house to collect something else. OK?'

He nodded and drove to Greville's house skilfully, but slowed just before we reached it and pointed to Greville's car, still standing by the kerb.

'See?' he said. 'It's been broken into.'

He found a parking place and we went back to look. The heavily locked boot had been jemmied open and now wouldn't close again.

'Good job we took the things out,' I said. 'I suppose they are still in my car.'

He shook his head. 'In our house, under the stairs. Our Mum said to do it, with your car outside our door all night. Dodgy neighbourhood, round our part.'

'Very thoughtful,' I said.

He nodded. 'Smart, our Mum.'

He came with me into Greville's garden, holding the gate open.

'They done this place over proper,' he said, producing the three keys from his pocket. 'Want me to?'

He didn't wait for particular assent but went up the steps and undid the locks. Daylight: no floods, no dog.

He waited in the hall while I went along to the little sitting room to collect the tapes. It all looked forlorn in there, a terrible mess made no better by time. I put the featherweight cassettes in my pocket and left again, thinking that tidying up was a long way down my urgency list. When the ankle had altogether stopped hurting; maybe then. When the insurance people had seen it, if they wanted to.

I had brought with me a note which I left prominently on the lowest step of the staircase, where anyone coming into the house would see it.

'Dear Mrs P. I'm afraid there is bad news for you. Don't clean the house. Telephone Saxony Franklin Ltd instead.'

I'd added the number in case she didn't know it by heart, and I'd warned Annette to go gently with anyone ringing. Nothing else I could do to cushion the shock.

Brad locked the front door and we set off again to Lambourn. He had done enough talking for the whole journey and we travelled in customary silence, easy if not comrades.

Milo was striding about in the yard, expending

energy to no purpose. He yanked the passenger side door of my car open and scowled in at Brad, more as a reflection of his general state of mind, I gathered, than from any particular animosity.

I retrieved the crutches and stood up, and he told me it was high time I threw them away.

'Calm down,' I said.

'Don't patronize me.'

'Is Phil here?'

Phil was Phil Urquhart, veterinary surgeon, pill pusher to the stable.

'No, he isn't,' Milo said crossly, 'but he's coming back. The damned horse won't give a sample. And for a start, you can tell me whether it is or isn't Dozen Roses. His passport matches, but I'd like to be sure.'

He strode away towards a box in one corner of the yard and I followed and looked where he looked, over the bottom half of the door.

Inside the box were an obstinate-looking horse and a furious red-faced lad. The lad held a pole which had on one end of it an open plastic bag on a ring, like a shrimping net. The plastic bag was clean and empty.

I chuckled.

'It's all right for you,' Milo said sharply. 'You haven't been waiting for more than two hours for the damned animal to stale.'

'On Singapore racecourse, one time,' I said, 'they got a sample with nicotine in it. The horse didn't smoke, but the lad did. He got tired of waiting for the horse and just supplied the sample himself.'

'Very funny,' Milo said repressively.

'This often takes hours, though, so why the rage?'

It sounded always so simple, of course, to take a regulation urine sample from two horses after every race, one nearly always from the winner. In practice, it meant waiting around for the horses to oblige. After two hours of non-performance, blood samples were taken instead, but blood wasn't as easy to come by. Many tempers were regularly lost while the horses made up their minds.

'Come away,' I said, 'he'll do it in the end. And he's definitely the horse that ran at York. Dozen Roses without doubt.'

He followed me away reluctantly and we went into the kitchen where Milo switched lights on and asked me if I'd like a drink.

'Wouldn't mind some tea,' I said.

'Tea? At this hour? Well, help yourself.' He watched me fill the kettle and set it to boil. 'Are you off booze for ever?'

'No.'

'Thank God.'

Phil Urquhart's car scrunched into the yard and pulled up outside the window, and he came breezing into the kitchen asking if there were any results. He read Milo's scowl aright and laughed.

'Do you think the horse is doped?' I asked him.

'Me? No, not really. Hard to tell. Milo thinks so.'

He was small and sandy-haired, and about thirty, the grandson of a three-generation family practice, and to my mind the best of them. I caught myself thinking that when I in the future trained here in Lambourn, I would want him for my horses. An odd thought. The future planning itself behind my back.

'I hear we're lucky you're still with us,' he said. 'An impressive crunch, so they say.' He looked at me assessingly with friendly professional eyes. 'You've a few rough edges, one can see.'

'Nothing that will stop him racing,' Milo said crisply.

Phil smiled. 'I detect more alarm than sympathy.'

'Alarm?'

'You've trained more winners since he came here.'

'Rubbish,' Milo said.

He poured drinks for himself and Phil, and I made my tea; and Phil assured me that if the urine passed all tests he would give the thumbs up to Dozen Roses.

'He may just be showing the effects of the hard race he had at York,' he said. 'It might be that he's always like this. Some horses are, and we don't know how much weight he lost.'

'What will you get the urine tested for?' I asked.

He raised his eyebrows. 'Barbiturates, in this case.'

'At York,' I said thoughtfully, 'one of Nicholas Loder's owners was walking around with a nebulizer in his pocket. A kitchen baster, to be precise.'

'An owner?' Phil asked, surprised.

'Yes. He owned the winner of the five-furlong sprint. He was also in the saddling box with Dozen Roses.'

Phil frowned. 'What are you implying?'

'Nothing. Merely observing. I can't believe he interfered with the horse. Nicholas Loder wouldn't have let him. The stable money was definitely on. They wanted to win, and they knew if it won it would be tested. So the only question is, what could you give a horse that wouldn't disqualify it? Give it via a nebulizer just before a race?'

'Nothing that would make it go faster. They test for all stimulants.'

'What if you gave it, say, sugar? Glucose? Or adrenalin?'

'You've a criminal mind!'

'I just wondered.'

'Glucose would give energy, as to human athletes. It wouldn't increase speed, though. Adrenalin is more tricky. If it's given by injection you can see it, because the hairs stand up all round the puncture. But straight into the mucous membranes ... well, I suppose it's possible.'

'And no trace.'

He agreed. 'Adrenalin pours into a horse's bloodstream naturally anyway, if he's excited. If he wants to win. If he feels the whip. Who's to say how much? If you suspected a booster, you'd have to take a blood sample in the winner's enclosure, practically, and even then you'd have a hard job proving any reading was excessive.

Adrenalin levels vary too much. You'd even have a hard job proving extra adrenalin made any difference at all.' He paused and considered me soberly. 'You do realize that you're saying that if anything was done, Nicholas Loder condoned it?'

'Doesn't seem likely, does it?'

'No, it doesn't,' he said. 'If he were some tin-pot little crook, well then, maybe, but not Nicholas Loder with his Classic winners and everything to lose.'

'Mm.' I thought a bit. 'If I asked, I could get some of the urine sample that was taken from Dozen Roses at York. They always make it available to owners for private checks. To my brother's company, that is to say, in this instance.' I thought a bit more. 'When Nicholas Loder's friend dropped his baster, Martha Ostermeyer handed the bulb part back to him, but then Harley Ostermeyer picked up the tube part and gave it to me. But it was clean. No trace of liquid. No adrenalin. So I suppose it's possible he might have used it on his own horse and still had it in his pocket, but did nothing to Dozen Roses.'

They considered it.

'You could get into a lot of trouble making unfounded accusations,' Phil said.

'So Nicholas Loder told me.'

'Did he? I'd think twice, then, before I did. It wouldn't do you much good generally in the racing world, I shouldn't think.'

'Wisdom from babes,' I said, but he echoed my thoughts.

'Yes, old man.'

'I kept the baster tube,' I said, shrugging, 'but I guess I'll do just what I did at the races, which was nothing.'

'As long as Dozen Roses tests clean both at York and here, that's likely best,' Phil said, and Milo, for all his earlier pugnaciousness, agreed.

A commotion in the darkening yard heralded the success of the urine mission and Phil went outside to unclip the special bag and close its patented seal. He wrote and attached the label giving the horse's name, the location, date and time and signed his name.

'Right,' he said, 'I'll be off. Take care.' He loaded himself, the sample and his gear into his car and with economy of movement scrunched away. I followed soon after with Brad still driving, but decided again not to go home.

'You saw the mess in London,' I said. 'I got knocked out by whoever did that. I don't want to be in if they come to Hungerford. So let's go to Newbury instead, and try The Chequers.'

Brad slowed, his mouth open.

'A week ago yesterday,' I said, 'you saved me from a man with a knife. Yesterday someone shot at the car I was in and killed the chauffeur. It may not have been your regulation madman. So last night I slept in Swindon, tonight in Newbury.'

'Yerss,' he said, understanding.

'If you'd rather not drive me any more, I wouldn't blame you.'

After a pause, with a good deal of stalwart resolution, he made a statement. 'You need me.'

'Yes,' I said. 'Until I can walk properly, I do.'

'I'll drive you, then.'

'Thanks,' I said, and meant it wholeheartedly, and he could hear that, because he nodded twice to himself emphatically and seemed even pleased.

The Chequers Hotel having a room free, I booked in for the night. Brad took himself home in my car, and I spent most of the evening sitting in an armchair upstairs learning my way round the Wizard.

Computers weren't my natural habitat like they were Greville's and I hadn't the same appetite for them. The Wizard's instructions seemed to take it for granted that everyone reading them would be computer-literate, so it probably took me longer than it might have done to get results.

What was quite clear was that Greville had used the gadget extensively. There were three separate telephone and address lists, the world-time clock, a system for entering daily appointments, a prompt for anniversaries, a calendar flashing with the day's date, and provision for storing oddments of information. By plugging in the printer, and after a few false starts, I ended with long printed lists of everything held listed under all the headings, and read them with growing frustration.

None of the addresses or telephone numbers seemed to have anything to do with Antwerp or with diamonds, though the 'Business Overseas' list contained many gem merchants' names from all round the world. None of the appointments scheduled, which stretched back six weeks or more, seemed to be relevant, and there were no entries at all for the Friday he'd gone to Ipswich. There was no reference to *Koningin Beatrix*.

I thought of my question to June the day she'd found her way to 'pearl': what if it were all in there, but stored in secret?

The Wizard's instruction manual, two hundred pages long, certainly did give lessons in how to lock things away. Entries marked 'secret' could only be retrieved by knowing the password which could be any combination of numbers and letters up to seven in all. Forgetting the password meant bidding farewell to the entries: they could never be seen again. They could be deleted unseen, but not printed or brought to the screen.

One could tell if secret files were present, the book said, by the small symbol s, which could be found on the lower right-hand side of the screen. I consulted Greville's screen and found the s there, sure enough.

It would be, I thought. It would have been totally unlike him to have had the wherewithal for secrecy and not used it.

Any combination of numbers or letters up to seven . . .

The book suggested 1234, but once I'd sorted out the

opening moves for unlocking and entered 1234 in the space headed 'Secret Off', all I got was a quick dusty answer, 'Incorrect Password'.

Damn him, I thought, wearily defeated. Why couldn't he make any of it easy?

I tried every combination of letters and numbers I thought he might have used but got absolutely nowhere. Clarissa was too long, 12Roses should have been right but wasn't. To be right, the password had to be entered exactly as it had been set, whether in capital letters or lower case. It all took time. In the end I was ready to throw the confounded Wizard across the room, and stared at its perpetual 'Incorrect Password' with hatred.

I finally laid it aside and played the tiny tape recorder instead. There was a lot of office chat on the tapes and I couldn't think why Greville should have bothered to take them home and hide them. Long before I reached the end of the fourth side, I was asleep.

I woke stiffly after a while, unsure for a second where I was. I rubbed my face, looked at my watch, thought about all the constructive thinking I was supposed to be doing and wasn't, and rewound the second of the baby tapes to listen to what I'd missed. Greville's voice, talking business to Annette.

The most interesting thing, the only interesting thing about those tapes, I thought, was Greville's voice. The only way I would ever hear him again.

'. . . going out to lunch,' he was saying. 'I'll be back by two-thirty.'

Annette's voice said, 'Yes, Mr Franklin.'

A click sounded on the tape.

Almost immediately, because of the concertina-ing of time by the voice-activated mechanism, a different voice said, 'I'm in his office now and I can't find them. He hides everything, he's security mad, you know that.' Click. 'I can't ask. He'd never tell me, and I don't think he trusts me.' Click. 'Po-faced Annette doesn't sneeze unless he tells her to. She'd never tell me anything.' Click. 'I'll try. I'll have to go, he doesn't like me using this phone, he'll be back from lunch any second.' Click.

End of tape.

Bloody hell, I thought. I rewound the end of the tape and listened to it again. I knew the voice, as Greville must have done. He'd left the recorder on, I guessed by mistake, and he'd come back and listened, with I supposed sadness, to treachery. It opened up a whole new world of questions and I went slowly to bed groping towards answers.

I lay a long time awake. When I slept, I dreamed the usual surrealist muddle and found it no help, but around dawn, awake again and thinking of Greville, it occurred to me that there was one password I hadn't tried because I hadn't thought of his using it.

The Wizard was across the room by the armchair. Impelled by curiosity I turned on the light, rolled out of bed and hopped over to fetch it. Taking it back with me, I switched it on, pressed the buttons, found 'Secret Off' and into the offered space typed the word Greville had written on the last page of his racing diary, below the numbers of his passport and national insurance.

DEREK, all in capital letters.

I typed DEREK and pressed Enter, and the Wizard with resignation let me into its data.

CHAPTER FIFTEEN

I began printing out everything in the secret files as it seemed from the manual that, particularly as regarded the expense organizer, it was the best way to get at the full information stored there.

Each category had to be printed separately, the baby printer clicking away line by line and not very fast. I watched its steady output with fascination, hoping the small roll of paper would last to the end, as I hadn't any more.

From the Memo section, which I printed first, came a terse note, 'Check, don't trust.'

Next came a long list of days and dates which seemed to bear no relation to anything. Monday, 30 January, Wednesday, 8 March ... Mystified I watched the sequence lengthen, noticing only that most of them were Mondays, Tuesdays or Wednesdays, five or six weeks apart, sometimes less, sometimes longer. The list ended five weeks before his death, and it began ... It began, I thought blankly, four years earlier. Four years ago; when he first met Clarissa.

I felt unbearable sadness for him. He'd fallen in love with a woman who wouldn't leave home for him, whom he hadn't wanted to compromise: he'd kept a record, I was certain, of every snatched day they'd spent together, and hidden it away as he had hidden so much else. A whole lot of roses, I thought.

The Schedule section, consulted next, contained appointments not hinted at earlier, including the delivery of the diamonds to his London house. For the day of his death there were two entries: the first, 'Ipswich. Orwell Hotel, P. 3.30 pm', and the second, 'Meet *Koningin Beatrix* 6.30 pm, Harwich.' For the following Monday he had noted, 'Meet C King's Cross 12.10 Lunch Luigi's.'

Meet C at King's Cross . . . He hadn't turned up, and she'd telephoned his house, and left a message on his answering machine, and sometime in the afternoon she'd telephoned his office to ask for him. Poor Clarissa. By Monday night she'd left the ultra-anxious second message, and on Tuesday she had learned he was dead.

The printer whirred and produced another entry, for the Saturday after. 'C and Dozen Roses both at York! Could I go? Not wise. Check TV.'

The printer stopped, as Greville's life had done. No more appointments on record.

Next I printed the Telephone sections, Private, Business and Business Overseas. Private contained only Knightwood. Business was altogether empty, but from Business Overseas I watched with widening eyes the emergence of five numbers and addresses in Antwerp. One was van Ekeren, one was Guy Servi: three were so far unknown to me. I breathed almost painfully with exultation, unable to believe Greville had entered them there for no purpose.

I printed the Expense Manager's secret section last as it was the most complicated and looked the least promising, but the first item that emerged was galvanic.

> Antwerp say 5 of the first
> batch of rough are CZ.
> Don't want to believe it.
> Infinite sadness.
> Priority 1.
> Arrange meetings. Ipswich?
> Undecided. Damnation!

I wished he had been more explicit, more specific, but he'd seen no need to be. It was surprising he'd written so much. His feelings must have been strong to have been entered at all. No other entries afterwards held any comment but were short records of money spent on courier services with a firm called Euro-Securo, telephone number supplied. In the middle of those the paper ran out. I brought the rest of the stored information up on to the screen and scrolled through it, but there was nothing else disturbing.

I switched off both baby machines and reread the long curling strip of printing from the beginning, afterwards flattening it out and folding it to fit a shirt pocket. Then I dressed, packed, breakfasted, waited for Brad and travelled to London hopefully.

The telephone calls to Antwerp had to be done from the Saxony Franklin premises because of the pre-cautionary checking back. I would have preferred more privacy than Greville's office but couldn't achieve it, and one of the first things I asked Annette that morning was whether my brother had had one of those gadgets that warned you if someone was listening to your conversation on an extension. The office phones were all interlinked.

'No, he didn't,' she said, troubled.

'He could have done with one,' I said.

'Are you implying that we listened when he didn't mean us to?'

'Not you,' I assured her, seeing her resentment of the suggestion. 'But yes, I'd think it happened. Anyway, at some point this morning, I want to make sure of not being overheard, so when that call comes through per-haps you'll all go into the stock-room and sing Rule Britannia.'

Annette never made jokes. I had to explain I didn't mean sing literally. She rather huffily agreed that when I wanted it, she would go round the extensions checking against eavesdroppers.

I asked her why Greville hadn't had a private line in any case, and she said he had had one earlier but they now used that for the fax machine.

'If he wanted to be private,' she said, 'he went down to the yard and telephoned from his car.'

There, I supposed, he would have been safe also from people with sensitive listening devices, if he'd suspected their use. He had been conscious of betrayal, that was for sure.

I sat at Greville's desk with the door closed and matched the three unknown Antwerp names from the Wizard with the full list June had provided, and found that all three were there.

The first and second produced no results, but from the third, once I explained who I was, I got the customary response about checking the files and calling back. They did call back, but the amorphous voice on the far end was cautious to the point of repression.

'We at Maarten-Pagnier cannot discuss anything at all with you, monsieur,' he said. 'Monsieur Franklin gave express orders that we were not to communicate with anyone in his office except himself.'

'My brother is dead,' I said.

'So you say, monsieur. But he warned us to beware of any attempt to gain information about his affairs and we cannot discuss them.'

'Then please will you telephone to his lawyers and get their assurance that he's dead and that I am now managing his business?'

After a pause the voice said austerely, 'Very well, monsieur. Give us the name of his lawyers.'

I did that and waited for ages during which time

three customers telephoned with long orders which I wrote down, trying not to get them wrong from lack of concentration.

Then there was a frantic call from a nearly incoherent woman who wanted to speak to Mr Franklin urgently.

'Mrs P?' I asked tentatively.

Mrs P it was. Mrs Patterson, she said. I gave her the abysmal news and listened to her telling me what a fine nice gentleman my brother had been, and oh dear, she felt faint, had I seen the mess in the sitting room?

I warned her that the whole house was the same. 'Just leave it,' I said. 'I'll clean it up later. Then if you could come after that to hoover and dust, I'd be very grateful.'

Calming a little, she gave me her phone number. 'Let me know, then,' she said. 'Oh dear, oh dear.'

Finally the Antwerp voice returned and, begging him to hold on, I hopped over to the door, called Annette, handed her the customers' orders and said this was the moment for securing the defences. She gave me a disapproving look as I again closed the door.

Back in Greville's chair I said to the voice, 'Please, monsieur, tell me if my brother had any dealings with you. I am trying to sort out his office but he has left too few records.'

'He asked us particularly not to send any records of the work we were doing for him to his office.'

'He, er, what?' I said.

316

'He said he could not trust everyone in his office as he would like. Instead, he wished us to send anything necessary to the fax machine in his car, but only when he telephoned from there to arrange it.'

'Um,' I said, blinking, 'I found the fax machine in his car but there were no statements or invoices or anything from you.'

'I believe if you ask his accountants, you may find them there.'

'Good grief.'

'I beg your pardon, monsieur?'

'I didn't think of asking his accountants,' I said blankly.

'He said for tax purposes . . .'

'Yes, I see.' I hesitated. 'What exactly were you doing for him?'

'Monsieur?'

'Did he,' I asked a shade breathlessly, 'send you a hundred diamonds, colour H, average uncut weight three point two carats, to be cut and polished?'

'No, monsieur.'

'Oh.' My disappointment must have been audible.

'He sent twenty-five stones, monsieur, but five of them were not diamonds.'

'Cubic zirconia,' I said, enlightened.

'Yes, monsieur. We told Monsieur Franklin as soon as we discovered it. He said we were wrong, but we were not, monsieur.'

'No,' I agreed. 'He did leave a note saying five of the first batch were CZ.'

'Yes, monsieur. He was extremely upset. We made several enquiries for him, but he had bought the stones from a sightholder of impeccable honour and he had himself measured and weighed the stones when they were delivered to his London house. He sent them to us in a sealed Euro-Securo courier package. We assured him that the mistake could not have been made here by us, and it was then, soon after that, that he asked us not to send or give any information to anyone in his . . . your . . . office.' He paused. 'He made arrangements to receive the finished stones from us, but he didn't meet our messenger.'

'Your messenger?'

'One of our partners, to be accurate. We wished to deliver the stones to him ourselves because of the five disputed items, and Monsieur Franklin thought it an excellent idea. Our partner dislikes flying, so it was agreed he should cross by boat and return the same way. When Monsieur Franklin failed to meet him he came back here. He is elderly and had made no provision to stay away. He was . . . displeased . . . at having made a tiring journey for nothing. He said we should wait to hear from Monsieur Franklin. Wait for fresh instructions. We have been waiting, but we've been puzzled. We didn't try to reach Monsieur Franklin at his office as he had forbidden us to do that, but we were considering asking someone else to try on our behalf. We are very sorry to hear of his death. It explains everything, of course.'

I said, 'Did your partner travel to Harwich on the *Koningin Beatrix*?'

'That's right, monsieur.'

'He brought the diamonds with him?'

'That's right, monsieur. And he brought them back. We will now wait your instructions instead.'

I took a deep breath. Twenty of the diamonds at least were safe. Five were missing. Seventy-five were . . . *where*?

The Antwerp voice said, 'It's to be regretted that Monsieur Franklin didn't see the polished stones. They cut very well. Twelve tear drops of great brilliance, remarkable for that colour. Eight were not suitable for tear drops, as we told Monsieur Franklin, but they look handsome as stars. What shall we do with them, monsieur?'

'When I've talked to the jeweller they were cut for, I'll let you know.'

'Very good, monsieur. And our account? Where shall we send that?' He mentioned considerately how much it would be.

'To this office,' I said, sighing at the prospect. 'Send it to me marked "Personal".'

'Very good, monsieur.'

'And thank you,' I said. 'You've been very helpful.'

'At your service, monsieur.'

I put the receiver down slowly, richer by twelve

glittering tear drops destined to hang and flash in sunlight, and by eight handsome stars that might twinkle in
a fantasy of rock crystal. Better than nothing, but not
enough to save the firm.

Using the crutches, I went in search of Annette and
asked her if she would please find Prospero Jenks, wherever he was, and make another appointment for me,
that afternoon if possible. Then I went down to the yard,
taking a tip from Greville, and on the telephone in my
car put a call through to his accountants.

Brad, reading a golfing magazine, paid no attention.

Did he play golf, I asked?

No, he didn't.

The accountants helpfully confirmed that they had
received envelopes both from my brother and from
Antwerp, and were holding them unopened, as
requested, pending further instructions.

'You'll need them for the general accounts,' I said.
'So would you please just keep them?'

Absolutely no problem.

'On second thoughts,' I said, 'please open all the
envelopes and tell me who all the letters from Antwerp
have come from.'

Again no problem: but the letters were all either
from Guy Servi, the sightholder, or from Maarten-
Pagnier, the cutters. No other firms. No other safe
havens for seventy-five rocks.

I thanked them, watched Brad embark on a learned

comparison of Ballesteros and Faldo, and thought about disloyalty and the decay of friendship.

It was restful in the car, I decided. Brad went on reading. I thought of robbery with violence and violence without robbery, of being laid out with a brick and watching Simms die of a bullet meant for me, and I wondered whether, if I were dead, anyone could find what I was looking for, or whether they reckoned they now couldn't find it if I were alive.

I stirred and fished in a pocket and gave Brad a cheque I'd written out for him upstairs.

'What's this?' he said, peering at it.

I usually paid him in cash, but I explained I hadn't enough for what I owed him, and cash dispensers wouldn't disgorge enough all at once and we hadn't recently been in Hungerford when the banks were open, as he might have noticed.

'Give me cash later,' he said, holding the cheque out to me. 'And you paid me double.'

'For last week and this week,' I nodded. 'When we get to the bank I'll swap it for cash. Otherwise, you could bring it back here. It's a company cheque. They'd see you got cash for it.'

He gave me a long look.

'Is this because of guns and such? In case you never get to the bank?'

I shrugged. 'You might say so.'

He looked at the cheque, folded it deliberately and stowed it away. Then he picked up the magazine and

stared blindly at a page he'd just read. I was grateful for
the absence of comment or protest, and in a while said
matter-of-factly that I was going upstairs for a bit, and
why didn't he get some lunch.

He nodded.

'Have you got enough money for lunch?'

'Yerss.'

'You might make a list of what you've spent. I've
enough cash for that.'

He nodded again.

'OK, then,' I said. 'See you.'

Upstairs, Annette said she had opened the day's post
and put it ready for my attention, and she'd found Prospero Jenks and he would be expecting me in the
Knightsbridge shop any time between three and six.

'Great.'

She frowned. 'Mr Jenks wanted to know if you were
taking him the goods Mr Franklin bought for him. Grev
– he always calls Mr Franklin, Grev. I do wish he
wouldn't – I asked what he meant about goods and
he said you would know.'

'He's talking about diamonds,' I said.

'But we haven't . . .' She stopped and then went on
with a sort of desperate vehemence. 'I *wish* Mr Franklin
was here. Nothing's the same without him.'

She gave me a look full of her insecurity and doubt
of my ability and plodded off into her own domain and
I thought that with what lay ahead I'd have preferred a

vote of confidence: and I too, with all my heart, wished Greville back.

The police from Hungerford telephoned, given my number by Milo's secretary. They wanted to know if I had remembered anything more about the car driven by the gunman. They had asked the family in the family car if they had noticed the make and colour of the last car they'd seen coming towards them before they rounded the bend and crashed into the Daimler, and one of the children, a boy, had given them a description. They had also, while the firemen and others were trying to free me, walked down the row of spectator cars asking them about the last car they'd seen coming towards them. Only the first two drivers had seen a car at all, that they could remember, and they had no help-ful information. Had I any recollection, however vague, as they were trying to piece together all the impressions they'd been given?

'I wish I could help,' I said, 'but I was talking to Mr and Mrs Ostermeyer, not concentrating on the road. It winds a bit, as you know, and I think Simms had been waiting for a place where he could pass the car in front, but all I can tell you, as on Sunday, is that it was a greyish colour and fairly large. Maybe a Mercedes. It's only an impression.'

'The child in the family car says it was a grey Volvo travelling fast. The bus driver says the car in question was travelling slowly before the Daimler tried to pass it, and he was aiming to pass also at that point, and was accelerating to do so, which was why he rammed the Daimler so hard. He says the car was silver grey and accelerated away at high speed, which matched what the child says.'

'Did the bus driver,' I asked, 'see the gun or the shots?'

'No, sir. He was looking at the road ahead and at the Daimler, not at the car he intended to pass. Then the Daimler veered sharply, and bounded off the wall straight into his path. He couldn't avoid hitting it, he said. Do you confirm that, sir?'

'Yes. It happened so fast. He hadn't a chance.'

'We are asking in the neighbourhood for anyone to come forward who saw a grey four-door saloon, possibly a Volvo, on that road on Sunday afternoon, but so far we have heard nothing new. If you remember anything else, however minor, let us know.'

I would, I said.

I put the phone down wondering if Vaccaro's shotdown pilots had seen the make of car from which their deaths had come spitting. Anyone seeing those murders would, I supposed, have been gazing with uncomprehending horror at the falling victims, not dashing into the road to peer at a fast disappearing number plate.

No one had heard any shots on Sunday. No one had heard the shots, the widow had told Greville, when her husband was killed. A silencer on a gun in a moving car . . . a swift pfftt . . . curtains.

It couldn't have been Vaccaro who shot Simms. Vaccaro didn't make sense. Someone with the same anti-social habits, as in Northern Ireland and elsewhere. A copycat. Plenty of precedent.

Milo's secretary had been busy and given my London number also to Phil Urquhart who came on the line to tell me that Dozen Roses had tested clean for barbiturates and he would give a certificate of soundness for the sale.

'Fine,' I said.

'I've been to examine the horse again this morning. He's still very docile. It seems to be his natural state.'

'Mm.'

'Do I hear doubt?'

'He's excited enough every time cantering down to the start.'

'Natural adrenalin,' Phil said.

'If it was anyone but Nicholas Loder . . .'

'He would never risk it,' Phil said, agreeing with me. 'But look . . . there are things that potentiate adrenalin, like caffeine. Some of them are never tested for in racing, as they are not judged to be stimulants. It's your money that's being spent on the tests I've done for you. We have some more of that sample of urine. Do you want me to get different tests done, for things not usually looked for? I mean, do you really think Nicholas Loder gave the horse something, and if you do, do you want to know about it?'

'It was his owner, a man called Rollway, who had the baster, not Loder himself.'

'Same decision. Do you want to spend more, or not bother? It may be money down the drain, anyway. And if you get any results, what then? You don't want to get the horse disqualified, that wouldn't make sense.'

'No . . . it wouldn't.'

'What's your problem?' he asked. 'I can hear it in your voice.'

'Fear,' I said. 'Nicholas Loder was afraid.'

'Oh.' He was briefly silent. 'I could get the tests done anonymously, of course.'

'Yes. Get them done, then. I particularly don't want to sell the Ostermeyers a lemon, as she would say. If Dozen Roses can't win on his own merits, I'll talk them out of the idea of owning him.'

'So you'll pay for negative results?'

'I will indeed.'

'While I was at Milo's this morning,' he said, 'he was talking to the Ostermeyers in London, asking how they were and wishi ng them a good journey. They were still a bit wobbly from the crash, it seems.'

'Surprising if they weren't.'

'They're coming back to England though to see Datepalm run in the Hennessy. How's your ankle?'

'Good as new by then.'

'Bye then.' I could hear his smile. 'Take care.'

He disconnected and left me thinking that there still were good things in the world, like the Ostermeyers' faith and riding Datepalm in the Hennessy, and I stood up and put my left foot flat on the floor for a progress report.

It wasn't so bad if I didn't lean any weight on it, but there were still jabbingly painful protests against attempts to walk. Oh well, I thought, sitting down again, give it another day or two. It hadn't exactly had a therapeutic week and was no doubt doing its best against odds. On Thursday, I thought, I would get rid of the crutches. By Friday, definitely. Any day after that I'd be running. Ever optimistic. It was the belief that cured.

The ever-busy telephone rang again, and I answered it with 'Saxony Franklin?' as routine.

'Derek?'

'Yes,' I said.

Clarissa's unmistakable voice said, 'I'm in London. Could we meet?'

I hadn't expected her so soon, I thought. I said, 'Yes, of course. Where?'

'I thought ... perhaps ... Luigi's. Do you know Luigi's bar and restaurant?'

'I don't,' I said slowly, 'but I can find it.'

'It's in Swallow Street near Piccadilly Circus. Would you mind coming at seven, for a drink?'

'And dinner?'

'Well ...'

'And dinner,' I said.

I heard her sigh, 'Yes. All right,' as she disconnected, and I was left with a vivid understanding both of her compulsion to put me where she had been going to meet Greville and of her awareness that perhaps she ought not to.

I could have said no, I thought. I could have, but hadn't. A little introspection revealed ambiguities in my response to her also, like did I want to give comfort, or to take it.

By three-thirty I'd finished the paperwork and filled an order for pearls and another for turquoise and relocked the vault and got Annette to smile again, even if faintly. At four, Brad pulled up outside Prospero Jenks's shop in Knightsbridge and I put the telephone ready to let him know when to collect me.

Prospero Jenks was where I'd found him before, sitting in shirtsleeves at his workbench. The discreet dark-suited man, serving customers in the shop, nodded me through.

'He's expecting you, Mr Franklin.'

Pross stood up with a smile on his young-old Peter Pan face and held out his hand, but let it fall again as I waggled a crutch handle at him instead.

'Glad to see you,' he said, offering a chair, waiting while I sat. 'Have you brought my diamonds?' He sat down again on his own stool.

'No. Afraid not.'

He was disappointed. 'I thought that was what you were coming for.'

'No, not really.'

I looked at his long efficient workroom with its little drawers full of unset stones and thought of the marvels he produced. The big notice on the wall still read 'NEVER TURN YOUR BACK TO CUSTOMERS. ALWAYS WATCH THEIR HANDS.'

I said, 'Greville sent twenty-five rough stones to Antwerp to be cut for you.'

'That's right.'

'Five of them were cubic zirconia.'

'No, no.'

'Did you,' I asked neutrally, 'swap them over?'

The half-smile died out of his face, which grew stiff and expressionless. The bright blue eyes stared at me and the lines deepened across his forehead.

'That's rubbish,' he said. 'I'd never do anything stupid like that.'

I didn't say anything immediately and it seemed to give him force.

'You can't come in here making wild accusations. Go on, get out, you'd better leave.' He half-rose to his feet.

I said, not moving, 'When the cutters told Greville five of the stones were cubic zirconia, he was devastated. Very upset.'

I reached into my shirt pocket and drew out the print-out from the Wizard.

'Do you want to see?' I asked. 'Read there.'

After a hesitation he took the paper, sat back on the stool and read the entry:

Antwerp say 5 of the first
batch of rough are CZ.

Don't want to believe it.
Infinite sadness.
Priority 1.
Arrange meetings. Ipswich?
Undecided. Damnation!

'Greville used to write his thoughts in a notebook,' I said. 'In there it says, "Infinite sadness is not to trust an old friend." '

'So what?'

'Since Greville died,' I said, 'someone has been trying to find his diamonds, to steal them from me. That someone had to be someone who knew they were there to be found. Greville kept the fact that he'd bought them very quiet for security reasons. He didn't tell even his staff. But of course you yourself knew, as it was for you he bought them.'

He said again, 'So what?'

'If you remember,' I said, still conversationally, 'someone broke into Greville's office after he died and stole things like an address book and an appointments diary. I began to think the thief had also stolen any other papers which might point to where the diamonds were, like letters or invoices. But I know now there weren't any such papers to be found there, because Greville was full of distrust. His distrust dated from the day the Antwerp cutters told him five of his stones were cubic zirconia, which was about three weeks before he died.'

Pross, Greville's friend, said nothing.

'Greville bought the diamonds,' I went on, 'from a sightholder based in Antwerp who sent them by messenger to his London house. There he measured them and weighed them and signed for them. Then it would be reasonable to suppose that he showed them to you, his customer. Or showed you twenty-five of them, perhaps. Then he sent that twenty-five back to Antwerp by the Euro-Securo couriers. Five diamonds had mysteriously become cubic zirconia, and yes, it was an entirely stupid thing to do, because the substitution was bound to be discovered almost at once, and you knew it would be. Had to be. I'd think you reckoned Greville would never believe it of you, but would swear the five stones had to have been swapped by someone in the couriers or the cutters in Antwerp, and he would collect the insurance in due course, and that would be that. You would be five diamonds to the good, and he would have lost nothing.'

'You can't prove it,' he said flatly.

'No, I can't prove it. But Greville was full of sorrow and distrust, and why should he be if he thought his stones had been taken by strangers?'

I looked with some of Greville's own sadness at Prospero Jenks. A likeable, entertaining genius whose feelings for my brother had been strong and long-lasting, whose regret at his death had been real.

'I'd think,' I said, 'that after your long friendship, after all the treasures he'd brought you, after the pink and green tourmaline, after your tremendous success, that he could hardly bear your treachery.'

'Stop it,' he said sharply. 'It's bad enough . . .'

He shut his mouth tight and shook his head, and seemed to sag internally.

'He forgave me,' he said.

He must have thought I didn't believe him.

He said wretchedly, 'I wished I hadn't done it almost from the beginning, if you want to know. It was just an impulse. He left the diamonds here while he went off to do a bit of shopping, and I happened to have some rough CZ the right size in those drawers, as I often do, waiting for when I want special cutting, and I just . . . exchanged them. Like you said. I didn't think he'd lose by it.'

'He knew, though,' I said. 'He knew you, and he knew a lot about thieves, being a magistrate. Another of the things he wrote was, "If laws are inconvenient, ignore them, they don't apply to you." '

'Stop it. Stop it. He forgave me.'

'When?'

'In Ipswich. I went to meet him there.'

I lifted my head. 'Ipswich. Orwell Hotel, P. 3.30 pm,' I said.

'What? Yes.' He seemed unsurprised that I should know. He seemed to be looking inwards to an unendurable landscape.

'I saw him die,' he said.

CHAPTER SIXTEEN

'I saw the scaffolding fall on him,' he said.

He'd stunned me to silence.

'We talked in the hotel. In the lounge there. It was almost empty . . . then we walked down the street to where I'd left my car. We said goodbye. He crossed the road and walked on, and I watched him. I wanted him to look back and wave . . . but he didn't.'

Forgiveness was one thing, I thought, but friendship had gone. What did he expect? Absolution and comfort? Perhaps Greville in time would have given those too, but I couldn't.

Prospero Jenks with painful memory said, 'Grev never knew what happened . . . There wasn't any warning. Just a clanging noise and metal falling and men with it. Crashing down fast. It buried him. I couldn't see him . . . I ran across the road to pull him and there were bodies . . . and he . . . he . . . I thought he was dead already. His head was bleeding . . . there was a metal bar in his stomach and another had ripped into his leg . . . it was . . . I can't . . . I try to forget but I see it all the time.'

I waited and in a while he went on.

'I didn't move him. Couldn't. There was so much blood . . . and a man lying over his legs . . . and another man groaning. People came running . . . then the police . . . it was just chaos . . .'

He stopped again, and I said, 'When the police came, why didn't you stay with Greville and help him? Why didn't you identify him to them, even?'

His genuine sorrow was flooded with a shaft of alarm. The dismay was momentary, and he shrugged it off.

'You know how it is.' He gave me a little-boy shame-faced look, much the same as when he'd admitted to changing the stones. 'Don't get involved. I didn't want to be dragged in . . . I thought he was dead.'

Somewhere along the line, I thought, he was lying to me. Not about seeing the accident: his description of Greville's injuries had been piercingly accurate.

'Did you simply . . . drive off?' I asked bleakly.

'No, I couldn't. Not for ages. The police cordoned off the street and took endless statements. Something about criminal responsibility and insurance claims. But I couldn't help them. I didn't see why the scaffolding fell. I felt sick because of the blood . . . I sat in my car till they let us drive out. They'd taken Grev off in an ambulance before that . . . and the bar was still sticking out of his stomach . . .'

The memory was powerfully reviving his nausea.

'You knew by then that he was still alive,' I said.

He was shocked. 'How? How could I have known?'

'They hadn't covered his face.'

'He was dying. Anyone could see. His head was dented . . . and bleeding . . .'

Dead men don't bleed, I thought, but didn't say it. Prospero Jenks already looked about to throw up, and I wondered how many times he actually had, in the past eleven days.

Instead, I said, 'What did you talk about in the Orwell Hotel?'

He blinked. 'You know what.'

'He accused you of changing the stones.'

'Yes.' He swallowed. 'Well, I apologized. Said I was sorry. Which I was. He could see that. He said why did I do it when I was bound to be found out, but when I did it, it was an impulse, and I didn't think I'd be found out, like I told you.'

'What did he say?'

'He shook his head as if I were a baby. He was sad more than angry. I said I would give the diamonds back, of course, and I begged him to forgive me.'

'Which he did?'

'Yes, I told you. I asked if we could go on trading together. I mean, no one was as good as Grev at finding marvellous stones, and he always loved the things I made. It was good for both of us. I wanted to go back to that.'

Going back was one of life's impossibilities, I thought. Nothing was ever the same.

'Did Greville agree?' I asked.

'Yes. He said he had the diamonds with him but he had arrangements to make. He didn't say what. He said he would come here to the shop at the beginning of the week and I would give him his five stones and pay for the tear drops and stars. He wanted cash for them, and he was giving me a day or two to find the money.'

'He didn't usually want cash for things, did he? You sent a cheque for the spinel and rock crystal.'

'Yes, well . . .' Again the quick look of shame, 'He said cash in future, as he couldn't trust me. But you didn't know that.'

Greville certainly hadn't trusted him, and it sounded as if he'd said he had the diamonds with him when he knew they were at that moment on a boat crossing the North Sea. Had he said that, I wondered? Perhaps Prospero Jenks had misheard or misunderstood, but he'd definitely believed Greville had had the diamonds with him.

'If I give you those diamonds now, then that will be the end of it?' he said. 'I mean, as Grev had forgiven me, you won't go back on that and make a fuss, will you? Not the police . . . Grev wouldn't have wanted that, you know he wouldn't.'

I didn't answer. Greville would have to have balanced his betrayed old friendship against his respect for the law, and I supposed he wouldn't have had Prospero prosecuted, not for a first offence, admitted and regretted.

Prospero Jenks gave my silence a hopeful look, rose from his stool and crossed to the ranks of little drawers. He pulled one open, took out several apparently unimportant packets and felt deep inside with a searching hand. He brought out a twist of white gauze fastened with a band of sticky tape and held it out for me.

'Five diamonds,' he said. 'Yours.'

I took the unimpressive little parcel which most resembled the muslin bag of herbs cooks put in stews, and weighed it in my hand. I certainly couldn't myself tell CZ from C and he could see the doubt in my face.

'Have them appraised,' he said with unjustified bitterness, and I said we would weigh them right there and then and he would write out the weight and sign it.

'Grev didn't . . .'

'More fool he. He should have done. But he trusted you. I don't.'

'Come on, Derek.' He was cajoling; but I was not Greville.

'No. Weigh them,' I said.

With a sigh and an exaggerated shrug he cut open the little bag when I handed it back to him, and on small fine scales weighed the contents.

It was the first time I'd actually seen what I'd been searching for, and they were unimposing, to say the least. Five dull-looking greyish pieces of crystal the size of large misshapen peas without a hint of the fire waiting within. I watched the weighing carefully and took them myself off the scales, wrapping them in a fresh square of gauze which Prospero handed me and fastening them safely with sticky tape.

'Satisfied?' he said with a touch of sarcasm, watching me stow the bouquet garni in my trouser pocket.

'No. Not really.'

'They're the genuine article,' he protested. He signed the paper on which he'd written their combined weight, and gave it to me. 'I wouldn't make that mistake again.' He studied me. 'You're much harder than Grev.'

'I've reason to be.'

'What reason?'

'Several attempts at theft. Sundry assaults.'

His mouth opened.

'Who else?' I said.

'But I've never ... I didn't ...' He wanted me to believe him. He leaned forward with earnestness. 'I don't know what you're talking about.'

I sighed slightly. 'Greville hid the letters and invoices dealing with the diamonds because he distrusted someone in his office. Someone that he guessed was running to you with little snippets of information. Someone who would spy for you.'

'Nonsense.' His mouth seemed dry, however.

I pulled out of a pocket the microcassette recorder and laid it on his workbench.

'This is voice activated,' I said. 'Greville left it switched on one day when he went to lunch, and this is what he found on the tape when he returned.' I pressed the switch and the voice that was familiar to both of us spoke revealing forth:

'I'm in his office now and I can't find them. He hides everything, he's security mad, you know that. I can't ask. He'd never tell me, and I don't think he trusts me. Po-faced Annette doesn't sneeze unless he tells her to . . .'

Jason's voice, full of the cocky street-smart aggression that went with the orange spiky hair, clicked off eventually into silence. Prospero Jenks worked some saliva into his mouth and carefully made sure the recorder was not still alive and listening.

'Jason wasn't talking to me,' he said unconvincingly. 'He was talking to someone else.'

'Jason was the regular messenger between you and Greville,' I said. 'I sent him round here myself last week. Jason wouldn't take much seducing to bring you information along with the merchandise. But Greville found out. It compounded his sense of betrayal. So when you and he were talking in the Orwell at Ipswich, what was his opinion of Jason?'

He made a gesture of half-suppressed fury.

'I don't know how you know all this,' he said.

It had taken nine days and a lot of searching and a good deal of guessing at possibilities and probabilities, but the pattern was now a reliable path through at least part of the maze, and no other interpretation that I could think of explained the facts.

I said again, 'What did he say about Jason?'

Prospero Jenks capitulated. 'He said he'd have to leave Saxony Franklin. He said it was a condition of us ever doing business again. He said I was to tell Jason not to turn up for work on the Monday.'

'But you didn't do that,' I said.

'Well, no.'

'Because when Greville died, you decided to try to steal not only five stones but the lot.'

The blue eyes almost smiled. 'Seemed logical, didn't it?' he said. 'Grev wouldn't know. The insurance would pay. No one would lose.'

Except the underwriters, I thought. But I said, 'The diamonds weren't insured. Are not now insured. You were stealing them directly from Greville.'

He was almost astounded, but not quite.

'Greville told you that, didn't he?' I guessed.

Again the little-boy shame. 'Well, yes, he did.'

'In the Orwell?'

'Yes.'

'Pross,' I said, 'did you ever grow up?'

'You don't know what growing up is. Growing up is being ahead of the game.'

'Stealing without being found out?'

'Of course. Everyone does it. You have to make what you can.'

'But you have this marvellous talent,' I said.

'Sure. But I make things for money. I make what people like. I take their bread, whatever they'll pay. Sure, I get a buzz when what I've made is brilliant, but I

340

wouldn't starve in a garret for art's sake. Stones sing to me. I give them life. Gold is my paintbrush. All that, sure. But I'll laugh behind people's backs. They're gullible. The day I understood all customers are suckers is the day I grew up.'

I said, 'I'll bet you never said all that to Greville.'

'Do me a favour. Grev was a saint, near enough. The only truly good person through and through I've ever known. I wish I hadn't cheated him. I regret it something rotten.'

I listened to the sincerity in his voice and believed him, but his remorse had been barely skin deep, and nowhere had it altered his soul.

'Jason,' I said, 'knocked me down outside St Catherine's Hospital and stole the bag containing Greville's clothes.'

'No.' The Jenks' denial was automatic, but his eyes were full of shock.

I said, 'I thought at the time it was an ordinary mugging. The attacker was quick and strong. A friend who was with me said the mugger wore jeans and a woolly hat, but neither of us saw his face. I didn't bother to report it to the police because there was nothing of value in the bag.'

'So how can you say it was Jason?'

I answered his question obliquely.

'When I went to Greville's firm to tell them he was dead,' I said, 'I found his office had been ransacked. As you know. The next day I discovered that Greville had bought diamonds. I began looking for them, but there was no paperwork, no address book, no desk diary, no reference to or appointments with diamond dealers. I couldn't physically find the diamonds either. I spent three days searching in the vault, with Annette and June, her assistant, telling me that there never were any diamonds in the office, Greville was far too security-conscious. You yourself told me the diamonds were intended for you, which I didn't know until I came here. Everyone in the office knew I was looking for diamonds, and at that point Jason must have told you I was looking for them, which informed you that I didn't know where they were.'

He watched my face with his mouth slightly open, no longer denying, showing only the stunned disbelief of the profoundly found out.

'The office staff grew to know I was a jockey,' I said, 'and Jason behaved to me with an insolence I thought inappropriate, but I now think his arrogance was the result of his having had me face down on the ground under his foot. He couldn't crow about that, but his belief in his superiority was stamped all over him. I asked the office staff not to unsettle the customers by telling them that they were now trading with a jockey not a gemmologist, but I think it's certain that Jason told *you*.'

'What makes you think that?' He didn't say it hadn't happened.

'You couldn't get into Greville's house to search it,' I

said, 'because it's a fortress. You couldn't swing any sort of wrecking ball against the windows because the grilles inside made it pointless, and anyway they're wired on a direct alarm to the police station. The only way to get into that house is by key, and I had the keys. So you worked out how to get me there, and you set it up through the trainer I ride for, which is how I know you were aware I was a jockey. Apart from the staff, no one else who knew I was a jockey knew I was looking for diamonds, because I carefully didn't tell them. Come to the telephone in Greville's house for information about the diamonds, you said, and I obediently turned up, which was foolish.'

'But I never went to Greville's house . . .' he said.

'No, not you, Jason. Strong and fast in the motorcycle helmet which covered his orange hair, butting me over again just like old times. I saw him vault the gate on the way out. That couldn't have been you. He turned the house upside down but the police didn't think he'd found what he was looking for, and I'm sure he didn't.'

'Why not?' he asked, and then said, 'That's to say . . .'

'Did you mean Jason to kill me?' I asked flatly.

'No! Of course not!' The idea seemed genuinely to shock him.

'He could have done,' I said.

'I'm not a murderer!' His indignation, as far as I could tell, was true and without reservation, quite different from his reaction to my calling him a thief.

'What were you doing two days ago, on Sunday afternoon?' I said.

'What?' He was bewildered by the question but not alarmed.

'Sunday afternoon,' I said.

'What about Sunday afternoon? What are you talking about?'

I frowned. 'Never mind. Go back to Saturday night. To Jason giving me concussion with half a brick.'

The knowledge of that was plain to read. We were again on familiar territory.

'You can kill people,' I said, 'hitting them with bricks.'

'But he said . . .' He stopped dead.

'You might as well go on,' I said reasonably, 'we both know that what I've said is what happened.'

'Yes, but . . . what are you going to do about it?'

'I don't know yet.'

'I'll deny everything.'

'What did Jason say about the brick?'

He gave a hopeless little sigh. 'He said he knew how to knock people out for half an hour. He'd seen it done in street riots, he said, and he'd done it himself. He said it depended on where you hit.'

'You can't time it,' I objected.

'Well, that's what he said.'

He hadn't been so wrong, I supposed. I'd beaten his estimate by maybe ten minutes, not more.

'He said you'd be all right afterwards,' Pross said.

'He couldn't be sure of that.'

'But you are, aren't you?' There seemed to be a tinge of regret that I hadn't emerged punch drunk and unable to hold the present conversation. Callous and irresponsible, I thought, and unforgivable, really. Greville had forgiven treachery; and which was worse?

'Jason knew which office window to break,' I said, 'and he came down from the roof. The police found marks up there.' I paused. 'Did he do that alone, or were you with him?'

'Do you expect me to tell you?' he said incredulously.

'Yes, I do. Why not? You know what plea bargaining is, you just tried it with five diamonds.'

He gave me a shattered look and searched his common sense; not that he had much of it, when one considered.

Eventually, without shame, he said, 'We both went.'

'When?'

'That Sunday. Late afternoon. After he brought Grev's things back from Ipswich and they were a waste of time.'

'You found out which hospital Greville was in,' I said, 'and you sent Jason to steal his things because you believed they would include the diamonds which Greville had told you he had with him, is that right?'

He rather miserably nodded. 'Jason phoned me from the hospital on the Saturday and said Grev wasn't dead yet but that this brother had turned up, some frail old

345

creature on crutches, and it was good because he'd be an easy mark . . . which you were.'

'Yes.'

He looked at me and repeated, 'Frail old creature,' and faintly smiled, and I remembered his surprise at my physical appearance when I'd first come into this room. Jason, I supposed, had seen only my back view and mostly at a distance. I certainly hadn't noticed anyone lurking, but I probably wouldn't at the time have noticed half a ship's company standing at attention. Being with the dying, seeing the death, had made ordinary life seem unreal and unimportant, and it had taken me until hours after Jason's attack to lose that feeling altogether.

'All right,' I said, 'so Jason came back empty-handed. What then?'

He shrugged. 'I thought I'd probably got it wrong. Grev couldn't have meant that he had the diamonds with him.' He frowned. 'I thought that was what he said, though.'

I enlightened him. 'Greville was on his way to Harwich to meet a diamond cutter coming from Antwerp by ferry, who was bringing your diamonds with him. Twelve tear drops and eight stars.'

'Oh.' His face cleared momentarily with pleasure but gloom soon returned. 'Well, I thought it was worth looking in his office, though Jason said he never kept anything valuable there. But for diamonds . . . so many diamonds . . . it was worth a chance. Jason didn't take much persuading. He's a violent young bugger . . .'

I wondered fleetingly if that description mightn't be positively and scatologically accurate.

'So you went up to the roof in the service lift,' I said, 'and swung some sort of pendulum at the packing room window.'

He shook his head. 'Jason brought grappling irons and a rope ladder and climbed down that to the window, and broke the glass with a baseball bat. Then when he was inside I threw the hooks and the ladder down into the yard, and went down in the lift to the eighth floor, and Jason let me in through the staff door. But we couldn't get into the stock-rooms because of Grev's infernal electronic locks or into the showroom, same reason. And that vault . . . I wanted to try to beat it open with the bat but Jason said the door is six inches thick.' He shrugged. 'So we had to make do with papers . . . and we couldn't find anything about diamonds. Jason got angry . . . we made quite a mess.'

'Mm.'

'And it was all a waste of time. Jason said what we really needed was something called a Wizard, but we couldn't find that either. In the end, we simply left. I gave up. Grev had been too careful. I got resigned to not having the diamonds unless I paid for them. Then Jason said you were hunting high and low for them, and I got interested again. Very. You can't blame me.'

I could and did, but I didn't want to switch off the fountain.

'And then,' he said, 'like you guessed, I inveigled you into Grev's garden, and Jason had been waiting ages there getting furious you took so long. He let his anger out on the house, he said.'

'He made a mess there too, yes.'

'Then you woke up and set the alarms off and Jason said he was getting right nervous by then and he wasn't going to wait around for the handcuffs. So Grev had beaten us again . . . and he's beaten you too, hasn't he?' He looked at me shrewdly. 'You haven't found the diamonds either.'

I didn't answer him. I said, 'When did Jason break into Greville's car?'

'Well . . . when he finally found it in Greville's road. I'd looked for it at the hotel and round about in Ipswich, but Grev must have hired a car to drive there because his own car won't start.'

'When did you discover that?'

'Saturday. If the diamonds had been in it, we wouldn't have needed to search the house.'

'He wouldn't have left a fortune in the street,' I said.

Pross shook his head resignedly. 'You'd already looked there, I suppose.'

'I had.' I considered him. 'Why Ipswich?' I said.

'What?'

'Why the Orwell Hotel at Ipswich, particularly? Why did he want you to go there?'

348

'No idea,' he said blankly. 'He didn't say. He'd often ask me to meet him in odd places. It was usually because he'd found some heirloom or other and wanted to know if the stones would be of use to me. An ugly old tiara once, with a boring yellow diamond centrepiece filthy from neglect. I had the stone recut and set it as the crest of a rock crystal bird and hung it in a golden cage . . . it's in Florida, in the sun.'

I was shaken with the pity of it. So much soaring priceless imagination and such grubby, perfidious greed.

I said, 'Had he found you a stone in Ipswich?'

'No. He told me he'd asked me to come there because he didn't want us to be interrupted. Somewhere quiet, he said. I suppose it was because he was going to Harwich.'

I nodded. I supposed so also, though it wasn't on the most direct route which was further south, through Colchester. But Ipswich was where Greville had chosen, by freak mischance.

I thought of all Pross had told me, and was struck by one unexplored and dreadful possibility.

'When the scaffolding fell,' I said slowly, 'when you ran across the road and found Greville lethally injured . . . when he was lying there bleeding with the metal bar in him . . . did you steal his wallet?'

Pross's little-boy face crumpled and he put up his hands to cover it as if he would weep. I didn't believe in the tears and the remorse. I couldn't bear him any longer. I stood up to go.

349

'You thought he might have diamonds in his wallet,' I said bitterly. 'And then, even then, when he was dying, you were ready to rob him.'

He said nothing. He in no way denied it.

I felt such anger on Greville's behalf that I wanted suddenly to hurt and punish the man before me with a ferocity I wouldn't have expected in myself, and I stood there trembling with the self-knowledge and the essential restraint, and felt my throat close over any more words.

Without thinking, I put my left foot down to walk out and felt the pain as an irrelevance, but then after three steps used the crutches to make my way to his doorway and round the screen into the shop and through there out onto the pavement, and I wanted to yell and scream at the bloody injustice of Greville's death and the wickedness of the world and call down the rage of angels.

CHAPTER SEVENTEEN

I stood blindly on the pavement oblivious to the pas-
sers-by finding me an obstacle in their way. The swamp-
ing tidal wave of fury and desolation swelled and broke
and gradually ebbed, leaving me still shaking from its
force, a tornado in the spirit.

I loosened a jaw I hadn't realized was clamped tight
shut and went on feeling wretched.

A grandmotherly woman touched my arm and said,
'Do you need help?' and I shook my head at her kind-
ness because the help I needed wasn't anyone's to give.
One had to heal from the inside: to knit like bones.

'Are you all right?' she asked again, her eyes concerned.

'Yes.' I made an effort. 'Thank you.'

She looked at me uncertainly, but finally moved on,
and I took a few sketchy breaths and remembered with
bathos that I needed a telephone if I were ever to move
from that spot.

A hairdressing salon having (for a consideration) let
me use their instrument, Brad came within five minutes

to pick me up. I shoved the crutches into the back and climbed wearily in beside him, and he said, 'Where to?' giving me a repeat of the grandmotherly solicitude in his face if not his words.

'Uh,' I said. 'I don't know.'

'Home?'

'No . . .' I gave it a bit of thought. I had intended to go to Greville's house to change into my suit that was hanging in his wardrobe before meeting Clarissa at seven, and it still seemed perhaps the best thing to do, even if my energy for the project had evaporated.

Accordingly we made our way there, which wasn't far, and when Brad stopped outside the door, I said, 'I think I'll sleep here tonight. This house is as safe as anywhere. So you can go on to Hungerford now, if you like.'

He didn't look as if he liked, but all he said was, 'I come back tomorrow?'

'Yes, please,' I agreed.

'Pick you up. Take you to the office?'

'Yes, please.'

He nodded, seemingly reassured that I still needed him. He got out of the car with me and opened the gate, brought my overnight bag and came in with me to see, upstairs and down, that the house was safely empty of murderers and thieves. When he'd departed I checked that all the alarms were switched on and went up to Greville's room to change.

I borrowed another of his shirts and a navy silk tie,

and shaved with his electric razor which was among the things I'd picked up from the floor and had put on his white chest of drawers, and brushed my hair with his brushes for the same reason, and thought with an odd frisson that all of these things were mine now, that I was in his house, in his room, in his clothes . . . in his life.

I put on my own suit, because his anyway were too long, and came across the tube of the baster, still there in an inner breast pocket. Removing it, I left it among the jumble on the dressing chest and checked in the looking glass on the wall that Franklin, Mark II, wouldn't entirely disgrace Franklin, Mark I. He had looked in that mirror every day for three months, I supposed. Now his reflection was my reflection and the man that was both of us had dark marks of tiredness under the eyes and a taut thinness in the cheeks, and looked as if he could do with a week's lying in the sun. I gave him a rueful smile and phoned for a taxi, which took me to Luigi's with ten minutes to spare.

She was there before me all the same, sitting at a small table in the bar area to one side of the restaurant, with an emptyish glass looking like vodka on a prim mat in front of her. She stood up when I went in and offered me a cool cheek for a polite social greeting, inviting me with a gesture to sit down.

'What will you drink?' she asked formally, but battling, I thought, with an undercurrent of diffidence.

I said I would pay for our drinks and she said no, no, this was her suggestion. She called the waiter and said,

'Double water?' to me with a small smile and when I nodded ordered Perrier with ice and fresh lime-juice for both of us.

I was down by then to only two or three Distalgesics a day and would soon have stopped taking them, though the one I'd just swallowed in Greville's house was still an inhibitor for the evening. I wondered too late which would have made me feel better, a damper for the ankle or a large scotch everywhere else.

Clarissa was wearing a blue silk dress with a double-strand pearl necklace, pearl, sapphire and diamond earrings and a sapphire and diamond ring. I doubted if I would have noticed those, in the simple old jockey days. Her hair, smooth as always, curved in the expensive cut and her shoes and handbag were quiet black calf. She looked as she was, a polished, well-bred woman of forty or so, nearly beautiful, slender, with generous eyes.

'What have you been doing since Saturday?' she asked, making conversation.

'Peering into the jaws of death. What have you?'

'We went to . . .' She broke off. '*What* did you say?'

'Martha and Harley Ostermeyer and I were in a car crash on Sunday. They're OK, they went back to America today, I believe. And I, as you see, am here in one piece. Well . . . almost one piece.'

She was predictably horrified and wanted to hear all the details, and the telling at least helped to evaporate any awkwardness either of us had been feeling at the meeting.

'Simms was *shot*?'

'Yes.'

'But . . . do the police know who did it?'

I shook my head. 'Someone in a large grey Volvo, they think, and there are thousands of those.'

'Good heavens.' She paused. 'I didn't like to comment, but you look . . .' She hesitated, searching for the word.

'Frazzled?' I suggested.

'Smooth.' She smiled. 'Frazzled underneath.'

'It'll pass.'

The waiter came to ask if we would be having dinner and I said yes, and no argument, the dinner was mine. She accepted without fuss, and we read the menus.

The fare was chiefly Italian, the decor cosmopolitan, the ambience faintly European tamed by London. A lot of dark red, lamps with glass shades, no wallpaper music. A comfortable place, nothing dynamic. Few diners yet, as the hour was early.

It was not, I was interested to note, a habitual rendezvous place for Clarissa and Greville: none of the waiters treated her as a regular. I asked her about it and, startled, she said they had been there only two or three times, always for lunch.

'We never went to the same place often,' she said. 'It wouldn't have been wise.'

'No.'

She gave me a slightly embarrassed look. 'Do you disapprove of me and Greville?'

'No,' I said again. 'You gave him joy.'

'Oh.' She was comforted and pleased. She said with a certain shyness, 'It was the first time I'd fallen in love. I suppose you'll think that silly. But it was the first time for him, too, he said. It was ... truly *wonderful*. We were like ... as if twenty years younger ... I don't know if I can explain. Laughing. Lit up.'

'As far as I can see,' I said, 'the thunderbolt strikes at any age. You don't have to be teenagers.'

'Has it ... struck you?'

'Not since I was seventeen and fell like a ton of bricks for a trainer's daughter.'

'What happened?'

'Nothing much. We laughed a lot. Slept together, a bit clumsily at first. She married an old man of twenty-eight. I went to college.'

'I met Henry when I was eighteen. He fell in love with me ... pursued me ... I was flattered ... and he was so very good looking ... and kind.'

'He still is,' I said.

'He'd already inherited his title. My mother was ecstatic ... she said the age difference didn't matter ... so I married him.' She paused. 'We had a son and a daughter, both grown up now. It hasn't been a bad life, but before Greville, incomplete.'

'A better life than most,' I said, aiming to comfort.

'You're very like Greville,' she said unexpectedly. 'You look at things straight, in the same way. You've his sense of proportion.'

'We had realistic parents.'

'He didn't speak about them much, only that he became interested in gemstones because of the museums his mother took him to. But he lived in the present and he looked outward, not inward, and I loved him to distraction and in a way I didn't know him . . .' She stopped and swallowed and seemed determined not to let emotion intrude further.

'He was like that with me too,' I said. 'With everyone, I think. It didn't occur to him to give running commentaries on his actions and feelings. He found everything else more interesting.'

'I do miss him,' she said.

'What will you eat?' I asked.

She gave me a flick of a look and read the menu without seeing it for quite a long time. In the end she said with a sigh, 'You decide.'

'Did Greville?'

'Yes.'

'If I order fried zucchini as a starter, then fillet steak in pepper sauce with linguine tossed in olive oil with garlic, will that do?'

'I don't like garlic. I like everything else. Unusual. Nice.'

'OK. No garlic.'

We transferred to the dining room before seven-thirty and ate the proposed programme, and I asked if she were returning to York that night: if she had a train to catch, if that was why we were eating early.

'No, I'm down here for two nights. Tomorrow I'm going to an old friend's wedding, then back to York on Thursday morning.' She concentrated on twirling linguine onto her fork. 'When Henry and I come to London together we always stay at the Selfridge Hotel, and when I come alone I stay there also. They know us well there. When I'm there alone they don't present me with an account, they send it to Henry.' She ate the forkful of linguine. 'I tell him I go to the cinema and eat in snack bars . . . and he knows I'm always back in the hotel before midnight.'

There was a good long stretch of time between this dinner and midnight.

I said, 'Every five weeks or so, when you came down to London alone, Greville met you at King's Cross, isn't that right, and took you to lunch?'

She said in surprise, 'Did he tell you?'

'Not face to face. Did you ever see that gadget of his, the Wizard?'

'Yes, but . . .' She was horrified. 'He surely didn't put me in it?'

'Not by name, and only under a secret password. You're quite safe.'

She twiddled some more with the pasta, her eyes down, her thoughts somewhere else.

'After lunch,' she said, with pauses, 'if I had appointments, I'd keep them, or do some shopping . . . something to take home. I'd register at the hotel and change, and go to Greville's house. He used to have the flat, of course, but the house was much better. When he came, we'd have drinks . . . talk . . . maybe make love. We'd go to dinner early, then back to his house.' Her voice stopped. She still didn't look up.

I said, 'Do you want to go to his house now, before midnight?'

After a while, she said, 'I don't know.'

'Well . . . would you like coffee?'

She nodded, still not meeting my eyes, and pushed the linguine away. We sat in silence while waiters took away the plates and poured into cups, and if she couldn't make up her mind, nor could I.

In the end I said, 'If you like, come to Greville's house now. I'm sleeping there tonight, but that's not a factor. Come if you like, just to be near him, to be with him as much as you can for maybe the last time. Lie on his bed. Weep for him. I'll wait for you downstairs . . . and take you safely to your hotel before the fairy coach changes back to a pumpkin.'

'Oh!' She turned what had been going to be a sob into almost a laugh. 'Can I really?'

'Whenever you like.'

'Thank you, then. Yes.'

'I'd better warn you,' I said, 'it's not exactly tidy.' I told her what she would find, but she was inconsolable at the sight of the reality.

'He would have hated this,' she said. 'I'm so glad he didn't see it.'

We were in the small sitting room, and she went

round picking up the pink and brown stone bears, restoring them to their tray.

'I gave him these,' she said. 'He loved them. They're rhodonite, he said.'

'Take them to remember him by. And there's a gold watch you gave him, if you'd like that too.'

She paused with the last bear in her hand and said, 'You're very kind to me.'

'It's not difficult. And he'd have been furious with me if I weren't.'

'I'd love the bears. You'd better keep the watch, because of the engraving.'

'OK,' I said.

'I think,' she said with diffidence, 'I'll go upstairs now.'

I nodded.

'Come with me,' she said.

I looked at her. Her eyes were wide and troubled, but not committed, not hungry. Undecided. Like myself.

'All right,' I said.

'Is there chaos up there too?'

'I picked some of it up.'

She went up the stairs ahead of me at about four times my speed, and I heard her small moan of distress at the desecration of the bedroom. When I joined her, she was standing forlornly looking around, and with naturalness she turned to me and put her arms loosely round my waist, laying her head on my shoulder. I shed the confounded crutches and hugged her tight in grief for her and for Greville and we stood there for a long minute in mutual and much needed comfort.

She let her arms fall away and went over to sit on the bed, smoothing a hand over the black and white chequer-board counterpane.

'He was going to change this room,' she said. 'All this drama . . .' She waved a hand at the white furniture, the black carpet, one black wall . . . 'It came with the house. He wanted me to choose something softer, that I would like. But this is how I'll always remember it.'

She lay down flat, her head on the pillows, her legs toward the foot of the bed, ankles crossed. I half-hopped, half-limped across the room and sat on the edge beside her.

She watched me with big eyes. I put my hand flat on her stomach and felt the sharp internal contraction of muscles.

'Should we do this?' she said.

'I'm not Greville.'

'No . . . Would he mind?'

'I shouldn't think so.' I moved my hand, rubbing a little. 'Do you want to go on?'

'Do you?'

'Yes,' I said.

She sat up fast and put her arms round my neck in a sort of released compulsion.

'I do want this,' she said. 'I've wanted it all day. I've been pretending to myself, telling myself I shouldn't, but yes, I do want this passionately, and I know you're not Greville, I know it will be different, but this is the only way I can love him . . . and can you bear it, can you understand it, if it's him I love?'

I understood it well, and I minded not at all.

I said, smiling, 'Just don't *call* me Greville. It would be the turn-off of the century.'

She took her face away from the proximity of my ear and looked me in the eyes, and her lips too, after a moment, were smiling.

'Derek,' she said deliberately, 'make love to me. Please.'

'Don't beg,' I said.

I put my mouth on hers and took my brother's place.

As a memorial service it was quite a success. I lay in the dark laughing in my mind at that disgraceful pun, wondering whether or not to share it with Clarissa.

The catharsis was over, and her tears. She lay with her head on my chest, lightly asleep, contented, as far as I could tell, with the substitute loving. Women said men were not all the same in the dark, and I knew both where I'd surprised her and failed her, known what I'd done like Greville and not done like Greville from the instinctive releases and tensions of her reactions.

Greville, I now knew, had been a lucky man, though whether he had himself taught her how to give exquisite pleasure was something I couldn't quite ask. She knew, though, and she'd done it, and the feeling of her featherlight tattooing fingers on the base of my spine at the moment of climax had been a revelation. Knowledge marched on, I thought. Next time, with anyone else, I'd know what to suggest.

Clarissa stirred and I turned my wrist over, seeing the fluorescent hands of my watch.

'Wake up,' I said affectionately. 'It's Cinderella time.'

'Ohh . . .'

I stretched out a hand and turned on a bedside light. She smiled at me sleepily, no doubts remaining.

'That was all right,' she said.

'Mm. Very.'

'How's the ankle?'

'What ankle?'

She propped herself on one elbow, unashamed of nakedness, and laughed at me. She looked younger and sweeter, and I was seeing, I knew, what Greville had seen, what Greville had loved.

'Tomorrow,' she said, 'my friend's wedding will be over by six or so. Can I come here again?' She put her fingers lightly on my mouth to stop me answering at once. 'This time was for him,' she said. 'Tomorrow for us. Then I'll go home.'

'For ever?'

'Yes, I think so. What I had with Greville was unforgettable and unrepeatable. I decided on the train coming down here that whatever happened with you, or didn't happen, I would live with Henry, and do my best there.'

'I could easily love you,' I said.

'Yes, but don't.'

I knew she was right. I kissed her lightly.

'Tomorrow for us,' I agreed. 'Then goodbye.'

When I went into the office in the morning, Annette told me crossly that Jason hadn't turned up for work, nor had he telephoned to say he was ill.

Jason had been prudent, I thought. I'd have tossed him down the lift shaft, insolence, orange hair and all, given half an ounce of provocation.

'He won't be coming back,' I said, 'so we'll need a replacement.'

She was astonished. 'You can't sack him for not turning up. You can't sack him for anything without paying compensation.'

'Stop worrying,' I said, but she couldn't take that advice.

June came zooming into Greville's office waving a tabloid newspaper and looking at me with wide incredulous eyes.

'Did you know you're in the paper? Lucky to be alive, it says here. You didn't say anything about it!'

'Let's see,' I said, and she laid the *Daily Sensation* open on the black desk.

There was a picture of the smash in which one could more or less see my head inside the Daimler, but not recognizably. The headline read: 'Driver shot, jockey lives', and the piece underneath listed the lucky-to-be-alive passengers as Mr and Mrs Ostermeyer of Pittsburgh, America, and ex-champion steeplechase jockey Derek Franklin. The police were reported to be interested in a grey Volvo seen accelerating from the scene, and also to have recovered two bullets from the bodywork of the Daimler. After that titbit came a rehash of the Hungerford massacre and a query, 'Is this a copycat killing?' and finally a picture of Simms looking happy: 'Survived by wife and two daughters who were last night being comforted by relatives'.

Poor Simms. Poor family. Poor every shot victim in Hungerford.

'It happened on Sunday,' June exclaimed, 'and you came here on Monday and yesterday as if nothing was wrong. No wonder you looked knackered.'

'June!' Annette disapproved of the word.

'Well, he did. Still does.' She gave me a critical, kindly, motherly-sister inspection. 'He could have been killed, and then what would we all have done here?'

The dismay in Annette's face was a measure, I supposed, of the degree to which I had taken over. The place no longer felt like a quicksand to me either and I was beginning by necessity to get a feel of its pulse.

But there was racing at Cheltenham that day. I turned the pages of the newspaper and came to the runners and riders. That was where my name belonged, not on Saxony Franklin cheques. June looked over my shoulder and understood at least something of my sense of exile.

'When you go back to your own world,' she said, rephrasing her thought and asking it seriously, 'what will we do here?'

'We have a month,' I said. 'It'll take me that time to get fit.' I paused. 'I've been thinking about that problem, and, er, you might as well know, both of you, what I've decided.'

They both looked apprehensive, but I smiled to reassure them.

'What we'll do,' I said, 'is this. Annette will have a new title, which will be Office Manager. She'll run things generally and keep the keys.'

She didn't look displeased. She repeated 'Office Manager' as if trying it on for size.

I nodded. 'Then I'll start looking from now on for a business expert, someone to oversee the cash flow and do the accounts and try to keep us afloat. Because it's going to be a struggle, we can't avoid that.'

They both looked shocked and disbelieving. Cash flow seemed never to have been a problem before.

'Greville did buy diamonds,' I said regretfully, 'and so far we are only in possession of a quarter of them. I can't find out what happened to the rest. They cost the firm altogether one and a half million dollars, and we'll still owe the bank getting on for three-quarters of that sum when we've sold the quarter we have.'

Their mouths opened in unhappy unison.

'Unless and until the other diamonds turn up,' I said, 'we have to pay interest on the loan and persuade the bank that somehow or other we'll climb out of the hole. So we'll want someone we'll call the Finance Manager, and we'll pay him out of part of what used to be Greville's own salary.'

They began to understand the mechanics, and nodded.

'Then,' I said, 'we need a gemmologist who has a feeling for stones and understands what the customers like and need. There's no good hoping for another Greville, but we will create the post of Merchandise Manager, and that,' I looked at her, 'will be June.'

She blushed a fiery red. 'But I can't . . . I don't know enough.'

'You'll go on courses,' I said. 'You'll go to trade fairs. You'll travel. You'll do the buying.'

I watched her expand her horizons abruptly and saw the sparkle appear in her eyes.

'She's too young,' Annette objected.

'We'll see,' I said, and to June I added, 'You know what sells. You and the Finance Manager will work together to make us the best possible profit. You'll still work the computer, and teach Lily or Tina how to use it for when you're away.'

'Tina,' she said, 'she's quicker.'

'Tina, then.'

'What about you?' she asked.

'I'll be General Manager. I'll come when I can, at

least twice a week for a couple of hours. Everyone will tell me what's going on and we will all decide what is best to be done, though if there's a disagreement I'll have the casting vote. Right or wrong will be my responsibility, not yours.'

Annette, nevertheless troubled, said, 'Surely you yourself will need Mr Franklin's salary.'

I shook my head. 'I earn enough riding horses. Until we're solvent here, we need to save every penny.'

'It's an adventure!' June said, enraptured.

I thought it might be a very long haul and even in the end impossible, but I couldn't square it with the consciousness of Greville all around me not to try.

'Well,' I said, putting a hand in a pocket and bringing out a twist of gauze, 'we have here five uncut diamonds which cost about seventy-five thousand dollars altogether.'

They more or less gasped.

'How do we sell them?' I said.

After a pause, Annette said, 'Interest a diamantaire.'

'Do you know how to do that?'

After another moment's hesitation, she nodded.

'We can give provenance,' I said. 'Copies of the records of the original sale are on their way here from Guy Servi in Antwerp. They might be here tomorrow. Sight-box number and so on. We'll put these stones in the vault until the papers arrive, then you can get cracking.'

She nodded, but fearfully.

'Cheer up,' I said. 'It's clear from the ledgers that Saxony Franklin is normally a highly successful and profitable business. We'll have to cut costs where we can, that's all.'

'We could cut out Jason's salary,' Annette said unexpectedly. 'Half the time Tina's been carrying the heavy boxes, anyway, and I can do the hoovering myself.'

'Great,' I said with gratitude. 'If you feel like that, we'll succeed.'

The telephone rang and Annette answered it briefly.

'A messenger has left a packet for you down at the front desk,' she said.

'I'll go for it,' June said, and was out of the door on the words, returning in her usual short time with a brown padded jiffy bag, not very large, addressed simply to Derek Franklin in neat handwriting, which she laid before me with a flourish.

'Mind it's not a bomb,' she said facetiously as I picked it up, and I thought with an amount of horror that it was a possibility I hadn't thought of.

'I didn't mean it,' she said teasingly, seeing me hesitate. 'Do you want me to open it?'

'And get your hands blown off instead?'

'Of course it's not a bomb,' Annette said uneasily.

'Tell you what,' June said, 'I'll fetch the shears from the packing room.' She was gone for a few seconds. 'Alfie says,' she remarked, returning, 'we ought to put it in a bucket of water.'

She gave me the shears, which were oversized scissors that Alfie used for cutting cardboard, and for all her disbelief she and Annette backed away across the room while I sliced the end off the bag.

There was no explosion. Complete anti-climax. I shook out the contents which proved to be two objects and one envelope.

One of the objects was the microcassette recorder that I'd left on Prospero Jenks's workbench in my haste to be gone.

The other was a long black leather wallet almost the size of the Wizard, with gold initials G.S.F. in one corner and an ordinary brown rubber band holding it shut.

'That's Mr Franklin's,' Annette said blankly, and June, coming to inspect it, nodded.

I peeled off the rubber band and laid the wallet open on the desk. There was a business card lying loose inside it with Prospero Jenks's name and shops on the front, and on the reverse the single word, 'Sorry.'

'Where did he get Mr Franklin's wallet from?' Annette asked, puzzled, looking at the card.

'He found it,' I said.

'He took his time sending it back,' June said tartly.

'Mm.'

The wallet contained a Saxony Franklin chequebook, four credit cards, several business cards and a small pack of banknotes, which I guessed were fewer in number than when Greville set out.

The small excitement over, Annette and June went off to tell the others the present and future state of the nation, and I was alone when I opened the envelope.

CHAPTER EIGHTEEN

Pross had sent me a letter and a certified bank draft: instantly cashable money.

I blinked at the numbers on the cheque and reread them very carefully. Then I read the letter.

It said:

Derek,

This is a plea for a bargain, as you more or less said. The cheque is for the sum I agreed with Grev for the twelve tear drops and eight stars. I know you need the money, and I need those stones.

Jason won't be troubling you again. I'm giving him a job in one of my workrooms.

Grev wouldn't have forgiven the brick, though he might the wallet. For you it's the other way round. You're very like him. I wish he hadn't died.

Pross.

What a mess, I thought. I did need the money, yet if I accepted it I was implicitly agreeing not to take any action against him. The trouble about taking action against him was that however much I might want to I didn't know that I could. Apart from difficulties of evidence, I had more or less made a bargain that for information he would get inaction, but that had been before the wallet. It was perceptive of him, I thought, to see that it was betrayal and attacks on our *brother* that would anger both Greville and me most.

Would Greville want me to extend, if not forgiveness, then at least suspended revenge? Would Greville want me to confirm his forgiveness or to rise up in wrath and tear up the cheque . . .

In the midst of these sombre squirrelling thoughts the telephone rang and I answered it.

'Elliot Trelawney here,' the voice said.

'Oh, hello.'

He asked me how things were going and I said life was full of dilemmas. Ever so, he said with a chuckle.

'Give me some advice,' I said on impulse, 'as a magistrate.'

'If I can, certainly.'

'Well. Listen to a story, then say what you think.'

'Fire away.'

'Someone knocked me out with a brick . . .' Elliot made protesting noises on my behalf, but I went on, 'I know now who it was, but I didn't then, and I didn't see his face because he was masked. He wanted to steal a particular thing from me, but although he made a mess in the house searching, he didn't find it, and so didn't rob me of anything except consciousness. I guessed later who it was, and I challenged another man with having sent him to attack me. That man didn't deny it to me, but he said he would deny it to anyone else. So . . . what do I do?'

'Whew.' He pondered. 'What do you want to do?'

'I don't know. That's why I need the advice.'

'Did you report the attack to the police at the time?'

'Yes.'

'Have you suffered serious after-effects?'

'No.'

'Did you see a doctor?'

'No.'

He pondered some more. 'On a practical level you'd find it difficult to get a conviction, even if the prosecution service would bring charges of actual bodily harm. You couldn't swear to the identity of your assailant if you didn't see him at the time, and as for the other man, conspiracy to commit a crime is one of the most difficult charges to make stick. As you didn't consult a doctor, you're on tricky ground. So, hard as it may seem, my advice would be that the case wouldn't get to court.'

I sighed. 'Thank you,' I said.

'Sorry not to have been more positive.'

'It's all right. You confirmed what I rather feared.'

'Fine then,' he said. 'I rang to thank you for sending the Vaccaro notes. We held the committee meeting and turned down Vaccaro's application, and now we find we needn't have bothered because on Saturday night he was arrested and charged with attempting to import illegal substances. He's still in custody, and America is asking for him to be extradited to Florida where he faces murder charges and perhaps execution. And we nearly gave him a gambling licence! Funny old world.'

'Hilarious.'

'How about our drink in The Rook and Castle?' he suggested. 'Perhaps one evening next week?'

'OK.'

'Fine,' he said. 'I'll ring you.'

I put the phone down thinking that if Vaccaro had been arrested on Saturday evening and held in custody, it was unlikely he'd shot Simms from a moving car in Berkshire on Sunday afternoon. But then, I'd never really thought he had.

Copycat. Copycat, that's what it had been.

Pross hadn't shot Simms either. Had never tried to kill me. The Peter-Pan face upon which so many emotions could be read had shown a total blank when I'd asked him what he was doing on Sunday afternoon.

The shooting of Simms, I concluded, had been random violence like the other murders in Hungerford. Pointless and vicious; malignant, lunatic and impossible to explain.

I picked up the huge cheque and looked at it. It would solve all immediate problems: pay the interest already due, the cost of cutting the diamonds and more than a fifth of the capital debt. If I didn't take it, we would no doubt sell the diamonds later to someone else, but they had been cut especially for Prospero Jenks's fantasies and might not easily fit necklaces and rings.

A plea. A bargain. A chance that the remorse was at least half real. Or was he taking me again for a sucker?

I did some sums with a calculator and when Annette came in with the day's letters I showed her my figures and the cheque and asked her what she thought.

'That's the cost price,' I pointed. 'That's the cost of cutting and polishing. That's for delivery charges. That's for loan interest and VAT. If you add those together and subtract them from the figure on this cheque, is that the sort of profit margin Greville would have asked?'

Setting prices was something she well understood, and she repeated my steps on the calculator.

'Yes,' she said finally; 'it looks about right. Not over-generous, but Mr Franklin would have seen this as a service for commission, I think. Not like the rock crystal, which he bought on spec, which had to help pay for his journeys.' She looked at me anxiously. 'You understand the difference?'

'Yes,' I said. 'Prospero Jenks says this is what he and Greville agreed on.'

'Well then,' she said, relieved, 'he wouldn't cheat you.'

I smiled with irony at her faith. 'We'd better bank this cheque, I suppose,' I said, 'before it evaporates.'

'I'll do it at once,' she declared. 'With a loan as big as you said, every minute costs us money.'

She put on her coat and took an umbrella to go out

with, as the day had started off raining and showed no signs of relenting.

It had been raining the previous night when Clarissa had been ready to leave, and I'd had to ring three times for a taxi, a problem Cinderella didn't seem to have encountered. Midnight had come and gone when the wheels had finally arrived, and I'd suggested meanwhile that I lend her Brad and my car for going to her wedding.

I didn't need to, she said. When she and Henry were in London, they were driven about by a hired car firm. The car was already ordered to take her to the wedding which was in Surrey. The driver would wait for her and return her to the hotel, and she'd better stick to the plan, she said, because the bill for it would be sent to her husband.

'I always do what Henry expects,' she said, 'then there are no questions.'

'Suppose Brad picks you up from the Selfridge after you get back?' I said, packing the little stone bears and giving them to her in a carrier. 'The forecast is lousy and if it's raining you'll have a terrible job getting a taxi at that time of day.'

She liked the idea except for Brad's knowing her name. I assured her he never spoke unless he couldn't avoid it, but I told her I would ask Brad to park somewhere near the hotel. Then she could call the car phone's number when she was ready to leave, and Brad would beetle up at the right moment and not need to know her name or ask for her at the desk.

As that pleased her, I wrote down the phone number and the car's number plate so that she would recognize the right pumpkin, and described Brad to her; going bald, a bit morose, an open-necked shirt, a very good driver.

I couldn't tell Brad's own opinion of the arrangement. When I'd suggested it in the morning on the rainy way to the office, he had merely grunted which I'd taken as preliminary assent.

When he'd brought Clarissa, I thought as I looked through the letters Annette had given me, he could go on home, to Hungerford, and Clarissa and I might walk along to the restaurant at the end of Greville's street where he could have been known but I was not, and after an early dinner we would return to Greville's bed, this time for us, and we'd order the taxi in better time . . . perhaps.

I was awoken from this pleasant daydream by the ever-demanding telephone, this time with Nicholas Loder on the other end spluttering with rage.

'Milo says you had the confounded cheek,' he said, 'to have Dozen Roses dope-tested.'

'For barbiturates, yes. He seemed very sleepy. Our vet said he'd be happier to know the horse hadn't been tranquillized for the journey before he gave him an all-clear certificate.'

'I'd never give a horse tranquillizers,' he declared.

'No, none of us really thought so,' I said pacifyingly, 'but we decided to make sure.'

'It's shabby of you. Offensive. I expect an apology.'

'I apologize,' I said sincerely enough, and thought guiltily of the further checks going on at that moment.

'That's not good enough,' Nicholas Loder said huffily.

'I was selling the horse to good owners of Milo, people I ride for,' I said reasonably. 'We all know you disapproved. In the same circumstances, confronted by a sleepy horse, you'd have done the same, wouldn't you? You'd want to be sure what you were selling.'

Weigh the merchandise, I thought. Cubic zirconia, size for size, was one point seven times heavier than diamond. Greville had carried jewellers' scales in his car on his way to Harwich, presumably to check what the *Koningin Beatrix* was bringing.

'You've behaved disgustingly,' Nicholas Loder said. 'When did you see the horse last? And when next?'

'Monday evening, last. Don't know when next. As I told you, I'm tied up a bit with Greville's affairs.'

'Milo's secretary said I'd find you in Greville's office,' he grumbled. 'You're never at home. I've got a buyer for Gemstones, I think, though you don't deserve it. Where will you be this evening, if he makes a definite offer?'

'In Greville's house, perhaps.'

'Right, I have the number. And I want a written apology from you about those dope tests. I'm so angry I can hardly be civil to you.'

He hardly was, I thought, but I was pleased enough about Gemstones. The money would go into the firm's coffers and hold off bankruptcy a little while longer. I still held the Ostermeyers' cheque for Dozen Roses, waiting for Phil Urquhart's final clearance before cashing it. The horses would make up for a few of the missing diamonds. Looking at it optimistically, saying it quickly, the millstone had been reduced to near one million dollars.

June out of habit brought me a sandwich for lunch. She was walking with an extra bounce, with unashamed excitement. Way down the line, I thought, if we made it through the crisis, what then? Would I simply sell the whole of Saxony Franklin as I'd meant or keep it and borrow against it to finance a stable, as Greville had financed the diamonds? I wouldn't hide the stable! Perhaps I would know enough by then to manage both businesses on a sound basis: I'd learned a good deal in ten days. I had also, though I found it surprising, grown fond of Greville's firm. If we saved it, I wouldn't want to let it go.

If I went on riding until solvency dawned I might be the oldest jump jockey in history . . .

Again the telephone interrupted the daydreams, and I'd barely made a start on the letters.

It was a man with a long order for cabochons and beads. I hopped to the door and yelled for June to pick up the phone and to put the order on the computer, and Alfie came along to complain we were running out of heavy duty binding tape and to ask why we'd ever needed Jason. Tina did his work in half the time without the swear words.

Annette almost with gaiety hoovered everywhere, though I thought I would soon ask Tina to do it instead. Lily came with downcast eyes to ask meekly if she could have a title also. Stock-room Manager? she suggested.

'Done!' I said with sincere pleasure; and before the day was out we had a Shipment Manager (Alfie) and an Enabling Manager (Tina), and it seemed to me that such a spirit had been released there that the enterprise was now flying. Whether the euphoria would last or not was next week's problem.

I telephoned Maarten-Pagnier in Antwerp and discussed the transit of twelve tear drops, eight stars and five fakes.

'Our customer has paid us for the diamonds,' I said. 'I'd like to be able to tell him when we could get them to him.'

'Do you want them sent direct to him, monsieur?'

'No. Here to us. We'll pass them on.' I asked if he would insure them for the journey and send them by Euro-Securo; no need to trouble his partner again personally as we did not dispute that five of the stones sent to him had been cubic zirconia. The real stones had been returned to us, I said.

'I rejoice for you, monsieur. And shall we expect a further consignment for cutting? Monsieur Franklin intended it.'

'Not at the moment, I regret.'

'Very well, monsieur. At any time, we are at your service.'

After that I asked Annette if she could find Prospero Jenks to tell him his diamonds would be coming. She ran him to earth in one of his workrooms and appeared in my doorway saying he wanted to speak to me personally.

With inner reluctance I picked up the receiver. 'Hello, Pross,' I said.

'Truce, then?' he asked.

'We've banked the cheque. You'll get the diamonds.'

'When?'

'When they get here from Antwerp. Friday, maybe.'

'Thanks.' He sounded fervently pleased. Then he said with hesitation, 'You've got some light blue topaz, each fifteen carats or more, emerald cut, glittering like water . . . can I have it? Five or six big stones, Grev said. I'll take them all.'

'Give it time,' I said, and God, I thought, what unholy nerve.

'Yes, well, but you and I need each other,' he protested.

'Symbiosis?' I said.

'What? Yes.'

It had done Greville no harm in the trade, I'd gathered, to be known as the chief supplier of Prospero Jenks. His firm still needed the cachet as much as the cash. I'd taken the money once. Could I afford pride?

'If you try to steal from me one more time,' I said, 'I not only stop trading with you, I make sure everyone knows why. Everyone from Hatton Garden to Pelikanstraat.'

'Derek!' He sounded hurt, but the threat was a dire one.

'You can have the topaz,' I said. 'We have a new gemmologist who's not Greville, I grant you, but who knows what you buy. We'll still tell you what special stones we've imported. You can tell us what you need. We'll take it step by step.'

'I thought you wouldn't!' He sounded extremely relieved. 'I thought you'd never forgive me the wallet. Your face . . .'

'I don't forgive it. Or forget. But after wars, enemies trade.'

It always happened, I thought, though cynics might mock. Mutual benefit was the most powerful of bridge-builders, even if the heart remained bitter. 'We'll see how we go,' I said again.

'If you find the other diamonds,' he said hopefully, 'I still want them.' Like a little boy in trouble, I thought, trying to charm his way out.

Disconnecting, I ruefully smiled. I'd made the same inner compromise that Greville had, to do business with the treacherous child, but not to trust him. To supply the genius in him, and look to my back.

June came winging in and I asked her to go along to the vault to look at the light blue large-stone topaz which I well remembered. 'Get to know it while it's still here. I've sold it to Prospero Jenks.'

'But I don't go into the vault,' she said.

'You do now. You'll go in there every day from now on at spare moments to learn the look and feel of the faceted stones, like I have. Topaz is slippery, for instance. Learn the chemical formulas, learn the cuts and the weights, get to know them so that if you're offered unusual faceted stones anywhere in the world, you can check them against your knowledge for probability.'

Her mouth opened.

'You're going to buy the raw materials for Prospero Jenks's museum pieces,' I said. 'You've got to learn fast.'

Her eyes stretched wide as well, and she vanished.

With Annette I finished the letters.

At four o'clock I answered the telephone yet again, and found myself talking to Phil Urquhart, whose voice sounded strained.

'I've just phoned the lab for the results of Dozen Roses's tests.' He paused. 'I don't think I believe this.'

'What's the matter?' I asked.

'Do you know what a metabolite is?'

'Only vaguely.'

'What then?' he said.

'The result of metabolism, isn't it?'

'It is,' he said. 'It's what's left after some substance or other has broken down in the body.'

'So what?'

'So,' he said reasonably, 'if you find a particular metabolite in the urine, it means a particular substance was earlier present in the body. Is that clear?'

'Like viruses produce special antibodies, so the presence of the antibodies proves the existence of the viruses?'

'Exactly,' he said, apparently relieved I understood. 'Well, the lab found a metabolite in Dozen Roses's urine. A metabolite known as benzyl ecognine.'

'Go on,' I urged, as he paused. 'What is it the metabolite *of*?'

'Cocaine,' he said.

I sat in stunned disbelieving silence.

'Derek?' he said.

'Yes.'

'Racehorses aren't routinely tested for cocaine because it isn't a stimulant. Normally a racehorse could be full of cocaine and no one would know.'

'If it isn't a stimulant,' I said, loosening my tongue, 'why give it to them?'

'If you *believed* it was a stimulant, you might. Knowing it wouldn't be tested for.'

'How could you believe it?'

'It's one of the drugs that potentiates adrenalin. I particularly asked the lab to test for all drugs like that because of what you said about adrenalin yourself. What happens with a normal adrenalin surge is that after a while an enzyme comes along to disperse some of it while much gets stored for future use. Cocaine blocks the storage uptake, so the adrenalin goes roaring round the body for much longer. When the cocaine decays, its chief metabolic product is benzyl ecognine which is what the lab found in its gas chromatograph analyser this afternoon.'

'There were some cases in America...' I said vaguely.

'It's still not part of a regulation dope test even there.'

'But my God,' I said blankly, 'Nicholas Loder must have known.'

'Almost certainly, I should think. You'd have to administer the cocaine very soon before the race, because its effect is short lived. One hour, an hour and a half at most. It's difficult to tell, with a horse. There's no data. And although the metabolite would appear in the blood and the urine soon after that, the metabolite itself would be detectable for probably not much longer than forty-eight hours, but with a horse, that's still a guess. We took the sample from Dozen Roses on Monday evening about fifty-two hours after he'd raced. The lab said the metabolite was definitely present, but they could make no estimate of how much cocaine had been assimilated. They told me all this very carefully. They have much more experience with humans. They say in humans the rush from cocaine is fast, lasts about forty minutes and brings little post-exhilaration depression.'

'Nice,' I said.

'In horses,' he went on, 'they think it would probably induce skittishness at once.'

I thought back to Dozen Roses's behaviour both at York and on the TV tapes. He'd certainly woken up dramatically between saddling box and starting gate.

'But,' Phil added, 'they say that at the most it might give more stamina, but not more speed. It wouldn't make the horse go faster, but just make the adrenalin push last longer.'

That might be enough sometimes, I thought. Sometimes you could feel horses 'die' under you near the finish, not from lack of ability, but from lack of perseverance, of fight. Some horses were content to be second. In them, uninhibited adrenalin might perhaps tip the balance.

Caffeine, which had the same potentiating effect, was a prohibited substance in racing.

'Why don't they test for cocaine?' I asked.

'Heaven knows,' Phil said. 'Perhaps because enough to wind up a horse would cost the doper too much to be practicable. I mean ... more than one could be sure of winning back on a bet. But cocaine's getting cheaper, I'm told. There's more and more of it around.'

'I don't know much about drugs,' I said.

'Where have you been?'

'Not my scene.'

'Do you know what they'd call you in America?'

'What?'

'Straight,' he said.

'I thought that meant heterosexual.'

He laughed. 'That too. You're straight through and through.'

'Phil,' I said, 'what do I do?'

He sobered abruptly. 'God knows. My job ends with passing on the facts. The moral decisions are yours. All I can tell you is that some time before Monday evening Dozen Roses took cocaine into his bloodstream.'

'Via a baster?' I said.

After a short silence he said, 'We can't be sure of that.'

'We can't be sure he didn't.'

'Did I understand right, that Harley Ostermeyer picked up the tube of the baster and gave it to you?'

'That's right,' I said. 'I still have it, but like I told you, it's clean.'

'It might look clean,' he said slowly, 'but if cocaine was blown up it in powder form, there may be particles clinging.'

I thought back to before the race at York.

'When Martha Ostermeyer picked up the blue bulb end and gave it back to Rollway,' I said, 'she was brushing her fingers together afterwards . . . she seemed to be getting rid of dust from her gloves.'

'Oh glory,' Phil said.

I sighed and said, 'If I give the tube to you, can you get it tested without anyone knowing where it came from?'

'Sure. Like the urine, it'll be anonymous. I'll get the lab to do another rush job, if you want. It costs a bit more, though.'

'Get it done, Phil,' I said. 'I can't really decide anything unless I know for sure.'

'Right. Are you coming back here soon?'

'Greville's business takes so much time. I'll be back at the weekend, but I think I'll send the tube to you by carrier, to be quicker. You should get it tomorrow morning.'

'Right,' he said. 'We might get a result late tomorrow. Friday at the latest.'

'Good, and er . . . don't mention it to Milo.'

'No, but why not?'

'He told Nicholas Loder we tested Dozen Roses for tranquillizers and Nicholas Loder was on my phone hitting the roof.'

'Oh God.'

'I don't want him knowing about tests for cocaine. I mean, neither Milo nor Nicholas Loder.'

'You may be sure,' Phil said seriously, 'they won't learn it from me.'

It was the worst dilemma of all, I thought, replacing the receiver.

Was cocaine a stimulant or was it not? The racing authorities didn't think so: didn't test for it. If I believed it didn't effect speed then it was all right to sell Dozen Roses to the Ostermeyers. If I thought he wouldn't have got the race at York without help, then it wasn't all right.

Saxony Franklin needed the Ostermeyers' money.

The worst result would be that, if I banked the money and Dozen Roses never won again and Martha and Harley ever found out I knew the horse had been given cocaine, I could say goodbye to any future Gold Cups or Grand Nationals on Datepalm. They wouldn't forgive the unforgivable.

Dozen Roses had seemed to me to run gamely at York and to battle to the end. I was no longer sure. I wondered now if he'd won all his four races spaced out, as the orthopod would have described it; as high as a kite.

At the best, if I simply kept quiet, banked the money and rode Dozen Roses to a couple of respectable victories, no one would ever know. Or I could inform the Ostermeyers privately, which would upset them.

There would be precious little point in proving to the world that Dozen Roses had been given cocaine (and of course I could do it by calling for a further analysis of the urine sample taken by the officials at York) because if cocaine weren't a specifically banned substance, neither was it a normal nutrient. Nothing that was not a normal nutrient was supposed to be given to thoroughbreds racing in Britain.

If I disclosed the cocaine, would Dozen Roses be disqualified for his win at York? If he were, would Nicholas Loder lose his licence to train?

If I caused so much trouble, I would be finished in racing. Whistleblowers were regularly fired from their jobs.

My advice to myself seemed to be, take the money, keep quiet, hope for the best.

Coward, I thought. Maybe stupid as well.

My thoughts made me sweat.

CHAPTER NINETEEN

June, her hands full of pretty pink beads from the stock-
room, said, 'What do we do about more rhodocrosite?
We're running out and the suppliers in Hong Kong
aren't reliable any more. I was reading in a trade magazine that a man in Germany has some of good quality.
What do you think?'

'What would Greville have done?' I asked.

Annette said regretfully, 'He'd have gone to Germany to see. He'd never start buying from a new source
without knowing who he was trading with.'

I said to June, 'Make an appointment, say who we
are, and book an air ticket.'

They both simultaneously said, 'But . . .' and stopped.

I said mildly, 'You never know whether a horse is
going to be a winner until you race it. June's going down
to the starting gate.'

June blushed and went away. Annette shook her
head doubtfully.

'I wouldn't know rhodocrosite from granite,' I said.

'June does. She knows its price, knows what sells. I'll trust that knowledge until she proves me wrong.'

'She's too young to make decisions,' Annette objected.

'Decisions are easier when you're young.'

Isn't that the truth, I thought wryly, rehearsing my own words. At June's age I'd been full of certainties. At June's age, what would I have done about cocaine-positive urine tests? I didn't know. Impossible to go back.

I said I would be off for the day and would see them all in the morning. Dilemmas could be shelved, I thought. The evening was Clarissa's.

Brad, I saw, down in the yard, had been reading the *Racing Post* which had the same photograph as the *Daily Sensation*. He pointed to the picture when I eased in beside him, and I nodded.

'That's your head,' he said.

'Mm.'

'Bloody hell,' he said.

I smiled. 'It seems a long time ago.'

He drove to Greville's house and came in with me while I went upstairs and put the baster tube into an envelope and then into a jiffy bag brought from the office for the purpose and addressed it to Phil Urquhart.

To Brad, downstairs again, I said, 'The Euro-Securo couriers' main office is in Oxford Street not very far from the Selfridge Hotel. This is the actual address . . .' I gave it to him. 'Do you think you can find it?'

'Yerss.' He was again affronted.

'I phoned them from the office. They're expecting this. You don't need to pay, they're sending the bill. Just get a receipt. OK?'

'Yerss.'

'Then pick up my friend from the Selfridge Hotel and bring her here. She'll phone for you, so leave it switched on.'

'Yerss.'

'Then go home, if you like.'

He gave me a glowering look but all he said was, 'Same time tomorrow?'

'If you're not bored.'

He gave me a totally unexpected grin. Unnerving, almost, to see that gloom-ridden face break up.

'Best time o' my life,' he said, and departed, leaving me literally gasping.

In bemusement, I went along to the little sitting room and tidied up a bit more of the mess. If Brad enjoyed waiting for hours reading improbable magazines it was all right by me, but I no longer felt in imminent danger of assault or death, and I could drive my car myself if I cared to, and Brad's days as bodyguard/chauffeur were numbered. He must realize it, I thought: he'd clung on to the job several times.

By that Wednesday evening there was a rapid improvement also in the ankle. Bones, as I understood it, always grew new soft tissue at the site of a fracture, as if to stick the pieces together with glue. After eight or nine days, the soft tissue began to harden, the bone getting progressively stronger from then on, and it was in that phase that I'd by then arrived. I laid one of the crutches aside in the sitting room and used the other like a walking stick, and put my left toe down to the carpet for balance if not to bear my full weight.

Distalgesic, I decided, was a thing of the past. I'd drink wine for dinner with Clarissa.

The front door bell rang, which surprised me. It was too early to be Clarissa: Brad couldn't have done the errand and got to the Selfridge and back in the time he'd been gone.

I hopped along to the door and looked through the peep-hole and was astounded to see Nicholas Loder on the doorstep. Behind him, on the path, stood his friend Rollo Rollway, looking boredly around at the small garden.

In some dismay I opened the door and Nicholas Loder immediately said, 'Oh, good. You're in. We happened to be dining in London so as we'd time to spare I thought we'd come round on the off-chance to discuss Gemstones, rather than negotiate on the telephone.'

'But I haven't named a price,' I said.

'Never mind. We can discuss that. Can we come in?' I shifted backwards reluctantly.

'Well, yes,' I said, looking at my watch. 'But not for long. I have another appointment pretty soon.'

'So have we,' he assured me. He turned round and

waved a beckoning arm to his friend. 'Come on, Rollo, he has time to see us.'

Rollway, looking as if the enterprise were not to his liking, came up the steps and into the house. I turned to lead the way along the passage, ostentatiously not closing the front door behind them as a big hint to them not to stay long.

'The room's in a mess,' I warned them over my shoulder, 'we had a burglar.'

'We?' Nicholas Loder said.

'Greville and I.'

'Oh.'

He said, 'Oh' again when he saw the chrysanthemum pot wedged in the television, but Rollway blinked around in an uninterested fashion as if he saw houses in chaos every day of the week.

Rollway at close quarters wasn't any more attractive than Rollway at a distance: a dull dark lump of a man, thickset, middle-aged and humourless. One could only explain his friendship with the charismatic Loder, I thought, in terms of trainer-owner relationship.

'This is Thomas Rollway,' Nicholas Loder said to me, making belated introductions. 'One of my owners. He's very interested in buying Gemstones.'

Rollway didn't look very interested in anything.

'I'd offer you a drink,' I said, 'but the burglar broke all the bottles.'

Nicholas Loder looked vaguely at the chunks of glass

on the carpet. There had been no diamonds in the bottles. Waste of booze.

'Perhaps we could sit down,' he said.

'Sure.'

He sat in Greville's armchair and Rollway perched on the arm of the second armchair which effectively left me the one upright hard one. I sat on the edge of it, wanting them to hurry, laying the second crutch aside.

I looked at Loder, big, light-haired with brownish eyes, full of ability and not angry with me as he had been in the recent past. It was almost with guilt that I thought of the cocaine analyses going on behind his back when his manner towards me was more normal than at any time since Greville's death. If he'd been like that from the beginning, I'd have seen no reason to have had the tests done.

'Gemstones,' he said, 'what do you want for him?'

I'd seen in the Saxony Franklin ledgers what Gemstones had cost as a yearling, but that had little bearing on his worth two years later. He'd won one race. He was no bright star. I doubled his cost and asked for that.

Nicholas Loder laughed with irony. 'Come on, Derek. Half.'

'Half is what he cost Greville originally,' I said.

His eyes narrowed momentarily and then opened innocently. 'So we've been doing our homework!' He actually smiled. 'I've promised Rollo a reasonable horse at a reasonable price. We all know Gemstones is no world-beater, but there are more races in him. His cost price is perfectly fair. More than fair.'

I thought it quite likely was indeed fair, but Saxony Franklin needed every possible penny.

'Meet me halfway,' I said, 'and he's yours.'

Nicholas raised his eyebrows at his friend for a decision. 'Rollo?'

Rollo's attention seemed to be focused more on the crutch I'd earlier propped unused against a wall rather than on the matter in hand.

'Gemstones is worth that,' Nicholas Loder said to him judiciously, and I thought in amusement that he would get me as much as he could in order to earn himself a larger commission. Trade with the enemy, I thought: build mutual-benefit bridges.

'I don't want Gemstones at any price,' Rollo said, and they were the first words he'd uttered since arriving. His voice was harsh and curiously flat, without inflection. Without emotion, I thought.

· Nicholas Loder protested, 'But that's why you wanted to come here! It was your idea to come here.'

Thomas Rollway, as if absentmindedly, stood and picked up the abandoned crutch, turning it upside down and holding it by the end normally near the floor. Then, as if the thought had at that second occurred to him, he bent his knees and swung the crutch round forcefully in a scything movement a bare four inches above the carpet.

It was so totally unexpected that I wasn't quick

enough to avoid it. The elbow-rest and cuff crashed into my left ankle and Rollway came after it like a bull, kicking, punching, overbalancing me, knocking me down.

I was flabbergasted more than frightened, and then furious. It seemed senseless, without reason, unprovoked, out of any sane proportion. Over Rollway's shoulder I glimpsed Nicholas Loder looking dumbfounded, his mouth and eyes stretched open, uncomprehending.

As I struggled to get up, Thomas Rollway reached inside his jacket and produced a handgun; twelve inches of it at least, with the thickened shape of a silencer on the business end.

'Keep still,' he said to me, pointing the barrel at my chest.

A gun . . . Simms . . . I began dimly to understand and to despair pretty deeply.

Nicholas Loder was shoving himself out of his armchair. 'What are you doing?' His voice was high with alarm, with rising panic.

'Sit down, Nick,' his friend said. 'Don't get up.' And such was the grindingly heavy tone of his unemotional voice that Nicholas Loder subsided, looking overthrown, not believing what was happening.

'But you came to buy his horse,' he said weakly.

'I came to kill him.'

Rollway said it dispassionately, as if it were nothing. But then, he'd tried to before.

Loder's consternation became as deep as my own.

Rollway moved his gun and pointed it at my ankle. I immediately shifted it, trying desperately to get up, and he brought the spitting end back fast into alignment with my heart.

'Keep still,' he said again. His eyes coldly considered me as I half-sat, half-lay on the floor, propped on my elbow and without any weapon within reach, not even the one crutch I'd been using. Then, with as little warning as for his first attack, he stamped hard on my ankle and for good measure ground away with his heel as if putting out a cigarette butt. After that he left his shoe where it was, pressing down on it with his considerable weight.

I swore at him and couldn't move, and thought idiotically, feeling things give way inside there, that it would take me a lot longer now to get fit, and that took my mind momentarily off a bullet that I would feel a lot less, anyway.

'But *why*?' Nicholas Loder asked, wailing. 'Why are you doing this?'

Good question.

Rollway answered it.

'The only successful murders,' he said, 'are those for which there appears to be no motive.'

It sounded like something he'd learned on a course. Something surrealistic. Monstrous.

Nicholas Loder, sitting rigidly to my right in Greville's chair, said with an uneasy attempt at a laugh,

'You're kidding, Rollo, aren't you? This is some sort of joke?'

Rollo was not kidding. Rollo, standing determinedly on my ankle between me and the door, said to me, 'You picked up a piece of my property at York races. When I found it was missing I went back to look for it. An official told me you'd put it in your pocket. I want it back.'

I said nothing.

Damn the official, I thought. So helpful. So deadly. I hadn't even noticed one watching.

Nicholas Loder, bewildered, said, 'What piece of property?'

'The tube part of the nebulizer,' Rollway told him.

'But that woman, Mrs Ostermeyer, gave it back to you.'

'Only the bulb. I didn't notice the tube had dropped as well. Not until after the race. After the Stewards' enquiry.'

'But what does it matter?'

Rollway pointed his gun unwaveringly at where it would do me fatal damage and answered the question without taking his gaze from my face.

'You yourself, Nick,' he informed him, 'told me you were worried about Franklin, he was observant and too bright.'

'But that was because I gelded Dozen Roses.'

'So when I found he had the nebulizer, I asked one or two other people their opinion of Derek Franklin as a person, not a jockey, and they all said the same. Brainy. Intelligent. Bright.' He paused. 'I don't like that.'

I was thinking that through the door, down the passage and in the street there was sanity and Wednesday and rain and rush hour all going on as usual. Saturn was just as accessible.

'I don't believe in waiting for trouble,' Rollway said. 'And dead men can't make accusations.' He stared at me. 'Where's the tube?'

I didn't answer for various reasons. If he took murder so easily in his stride and I told him I'd sent the tube to Phil Urquhart I could be sentencing Phil to death too, and besides, if I opened my mouth for any reason, what might come out wasn't words at all but something between a yell and a groan, a noise I could hear loudly in my head but which wasn't important either, or not as important as getting out of the sickening prospect of the next few minutes.

'But he would never have suspected . . .' Loder feebly said.

'Of course he did. Anyone would. Why do you think he's had that bodyguard glued to him? Why do you think he's been dodging about so I can't find him and not going home? And he had the horse's urine taken in Lambourn for testing, and there's the official sample too at York. I tell you, I'm not waiting for him to make trouble. I'm not going to gaol, I'll tell you.'

'But you wouldn't.'

'Be your age, Nick,' Rollway said caustically, 'I import the stuff. I take the risks. And I get rid of trouble as soon as I see it. If you wait too long, trouble can destroy you.'

Nicholas Loder said in wailing protest, 'I told you it wasn't necessary to give it to horses. It doesn't make them go faster.'

'Rubbish. You can't tell, because it isn't much done. No one can afford it except people like me. I'm swamped with the stuff at the moment, it's coming in bulk from the Medellin cartel in Madrid . . . *Where's the tube?*' he finished, bouncing his weight up and down.

If not telling him would keep me alive a bit longer, I wasn't going to try telling him I'd thrown it away.

'You can't just shoot him,' Nicholas Loder said despairingly. 'Not with me watching.'

'You're no danger to me, Nick,' Rollway said flatly. 'Where would you go for your little habit? One squeak from you would mean your own ruin. I'd see you went down for possession. For conniving with me to drug horses. They'd take your licence away for that. Nicholas Loder, trainer of Classic winners, down in the gutter.' He paused. 'You'll keep quiet, we both know it.'

The threats were none the lighter for being uttered in a measured unexcited monotone. He made my hair bristle. Heaven knew what effect he had on Loder.

He wouldn't wait much longer, I thought, for me to tell him where the tube was: and maybe the tube would in the end indeed be his downfall because Phil knew

whose it was, and that the Ostermeyers had been witnesses, and if I were found shot perhaps he would light
a long fuse ... but it wasn't of much comfort at that
moment.

With the strength of desperation I rolled my body
and with my right foot kicked hard at Rollway's leg. He
grunted and took his weight off my ankle and I pulled
away from him, shuffling backwards, trying to reach the
chair I'd been sitting on to use it as a weapon against
him, or at least not to lie there supinely waiting to be
slaughtered, and I saw him recover his rocked balance
and begin to straighten his arm, aiming and looking
along the barrel so as not to miss.

That unmistakable stance was going to be the last
thing I would see: and the last emotion I would feel
would be the blazing fury of dying for so pointless a
cause.

Nicholas Loder, also seeing that it was the moment
of irretrievable crisis, sprang with horror from the armchair and shouted urgently, 'No, no, Rollo. No, don't do
it!'

It might have been the droning of a gnat for all the
notice Rollo paid him.

Nicholas Loder took a few paces forward and grabbed at Rollway and at his aiming arm.

I took the last opportunity to get my hands on
something ... anything ... got my fingers on a crutch.

'I won't let you,' Nicholas Loder frantically persisted.
'You mustn't!'

Rollo shook him off and swung his gun back to me.

'No.' Loder was terribly disturbed. Shocked. Almost frenzied. 'It's wrong. I won't let you.' He put his body against Rollway's, trying to push him away.

Rollway shrugged him off, all bull-muscle and undeterrable. Then, very fast, he pointed the gun straight at Nicholas Loder's chest and without pausing pulled the trigger. Pulled it twice.

I heard the rapid phut, phut. Saw Nicholas Loder fall, saw the blankness on his face, the absolute astonishment.

There was no time to waste on terror, though I felt it. I gripped the crutch I'd reached and swung the heavier end of it at Rollway's right hand, and landed a blow fierce enough to make him drop the gun.

It fell out of my reach.

I stretched for it and rolled and scrambled but he was upright and much faster, and he bent down and took it into his hand again with a tight look of fury as hot as my own.

He began to lift his arm again in my direction and again I whipped at him with the crutch and again hit him. He didn't drop the gun that time but transferred it to his left hand and shook out the fingers of his right hand as if they hurt, which I hoped to God they did.

I slashed at his legs. Another hit. He retreated a couple of paces and with his left hand began to take aim. I slashed at him. The gun barrel wavered. When he pulled the trigger, the flame spat out and the bullet missed me.

He was still between me and the door.

Ankle or not, I thought, once I was on my feet I'd smash him down and out of the way and run, run . . . run into the street . . .

I had to get up. Got as far as my knees. Stood up on my right foot. Put down the left. It wasn't a matter of pain. I didn't feel it. It just buckled. It needed the crutch's help . . . and I needed the crutch to fight against his gun, to hop and shuffle forward and hack at him, to put off the inevitable moment, to fight until I was dead.

A figure appeared abruptly in the doorway, seen peripherally in my vision.

Clarissa.

I'd forgotten she was coming.

'Run,' I shouted agonizedly. 'Run. Get away.'

It startled Rollway. I'd made so little noise. He seemed to think the instructions were for himself. He sneered. I kept my eyes on his gun and lunged at it, making his aim swing wide again at a crucial second. He pulled the trigger. Flame. Phut. The bullet zipped over my shoulder and hit the wall.

'Run,' I yelled again with fearful urgency. 'Quick. Oh, be quick.'

Why didn't she run? He'd see her if he turned.

He would kill her.

Clarissa didn't run. She brought her hand out of her raincoat pocket holding a thing like a black cigar and she swung her arm in a powerful arc like an avenging fury. Out of the black tube sprang the fearsome telescopic silvery springs with a knob on the end, and the kiyoga smashed against the side of Rollway's skull.

He fell without a sound. Fell forward, cannoning into me, knocking me backwards. I ended on the floor, sitting, his inert form stomach-down over my shins.

Clarissa came down on her knees beside me, trembling violently, very close to passing out. I was breathless, shattered, trembling like her. It seemed ages before either of us was able to speak. When she could, it was a whisper, low and distressed.

'Derek . . .'

'Thanks,' I said jerkily, 'for saving my life.'

'Is he dead?' She was looking with fear at Rollway's head, strain in her eyes, in her neck, in her voice.

'I don't care if he is,' I said truthfully.

'But I . . . I hit him.'

'I'll say I did it. Don't worry. I'll say I hit him with the crutch.'

She said waveringly, 'You can't.'

'Of course I can. I meant to, if I could.'

I glanced over at Nicholas Loder, and Clarissa seemed to see him for the first time. He was on his back, unmoving.

'Dear God,' she said faintly, her face even paler. 'Who's that?'

I introduced her posthumously to Nicholas Loder, racehorse trainer, and then to Thomas Rollway, drug baron. They'd squirted cocaine into Dozen Roses, I said, struggling for lightness. I'd found them out. Rollway wanted me dead rather than giving evidence against him. He'd said so.

Neither of the men contested the charges, though Rollway at least was alive, I thought. I could feel his breathing on my legs. A pity, on the whole. I told Clarissa which made her feel a shade happier.

Clarissa still held the kiyoga. I touched her hand, brushing my fingers over hers, grateful beyond expression for her courage. Greville had given her the kiyoga. He couldn't have known it would keep me alive. I took it gently out of her grasp and let it lie on the carpet.

'Phone my car,' I said. 'If Brad hasn't gone too far, he'll come back.'

'But . . .'

'He'll take you safely back to the Selfridge. Phone quickly.'

'I can't just . . . leave you.'

'How would you explain being here, to the police?'

She looked at me in dismay and obstinacy. 'I can't . . .'

'You must,' I said. 'What do you think Greville would want?'

'Oh . . .' It was a long sigh of grief, both for my brother and, I thought, for the evening together that she and I were not now going to have.

'Do you remember the number?' I said.

'Derek . . .'

'Go and do it, my dear love.'

She got blindly to her feet and went over to the telephone. I told her the number, which she'd forgotten. When the impersonal voice of the radio-phone operator said as usual after six or seven rings that there was no reply, I asked her to dial the number again, and yet again. With luck, Brad would reckon three calls spelled emergency.

'When we got here,' Clarissa said, sounding stronger, 'Brad told me there was a grey Volvo parked not far from your gate. He was worried, I think. He asked me to tell you. Is it important?'

God in heaven . . .

'Will that phone stretch over here?' I said. 'See if it will. Push the table over. Pull the phone over here. If I ring the police from here, and they find me here, they'll take the scene for granted.'

She tipped the table on its side, letting the answering machine fall to the floor, and pulled the phone to the end of its cord. I still couldn't quite reach it, and edged round a little in order to do so, and it hurt, which she saw.

'Derek!'

'Never mind.' I smiled at her, twistedly, making a joke of it. 'It's better than death.'

'I can't leave you.' Her eyes were still strained and she was still visibly trembling, but her composure was on the way back.

'You damned well can,' I said. 'You have to. Go out to the gate. If Brad comes, get him to toot the horn, then I'll know you're away and I'll phone the police. If he doesn't come ... give him five minutes, then walk ... walk and get a taxi ... Promise?'

I picked up the kiyoga and fumbled with it, trying to concertina it shut. She took it out of my hands, twisted it, banged the knob on the carpet and expertly returned it closed to her pocket.

'I'll think of you, and thank you,' I said, 'every day that I live.'

'At four-twenty,' she said as if automatically, and then paused and looked at me searchingly. 'It was the time I met Greville.'

'Four-twenty,' I said, and nodded. 'Every day.'

She knelt down again beside me and kissed me, but it wasn't passion. More like farewell.

'Go on,' I said. 'Time to go.'

She rose reluctantly and went to the doorway, pausing there and looking back. Lady Knightwood, I thought, a valiant deliverer with not a hair out of place.

'Phone me,' I said, 'one day soon?'

'Yes.'

She went quietly down the passage but wasn't gone long. Brad himself came bursting into the room with Clarissa behind him like a shadow.

Brad almost skidded to a halt, the prospect before him enough to shock even the garrulous to silence.

'Strewth,' he said economically.

'As you say,' I replied.

Rollway had dropped his gun when he fell but it still lay not far from his left hand. I asked Brad to move it further away in case the drug man woke up.

'Don't touch it,' I said sharply as he automatically reached out a hand, bending down. 'Your prints would be an embarrassment.'

He made a small grunt of acknowledgement and Clarissa wordlessly held out a tissue with which Brad gingerly took hold of the silencer and slid the gun across the room to the window.

'What if he does wake up?' he said, pointing to Rollway.

'I give him another clout with the crutch.'

He nodded as if that were normal behaviour.

'Thanks for coming back,' I said.

'Didn't go far. You've got a Volvo . . .'

I nodded.

'Is it the one?'

'Sure to be,' I said.

'Strewth.'

'Take my friend back to the Selfridge,' I said. 'Forget she was here. Forget you were here. Go home.'

'Can't leave you,' he said. 'I'll come back.'

'The police will be here.'

As ever, the thought of policemen made him uneasy. 'Go on home,' I said. 'The dangers are over.'

He considered it. Then he said hopefully, 'Same time tomorrow?'

I moved my head in amused assent and said wryly, 'Why not?'

He seemed satisfied in a profound way, and he and Clarissa went over to the doorway, pausing there and looking back, as she had before. I gave them a brief wave, and they waved back before going. They were both, incredibly, smiling.

'Brad!' I yelled after him.

He came back fast, full of instant alarm.

'Everything's fine,' I said. 'Just fine. But don't shut the front door behind you. I don't want to have to get up to let the police in. I don't want them smashing the locks. I want them to walk in here nice and easy.'

CHAPTER TWENTY

It was a long dreary evening, but not without humour.

I sat quietly apart most of the time in Greville's chair, largely ignored while relays of people came and efficiently measured, photographed, took fingerprints and dug bullets out of the walls.

There had been a barrage of preliminary questions in my direction which had ended with Rollway groaning his way back to consciousness. Although the police didn't like advice from a civilian, they did, at my mild suggestion, handcuff him before he was fully awake, which was just as well, as the bullish violence was the first part of his personality to surface. He was on his feet, threshing about, mumbling, before he knew where he was.

While a policeman on each side of him held his arms, he stared at me, his eyes slowly focusing. I was still at that time on the floor, thankful to have his weight off me. He looked as if he couldn't believe what was happening, and in the same flat uninflected voice as before, called me a bastard, among other things not as innocuous.

'I knew you were trouble,' he said. He was still too groggy to keep a rein on his tongue. 'You won't live to give evidence, I'll see to that.'

The police phlegmatically arrested him formally, told him his rights and said he would get medical attention at the police station. I watched him stumble away, thinking of the irony of the decision I'd made earlier not to accuse him of anything at all, much less, as now, of shooting people. I hadn't known he'd shot Simms. I hadn't feared him at all. It didn't seem to have occurred to him that I might not act against him on the matter of cocaine. He'd been ready to kill to prevent it. Yet I hadn't suspected him even of being a large-scale dealer until he'd boasted of it.

While the investigating activity went on around me, I wondered if it were because drug runners cared so little for the lives of others that they came so easily to murder.

Like Vaccaro, I thought, gunning down his renegade pilots from a moving car. Perhaps that was an habitual mode of clean-up among drug kings. Copycat murder, everyone had thought about Simms, and everyone had been right.

People like Rollway and Vaccaro held other people's lives cheap because they aimed anyway at destroying them. They made addiction and corruption their business, wilfully intended to profit from the collapse and unhappiness of countless lives, deliberately enticed young people onto a one-way misery trail. I'd read that people could snort cocaine for two or three years before the physical damage hit. The drug growers, shippers, wholesalers knew that. It gave them time for steady selling. Their greed had filthy feet.

The underlying immorality, the aggressive callousness had themselves to be corrupting; addictive. Rollway had self destructed, like his victims.

I wondered how people grew to be like him. I might condemn them, but I didn't understand them. They weren't happy-go-lucky dishonest, like Pross. They were uncaring and cold. As Eliot Trelawney had said, the logic of criminals tended to be weird. If I ever added to Greville's notebook, I thought, it would be something like 'The ways of the crooked are mysterious to the straight', or even 'What makes the crooked crooked and the straight straight?' One couldn't trust the sociologists' easy answers.

I remembered an old story I'd heard sometime. A scorpion asked a horse for a ride across a raging torrent. Why not? said the horse, and obligingly started to swim with the scorpion on his back. Halfway across, the scorpion stung the horse. The horse, fatally poisoned, said, 'We will both drown now. Why did you do that?' And the scorpion said, 'Because it's my nature.'

Nicholas Loder wasn't going to worry or wonder about anything any more; and his morality, under stress, had risen up unblemished and caused his death. Injustice and irony everywhere, I thought, and felt regret for the man who couldn't acquiesce in my murder.

He had taken cocaine himself, that much was clear. He'd become perhaps dependent on Rollway, had perhaps been more or less blackmailed by him into allowing his horses to be tampered with. He'd been frightened I would find him out: but in the end he hadn't been evil, and Rollway had seen it, had seen he couldn't trust him to keep his mouth shut after all.

Through Loder, Rollway had known where to find me on Sunday afternoon, and through him he'd known where to find me this Wednesday evening. Yet Nicholas Loder hadn't knowingly set me up. He'd been used by his supposed friend; and I hadn't seen any danger in reporting on Sunday morning that I'd be lunching with Milo and the Ostermeyers or saying I would be in Greville's house ready for Gemstones bids.

I hadn't specifically been keeping myself safe from Rollway, whatever he might believe, but from an unidentified enemy, someone *there* and dangerous, but unrecognized.

Irony everywhere . . .

I thought about Martha and Harley and the cocaine in Dozen Roses. I would ask them to keep the horse and race him, and I'd promise that if he never did any good I would give them their money back and send him to auction. What the Jockey Club and the racing press would have to say about the whole mess boggled the mind. We might still lose the York race: would have to, I guessed.

I thought of Clarissa in the Selfridge Hotel struggling to behave normally with a mind filled with visions of violence. I hoped she would ring up her Henry, reach back to solid ground, mourn Greville peacefully, be glad she'd saved his brother. I would leave the Wizard's alarm set to four-twenty pm, and remember them both when I heard it: and one could say it was sentimental, that their whole affair had been packed with sentimental behaviour, but who cared, they'd enjoyed it, and I would endorse it.

At some point in the evening's proceedings, a highly senior plain-clothes policeman arrived whom everyone else deferred to and called sir.

He introduced himself as Superintendent Ingold and invited a detailed statement from me, which a minion wrote down. The superintendent was short, piercing, businesslike, and considered what I said with pauses before his next question, as if internally computing my answers. He was also, usefully, a man who liked racing: who sorrowed over Nicholas Loder and knew of my existence.

I told him pretty plainly most of what had happened, omitting only a few things: the precise way Rollway had asked for his tube, and Clarissa's presence, and the dire desperation of the minutes before she'd arrived. I made that hopeless fight a lot shorter, a lot easier, a rapid knock-out.

'The crutches?' he enquired. 'What are they for?'

'A spot of trouble with an ankle at Cheltenham.'

'When was that?'

'Nearly two weeks ago.'

He merely nodded. The crutch handles were quite heavy enough for clobbering villains, and he sought no other explanation.

It all took a fair while, with the pauses and the writing. I told him about the car crash near Hungerford. I said I thought it possible that it had been Rollway who shot Simms. I said that of course they would compare the bullets the Hungerford police had taken from the Daimler with those just now dug out of Greville's walls, and those no doubt to be retrieved from Nicholas Loder's silent form. I wondered innocently what sort of car Rollway drove. The Hungerford police, I told the superintendent, were looking for a grey Volvo.

After a pause a policeman was despatched to search the street. He came back wide-eyed with his news and was told to put a cordon round the car and keep the public off.

It was by then well past dark. Every time the police or officials came into the house, the mechanical dog started barking and the lights repeatedly blazed on. I thought it amusing which says something for my light-headed state of mind but it wore the police nerves to irritation.

'The switches are beside the front door,' I said to one of them eventually. 'Why don't you flip them all up?'

They did, and got peace.

'Who threw the flower-pot into the television?' the superintendent wanted to know.

'Burglars. Last Saturday. Two of your men came round.'

'Are you ill?' he said abruptly.

'No. Shaken.'

He nodded. Anyone would be, I thought.

One of the policemen mentioned Rollway's threat that I wouldn't live to give evidence. To be taken seriously, perhaps.

Ingold looked at me speculatively. 'Does it worry you?'

'I'll try to be careful.'

He smiled faintly. 'Like on a horse?' The smile disappeared. 'You could do worse than hire someone to mind your back for a while.'

I nodded my thanks. Brad, I thought dryly, would be ecstatic.

They took poor Nicholas Loder away. I would emphasize his bravery, I thought, and save what could be saved of his reputation. He had given me, after all, a chance of life.

Eventually the police wanted to seal the sitting room, although the superintendent said it was a precaution only: the events of the evening seemed crystal clear.

He handed me the crutches and asked where I would be going.

'Upstairs to bed,' I said.

'Here?' He was surprised. 'In this house?'

'This house,' I said, 'is a fortress. Until one lowers the drawbridge, that is.'

They sealed the sitting room, let themselves out, and left me alone in the newly quiet hallway.

I sat on the stairs and felt awful. Cold. Shivery. Old and grey. What I needed was a hot drink to get warm from inside, and there was no way I was going down to the kitchen. Hot water from the bathroom tap upstairs would do fine, I thought.

As happened in many sorts of battle, it wasn't the moment of injury that was worst, but the time a couple of hours later when the body's immediate natural anaesthetic properties subsided and let pain take over: nature's marvellous system for allowing a wild animal to flee to safety before hiding to lick its wounds with healing saliva. The human animal was no different. One needed the time to escape, and one needed the pain afterwards to say something was wrong.

At the moment of maximum adrenalin, fight-or-flight, I'd believed I could run on that ankle. It had been mechanics that had defeated me, not instinct, not willingness. Two hours later, the idea of even standing on it was impossible. Movement alone became breathtaking. I'd sat in Greville's chair for another two long hours after that, concentrating on policemen, blanking out feeling.

With them gone, there was no more pretending. However much I might protest in my mind, however much rage I might feel, I knew the damage to bones and ligaments was about as bad as before. Rollway had cracked them apart again. Back to square one . . . and the Hennessy only four and a half weeks away . . . and I was bloody well going to ride Datepalm in it, and I wasn't going to tell anyone about tonight's little stamping-ground, no one knew except Rollway and he wouldn't boast about that.

If I stayed away from Lambourn for two weeks, Milo wouldn't find out; not that he would himself care all that much. If he didn't know, though, he couldn't mention it to anyone else. No one expected me to be racing again for another four weeks. If I simply stayed in London for two of those and ran Greville's business, no one would comment. Then once I could walk I'd go down to Lambourn and ride every day . . . get physiotherapy, borrow the Electrovet . . . it could be done . . . piece of cake.

Meanwhile there were the stairs.

Up in Greville's bathroom, in a zipped bag with my washing things, I would find the envelope the orthopaedic surgeon had given me, which I'd tucked into a waterproof pocket and travelled around with ever since. In the envelope, three small white tablets not as big as aspirins, more or less with my initials on: DF 1-1-8s. Only as a last resort, the orthopod had said.

Wednesday evening, I reckoned, qualified.

I went up the stairs slowly, backwards, sitting down,

hooking the crutches up with me. If I dropped them, I thought, they would slither down to the bottom again. I wouldn't drop them.

It was pretty fair hell. I reminded myself astringently that people had been known to crawl down mountains with much worse broken bones: they wouldn't have made a fuss over one little flight upwards. Anyway, there had to be an end to everything, and eventually I sat on the top step, with the crutches beside me, and thought that the DF 1–1–8s weren't going to fly along magically to my tongue. I had still got to get them.

I shut my eyes and put both hands round my ankle on top of the bandage. I could feel the heat and it was swelling again already, and there was a pulse hammering somewhere.

Damn it, I thought. God bloody damn it. I was used to this sort of pain, but it never made it any better. I hoped Rollway's head was banging like crazy.

I made it to the bathroom, ran the hot water, opened the door of the capacious medicine cabinet, pulled out and unzipped my bag.

One tablet, no pain, I thought. Two tablets, spaced out. Three tablets, unconscious.

Three tablets had definite attractions but I feared I might wake in the morning needing them again and wishing I'd been wiser. I swallowed one with a glassful of hot water and waited for miracles.

The miracle that actually happened was extraordinary but had nothing to do with the pills.

I stared at my grey face in the looking glass over the basin. Improvement, I thought after a while, was a long time coming. Perhaps the damned things didn't work.

Be patient.

Take another . . .

No. Be patient.

I looked vaguely at the objects in the medicine cupboard. Talc. Deodorant. Shaving cream. Shaving cream. Most of one can of shaving cream had been squirted all over the mirror by Jason. A pale blue and grey can: 'Unscented,' it said.

Greville had an electric razor as well, I thought inconsequentially. It was on the dressing chest. I'd borrowed it that morning. Quicker than a wet shave, though not so long lasting.

The damn pill wasn't working.

I looked at the second one longingly.

Wait a bit.

Think about something else.

I picked up the second can of shaving cream which was scarlet and orange and said: 'Regular Fragrance'. I shook the can and took off the cover and tried to squirt foam onto the mirror.

Nothing happened. I shook it. Tried again. Nothing at all.

Guile and misdirection, I thought. Hollow books and green stone boxes with keyholes but no keys. Safes in concrete, secret drawers in desks . . . Take nothing at face value. Greville's mind was a maze ... *and he wouldn't have used scented shaving cream.*

I twisted the shaving cream can this way and that and the bottom ring moved and began to turn in my hand. I caught my breath. Didn't really believe it. I went on turning ... unscrewing.

It would be another empty hiding place, I told myself. Get a grip on hope. I unscrewed the whole bottom off the can, and from a nest of cottonwool a chamois leather pouch fell out into my hand.

Well, all right, I thought, but it wouldn't be diamonds.

With the help of the crutches I took the pouch into the bedroom and sat on Greville's bed, and poured onto the counterpane a little stream of dullish-looking pea-sized lumps of carbon.

I almost stopped breathing. Time stood still. I couldn't believe it. Not after everything ...

With shaking fingers I counted them, setting them in small clumps of five.

Ten ... fifteen ... twenty ... twenty-five.

Twenty-five meant I'd got fifty per cent. Half of what Greville had bought. With half, Saxony Franklin would be safe. I offered heartbursting thanks to the fates. I came dangerously near to crying.

Then, with a sense of revelation, I knew where the rest were. Where they had to be. Greville really had taken them with him to Ipswich, as he'd told Pross. I guessed he'd taken them thinking he might give them to the Maarten-Pagnier partner to take back to Antwerp for cutting.

I'd searched through the things in his car and had found nothing, and I'd held his diamonds in my hand and not known it.

They were . . . they had to be . . . in that other scarlet and orange can, in the apparent can of shaving cream in his overnight bag, safe as Fort Knox under the stairs of Brad's mum's house in Hungerford. She'd taken all Greville's things in off the street out of my car to keep them safe in a dodgy neighbourhood. In memory, I could hear Brad's pride in her.

'Smart, our Mum . . .'

The DF 1–1–8 was at last taking the edge off the worst.

I rolled the twenty-five precious pebbles around under my fingers with indescribable joy and thought how relieved Greville would have been. Sleep easy, pal, I told him, uncontrollably smiling. I've finally found them.

He'd left me his business, his desk, his gadgets, his enemies, his horses, his mistress. Left me Saxony Franklin, the Wizard, the shaving cream cans, Prospero Jenks and Nicholas Loder, Dozen Roses, Clarissa.

I'd inherited his life and laid him to rest; and at that moment, though I might hurt and I might throb, I didn't think I had ever been happier.

TRIAL RUN

Thanks
to
Andrew and Andrew

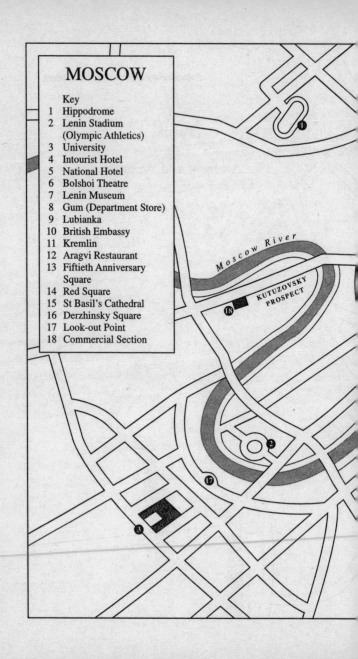

MOSCOW

Key
1 Hippodrome
2 Lenin Stadium
   (Olympic Athletics)
3 University
4 Intourist Hotel
5 National Hotel
6 Bolshoi Theatre
7 Lenin Museum
8 Gum (Department Store)
9 Lubianka
10 British Embassy
11 Kremlin
12 Aragvi Restaurant
13 Fiftieth Anniversary
    Square
14 Red Square
15 St Basil's Cathedral
16 Derzhinsky Square
17 Look-out Point
18 Commercial Section

Moscow River

KUTUZOVSKY
PROSPECT

CHAPTER ONE

I could think of three good reasons for not going to Moscow, one of which was twenty-six, blonde, and upstairs unpacking her suitcase.

'I can't speak Russian,' I said.

'Of course not.'

My visitor took a genteel sip of pink gin, sighing slightly over my obtuseness. His voice was condescending.

'No one would expect you to speak Russian.'

He had come by appointment, introduced on the telephone by the friend of a friend. He said his name was Rupert Hughes-Beckett; that it was a matter of some ... ah ... delicacy. That he would be glad of my help, if I could spare him half an hour.

The word 'mandarin' had drifted into my mind when I opened the front door to his ring, and every gesture, every intonation since then had deepened the impression. A man of about fifty, tall and spare, with uncreased clothes and quiet shoes. An aura of unflappable civilized composure. A cultivated voice speaking

1

without much lip movement, as if a muscular tightening round the mouth area could in itself prevent the issue of incautious words. There was control, too, in every movement of his hands and even in the way he used his eyes, rationing their forays into small courteous glances at my background between longer disciplined concentrations on my face, the backs of his own hands, or the glass holding his drink.

I had met many men of his type, and liked many, too, but to Rupert Hughes-Beckett I felt an antipathy I couldn't pin down. Its effect, however, was all too plain: I wished to say no to his proposals.

'It would not take a great deal of your time,' he said patiently. 'A week ... two weeks, we calculate, at a maximum.'

I mustered a careful politeness to match his own. 'Why don't you go yourself?' I said. 'You would have better access than I.'

The faintest hint of impatience twitched in his eyes. 'It is thought better to send someone who is intimate with ... ah ... horses.'

Ribald replies got no further than a laugh in the mind. Rupert Hughes-Beckett would not have been amused. I perceived, also, from the disapproving way he said 'horses', that he was as unenthusiastic about his present errand as I was. It did nothing to warm me towards him, but at least it explained why I instinctively disliked him. He had done his well-trained best, but hadn't in that one word been able to disguise his

inner feeling of superciliousness: and I had met that
stance far too often to mistake it.

'No cavaliers in the Foreign Office?' I said flippantly.

'I beg your pardon?'

'Why me?' I said: and heard in the question all the
despair of the unwillingly chosen. Why *me*? I don't
want it. Take it away. Pick someone else. Leave me
alone.

'I gather it was felt you should be approached
because you have . . . ah . . . *status*,' he said, and smiled
faintly as if deprecating such an extravagant statement.
'And, of course,' he added, 'the time.'

A right kick in the guts, I thought; and kept my face
flat and still. Then I took off my glasses and squinted
at them against the light, as if trying to see if they were
clean, and then put them back on again. It was a
delaying tactic I had used all my life, most often uncon-
sciously, to give myself a space for thought: a habit
that had started when I was about six and a school-
master asked me in an arithmetic lesson what I had
done with the multiplicand.

I had pulled off my owl-like silver rims and stared at
his suddenly fuzzy outline while I thought wild panicky
thoughts. What on earth was a multiplicand?

'I haven't seen it, sir. It wasn't me, sir.'

His sardonic laugh had stayed with me down the
years. I had exchanged the silver rims for gold, and
then for plastic, and finally for tortoiseshell, but I still
took them off when I couldn't answer.

3

'I've got a cough,' I said. 'And it is November.'

The frivolousness of this excuse was measured by a deepening silence and a gradual reverential bowing of the Hughes-Beckett head over the crystal tumbler.

'I'm afraid that the answer is no,' I said.

He raised his head and gave me a calm civil inspection. 'There will be some disappointment,' he said. 'I might almost go as far as to say . . . ah . . . dismay.'

'Flatter someone else,' I said.

'It was felt that *you* . . .' He left the words unfinished, hanging in the air.

'Who felt?' I asked. 'Who, exactly, felt?'

He shook his head gently, put down the emptied glass, and rose to his feet.

'I will convey your reply.'

'And regrets,' I said.

'Very well, Mr Drew.'

'I wouldn't have been successful,' I said. 'I'm not an investigator. I'm a farmer.'

He gave me a sort of sideways down-the-nose look where a less inhibited man would have said, 'Come off it.'

I walked with him into the hall, helped him on with his coat, opened the front door, and watched him walk bareheaded through the icy dark to his waiting chauffeur-driven Daimler. He gave me, by way of farewell, merely a five-second full-frontal view of his bland expression through the window. Then the big car crunched away on the gravel towards the gate, and I coughed in the cold air and went back inside.

Emma was walking down the oval sweep of Regency staircase in her Friday evening come-for-the-weekend clothes: jeans, cotton check shirt, baggy sweater and cowboy boots. I wondered fleetingly whether, if the house stood for as long again, the girls of the twenty-second century would look as incongruous against those gracefully curving walls.

'Fish fingers and the telly, then?' she said.

'More or less.'

'You've got bronchitis again.'

'It isn't catching.'

She reached the bottom of the stairs and made without pause towards the kitchen. It always took a while with her for the brittle stresses of the week to drop away, and I was used to the jerky arrivals and the spiky brush-offs of the first few hours. I no longer tried to greet her with warmth. She wouldn't be kissed much before ten, nor loved before midnight, and she wouldn't relax until Saturday tea-time. Sunday we would slop around in easy contentment, and at six on Monday morning she would be gone.

Lady Emma Louders-Allen-Croft, daughter, sister and aunt of dukes, was 'into', as she would say, 'the working-girl ethos'. She was employed full-time, no favours, in a bustling London department store, where, despite her search for social abasement, she had recently been promoted to bed-linen buyer on the

5

second floor. Emma, blessed with organizational skills above the average, was troubled about her rise, a screw-up one could trace back directly to her own schooling, where she, in an expensive boarding-school for highborn young ladies, had been taught in fierily left-wing sociology lessons that brains were elitist and that manual work was the noble path to heaven.

Her search for immolation, which had led to exhausting years of serving at tables in cafés as well as behind the counters in shops, seemed to be as strong as ever. She would in no way have starved without employment, but might quite likely have gone to drink or pot.

I believed, and she knew I did, that someone with her abilities and restless drive should have taken a proper training, or at least gone to university, and contributed more than a pair of hands; but I had learned not to talk about it, as it was one of the many no-man's-lands which led to shrieks and sulks.

'Why the hell do you bother with that mixed-up kook?' my step-brother frequently asked. Because, as I never told him, a shot of undiluted life-force every couple of weekends was better for the heart than his monotonous daily jogging.

Emma was looking into the refrigerator, the light shining out of it on to her fine-boned face and thick platinum hair. Her eyebrows were so pale as to be invisible without pencil, and her lashes the same without mascara. Sometimes she made up her eyes like sunbursts; sometimes, like that evening, she let nature take its course. It depended on the tide of ideas.

'Haven't you any yoghurt?' she demanded.

I sighed. A flood of health foods was not my favourite. 'Nor wheatgerm either,' I said.

'Kelp,' she said firmly.

'What?'

'Seaweed. Compressed into tablets. Very good for you.'

'I'm sure.'

'Apple cider vinegar. Honey. Organically grown vegetables.'

'Are we off avocados and hearts of palm?'

She pulled out a chunk of Dutch cheese and scowled at it. 'They're imported. We should limit imports. We need a siege economy.'

'No more caviar?'

'Caviar is immoral.'

'Would it be immoral if it was plentiful and cheap?'

'Stop arguing. What did your visitor want? Are these crème caramels for supper?'

'Yes, they are,' I said. 'He wanted me to go to Moscow.'

She straightened up and glared at me. 'That's not very funny.'

'A month ago you said crème caramels were food for angels.'

'Don't be stupid.'

'He said he wanted me to go to Moscow on an

errand, not to embrace the Marxist–Leninist philosophy.'

She slowly shut the refrigerator door.

'What sort of errand?'

'He wanted me to look for somebody. But I'm not going.'

'Who?'

'He didn't say.' I turned away from her. 'Come and have a drink in the sitting room. There's a fire in there.'

She followed me back through the hall and folded herself into a large armchair with a glass of white wine.

'How are the pigs, geese, and mangold-wurzels?'

'Coming along nicely,' I said.

I had no pigs, geese, or, indeed, mangold-wurzels. I had a lot of beef cattle, three square miles of Warwickshire, and all the modern problems of the food producer. I had grown used to measuring yield in tonnes per hectare but was still unconvinced by government policies which paid me sometimes *not* to grow certain crops, and threatened to prosecute me if I did.

'And the horses?' Emma said.

'Ah well . . .'

I stretched out lazily in my chair and watched the light from the table lamp fall on her silvery head, and decided it was really high time I stopped wincing over the thought that I would be riding in no more races.

'I suppose I'll sell the horses,' I said.

'There's still hunting.'

'It's not the same. And these are not hunters. They're racehorses. They should be on a track.'

'You've trained them all these years ... why don't you just get someone else to ride them?'

'I only trained them because I was riding them. I don't want to do it for anyone else.'

She frowned. 'I can't imagine you without horses.'

'Well,' I said, 'nor can I.'

'It's a bloody shame.'

'I thought you subscribed to the "we know what's best for you and you'll damn well put up with it" school of thought.'

'People have to be protected from themselves,' she said.

'Why?'

She stared. 'Of course they do.'

'Safety precautions are a growth industry,' I said with some bitterness. 'Masses of restrictive legislation to stop people taking everyday risks ... and accidents go right on happening, and we have terrorists besides.'

'You're still in a right tizz, aren't you?'

'Yes.'

'I thought you'd got over it.'

'The first fury may have worn off,' I said. 'The resentment will last for ever.'

I had been lucky in my racing, lucky in my horses, and steeplechasing had taken me, as it had so many others, to soul-filling heights and depths of passion and fear and triumphant exaltation. Left to myself I would in that autumn have been busily racing at every opportunity and fixing my sights as usual on the big amateur events in the spring; for, while I hadn't the world's toughest physique when it came to chest infections, to which I was as maddeningly prone as cars to rust, I was still, at thirty-two, as muscularly strong as I would ever be. But someone, somewhere, had recently dreamed up the nannying concept that people should no longer be allowed to ride in jump races *wearing glasses*.

Of course, a lot of people thought it daft for anyone to race in glasses anyway, and I dare say they were right: but although I'd broken a few frames and suffered a few superficial cuts from them, I'd never damaged my actual eyes. And they were *my eyes*, Goddammit.

There were restrictions now on contact lenses, though not a total ban: but although I had tried and persevered to the point of perpetual inflammation, my eyes and contacts remained incompatible. So if I couldn't wear contacts, I could no longer race. So goodbye to twelve years' fun. Goodbye to endeavour, to speed, to mind-blowing exhilaration. Too bad, too bad about your misery, it's all for your own good.

The weekend drifted along on its normal course. A drive round the farm on Saturday morning, visit to the local Stratford-upon-Avon races in the afternoon, dinner with friends in the evening. Sunday morning, getting up late, we sprawled in the sitting room with logs on the fire, newspapers around like snow, and the prospect of toasted ham sandwiches for lunch. Two satisfactory nights had been passed, with another, one hoped, ahead. Emma was at her softest, and we were as near to a married state as we were ever likely to get.

Into this domestic calm drove Hughes-Beckett in his Daimler. The wheels crunched on the gravel: I stood up to see who had arrived, and Emma also. We watched the chauffeur and a man sitting beside him get out of the car and open the two rear doors. From one stepped Hughes-Beckett, looking apprehensively up the façade of the house, and from the other . . .

Emma's eyes widened. 'My God . . . isn't that . . . ?'

'Yes, it is.'

She swept a wild look round the cosy untidy room. 'You can't bring them in here.'

'No. The drawing room.'

'But . . . did you know they were coming?'

'Of course not.'

'Good heavens.'

We watched the two visitors stroll the few steps towards the front door. Talk about not taking no for an answer, I thought. This was wheeling up the big guns with a vengeance.

'Well, go on,' said Emma, 'see what they want.'

'I know what they want. You sit here by the fire

11

and do the crossword while I think of ways of telling them they can't have it.'

I went to the front door and opened it.

'Randall,' said the Prince, holding out his hand to be shaken. 'Well, at least you're at home. Can we come in?'

'Of course, sir.'

Hughes-Beckett followed him over the threshold with an expression compounded of humiliation and triumph: he might not have been able to persuade me himself, but he was going to take joy in seeing me capitulate to someone else.

I led them into the blue-and-gold formal drawing room where at least the radiators were functioning even if there was no welcoming fire.

'Now, Randall,' said the Prince. 'Please go to Moscow.'

'Can I offer your Royal Highness a drink?' I said.

'No, you can't. Now, Randall, sit down and listen, and stop beating about the bush.'

The cousin of the monarch parked his backside firmly on a silk-covered Regency sofa and waved Hughes-Beckett and me towards adjoining chairs. He was of my generation, though a year or two older, and we had met countless times over the years because of our common pleasure in horses. His taste had taken him more to hounds and to polo than racing, although we had galloped alongside in several point-to-points. He was strong-minded and direct, and could be bracing

12

to the point of bossiness, but I had also seen his tears over the broken-necked body of his favourite hunter.

We had met from time to time on indoor social occasions, but we were not close private personal friends, and before that day he had not been to my house, nor I to his.

'My wife's brother,' he said. 'Johnny Farringford. You know him, don't you?'

'We've met,' I said. 'I don't really know him.'

'He wants to ride in the next Olympics. In Moscow.'

'Yes, sir. So Mr Hughes-Beckett said.'

'In the Three-Day Event.'

'Yes.'

'Well, Randall, there's this problem... what you might call, a *question mark*... We can't let him go to Russia unless it's cleared up. We simply can't... or at least, I simply *won't*... have him going there if the whole thing is going to blow up in our faces. I am not, positively not, going to let him go if there is any chance of an... *incident*... which would be in a way embarrassing to... er... other members of my family. Or to the British nation as a whole.' He cleared his throat. 'Now I know Johnny is not in line to the throne or anything like that, but he is after all an earl and my brother-in-law, and as far as the Press of the world is concerned, that's fair game.'

'But, sir,' I said, protesting mildly, 'the Olympics are still some way off. I know Lord Farringford is good,

13

but he might not be selected, and then there would be no problem at all.'

The Prince shook his head. 'If the problem isn't dealt with, however good Johnny is, even if he's the best we've got, he will not be selected.'

I looked at him speculatively. 'You would prevent it?'

'Yes, I should.' His voice was positive. 'It would no doubt cause a great deal of friction in my own home, as both Johnny and my wife have set their hearts on his getting a place in the team. He has a real chance, too, I admit. He won several Events during the summer and he's been working hard at improving his dressage to international standards. I don't want to stand in his way ... In fact, that's why I'm here, asking you to be a good chap and find out what, if anything, there is to make it risky for him to go to Russia.'

'Sir,' I said, 'why me? Why not the diplomats?'

'They've passed the buck. They think, and I must say I agree, that a private individual is the best bet. If there is ... anything ... we don't want it in official records.'

I said nothing, but my disinclination must have been obvious.

'Look,' the Prince said, 'we've known each other a long time. You've twice the brains I have, and I trust you. I'm damned sorry about your eyesight, and all that, but you've got a lot of empty time to fill now, and if your agent can run your estate like clockwork while you chunter round Cheltenham and Aintree, he can do it while you go to Moscow.'

I said, 'I suppose you didn't get the no-glasses rule passed just so that I'd have time to go on your errand?'

He listened to the bitterness in my voice, and chuckled in his throat. 'Most likely it was all the other amateurs, who wanted you out of their daylight.'

'A couple have already sworn it wasn't.'

'Will you go, then?' he said.

I looked at my hands and bit my fingernails and took my glasses off and put them on again.

'I know you don't want to,' he said. 'But I don't know who else to ask.'

'Sir . . . well . . . can we leave it until the spring? I mean . . . you might think of someone better . . .'

'It's got to be now, Randall. Right this minute, in fact. We've got the chance of buying one of the top young German horses, a real cracker, for Johnny. We . . . that is, his trustees . . . I suppose I should explain . . . His money is in trust until he is twenty-five, which is still three years ahead, and although of course he has a generous living allowance, a big item like an Olympic-type horse needs to come out of the capital. Anyway, we will be happy to buy this horse, and we have an option on it, but they are pressing for a reply. We must say yes or no by Christmas. It is too expensive except for an all-out attempt at the Olympics, and we are damned lucky to have been given the few weeks' option. They've got other buyers practically queueing for it.'

I stood up restlessly, went to the window, and looked out at the cold November sky. Winter in Moscow, chasing someone's possible indiscretion, maybe digging up a lot of private dirt, was an absolutely revolting prospect.

'Please, Randall,' said the Prince. 'Please go. Just give it a try.'

Emma was standing by the sitting-room window watching the Daimler roll away down the drive. She glanced assessingly at my face.

'I see he suckered you,' she said.

'I'm still fighting a rearguard action.'

'You haven't a chance.'

She walked across the panelled room and sat on the long stool in front of the fire, stretching out her hands to the warmth. 'It's too ingrained in you. Service to the sovereign, and all that. Grandfather an equerry, aunt a lady-in-waiting. Stacks like them in your family for generations back. What hope have you got? When a Prince says jump, all your ancestors' genes spring to attention and salute.'

CHAPTER TWO

The Prince lived in a modest house only a shade larger than my own, but a hundred years older, and he opened his door to me himself, although he did have living-in staff, which I did not. But then, he also had a wife, three children and, apparently, six dogs. A Dalmatian and a whippet oozed between his legs and the doorposts and bowled over to give me a good sniffing as I climbed out of my Mercedes, with a yapping collection of terriers cantering along in their wake.

'Kick 'em out of your way,' advised the Prince loudly, waiting on his doorstep. 'Get *down*, Fingers, you spotted oaf.'

The Dalmatian paid little attention, but I reached the door unchewed. Shook the Prince's hand. Made the small bow. Followed him across the rugs of his pillared hall into an ample sort of study. Leather-bound books in tidy rows lined two of the walls, with windows, doors, portraits and fireplace leaving small surrounds of pale green emulsion on the others. On his big cluttered desk stood ranks of photographs in silver frames, and in one corner a huge white cyclamen in a copper bowl drooped its pale heads in the greyish light.

I knew, and the Prince knew I knew, that his act in opening his door to me himself was a very unusual token of appreciation. He really must have been quite extraordinarily relieved, I thought, that I had agreed to take even the partial step I had: and I wondered a bit uneasily about the size of the pitfalls which he knew would lie ahead.

'Good of you, Randall,' he said, waving me to a black leather armchair. 'Did you have a good drive? We'll rustle up some coffee in a minute . . .'

He sat in a comfortable swivel beside his desk and kept up the flow of courteous chatter. Johnny Farring-ford, he said, had promised to be there by ten-thirty: he took a quick look at his watch and no doubt found it was roughly fifteen minutes after that already. It was good of me to come, he said again. It was probably better, he said, that I shouldn't be tied in too closely with Johnny at this stage, so it was perhaps wiser we should meet at the Prince's house, and not at Johnny's, if I saw what he meant.

He was strongly built, fairly tall, brown-haired, blue-eyed, with the easy good looks of youth beginning to firm into the settled character of coming middle age. The eyebrows were bushier than five years earlier, the nose more pronounced, and the neck a little thicker. Time was turning him from an athlete into a figurehead, and giving me unwanted insights into mortality on a Monday morning.

Another quick look at his watch, this time accompanied by a frown. I thought hopefully that perhaps the precious Johnny wouldn't turn up at all, and I could go contentedly back home and forget the whole thing.

The two tall windows of the study looked out to the sweep of drive in front of the house, in the same way as those of my own sitting room. Perhaps the Prince, too, found it useful to have early warning of people calling: time to dodge, if he wanted.

My Mercedes was clearly in view on the wide expanse of raked gravel, standing alone, bluish-grey and quiet. While I idly watched, a white Rover suddenly travelled like an arrow across the uncluttered area, making straight for my car's back. As if in horror-struck inevitable slow-motion I waited helplessly for the crash.

There was a noise like the emptying of ten metal dustbins into a pulverizing plant, followed by the uninterrupted blowing of the horn, as the unconscious driver of the Rover slumped over the steering wheel.

'Christ!' said the Prince, appalled and leaping to his feet. 'Johnny!'

'My car!' I said, involuntarily betraying my regrettable priorities.

The Prince was fortunately already on his way to

the study door, and I followed on his heels across the hall, bursting into the fresh air after him at a run.

The reverberating crunch and the wailing horn had brought an assortment of horrified faces to the windows and to the fringe of the scene, but it was the Prince and I who reached the tangle first.

The front of the Rover had half mounted the back of my car in a sort of monstrous mechanical mating, so that the Rover's wheels were slightly off the ground. The whole arrangement looked most precarious, and an assaulting smell of petrol brought one face to face with possibilities.

'Get him out,' said the Prince urgently, tugging at the handle of the driver's door. 'God . . .'

The door had buckled under the impact, and was wedged shut. I raced round to the far side, and tried the passenger door. Same thing. If he'd tried, Johnny Farringford couldn't have hit my Mercedes any straighter.

The rear doors were locked. The hatchback also. The horn blew on, urgent and disturbing.

'Jesus,' shouted the Prince frantically. 'Get him out.'

I climbed up on to the concertina'd mess between the two vehicles and slithered through the space where the windscreen had been, carrying with me a shower of crumbling glass. Knelt on the passenger seat, and hauled the unconscious man off the horn button. The sudden quiet was a blessing, but there was nothing reassuring about Johnny Farringford's face.

I didn't wait to look beneath the blood. I stretched across behind him, supporting his lolling head, and pulled up the locking catch on the offside rear door. The Prince worked at it feverishly from the outside, but it took a contortionist manoeuvre from me and a fierce stamp from my heel to spring it open: the thought of sparks from the scraping metal was a vivid horror, as I could now hear, as well as scarcely breathe from, the flood of escaping petrol.

It didn't make it any better that it was the petrol from my own car, or that I'd filled the capacious tank that very morning.

The Prince put his head and shoulders into the Rover and thrust his wrists under his brother-in-law's armpits. I squirmed back into the buckled front space and disengaged the flopping feet from the clutter of clutch, brake and accelerator pedals. The Prince heaved with his considerable strength and I lifted the lower part of the inert body as best I could, and, between us, we shifted him over the back of his seat and out through the rear door. I let go of his legs as the Prince tugged him backwards, and he flopped out free on to the gravel like a calf from a cow.

God help him, I thought, if we've made any broken bones worse by our rough handling, but anything on the whole was better than incineration. I scrambled along Johnny Farringford's escape route with no signs of calm unhurried nonchalance.

Assistance had arrived in a houseman's coat and in

gardening clothes, and the victim was carried more carefully from then on.

'Take him away from the car,' the Prince was saying to them while turning back towards me. 'The petrol . . . Randall, get out, man.'

Superfluous advice. I'd never felt so slow, so awkward, so over-equipped with knees and elbows and ankle joints.

Whether the balance of one vehicle on the other was in any case unstable, or whether my far from delicate movements rocked it over the brink, the effect was the same: the Rover began to move while I was still inside it.

I could hear the Prince's voice, rising with apprehension, 'Randall . . .'

I got one foot out free: began to put my weight on it, and the Rover shifted further. I stumbled, hung on to the door frame, and pulled myself out by force of arms. Landed sideways on hip and elbow, sprawling and ungainly.

I rolled and put my feet where they ought to be, with my hands on the ground like a runner, to get a bit of purchase. Behind me the Rover's heavy weight crunched backwards and tore itself off my Mercedes with metal screeching violently on metal, but I dare say it was some form of electrical short-circuiting which let go with a shower of sparks like a hundred cigarette lighters in chorus.

The explosion threw the two cars apart and left both

of them burning like mini infernos. There was a hissing
noise in the air as the expanding vapour flashed into a
second's flame, and a positive roaring gust of hot wind,
which helped me onwards.

'Your hair's on fire,' observed the Prince, as I
reached him.

I rubbed a hand over it, and so it was. Rubbed with
both hands rather wildly and put the conflagration out.

'Thanks,' I said.

'Not at all.'

He grinned at me in an un-Princely and most human
fashion. 'And your glasses, I see, haven't shifted an
inch.'

A doctor and a private ambulance arrived in due
course for Johnny Farringford, but long before that
he had woken up and looked around him in bewilderment. He was lying, by that time, on the long
comfortable sofa in the family sitting room, attended
by the Princess, his sister, who was taking things
matter-of-factly and mopping his wounds with
impressive efficiency.

'What happened?' Farringford said, opening dazed
eyes.

Bit by bit they told him: he had driven his car across
a space as big as a tennis court, straight into the back
of my Mercedes. Nothing else in sight.

'Randall Drew,' added the Prince, making the intro-
duction.

'Oh.'

'Damn silly thing to do,' said the Princess disparag-
ingly, but in her concerned face I read the lifelong
protectiveness of older sister to little brother.

'I don't . . . remember.'

He looked at the red stains on the swabs which
were piling up on a tray beside him, at the blood
dripping from a cut on one finger, and appeared to be
going to be sick.

'He used to pass out at the sight of blood,' said his
sister. 'A good job he's grown out of it.'

Johnny Farringford's injuries had resolved themselves into numerous cuts to the face but no obviously
broken bones. However, he winced every time he
moved, pressing his arm across his waist as if to hold
himself together, which spoke to me rather remi-
niscently of cracked ribs.

He was a willowy, fairly tall young man with a great
deal of crinkly reddish hair extending into tufty bits of
beard down the outer sides of his jaw. His nose looked
thin and sharp, and an out-of-door tan sat oddly on his
skin over the pallor of shock.

'Creeping . . . shit,' he said suddenly.

'It could have been worse,' said the Prince,
dubiously.

'No . . .' Farringford said. 'They hit me.'

'Who did?' The Princess mopped a bleeding cut

and clearly thought the remark was the rambling of concussion.

'Those men ... I ...' He broke off and focused his dazed eyes with great deliberation on the Prince's face, as if the act of keeping his glance steady was also helping to reorganize his thoughts.

'I drove here ... after. I felt ... I was sweating. I remember turning in through the gates ... and seeing the house ...'

'Which men?' said the Prince.

'The ones you sent ... about the horse.'

'I didn't send any men.'

Farringford blinked slowly and re-established the concentrating stare.

'They came ... to the stable. Just when I was thinking ... time to come here ... see this fellow ... someone ... you want me to ...'

The Prince nodded. 'That's right. Randall Drew, here.'

'Yeah ... well ... Higgins had got my car out ... the Rover ... said I wanted the Porsche but something about new tyres ... so I just went into the yard ... to see if Groucho's legs OK ... which Lakeland said they were, but wanted to look myself, you know ... So there they were, saying could they have a word ... you'd sent them. I said I was in a hurry ... got into the Rover ... they just crowded in after me ... punched me ... one of them drove down the road, past the village ... then they stopped ... and the sods knocked me about ... gave them as good as I got ... but two to one ... no good, you know.'

'They robbed you?' the Prince said. 'We'll have to consider the police.' He looked worried. Police meant publicity, and unfavourable publicity was anathema to the Prince.

'No ...' Farringford closed his eyes. 'They said ... to keep away ... from Alyosha.'

'They *what*?' The Prince jerked as if he too had been hit.

'That's right ... knew you wouldn't like it ...'

'What else did they say?'

'Nothing. Bloody ironic ...' said Farringford rather faintly. 'It's you ... who wants Alyosha ... found ... Far as I'm concerned ... whole thing can stay ... buried.'

'Just rest,' said the Princess anxiously, wiping red oozing drops from his grazed forehead. 'Don't talk any more, Johnny, there's a lamb.' She looked up at the two of us, standing at the sofa's foot. 'What will you do about the cars?'

The Prince stared morosely at the two burnt-out wrecks and at five empty extinguishers which lay around like scarlet torpedoes. An acrid smell in the November air was all that was left of the thick column of smoke and flame which had risen higher than the rooftops. The firemen, still in the shape of houseman and gardener, stood in the background, looking smugly at their handiwork and waiting for the next gripping instalment.

'Do you suppose he fainted?' said the Prince.

'It sounds like it, sir,' I said. 'He said he was sweating. Not much fun being beaten up like that.'

'And he never could stand the sight of blood.'

The Prince traced with his eye the path the Rover would have taken with an unconscious driver had not my car been parked slap in the way.

'He'd've crashed into one of those beeches,' said the Prince. 'And his foot was on the accelerator . . .'

Across the lawn a double row of stately, mature trees stretched away from the house, thick with criss-crossing branches, and bare except for a last dusting of dried brown leaves. They had been planted, one would guess, as a break against the north-east winds, in an age when sculpture of the land was designed to delight the eye of future generations, and their sturdy trunks would have stopped a tank, let alone a Rover. They were lucky, I thought, to have survived where so many had fallen to drought, fungus and gales.

'I'm glad he didn't hit the beeches,' said the Prince, and left me unsure whether it was for Johnny's sake or theirs. 'Sorry about your car, of course. I hope it was insured, and all that? Better just tell the insurers it was a parking accident. Keep it simple. Cars get written off so easily, these days. You don't want to claim against Johnny, or anything like that, do you?'

27

I shook my head reassuringly. The Prince smiled faintly with relief and relaxed several notches.

'We don't want the place crawling with Press, do you see? Telephoto lenses ... Any sniff of this and they'd be down here in droves.'

'But too late for the action,' I said.

He looked at me in alarm. 'You won't say anything about us hauling Johnny out, will you? Not to anyone. I don't want the Press getting hold of a story like that. It really doesn't do.'

'Would you mind people knowing you would take a slight risk to rescue your wife's brother, sir?'

'Yes, I should,' he said positively. 'Don't you say a word, there's a good chap.' He cast a glance at my singed hair. 'And not so much of the "slight", come to that.' He put his head on one side. 'We could say you did it yourself, if you like.'

'No, sir, I don't like.'

'Didn't think you would. You wouldn't want them crawling all over you with their notebooks any more than I should.'

He turned away and with a movement of his hand that was more a suggestion than a command, he called over the hovering gardener.

'What do we do about all this, Bob?' he said.

The gardener was knowledgeable about breakdown trucks and suitable garages, and said he would fix it. His manner with the Prince was comfortable and spoke of long-term mutual respect, which would have irritated the anti-royalists no end.

'Don't know what I'd do without Bob,' confirmed the Prince as we walked back towards the house. 'If I ring up shops or garages and say who I am they either don't believe it and say yes, they're the Queen of Sheba, or else they're so fussed they don't listen properly and get everything wrong. Bob will get those cars shifted without any trouble, but if I tried to arrange it myself the first people to arrive would be the reporters.'

He stopped on the doorstep and looked back at the skeleton of what had been my favourite vehicle.

'We'll have to fix you a car to get home in,' he said. 'Lend you one.'

'Sir,' I said, 'who or what is Alyosha?'

'Ha!' he said explosively, his head turning to me sharply, his eyes suddenly shining. 'That's the first bit of interest you've shown without me actually forcing you into it.'

'I did say I would see what I could do.'

'Meaning to do as precious little as possible.'

'Well, I . . .'

'And looking as if you'd been offered rotting fish.'

'Er . . .' I said. 'Well . . . what about Alyosha?'

'That's just the *point*,' the Prince said. 'We don't *know* about Alyosha. That's just what I want you to find *out*.'

*

29

Johnny Farringford got himself out of hospital and back home pretty fast, and I drove over to see him three days after the accident.

'Sorry about your car,' he said, looking at the Range-Rover in which I had arrived. 'Bit of a buggers' muddle, what?'

He was slightly nervous, and still pale. The numerous facial cuts were healing with the quick crusts of youth and looked unlikely to leave permanent scars; and he moved as if the soreness still in his body was after all more a matter of muscle than bone. Nothing, I thought a shade ruefully, that would stop him training hard for the Olympics.

'Come in,' he said. 'Coffee, and all that.'

He led the way into a thatched cottage and we stepped straight into a room that deserved a magazine article on traditional country living. Stone-flagged floors, good rugs, heavy supporting beams, inglenook fireplace, exposed old bricks, and masses of sagging sofas and chairs in faded chintzy covers.

'This place isn't mine,' he said, sensing my inspection. 'It's rented. I'll get the coffee.'

He headed towards a door at the far end, and I slowly followed. The kitchen, where he was pouring boiling water into a filter pot, was as modern as money could make it.

'Sugar? Milk?' he said. 'Would you rather have tea?'

'Milk, please. Coffee's fine.'

He carried the loaded tray back into the living room

and put it on a low table in front of the fireplace. Logs were stacked there ready on a heap of old dead ash, but the fire, like the cottage itself, was cold. I coughed a couple of times and drank the hot liquid gratefully, warmed inside if not out.

'How are you feeling now?' I asked.

'Oh . . . all right.'

'Still shaken, I should imagine.'

He shivered. 'I understand I'm lucky to be alive. Good of you to dig me out, and all that.'

'It was your brother-in-law, as much as me.'

'Beyond the call of duty, one might say.'

He fidgeted with the sugar bowl and his spoon, making small movements for their own sake.

'Tell me about Alyosha,' I said.

He flicked a quick glance at my face and looked away, leaving me the certainty that what he mainly felt at that moment was depression.

'There's nothing to tell,' he said tiredly. 'Alyosha is just a name which cropped up in the summer. One of the German team died at Burghley in September, and someone said it was because of Alyosha who came from Moscow. Of course, there were enquiries and so on, but I never heard the results because I wasn't directly involved, do you see?'

'But . . . indirectly?' I suggested.

He gave me another quick glance and a faint smile. 'I knew him quite well. The German chap. One

31

does, do you see? One meets all the same people everywhere, at every international event.'

'Yes,' I said.

'Well . . . I went out with him one evening, to a club in London. I was stupid, I admit it, but I thought it was just a gambling club. He played backgammon, as I do. I had taken him to my club a few days earlier, you know, so I thought he was just repaying my, er, hospitality.'

'But it wasn't just a gambling club?' I said, prompting him as he lapsed into gloomy silence.

'No.' He sighed. 'It was full of, well . . . transvestites.' His depression increased. 'I didn't realize, at first. No one would have done. They all *looked* like women. Attractive. Pretty, even, some of them. We were shown to a table. It was dark. And there was this girl, in the spotlight, doing a striptease, taking off a lot of cloudy gold scarf things. She was beautiful . . . dark-skinned, but not black . . . marvellous dark eyes . . . the most stunning little breasts. She undressed right down to the skin and then did a sort of dance with a bright pink feathery boa thing . . . it was brilliant, really. One would see her backview totally naked, but when she turned round there was always the boa falling in the . . . er . . . strategic place. When it was over, and I was applauding, Hans leant across grinning like a monkey and said into my ear, that she was a boy.' He grimaced. 'I felt a complete fool. I mean . . . one doesn't mind seeing performances like that if one *knows*. But to be taken in . . .'

'Embarrassing,' I said, agreeing.

'I laughed it off,' he said. 'I mean, one has to, doesn't one? And there was sort of weird fascination, of course. Hans said he had seen the boy in a nightclub in West Berlin, and he had thought it might amuse me. He seemed to be enjoying my discomfiture. Thought it a huge joke. I had to pretend to take it well, do you see, because he was my host, but to be honest, I thought it a bit *off.*'

A spot of dented pride, I thought.

'The Event started two days after that,' he said, 'and Hans died the day after, after the cross-country.'

'How?' I asked. 'How did he die?'

'Heart attack.'

I was surprised. 'Wasn't he a bit young?'

'Yes,' Johnny said. 'Only thirty-six. Makes one think, doesn't it?'

'And then what happened?' I said.

'Oh . . . nothing, really. Nothing one could put one's finger on. But there were these rumours flying about, and I expect I was the last to hear them, that there was something *queer* about Hans, and about me as well. That we were, in fact, gay, if you see what I mean? And that a certain Alyosha from Moscow was jealous and had made a fuss with Hans, and because of it all he had a heart attack. And there was a *message*, do you see, that if I ever went to Moscow, Alyosha would be waiting.'

'What sort of message? I mean, in what form was it delivered?' I said.

He looked frustrated. 'But that's just it, the message itself was only a rumour. Everyone seemed to know it. I was told it by several people. I just don't know who started it.'

'Did you take it seriously?' I asked.

'No, of course I didn't. It's all rubbish. No one would have the slightest reason to be jealous of me when it came to Hans Kramer. In fact, you know, I more or less avoided him after that evening, as much as one could do without being positively boorish, do you see?'

I put my empty cup on the tray and wished I had worn a second sweater. Johnny himself seemed totally impervious to cold.

'But your brother-in-law,' I said, 'takes it very seriously indeed.'

He made a face. 'He's paranoid about the Press. Haven't you noticed?'

'He certainly doesn't seem to like them.'

'They *persecuted* him when he was trying to keep them off the scent of his romance with my sister. I thought it a bit of a laugh, really, but I suppose it wasn't to him. And then there was a lot of brouhaha, if you remember, because a fortnight after the engagement our mama upped and scarpered with her hairdresser.'

34

'I'd forgotten that,' I said.

'Just before I went to Eton,' Johnny said. 'It slightly deflated my confidence, do you see, at a point when a fellow needs all he can get.' He spoke flippantly, but the echo of a desperate hurt was clearly there. 'So they couldn't get married for months, and when they did, the papers raked up my mama's sex-life practically every day. And any time there's any real news story about any of us, up it pops again. Which is why HRH has this *thing*.'

'I can see,' I said soberly, 'why he wouldn't want you mixed up in a murky scandal at the Olympics with the eyes of the gossip columns swivelling your way like searchlights. Particularly with transvestite overtones.'

The Prince's alarm, indeed, seemed to me now to be entirely justified, but Johnny disagreed.

'There can't be any scandal, because there *isn't* any,' he said. 'The whole thing is absolutely stupid.'

'I think that's what your brother-in-law wants to prove, and the Foreign Office also, because anyone going to Russia is vulnerable, but anyone with a reputation for homosexual behaviour is a positive political risk, as it is still very much against the law there. They do want you to take part in the Olympics. They're trying to get me to investigate the rumours entirely for your sake.'

He compressed his mouth obstinately. 'But there isn't any need.'

'What about the men?' I said.

'What men?'

'The men who attacked you and warned you off Alyosha.'

'Oh.' He looked blank. 'Well ... I should think it's obvious that whoever Alyosha is, she doesn't want an investigation any more than I do. It will probably do her a lot of *harm* ... did you think of that?'

He stood up restlessly, picked up the tray, and carried it out to the kitchen. He rattled the cups out there for a bit and when he came back showed no inclination to sit down again.

'Come out and see the horses,' he said.

'Tell me about the men first,' I said persuasively.

'What about them?'

He put a foot on a pile of logs beside the fire and fiddled unnecessarily with the fire tongs.

'Were they English?'

He looked up in surprise. 'Well, I suppose so.'

'You heard them speak. What sort of accents did they have?'

'Ordinary. I mean ... well, you know ... ordinary working-class accents.'

'But they differ,' I said. He shook his head, but all accents differed, to my mind, to an infinitely variable degree.

'Well,' I said, 'were they Irish? Scots? Geordies? London? Birmingham? Liverpool? West Country? All those are easy.'

'London, then,' he said.

'Not foreign? Not Russian, for example?'

'No.' He seemed to see the point for the first time. 'They had a rough, sloppy way of speaking, swallowing all the consonants. Southern England. London or the south-east, I should think, or Berkshire.'

'The accent you hear around here, every day?'

'I suppose so, yes. Anyway, I didn't notice anything special about it.'

'What did they look like?'

'They were both big.' He arranged the fire irons finally in a tidy row and straightened to his full height. 'Taller than I am. They were just men. Nothing remarkable. No beards or limps or scars down the cheek. I'm awfully sorry to be so useless, but honestly I don't think I'd know them again if I passed them in the street.'

'But you would,' I guessed, 'if they walked into this room.'

'You mean I'd *feel* it was them?'

'I mean I expect you remember more than you think, and if your memory were jogged it would all come rushing back.'

He looked doubtful, but he said, 'If I do see them again, I'll certainly let you know.'

'They might of course return with another, er, warning,' I said thoughtfully. 'If you can't persuade your brother-in-law to drop the whole affair.'

'Christ, do you think so?' He swung his thin beaky nose towards the door as if expecting instant attack.

'You do say the most bloody comforting things, don't you?'

'The crude deterrent,' I said.

'What?'

'Biff bang.'

'Oh . . . yes.'

'Cheap and often effective,' I said.

'Yes, well. I mean . . . so what?'

'So who was it meant to deter? You, me, or your brother-in-law?'

He gave me a slow look behind which the alternatives seemed to be being inspected for the first time.

'See what you mean,' he said. 'But it's too subtle for me by half. Come out and see the horses. Now those I do understand. Even if they kill you, there's no malice.'

He shed a good deal of his nervousness and most of his depression as we walked the fifty yards across the country road to the stables. Horses were his natural element, and being among them obviously gave him comfort and confidence. I wondered whether his half-controlled jitters with me were simply because I was human, and not because of my errand.

The stable yard was a small quadrangle of elderly wooden boxes round an area of impacted clay and gravel. There were clipped patches of grass, a straggling tree, and empty tubs for flowers. Green paint, nearing the end of its life. A feeling that weeds would grow in the spring.

'When I inherit the lolly, I'll buy a better yard,' Johnny said, uncannily picking up my thoughts again. 'This is rented. Trustees, do you see.'

'It's a friendly place,' I said mildly.

'Unsuitable.'

The trustees however had put the money where it mattered, which was in four legs, head and tail. Although it was then the comparative rest period of their annual cycle, the five resident horses looked well-muscled and fit. For the most part bred by thoroughbred stallions out of hunter mares, they had looks as well as performance, and Johnny told me the history of each with a decisive and far from casual pride. I saw come alive in him for the first time the single-minded, driving fanaticism which had to be there: the essential fuel for Olympic fire.

Even the crinkly red hair seemed to crisp into tighter curls, though I dare say this was due to the dampness in the air. But there was nothing climatic about the zeal in the eye, the tautness of the jaw, or the intensity of his manner. Enthusiasm of that order was bound to be infectious. I found myself responding to it easily, and understood why everyone was so anxious to make his Russian journey possible.

'I've an outside chance for the British team with this fellow,' he said, briskly slapping the rounded quarters of a long-backed chestnut, and reeling off the fullest list of successes. 'But he's not top world class. I know that. I need something better. The German

39

horse. I've seen him. I really covet that horse.' He let out his breath abruptly and gave a small laugh, as if hearing his own obsession and wanting to disguise it. 'I do go on a bit.'

The self-depreciation in his voice showed nowhere in his healing face.

'I want a Gold,' he said.

CHAPTER THREE

My packing for Moscow consisted, in order of priority, of an army of defences for dicky lungs, mostly on a be-prepared-and-it-won't-happen basis; a thick woolly scarf; a spare pair of glasses; a couple of paperbacks; and a camera.

Emma surveyed my medicine box with a mixture of amusement and horror.

'You're a hypochondriac,' she said.

'Stop poking around. Everything in there is tidy.'

'Oh, sure. What are these?' She lifted a small plastic pill bottle and shook it.

'Ventolin tablets. Put them down.'

She opened the cap instead and shook one on to her palm.

'Pink and tiny. What do they do?'

'Help one breathe.'

'And these?' She picked up a small cylindrical tin and read the yellow label. 'Intal spincaps?'

'Help one breathe.'

41

'And this? And this?' She picked them out and laid them in a row. 'And these?'

'Ditto, ditto, ditto.'

'And a syringe, for God's sake. Why a syringe?'

'Last resort. If a shot of adrenalin doesn't work, one sends for the undertaker.'

'Are you serious?'

'No,' I said; but the truth was probably yes. I had never actually found out.

'What a fuss over a little cough.' She looked at the fearsome array of life-support systems with all the superiority of the naturally healthy.

'Gloomsville,' I agreed. 'And put them all back.'

She humoured me by replacing them with excessive care.

'You know,' she said, 'surely all these things are for asthma, not bronchitis.'

'When I get bronchitis, I get asthma.'

'And vice versa?'

I shook my head. 'How about hopping into bed?'

'At half-past four on a Sunday afternoon with an invalid?'

'It's been done before.'

'So it has,' she agreed: and it was done again, with not a cough or a wheeze to be heard.

Rupert Hughes-Beckett, in his London office, the next morning, handed me an air ticket, a visa, a hotel reservation, and a sheet of names and addresses. Not enough.

'How about my answers?' I said.

'I'm afraid . . . ah . . . they are not yet available.'

'Why not?'

'The enquiries are still . . . ah . . . in hand.'

He was not meeting my eyes. He was finding the backs of his own hands as fascinating as he had in my sitting room. He must know every freckle, I thought. Every wrinkle and every vein.

'Do you mean you haven't even started?' I said incredulously. 'My letter must have reached you by last Tuesday at the latest. Six days ago.'

'With your visa photographs, yes. You must understand there are . . . ah . . . *problems* in obtaining a visa at such short notice.'

I said, 'What is the point of a visa if I don't have the information? And couldn't you have got both at once?'

'We thought . . . ah . . . the *telex*. At the Embassy. We can send you the answers as they reach us.'

'And I trot around there every five minutes to see if the carrier pigeon has fluttered into the loft?'

He smiled austerely, a minuscule movement of the severely controlled lips.

'You can telephone,' he said. 'The number is on that paper.' He leaned back a little in his five-star office chair and looked earnestly at his hand to see if the knuckle-to-wrist scenery had changed at all in the last half-minute. 'We did, of course, have a word with the doctor who attended Hans Kramer.'

'Well?' I prompted, as he seemed to have stopped there.

'He was the doctor in attendance at the Three-Day Event. He was seeing to a girl with a broken collarbone when someone came to tell him that one of the Germans had collapsed. He left the girl almost immediately, but by the time he reached him, Kramer was already dead. He tried heart massage, he says, and a suitable injection, and mouth-to-mouth resuscitation, but all to no avail. The body was ... ah ... cyanosed, and the cause of death was ... ah ... cardiac arrest.'

'Or in other words, heart attack.'

'Ah ... yes. There was an autopsy, of course. Natural causes. So sad in someone so young.'

None of this present caper would have been necessary, I thought moodily, if Hans Kramer had not been so inconsiderate as to drop in his tracks. There was nothing like death for spawning and perpetuating myths, and it looked certain the Alyosha crop had circulated simply because Kramer hadn't been around to deny them.

'The names and addresses of the rest of the German team?' I said.

'To follow.'

'And the names and addresses of the members of the Russian team which came over for the International Horse Trials at Burghley?'

44

'To follow.'

'And of the Russian observers?'

'To follow.'

I stared at him. The most hopeful lead I'd unearthed in several telephone calls to people in the Event world had been the frequent reference to 'the Russian observers': three men who in a semi-official capacity had attended a number of horse trials during the past season, not just the International Event for which their team had been entered. The reasons for their presence had been described variously as 'spying', 'seeing how Events should be run', 'nicking our best horses', and 'assessing the standard they had to reach to make the West look stupid at the Olympics'.

I said to Hughes-Beckett, 'The Prince told me you had agreed to do some of the spadework.'

'We will,' he said. 'But on the scene of international politics your errand is of limited importance. My office has been working this week on matters of greater urgency than . . . ah . . . horses.'

The same faint undisguisable contempt coloured his voice and pinched his nostrils.

'Do you expect me to succeed in this task?' I said.

He studied the back of his hand and didn't answer.

'Do you *wish* me to succeed?'

He lifted his gaze to my face as if it were a two-ton weight.

'I would be grateful if you would bear in mind that clearing the way for Lord Farringford to be able to be

45

considered for the Olympics, always supposing that he or his horse should prove to be good enough, is not something for which we would willingly sacrifice any . . . ah . . . bargaining positions with the Soviet Union. We would in particular not wish to find ourselves in the position of having to tender an *apology*.'

'It's a wonder you asked me to go,' I said.

'The Prince wished it.'

'And he leaned on you?'

Hughes-Beckett folded his mouth primly. 'It is not a totally unreasonable request. If we altogether disapproved of your errand we would not have helped in any way.'

'All right,' I said, rising to my feet and stowing the various papers into pockets. 'I take it that you would like me to go, which will prove you are not obstructive, and to ask a few harmless questions, and get some inconclusive answers, and for the Prince not to buy the German horse, and for Johnny Farringford not to be picked for the team, and for no one to make waves?'

He regarded me with all the world-weariness of a senior civil servant, saying nothing but meaning yes.

'We have reserved a room for you for two weeks,' he said. 'But of course you can return earlier if you wish.'

'Thanks.'

'And if you read that sheet of paper, you will find we have given you one or two . . . ah . . . contacts, who may be helpful.'

I glanced at the short list, which was headed by the British Embassy, Naberezhnaya Morisa Teresa 12.

'One of those lower down is a man concerned with training the Soviet team for the Olympic Three-Day Event.'

'Well,' I said, pleasantly surprised, 'that's better.'

He said with faint smugness, 'We have not been entirely idle, as you supposed.' He cleared his throat. 'The last name on the list is that of a student at Moscow University. He is English, and is there on an exchange visit for one year. He speaks Russian, of course. We have written to him to tell him you will be coming. He will be helpful if you need an interpreter, but we ask that nothing you do will prejudice his ... ah ... continued acceptance for the rest of the academic year.'

'As he is more important than horses?'

Hughes-Beckett achieved a remote and frosty smile. 'Most things are,' he said.

The ticket he had provided found me the next day sitting comfortably in the first class on an Aeroflot flight which arrived at six in the evening, local time. Most of my fellow travellers in the privileged cabin were black: Cubans, I idly wondered? But then, in a shifting world, they could be from anywhere: today's ally, tomorrow's exterminee. They wore superbly tailored suits with white shirts and elegant ties, and were met at the doors of the aeroplane on landing by extra-long limousines. Those of less note went through normal immigration procedures, but without, in my case, any great delay. The customs men waved me through as if uninterested, though on the next bench they seemed to be taking apart a man of much my age. Every scrap of paper was being read, every pocket emptied, and the lining of the suitcase closely examined. The object of these attentions bore them stolidly, without expression. No protest, no indignation, nor, as far as I could see, any apprehension. As I went on my way, one of the officers picked up a pair of underpants and carefully felt his way round the waistband.

I was thinking purposefully of taxis, but it transpired that I, too, had been provided with a reception committee. A girl in a brown coat and a fawn knitted hat approached me tentatively, and said, 'Mr Drew?'

She saw from my reaction that she had the right man. She said, 'My name is Natasha. I am from Intourist. We will be looking after you during your stay here. We have a car to take you to your hotel.' She turned towards a slightly older woman standing a pace or two away. 'This is my colleague, Anna.'

'How kind of you to take so much trouble,' I said politely. 'How did you know me?'

Natasha glanced matter-of-factly at a paper in her hand. 'Englishman, thirty-two years old, dark wavy hair, glasses with mottled brown frames, no moustache or beard, good clothes.'

'The car is outside,' Anna said. I thought that that

wasn't totally surprising, as cars usually were, at airports.

Anna was short, stocky, and soberly clad in a grey coat with a darker grey woolly hat. There was something forbidding in her face, a stiffness which continued downwards through the forward-thrusting abdomen to the functional toes of her boots. Her manner was welcoming enough, but would continue to be, I reckoned, only as long as I behaved as she thought I should.

'Do you have a hat?' Natasha said, solicitously. 'It is cold outside. You should have a fur hat.'

I had already had a taste of the climate in the scamper from aircraft to bus, and from bus to airport door. Most of the passengers seemed to have sprouted headgear on the flight and had emerged in black fur with ear-flaps, but I was huddled only into my fluffy scarf.

'You lose much body-heat through the head,' said Natasha seriously. 'Tomorrow you must buy a hat.'

'Very well,' I said.

She had splendid dark eyebrows and creamy-white skin, and wore smooth pale pink lipstick. A touch of humour would have put the missing sparkle into her brown eyes, but then a touch of humour in the Soviets would have transformed the world.

'You have not been to Moscow before?'

'No,' I said.

There was a group of four large men in dark overcoats standing by the exit doors. They were turned inwards towards each other as if in conversation, but their eyes were directed outwards, and none of them was talking. Natasha and Anna walked past them as if they were wallpaper.

'Who asked you to meet me?' I asked curiously.

'Our Intourist office,' Natasha said.

'But . . . who asked *them*?'

Both girls gave me a bland look and no answer, leaving me to gather that they didn't know, and that it was something they would not expect to know.

The car, which had a driver who spoke no English, travelled down straight wide empty roads towards the city, with wet snowflakes whirling thinly away in the headlights. The road surfaces were clear, but lumpy grey-white banks lined the verges. I shivered in my overcoat from aversion more than discomfort: it was warm enough in the car.

'It is not cold for the end of November,' Natasha said. 'Today it has been above freezing all day. Usually by now the snow has come for the winter, but instead we have had rain.'

The bus stops, I saw, had been built to deal with life below zero. They were enclosed in glass, and brightly lit inside; and in a few there were groups of inward-facing men, three, not four, who might or might not be there to catch a bus.

'If you wish,' Anna said, 'tomorrow you can make a conducted tour of the city by coach, and the next day there is a visit to the Exhibition of Economic Achievements.'

'We will do our best for tickets for the ballet and the opera,' said Natasha, nodding helpfully.

'There are always many English people in your hotel visiting Moscow on package holidays,' Anna said, 'and it will be possible for you to join them in a conducted tour of the Kremlin or other places of interest.'

I looked from one to the other and came to the conclusion that they were genuinely trying to be helpful.

'Thank you,' I said, 'but mostly I shall be visiting friends.'

'If you tell us where you want to go,' Natasha said earnestly, 'we will arrange it.'

My room at the Intourist Hotel was spacious enough for one person, with a bed along one side wall and a sofa along the other, but the same sized area with twin beds, glimpsed through briefly opened doors, must have been pretty cramped for two. I also had a wide shelf along the whole wall under the window, with a telephone and a table lamp on it; a chair, a built-in wardrobe, and a bathroom. Brown carpet, reddish patterned curtains, dark green sofa and bedcover. An ordinary, functional, adequate hotel room which could as well have been in Sydney, Los Angeles or Manchester for all its national flavour.

I unpacked my sparse belongings and looked at my watch. 'We have arranged your dinner for eight o'clock,' Anna had said. 'Please come to the restaurant then. I will be there to help you plan what you want to do tomorrow.' The nursemaiding care would have to be discouraged, I thought, but, as it was no part of my brief to cause immediate dismay, I decided to go along meekly. A short duty-free reviver, however, seemed a good idea.

I poured Scotch into a toothmug and sat on the sofa to drink it; and the telephone rang.

'Is that Mr Randall Drew?'

'Yes,' I said.

'Come to the bar of the National Hotel at nine o'clock,' said the voice. 'Leave your hotel, turn right, turn right at the street corner. The National Hotel will be on your right. Enter, leave your coat, climb the stairs, turn right. The bar is along the passage a short way, on the left. Nine o'clock. I'll see you, Mr Drew.'

The line clicked dead before I could say, 'Who are you?'

I went on drinking the Scotch. The only way to find out was to go.

After a while I took out the paper Hughes-Beckett had given me, and because the telephone seemed to be connected directly to an outside line, I dialled the number of the English student at the Russian university. A Russian voice answered, saying I knew not what.

'Stephen Luce,' I said distinctly. 'Please may I speak to Stephen Luce?'

The Russian voice said an English word, 'Wait,' and I waited. Three minutes later, by what seemed to me a minor miracle, a fresh English voice said, 'Yes? Who is it?'

'My name is Randall Drew,' I said. 'I—'

'Oh yes,' he interrupted. 'Where are you calling from?'

'My room at the Intourist Hotel.'

'What's your number? The telephone number, on the dial.'

I read it out.

'Right,' he said. 'I'd better meet you tomorrow. Twelve o'clock suit you? My lunch hour. In Red Square, in front of St Basil's Cathedral. OK?'

'Er, yes,' I said.

'Fine,' he said. 'Have to go now. Bye.' And he rang off.

It had to be catching, I thought. Something in the Moscow air. I dialled the number of the man concerned with training the Soviet team, and again a Russian voice answered. I asked in English for Mr Kropotkin, but this time without luck. After a couple of short silences at the other end, as I repeated my request, there was a burst of agitated incomprehensible speech, followed by a sharp decisive click.

I had better fortune with the British Embassy, and found myself talking to the cultural attaché.

'Sure,' he said in Etonian tones, 'we know all about you. Care to come for a drink tomorrow evening? Six o'clock suit you?'

'Perfectly,' I said. 'I . . .'

'Where are you calling from?' he said.

'My room at the Intourist Hotel.' I gave him the telephone number, unasked.

'Splendid,' he said. 'Look forward to seeing you.'

Again the swift click. I finished the Scotch and considered the shape of my telephone calls. My naïvety, I reflected, must, to the old hands in the city, have been frightening.

Anna waited, hovering, in the dining room, and came forward as I appeared. Unwrapped, she wore a green wool suit with rows of bronze-coloured beads, and would have fitted unremarkably into the London business scene. Her hair, with a few greys among the prevailing browns, was clean and well shaped, and she had the poise of one accustomed to plan and advise.

'You can sit here,' she said, indicating a stretch of tables beside a long row of windows. 'There are some English people sitting here, on a tour.'

'Thank you.'

'Now,' she said, 'tomorrow . . .'

'Tomorrow,' I said pleasantly, 'I thought I would walk around Red Square and the Kremlin, and perhaps GUM. I have a map and a guide book, and I'm sure I won't get lost.'

'But we can add you on to one of the guided tours,'

she said persuasively. 'There is a special two-hour tour of the Kremlin, with a visit to the Armoury.'

'I'd honestly rather not. I'm not a great one for museums and so on.'

She looked disapproving, but after another fruitless try, she told me that my lunch would be ready at one-thirty, when the Kremlin party returned. 'Then at two-thirty there is the bus tour of the city.'

'Yes,' I said. 'That will be fine.'

I saw as well as sensed the release of tension within her. Visitors who went their own way were clearly a problem, though I did not yet understand why. My semi-compliance, anyway, had temporarily earned me qualified good marks, and she said, as if promising sweeties to a child, that Bolshoi tickets for the opera were almost a certainty.

The tables, each set for four, began to fill up. A middle-aged couple from Lancashire joined me with enquiring smiles, closely followed by the man who had been picked clean by the customs officers. We all exchanged the sort of platitudes that strangers thrust together by chance use to demonstrate non-aggression, and the Lancashire lady commented on the extent of the airport search.

'We had to wait ever such a long time on the bus before you came out,' she said.

The unasked question floated in the air. The object of her curiosity, who was uniformed in jeans, jersey and longish hair, spooned sour cream into his borsch and took his time over replying.

'They took me off and searched me down to my skin,' he said finally, enjoying the sensationalism.

The Lancashire lady said 'ooh' in mock terror and was flatteringly impressed. 'What were they looking for?'

He shrugged. 'Don't know. There was nothing to find. I just let them get on with it, and in the end they said I could go.'

His name, he said, was Frank Jones. He taught in a school in Essex and it was his third trip to Russia. A great country, he said. The Lancashire couple regarded him doubtfully, and we all shaped up to some greyish meat of undiscernible origin. The ice cream coming later was better, but one would not, I thought, have made the journey for the gastronomic delights.

Duty done, I set off to the National Hotel in overcoat and woolly scarf, with sleet stinging my face and wetting my hair and a sharp wind invading every crevice. Pavements and roadway glistened with a wetness that was not yet ice, but the quality of the cold was all the same piercing, and I could feel it deep down inside my lungs. All it would take to abort the whole mission, I thought, would be a conclusive bout of bronchitis, and for a tempting minute I felt like opening my arms to the chill: but anything on the whole was probably better than coughing and spitting and looking at hotel bedroom walls.

The bar of the National Hotel was a matter of shady opulence, like an unmodernized Edwardian pub or a small London club gone slightly to seed. There were rugs on the floor, three long tables with eight or ten chairs round each, and a few separate small tables for three or four. Most of the chairs were occupied and there was a two-deep row in front of the bar which stretched across one end of the room. The voices around me spoke English, German, French and a lot of other tongues, but there was no one enquiring of every newcomer whether he was Randall Drew, newly arrived from England.

After an unaccosted few minutes I turned to the bar and in due course got myself a whisky. It was by then nine-fifteen. I drank for a while standing up, and then, when one of the small tables became free, sitting down; but I drank altogether alone. At nine thirty-five I bought a second drink, and at nine-fifty I reckoned that if all my investigating were to be as successful I wouldn't need bronchitis.

At two minutes to ten I looked at my watch and drained my glass, and a man detached himself from the row of drinkers at the bar and put two fresh tumblers on the table.

'Randall Drew?' he said, pulling up an empty chair and sitting down. 'Sorry to keep you waiting, sport.'

He had been there, I remembered, as long as I had; standing by the bar, exchanging words now and then with his neighbours and the barman, or looking down into his glass in the way of habitual pubbers, as if expecting to see the wisdom of the ages written in alcohol and water.

'Why did you?' I asked. 'Keep me waiting?'

The only reply I got was a grunt and an expressionless look from a pair of hard grey eyes. He pushed one of the tumblers my way and said it was my tipple, he thought. He was solid and in his forties, and wore his dark double-breasted jacket open, so that it flapped about him and hung forward when he moved. He had flatly combed black hair going a little thin on top, and a neck like a vigorous tree trunk.

'You want to be careful in Moscow,' he said.

'Mm,' I said. 'Do you have a name?'

'Herrick. Malcolm Herrick.' He paused, but I'd never heard of him. 'Moscow correspondent of the *Watch*.'

'How do you do,' I said politely, but neither of us offered a hand.

'This is no kids' playground, sport,' he said. 'I'm telling you for your own good.'

'Kind,' I murmured.

'You're here to ask damn fool questions about that four-letter Farringford.'

'Why four-letter?' I asked.

'I don't like him,' he said flatly. 'But that's neither here nor there. I've asked all the questions there are to ask about that shit, and there's damn all to find out. And if there'd been a smell there, I'd've found it.

There's no one like an old newshound, sport, if there's any dirt to be dug up about noble earls.'

Even his voice gave an impression of hard muscle. I wouldn't have liked to have him knock on my door, I thought, if I were caught in a newsworthy tragedy: he would be about as compassionate as a tornado.

'How come you've been looking?' I asked. 'And how did you know I was here, and on what errand, and staying at the Intourist? And how did you manage to telephone me within an hour of my arrival?'

He gave me another flat, hard, expressionless stare.

'We do want to know a lot, don't we, sport?' He took a mouthful of his drink. 'Little birds round at the Embassy. What else?'

'Go on,' I said, as he seemed to have stopped.

'Can't reveal sources,' he said automatically. 'But I'll tell you, sport, this is no new story. It's weeks since I did my bloodhound bit, and the Embassy staff have also put out their own feelers, and if you ask me they even set one of their Intelligence bods on to it on the quiet, on account of the queries that were popping up everywhere. It all turned out to be one big yawn. It's bloody silly sending you out here as well. Some fanatic in London doesn't seem to want to take "no story" for an answer, and "no story" is all the story there is.'

I took off my glasses and squinted at them against the light, and after a while put them on again.

'Well,' I said mildly, 'it's nice of you to bother to tell me all that, but I can't really go home straight away without *trying*, can I? I mean, they are paying my fare and expenses, and so on. But I wonder,' I went on tentatively, 'if perhaps you could tell me who you saw, so that I wouldn't duplicate a whole lot of wasteful legwork.'

'Christ, sport,' he exploded, 'you really do want your hand held, don't you?' He narrowed his eyes and compressed a firm mouth, and considered it. 'All right. There were three Russian observers in England last summer going round these damn fool horse trials. Officials from some minor committee set up here to arrange details of the equestrian events at the Games. I spoke to all three of them along at that vast Olympic committee centre they've got on Gorky Street, opposite the Red Army Museum. They had all seen Farringford riding at all the horse trials they had been to, but there was absolutely no link at all between Farringford and anything to do with Russia. *Niet, niet* and *niet*. Unanimous opinion.'

'Oh well,' I said resignedly, 'what about the Russian team which went to the international trials that were held at Burghley?'

'Those riders are unavailable, sport. You try interviewing a brick wall. The official reply that was given to the Embassy was that the Russian team had no contact with Farringford, minimum contact with any British civilians, and in any case did not speak English.'

I thought it over. 'And did you come across anything to do with a girl called Alyosha?'

He choked over his drink at the name, but it was apparently mirth, and his laugh held a definite hint of sneer.

'Alyosha, sport, is not a girl, for a start. Alyosha is a man's name. A diminutive. Like Dickie for Richard. Alyosha is a familiar version of Alexei.'

'Oh . . .'

'And if you fell for all that guff about the German who died having a boy friend from Moscow, you can forget it. Over here they still throw you in jug for it. There are as many homosexuals here as warts on a billiard ball.'

'And the rest of the German team? Did you reach them too, to ask questions?'

'The diplomats did. None of the Krauts knew a thing.'

'How many Alyoshas in Moscow?' I said.

'How many Dickies in London? The two cities are roughly the same size.'

'Have another drink?' I said.

He rose to his feet with the nearest he'd come to a smile, but the brief show of teeth raised no echoing glimmer in the eyes.

'I'll get them,' he said. 'You give me the cash.'

I gave him a fiver, which did the trick nicely with change to spare. Only Western foreign currency, the barman had told me, was acceptable in that bar. Roubles and Eastern bloc equivalents were no good. The bar was for non-Curtain visitors, to hand over as

61

big a contribution to the tourist trade as possible, all in francs, marks, dollars and yen. The change came back meticulously, and correctly, in the currency in which one had paid.

Malcolm Herrick loosened up a little over the second drink and told me a bit about working in Moscow.

'There used to be dozens of British correspondents here, but most of the papers have called them back. Only five or six of us left now, except for the news-agency guys. Reuters, and so on. The fact is, if anything big breaks in Moscow it's the outside world that hears about it first, and we get it fed back to us on the world news service on the radio. We might as well not be here for all the inside info we get for ourselves.'

'Do you yourself speak Russian?' I said.

'I do not. The Russians don't like Russian speakers working here.'

'Why ever not?' I said, surprised.

He looked at me pityingly. 'The system over here is to keep foreigners away from the Russians and Russians away from foreigners. Foreigners who work here full time have to live in compounds, with Russian guards on the gates. All the journalists, diplomats and news-agency people live in compounds. We even have our offices there. No need to go out, sport. The news comes in, courtesy of telex.'

He seemed to be more cynical than bitter. I wondered what sort of stories he wrote for the *Watch*, which was a newspaper more famous for its emotional crusades than its accuracy. It was also a paper I seldom read, as its racing columnist knew more about orchids than good things for Ascot.

We finished the drinks and stood up to depart.

'Thank you for your help,' I said. 'If I think of anything else, can I give you a ring? Are you in the phone book?'

He gave me a final flat grey stare in which there was a quality of dour triumph. I was not going to succeed where he had failed, his manner said, so I might as well retire at once.

'There's no telephone directory in Moscow,' he said.

My turn to stare.

'If you want to know a number,' he said, 'you have to ask Directory Enquiries. You probably have to tell them why you want the number, and if they don't approve of you knowing it, they won't give it to you.'

He pulled a spiral-bound reporters' notebook out of his pocket and wrote down his number, ripping off the page and handing it to me.

'And use a public telephone, sport. Not the one in your room.'

I scurried the two hundred yards back to the Intourist in heavier sleet which was turning to snow. I collected my keys, went up in the lift, and said 'good evening' in English to the plump lady who sat at a desk from which she could keep an eye on the corridor to the bedrooms. Anyone coming from the lifts to the rooms had to pass her. She gave me a stolid inspection and said what I supposed to be 'goodnight' in Russian.

My room was on the eighth floor, looking from the front of the hotel down to Gorky Street. I drew the curtains and switched on the reading lamp.

There was something indefinably different in the way my belongings lay tidily around it. I pulled open a drawer or two, and felt my skin contract in a primeval ripple down my back and legs.

While I had been out, someone had searched my room.

CHAPTER FOUR

I lay in bed with the lamp on and looked at the ceiling, and wondered why I should feel so disturbed. I was not one of those spies in or out of the cold who was entirely at home with people ferreting through their belongings, and probably felt deprived if they didn't. I had read and enjoyed all the books, and had hoisted in some of the jargon: mole, sleeper, spook, *et al*. But as for that world affecting me personally: that was as unexpected as a scorpion on the breakfast toast.

Yet I was in Moscow to ask questions. Perhaps that made me a legitimate target for irregular attention. And, of course, the most immediate questions remained unanswered, and, so far, unanswerable.

Who, exactly, had done the searching? And why?

There had been nothing of significance for anyone to find. The paper with potentially useful names and addresses had been in my pocket. I had concealed in my luggage no guns, no codes, no tiny technology, no anti-Soviet propaganda. I had been told it was illegal to import Bibles and crucifixes into Russia, and had not done so. I had brought no forbidden books, no pornography, and no newspapers. No drugs . . .

Drugs . . .

I fairly bounded out of bed and yanked open the drawer in which I'd stored my box of assorted air freight. Heaved a considerable sigh of relief, once the lid was open, to see the pills and inhalers and syringe and adrenalin ampoules all more or less in the positions Emma had given them. I couldn't for certain tell whether or not they had been inspected, but at least nothing was missing. A hypochondriac Emma might well call me, but the sad fact remained that at certain dire times the contents of that box were all that held off the Hereafter. The fates that had given me wealth had been niggardly on health: a silver spoon that bent easily. Even at my age, if one was prone to chest troubles, insurance premiums were loaded. If one's father and grandfather had both died young for lack of salbutamol or beclomethasone dipropionate, or sundry other later miracles, one discovered that actuaries' hearts were as hard as flint.

In between times, and to be fair there were far more in between times than troubles, I was as bursting with health and vigour as any other poor slob living in the damp, cold, misty, bronchitic climate of the British Isles.

I shut the box and replaced it in the drawer: climbed back into bed, switched out the light, and took off my glasses, folding them neatly to hand for the morning.

How soon, I wondered, could I decently make use of my return ticket?

Red Square looked greyish-brown, with snowflakes blowing energetically across it in a fiendish wind. I stood in front of St Basil's Cathedral taking photographs in light dim enough to develop them by, wondering if even the deep intense red of the huge brick walls of the Kremlin would make a mark on the emulsion. The vast slush-covered expanse, where sometimes the self-aggrandizing parades beat hell out of the road surface for newsreels, was on that day trodden only by miserable-looking groups of tourists, shepherded in straggling crocodiles to and from a group of buses parked nearby.

The Cathedral itself was small, a cluster of brilliantly coloured and encrusted onion-shaped domes on stalks of different height, like a fantasy castle out of Disney. Snow lay on the onions now, dimming the blues and greens and golds that sparkled on the picture postcards, but I stood there wondering how a nation which had produced a building of such joyous, magnificent imagination could have come to its latter-day greyness.

'Ivan the Great commissioned that cathedral,' said a voice behind my right shoulder. 'When it was finished he was overwhelmed with its beauty; and he put out the eyes of his architect, so that he should not design anything more splendid for anyone else.'

I turned slowly round. A shortish young man stood there, wearing a dark blue overcoat, a black fur hat, and an expectant expression on a round face.

Round brown eyes full of bright intelligence, alive in a way that Russian faces were not. A person, I judged, whose still soft outlines of youth hid a mind already sharply adult. I'd had a bit of the same trouble myself at the same age, ten years or so ago.

'Are you Stephen Luce?' I said.

A smile flickered and disappeared. 'That's right.'

'I would rather not have known about the architect.'

'Why?'

'I don't like horror movies.'

'Life is a horror movie,' he said. 'Do you want to see Lenin's tomb?' He half turned away and pointed an arm to the middle distance, where a queue were waiting outside a large box-like building halfway along the Kremlin wall. 'The Cathedral isn't a church now, it's some sort of store. You can go into the Tomb, though.'

'No, thank you.'

He moved off, however, in that direction, and I went with him.

'Over there,' he said, pointing to one side of the Tomb, 'is a small bust of Stalin, on a short pillar. It has recently appeared there, without any ceremony. You may think this is of no great note, but in point of fact it is very interesting. At one time Stalin was with Lenin in the Tomb. Revered, and all that. Then there was a spot of revisionism, and Stalin was the ultra *persona non grata*, so they took him out of the Tomb and put up a small statue outside, instead. Then they did a spot more revisionism, and removed even the statue, leaving nothing but a curt plaque in the ground where it had been. But now we have a new statue, back on the same spot. This one is not the old proud glare of world domination, but a downward-looking, pensive, low-profile sort of thing. Fascinating, don't you think?'

'What are you reading at the University?' I said.

'Russian history.'

I looked from the rebirth of Stalin to the dead cathedral. 'Tyrants come and go,' I said. 'Tyranny is constant.'

'Some things are best said in the open air.'

I looked at him straightly. 'How much will you help me?' I asked.

'Why don't you take some photographs?' he said. 'Behave like a tourist.'

'No one thinks I'm a tourist, unless having one's room searched is par for the packages.'

'Oh gee,' he said quaintly. 'In that case, let's just walk.'

At tourist pace we left Red Square and went towards the river. I huddled inside my coat and pulled my scarf up over my ears to meet the fur hat I had bought that morning, following Natasha's instructions.

'Why don't you untie the ear-flaps?' Stephen Luce

said, untying a black tape bow on top of his own head. 'Much warmer.' He pulled the formerly folded-up flaps down over his ears, and let the black tape ties dangle free. 'Don't tie the tapes under your chin,' he said, 'or they'll think you're a pouff.'

I pulled the flaps down and let the tapes flutter in the wind, as he did.

'What do you want me to do?' he said.

'Come with me to see some men about some horses.'

'When?'

'Mornings are best, for horse people.'

He took a minute over replying, then said doubtfully, 'I suppose I could cut tomorrow's lecture, just for once.'

How like Hughes-Beckett, I thought sardonically, to equip me with an interpreter whose time was measured in lunch hours and missed lectures. I glanced at the round, troubled face in its frame of black fur, and more or less decided then and there that my whole mission was impossible.

'Do you know Rupert Hughes-Beckett?' I said.

'Never heard of him.'

I sighed. 'Who was it who wrote to you, asking you to help me?'

'The Foreign Office. A man called Spencer. I know *him*. They are sponsoring me, sort of, you see. Through college. The idea being that eventually I'll work for them. Though I might not, in the end. It's all a bit suffocating, that diplomatic wax-works.'

We reached the approach to the bridge over the river, and Stephen threw out an arm in another of his generous gestures.

'Over there is the British Embassy,' he said, pointing.

I couldn't see much for snow. I took off my glasses, dried them as best I could on a handkerchief, and enjoyed for a minute or two a clearer look at the world.

'Turn off right at the far side of the bridge,' Stephen said. 'Go down the steps to the other road running beneath it, along beside the river, and the Embassy's that pale yellow building along there, giving a good imitation of Buckingham Palace.'

I told him I was going for a drink with the cultural attaché and he said the best of British luck, and not to miss seeing the Ambassador's loo, it had the best view of the Kremlin in the whole of Moscow.

'I say,' he said, as we went on over the bridge, 'do you mind telling me what you're actually here for?'

'Didn't they say?'

'No. Only to interpret, if necessary.'

I shook my head in frustration. 'Chasing a will-o'-the-wisp. Looking for a rumour called Alyosha. Some say he doesn't exist and others that he doesn't want to be found. All I have to do is find him, see who he is and what he is, and decide whether he poses any sort of threat to a chap who wants to ride in the Olympics.

And since you asked, I will now bore your ears off by telling you the whole story.'

He listened with concentration and his ears remained in place. When I'd finished he was walking with a springier step.

'Count me in, then,' he said. 'And hang the lectures. I'll borrow someone else's notes.' We turned at the end of the bridge to go back, and between the snowflakes I saw his dark brown eyes shining with humorous life. 'I thought you were here just fact-finding for the Games. In a general way, and semi-official. This is more fun.'

'I haven't thought so,' I said.

He laughed. 'Ve have vays of making you sit up and enjoy yourself.'

'Ve had better have vays of keeping it all very discreet.'

'Oh sure. Do you want the benefit of the immense experience of a lifetime of living in Moscow?'

'Whose?' I said.

'Mine, of course. I've been here eleven weeks. Lifetimes are comparative.'

'Fire away,' I said.

'Never do anything unusual. Never turn up when you're not expected, and always turn up if you are.'

I said, 'That doesn't sound very extraordinary.'

I received a bright amused shot from the brown eyes. 'Some English people touring here by car decided to go to a different town for a night from the one they had originally booked. Just an impulse. They were fined for it.'

'*Fined?*' I was amazed.

'Yes. Can you imagine a foreign tourist being fined in England because he went to Manchester instead of Birmingham? Can you imagine an English hotel doing anything but shrug if he didn't turn up? But everything here is regulated. There are masses of people just standing around watching other people, and they all report what they see, because that's their job. They are employed to watch. There's no unemployment here. Instead of handing a bloke dole money and letting him spend it in civilized ways like soccer and gambling and pubs, they give him a job watching. Two birds with one stone, and all that.'

'Standing in groups at airports and in bus shelters, and dotted around outside hotels?'

He grinned. 'So right. Those guys in bus stops are there to stop all foreign-registered cars going out of Moscow, to check their destinations and visas, because all foreigners need a visa to go more than thirty kilo-metres from the centre. Sometimes they stop Russian cars, but not often. Anyway, there's a joke here that you always see at least three Russians together when they've any regular contact with foreigners. One alone might be tempted, two might conspire, but if there are three, one will always inform.'

'Cynical.'

'And practical. What did you say you'd do today? I take it you have Intourist girls looking after you?'

'Natasha and Anna,' I said. 'I told them I'd be in the hotel to lunch and go on a bus tour of the city afterwards.'

'Then you'd better do it,' he said judiciously. 'I'm not sure they don't get into trouble if they lose their charge, so to speak.'

I paused at the centre of the bridge to look over the parapet at the iron-grey water. Snow speckled everything and filled the air like torn tissue-paper. To the right along the river bank stretched the long red beautiful walls of the Kremlin, with golden towers at intervals and vistas of golden onion domes inside. A walled city, a fortress, with defunct churches and active government offices and the daily tread of millions of tourists. To the left, on the opposite bank, the British Embassy.

'Better move on,' Stephen said. 'Two men standing still on a bridge in the snow . . . that's suspicious.'

'I don't believe it.'

'You'd be surprised.'

We walked on, however, and went back up the incline to Red Square.

'Job number one,' I said. 'Will you make a call for me?'

I showed him the Olympic team trainer's name and number, and we stopped at a glasss-walled telephone box. Telephone calls, it appeared, were cheap. Stephen brushed away my offered rouble and produced a two-kopek coin.

'What shall I say?' he asked.

'Say I'd like to see him tomorrow morning. Say I was very impressed with the Russian team at the International Horse Trials and would like to congratulate him and ask his advice. Say I'm frightfully important in the horse world. Lay it on a bit. He doesn't know me.' I gave him some well-known Eventing names. 'Say I'm a colleague of theirs.'

'Are you?' he said, dialling the number.

'I know them,' I said. 'That's why I was sent. Because I know the horse people.'

Someone answered at the other end, and Stephen launched into what was to me a vague jumble of noises. A softer-sounding language than I had for some reason expected. Pleasing.

He talked for quite some time, and listened, and talked, and listened, and talked, and finally rang off.

'Success,' he said. 'Eleven o'clock. Outside the stables, round the far side of the racecourse.'

'The Hippodrome,' I said.

'That's right.' His eyes gleamed. 'The Olympic horses exercise there on the track.'

'Fantastic,' I said, astounded. 'Bloody incredible.'

'And you were wrong about one thing,' Stephen said. 'He did know who you are. He said you went to ride in a race called the Pardubice in Czechoslovakia, and he saw you finish third. He seemed in point of fact to be quite pleased to be going to meet you.'

'Nice of him,' I said modestly.

Stephen spoilt it. 'Russians love a chance of talking to people from the outside. They see so few that they love it.'

We agreed that he should meet me outside the hotel the following morning, and his cheerfulness was catching.

'When you go on that bus tour,' he said as we parted, 'you'll stop in Derzhinsky Square. With a statue of Derzhinsky on a tall column. There's a big store for children there. What the guide won't tell you, though, is that the building next to it, across the street, is the Lubianka.'

There were taxis waiting outside the hotel but none of the drivers spoke English, and either they didn't understand the words 'British Embassy', or the address written in English script, or they understood but refused to take me there. In any case, I got a chorus of shaken heads, so in the end I walked. It was still snowing, but wetly, and what lay on the ground was slush. After a mile and a half of it my feet were soaking and icy and my mood deepening from cross to vile.

Following Stephen's instructions, I found the steps at the far side of the bridge and descended to the lower level, walking along there with dark heavy buildings on my left and the chest-high river wall on the right. When I, at length, reached the gateway of the Embassy, a Russian soldier stepped out of a sentry box and barred my way.

An odd argument then took place in which neither protagonist could understand a word the other said. I pointed vigorously at my watch, and to the Embassy door, and said, 'I am English,' several times very loudly, and got even crosser. The Russian finally, dubiously, stood back a pace and let me through into the short driveway. The huge front door of the Embassy itself was opened, with a lot less fuss, by a dark blue uniform with gilt buttons and braids.

Inside, the hall and stairs and visible doorways were rich with the glossy wood and glass and plaster mouldings of more elegant ages. There was also a large leather-topped desk behind which sat a one-man reception committee, and, standing near him, a tall languid man with noble bones and greying hair combed carefully backwards.

The dark blue uniform offered to relieve me of my coat and hat, and the man at the desk asked if he could help me.

'The cultural attaché?' I said. 'I've an appointment.'

The grey-haired man moved gently like a lily in the wind and said that the cultural attaché happened to be himself. He extended a limp hand and a medium smile, and I responded with the merest shade more warmth to both. He murmured platitudes about the weather and air travel while he made some internal judgements about me, but it appeared that I had passed his private tests, because he suddenly changed mental gears and asked with some charm whether I would care to see over the Embassy itself before we went to his office for a drink. His office, he explained, was in a separate building.

We climbed the stairs and made a tour of the reception rooms, and duly inspected the loo with the best view of the Kremlin. The cultural attaché, who had identified himself as Oliver Waterman, kept up a genial informed chatter as if he showed visitors round this route every day of the week: which, on reflection, perhaps he did. We ended, after a short windy outside walk, in a more modern-looking first-floor suite of carpeted book-lined offices, where he wasted no time in pouring hefty drinks.

'Don't know what we can do for you,' he said, settling deep into a leather armchair, and waving me to one similar. 'This Farringford business seems to be a fuss over nothing.'

'You hope,' I said.

He smiled thinly. 'True. But there's no fire without smoke, and we haven't had even a whiff.'

'Did you yourself interview the three Russian observers?' I asked.

'Er,' he said, clearing his throat and looking concerned. 'Which observers would those be?'

Resignedly I explained. His expression cleared

gradually as if a responsibility had been taken from him.

'But, you see,' he said pleasantly, 'we in the Embassy would not speak to them ourselves. We approached our opposite numbers for relevant information, and were informed that no one knew anything of any significance.'

'You couldn't have spoken to those men face to face in their own homes?'

He shook his head. 'It is actively discouraged, if not positively forbidden, for private contacts to take place.'

'Forbidden by them, or by us?'

'Bit of both. But by us, definitely.'

'So you never really get to know the Russian people, even though you live here?'

He shook his head without any visible regret. 'There is always a risk, in unofficial contacts.'

'So xenophobia works both ways?' I said.

He uncrossed his legs and recrossed them left over right. 'Fear of foreigners is older than the conscious mind,' he said, smiling as if he had said it often before. 'But, now, about your enquiries . . .'

The telephone at his elbow interrupted him. He picked up the receiver in a leisurely fashion after the third ring, and said merely, 'Yes?'

A slight frown creased his high smooth forehead. 'Very well, bring him round.' He replaced the receiver and continued with his former sentence. 'About your enquiries, we can offer you telex facilities, if you need them, and if you'll give me your room's telephone number I can ring you if any messages arrive for you.'

'I gave you the number,' I said.

'Oh, did you?' He looked vague. 'I'd better take it again, my dear chap.'

I repeated the number from memory, and he wrote it on a notepad.

'Let me see to your glass,' he said, splashing away with a lavish hand. 'And then perhaps you might meet one or two of my colleagues.'

There were the noises of people arriving downstairs. Oliver Waterman stood up and brushed his smooth hair back with the insides of both wrists; a gesture of preparing himself, I reckoned, more than any need for grooming.

There was one loud intrusive voice rising above a chorus of two others, one male, one female, and as they came up the stairs I found myself putting a name to it. With no sense of surprise I watched Malcolm Herrick advance through the doorway.

'Evening, Oliver,' he said confidently, and then, seeing me, 'Well, sport, if it isn't our sleuth. Made any progress?'

From a fleeting glance at Oliver Waterman's face I gathered that his reaction to Malcolm Herrick was much like mine. It was impossible not to attend to what Herrick said because of the physical force of his speech, the result no doubt of years of journalistic necessity; but there was no visible warmth behind the sociable words, and possibly even a little malice.

'Drink, Malcolm?' Oliver suggested, with true diplomatic civility.

'Couldn't be better.'

Oliver Waterman, bottle and glass in hand, made introducing motions between me and the other newcomers. 'Randall Drew . . . Polly Paget, Ian Young. They work here with me in this department.'

Polly Paget was a sensible-looking lady in flat shoes, past girlhood but not quite middle-aged, wearing her hair short and her cardigan long. She gave Oliver Waterman a small straightforward smile and accepted her drink before Herrick, as of right. He himself looked as if he thought attaché's assistants should be served after him.

If I hadn't been told Ian Young's name or heard him speak, I would have taken him for a Russian. I looked at him curiously, realizing how familiar I had already become with the skin texture and stillness of expression of the Moscow population. Ian Young had the same white heavyish face in which nothing discernible was going on. His voice, when he spoke, which at that time was very little, was unremarkably English.

Malcolm Herrick effortlessly dominated what conversation there was, telling Oliver Waterman, it seemed to me, just what he should do about a particularly boring row which had just broken out over a forthcoming visit of a prestigious orchestra.

When Polly Paget offered a suggestion, Herrick interrupted without listening and squashed her. Oliver Waterman said, 'Well, perhaps, yes, you may be right,' at intervals, while not looking Herrick in the eye except in the briefest of flashes, a sure sign of boredom or dislike. Ian Young sat looking at Herrick with an unnerving lack of response, by which Herrick was not in the least unnerved: and I drank my drink and thought of the wet walk back.

All possible juice extracted from the music scandal, Herrick switched his attention back to me.

'Well, then, sport, how's it going?'

'Slow to stop,' I said.

He nodded. 'Told you so. Too bad. That whole ground's been raked fine and there's not a pebble to be found. Wish there was. I need a decent story.'

'Or indecent, for preference,' Polly Paget said. Herrick ignored her.

'Did you talk to the *chef d'équipe*?' I said.

'Who?' said Oliver Waterman. I saw from Herrick's face that he hadn't, but also that he wasn't going to admit it unless forced to: and even then, I guessed, he would pooh-pooh the necessity.

I said to Oliver Waterman, 'Mr Kropotkin. The man who oversees the training of the horses and riders for the horse trials. The non-playing captain, so to speak. I was given his name by Rupert Hughes-Beckett.'

'So you'll be seeing him?' Waterman said.

'Yes, tomorrow morning. He seems to be all that's left.'

Ian Young stirred. 'I talked with him,' he said.

Every head turned his way. Thirty-five or so, I thought. Thick-set, brown-haired, wearing a crumpled grey suit and a blue-and-white-striped shirt with the points of the collar curling up like a dried sandwich. He raised his eyebrows and pursed his mouth, which for him was an excessive change of expression.

'In the course of the discreet preliminary enquiries required by the Foreign Office, I too was given his name. I talked with him pretty exhaustively. He knows nothing about any scandal to do with Farringford. A complete dead end.'

'There you are, then,' Waterman said, shrugging. 'As I said before, there's no fire. Not a spark.'

'Mm,' I said. 'It would be best that way. But there is a spark. Or there was, in England.' And I told them about Johnny Farringford being beaten up by two men who warned him to stay away from Alyosha.

Their faces showed differing levels of dismay and disbelief.

'But my dear chap,' said Oliver Waterman, recovering his former certainty, 'surely that means that this Alyosha, whoever he is, is absolutely determined not to be dropped into any sort of mess? So surely that makes it all the safer for Farringford to come to the Olympics?'

'Except,' I said apologetically, 'that of course

Farringford was also told in the summer that if he came to Moscow, Alyosha would be waiting to extract revenge for the stresses which gave Hans Kramer a heart attack.'

There was a short thoughtful silence.

'People change their minds,' said Polly Paget at length, judiciously. 'Maybe in the summer, when Kramer died, this Alyosha sounded off a bit hysterically, and now, on reflection, the last thing he wants is to be involved.'

Herrick shook his head impatiently, but it seemed to me the most sensible solution yet advanced.

'I really hope you're right,' I said. 'The only trouble will be proving it. And the only way to prove it, as it always has been, is for me to find Alyosha, and talk to him, and get from him his own positive assurance that he means Farringford no harm.'

Polly Paget nodded. Oliver Waterman looked mildly despairing, and Malcolm Herrick unmirthfully laughed.

'Good luck to you, then, sport,' he said. 'You'll be here till Doomsday. I tell you, I've looked for this bloody Alyosha, and he doesn't exist.'

I sighed a little and looked at Ian Young. 'And you?' I said.

'I've looked too,' he said. 'There isn't a trace.'

There seemed little else to say. The party broke up, and I asked Waterman if he could telephone for a taxi.

'My dear chap,' he said regretfully. 'They won't come here. They don't like to be contaminated by stopping

84

outside the British Embassy. You can probably catch an empty one on the main road, if you walk along to the bridge.'

We shook hands at his outer door, and, again swathed in overcoat and fur hat, I set off towards the guarded gate. It had stopped snowing at last, which improved the prospects slightly. Ian Young, however, called out after me and offered a lift in his car, which I gratefully agreed to. He sat stolidly behind his steering-wheel, dealing with darkness, falling snow and road-obscuring slush as if emotion had never been invented.

'Malcolm Herrick,' he said, still dead-pan, 'is a pain in the arse.'

He turned left out of the gate, and drove along beside the river.

'And you're stuck with him,' I said.

His silence was assent. 'He's a persistent burrower,' he said. 'Gets a story if it's there.'

'You're telling me to go home and forget it?'

'No,' he said, turning more corners. 'But don't stir up the Russians. They take fright very easily. When they're frightened they attack. People of great endurance, full of courage. But easily alarmed. Don't forget.'

'Very well,' I said.

'You have a man called Frank Jones sitting at your table at the hotel,' he said.

I glanced at him. His face was dead calm.

'Yes,' I said.

'Did you know he was in the KGB?'

I copied his impassiveness. I said, 'Did you know that you are going a very long way round to my hotel?'

He actually reacted: even went so far as to smile. 'How did you know?'

'Went on a bus tour. Studied the maps.'

'And does Frank Jones sit with you always?'

'So far,' I said, nodding. 'And a middle-aged couple from Lancashire. We sat together by chance at dinner yesterday, our first night here, and you know how it is, people tend to return to the same table. So yes, the same four of us have sat together today at breakfast and lunch. What makes you think he is in the KGB? He's as English as they come, and he was thoroughly searched at the airport on the way in.'

'Searched so that you could see, I suppose?'

'Yes,' I said, thinking. 'Everyone on the plane could see.'

'Cover,' he said. 'There's no mistake. He's not sitting at your table by accident. He came with you from England and he'll no doubt go back with you. Has he searched your room yet?'

I said nothing. Ian Young very faintly smiled again.

'I see he has,' he said. 'What did he find?'

'Clothes and cough mixture.'

'No Russian addresses or phone numbers?'

'I had them in my pocket,' I said. 'Such as they are.'

'Frank Jones,' he said, driving round back streets, 'has a Russian grandmother, who has spoken the language to him all his life. She married a British sailor, but her sympathies were all with the October Revolution. She recruited Frank in the cradle.'

'But if he is KGB,' I said, 'why do you let him ... operate?'

'Better the devil you know.' We swung into yet another deserted street. 'Every time he comes back we are alerted by our passport-control people back home. They send a complete passenger list of the flight he comes on, because he always travels with his business. So we scan it. We get someone out pronto to the airport to see where he goes. We follow. Tut tut. We see him book into the Intourist. We drift into the dining room. If it's safe, he also *sits* with his business. We see he's with you. We know all about you. We relax. We wish Frank well. We certainly don't want to disturb him. If his masters discovered we knew all about him, next time they'd send someone else. And then where would we be? When Frank comes, we know to pay attention. Worth his weight in roubles, Frank is, to us.'

We went slowly and quietly down a dark road. Snow fell and melted wetly as it touched the ground.

'What is he likely to do?' I said.

'About you? Report where you go, who you see, what you eat and how many times you crap before breakfast.'

'Sod,' I said.

'And don't ditch him unless you have to, and if you have to, for God's sake make it look accidental.'

87

I said doubtfully, 'I've had no practice at this sort of thing.'

'Obvious. You didn't notice him follow you from your hotel.'

'Did he?' I said, alarmed.

'He was walking up and down the Naberezhnaya waiting for you to come out. He saw you drive out with me. He'll go back to the Intourist and wait for you there.'

The lights from the dashboard shone dimly on his big impassive face. The economy of muscle movement extended, I had noticed, throughout his body. His head turned little upon his neck: his hands remained in one position on the steering wheel. He didn't shift in his seat, or drum with his fingers. In his heavy raincoat, thick leather gloves, and fur hat with the earflaps up, he looked every inch a Russian.

'What is your job here?' I said.

'Cultural assistant.' His voice gave away as little as his face. Ask silly questions, I thought.

He slowed the car still further and switched off the headlights, and, with the engine barely audible, swung into a cobbled courtyard, and stopped. Put on the handbrake. Half turned in his seat to face me.

'You'll be a few minutes late for dinner,' he said.

CHAPTER FIVE

He seemed to be in no hurry to explain. We sat in complete darkness listening to the irregular ticking of metal as the engine cooled to zero in the Moscow night. In time, as my eyes adjusted, I could see dark high buildings on each side, and some iron railings ahead, with bushes behind them.

'Where are we?' I said.

He didn't answer.

'Look . . .' I said.

He interrupted. 'When we get out of the car, do not talk. Follow me, but say nothing. There are always people standing in the shadows . . . if they hear you speak English, they will be suspicious. They'll report our visit.'

He opened the car door and stood up outside. He seemed to take it for granted that I should trust him, and I saw no particular reason not to. I stood up after him and closed the door quietly, as he had done, and followed where he led.

We walked towards the railings, which proved to

contain a gate. Ian Young opened it with a click of iron, and it swung on unoiled hinges with desolate little squeaks, falling shut behind us with a positive clink. Beyond it, a curving path led away between straggly bare-branched bushes, the dim light showing that in this forlorn public garden the snow lay greyly unmelted, covering everything thinly, like years of undisturbed dust.

There were a few seats beside the path, and glimpses of flat areas which might in summer be grass; but in late November the melancholy of such places could seep into the soul like fungus.

Ian Young walked purposefully onward, neither hurrying nor moving with caution: a man on a normal errand, not arousing suspicion.

At the far side of the garden we reached more railings and another gate. Again the opening click, the squeaks, the closing clink. Ian Young turned without pause to the right and set off along the slushy pavement.

In silence, I followed.

Lights from windows overhead revealed us to be in a residential road of large old buildings with alleys and small courtyards in between. Into one of these yards, cobbled and dark, Ian Young abruptly turned.

Again I went with him, unspeaking.

Scaffolding climbed the sides of the buildings there, and heaps of rubble cluttered the ground. We picked our way over broken bricks and metal tubing and scattered planks, going, as far as I could see, nowhere.

There was, however, a destination. To reach it, we had to step through the scaffolding and over an open ditch which looked like the preliminary earthworks of new drains: and on the far side of the mud and slush there was a heavy wooden door in a dark archway. Ian Young pushed the door, which seemed to have no fastening, and it opened with the easy grind of constant use.

Inside, out of the wind, there was a dimmish light in a bare grey entrance. Gritty concrete underfoot, no paint, no decoration of any kind on the greyish concrete walls. There was a flight of concrete steps leading upwards, and, beside them, a small lift in an ancient-looking cage.

Ian Young pulled open the outer and inner folding metal gates of the lift, and we stepped inside. He closed the gates, pushed the fourth-floor button, and forbade me, with his eye, to utter a word.

We emerged from the lift on to a bare landing; wooden-floored, not concrete. There were two closed doors, wooden, long ago varnished, one at each end of the rectangular space. Ian Young stepped to the left, and pressed the button of a bell.

The hallway was very quiet. One could not hear the sound of ringing when he pushed the button, as he did again, in a short-short-long rhythm. There were no voices murmuring behind the doors. No feet on the stairs. No feeling of nearby warmth and life. The lobby to limbo, I thought fancifully; and the door quietly opened.

A tall woman stood there, looking out with the lack of expression which I by now regarded as normal. She peered at Ian Young, and then, more lingeringly, at me. Her eyes travelled back again, enquiringly.

Ian Young nodded.

The woman stepped to one side, tacitly inviting us in. Ian Young went steadfastly over the threshold, and it was far too late for me to decide that on the other side of the door was where I had no wish to be. It swung shut behind me, and the woman slid a bolt.

Still no one spoke. Ian Young took off his coat and hat, and gestured for me to do the same. The woman hung them carefully on pegs in a row that already accommodated a good many similar garments.

She put a hand on Ian Young's arm and led the way along the passage of what seemed to be a private flat. Another closed wooden door was opened, and we went into a moderately sized living room.

There were five men there, standing up. Five pairs of eyes focused steadily on my face, five blank expressions covering who knew what thoughts.

They were all dressed tidily and much alike in shirts, jackets, trousers and indoor shoes, but they varied greatly in age and build. One of them, the slimmest, of about my own age, held himself rigid, as if facing an ordeal. The others were simply wary, standing like wild deer scenting the wind.

A man of about fifty, grey-haired and wearing glasses, stepped forward to greet Ian Young and give him a token hug.

He talked to him in Russian, and introduced him to the other four men in a mumble of long names I couldn't begin to catch. They nodded to him, each in turn. A little of the tension went out of the proceedings and small movements occurred in the herd.

'Evgeny Sergeevich,' Ian Young said. 'This is Randall Drew.'

The fiftyish man slowly extended his hand, which I shook. He was neither welcoming nor hostile, and in no hurry to commit himself either way. More dignity than power, I thought: and he was inspecting me with intensity, as if wishing to peer into my soul. He saw instead, I supposed, merely a thinnish, grey-eyed, dark-haired man in glasses, giving his own impression of a stone wall.

To me, Ian Young at last spoke. 'This is our host, Evgeny Sergeevich Titov. And our hostess, his wife, Olga Ivanovna.' He made a small semi-formal bow to the woman who had let us in. She gave him a steady look, and it seemed to me that the firmness of her features came from iron reserves within.

'Good evening,' I said, and she replied seriously in English, 'Good evening.'

The rigid young man, still tautly strung, said something urgently in Russian.

Ian Young turned to me. 'He is asking if we were followed. You can answer. Were we followed?'

'No,' I said.

'Why don't you think so?'

'No one followed us through the garden. The gates make an unmistakable noise. No one came through them after us.'

Ian Young turned away from me and spoke to the group in Russian. They listened to him with their eyes on me, and when he had finished they stirred, and began to move apart from each other, and to sit down. Only the rigid one remained standing, ready for flight.

'I have told them they can trust you,' Ian Young said. 'If I am wrong, I will kill you.'

His eyes were cool and steady, looking unwaveringly into mine. I listened to his words, which in other contexts would have been unbelievable and embarrassing, and I saw that he quite simply meant what he said.

'Very well,' I said.

A flicker of something I couldn't read moved in his mind.

'Please sit down,' Olga Ivanovna said, indicating a deep chair with arms on the far side of the room. 'Please sit down there.' She spoke the English words with a strong Russian accent, but that she knew any English at all put me to shame.

I walked across and sat where she pointed, knowing

that they had discussed and planned that I should be placed there, from where I couldn't escape unless they chose to let me go. The deep chair embraced me softly like a bolstered prison. I looked up and found Ian Young near me, looking down. I half closed my eyes, and faintly smiled.

'What do you expect?' he said.

'To learn why we are here.'

'You are not afraid.' Half a statement, half a question.

'No,' I said. 'They are.'

He glanced swiftly at the six Russians and then looked back, with concentration, at me.

'You are not the usual run of bloody fool,' he said.

The rigid young man, still also on his feet, said something impatiently to Ian Young. He nodded, looked from me to the rigid man and back again, took a visible breath, and entrusted me with a lot of dangerous knowledge.

'This is Boris Dmitrevich Telyatnikov,' he said.

The rigid young man raised his chin as if the name itself were an honour.

Ian Young said, 'Boris Dmitrevich rode in the Russian team at the International Horse Trials in England in September.'

It was a piece of information which had me starting automatically to my feet, but even the beginnings of the springing motion reawoke the alarm in all the watchers. Boris Dmitrevich took an actual step backwards.

I relaxed into the chair and looked as mild as possible, and the atmosphere of precarious trust crept gingerly back.

'Please tell him,' I said, 'that I am absolutely delighted to meet him.'

The same could obviously not be said for Boris Dmitrevich Telyatnikov, but I was there from their choice, not my own. I reckoned if they hadn't wanted to see me pretty badly, they wouldn't have put themselves at what they clearly felt was considerable risk.

Olga Ivanovna brought a hard wooden chair and placed it facing me, about four feet away. She then fetched another and placed it near me, at right angles. Ian Young took this seat next to me, and Boris Dmitrevich the one opposite.

While this was going on, I tool a look round the room, which had bookshelves over much of the wall space and cupboards over the rest. The single large window was obscured by solid wooden cream-painted shutters, fastened by a flat metal bar through slots. The floor was of bare wooden boards, dark stained, unpolished and clean. Furniture consisted of a table, an old sofa covered with a rug, several hard chairs, and the one deep comfortable one in which I sat. All the furniture, except for the two chairs repositioned for Boris Dmitrevich and Ian Young, was ranged round the walls against the bookshelves and cupboards, leaving the centre free. There were no softeners: no curtains, cushions, or indoor plants. Nothing extravagant, frivolous, or wasteful. Everything of ancient and sensible worth, giving an overall impression of shabbiness stemming from long use but not underlying poverty. A room belonging to people who chose to have it that way, not who could not afford anything different.

Ian Young carried on a short conversation with Boris Dmitrevich in impenetrable Russian, and then did a spot of translation, looking more worried than I liked.

'Boris wants to warn us,' he said, 'that what you are dealing with is not some tomfool scandal but something to do with killing people.'

'With *what*?'

He nodded. 'That's what he said.' He turned his head back to Boris, and they talked some more. It appeared, from the expressions all around me, that what Boris was saying was no news to anyone except Ian Young and myself.

Boris was built like a true horseman, of middle height, with strong shoulders and well-coordinated movements. He was good-looking, with straight black hair and ears very flat to his head. He spoke earnestly to Ian Young, his dark eyes flicking my way every few seconds as if to check that he could still risk my hearing what he had to tell.

'Boris says,' Ian Young said, the shock showing, 'that the German, Hans Kramer, was murdered.'

'No,' I said confidently. 'There was an autopsy. Natural causes.'

Ian shook his head. 'Boris says that someone has found a way of causing people to drop down dead from heart attacks. He says that the death of Hans Kramer was . . .' he turned back briefly to Boris to consult, and then back to me, ' . . . the death of Hans Kramer was a sort of demonstration.'

It seemed ridiculous. 'A demonstration of what?'

A longer chat ensued. Ian Young shook his head and argued. Boris began to make fierce chopping motions with his hands, and spots of colour appeared on his cheeks. I gathered that his information had at this point entered the realms of guesswork, and that Ian Young didn't believe what was being said. Time to take a pull back to the facts.

'Look,' I said, interrupting the agitated flow. 'Let's start at the beginning. I'll ask some questions, and you get me the answers. OK?'

'Yes,' Ian Young said, subsiding. 'Carry on.'

'Ask him how he travelled to England, and where he went, and where he stayed, and how his team fared in the finals.'

'But,' he said, puzzled, 'what has that to do with Hans Kramer?'

'Not much,' I said. 'But I know how the Russians travelled and where they stayed and how they fared, and I just want to do my own private bit of checking that Boris is who he says he is; and also if he talks about unloaded things like that he will calm down again and we can then get the beliefs without the passion.'

He blinked. 'My God,' he said.

'Ask him.'

'Yes.' He turned to Boris and delivered the question.

Boris answered impatiently that they travelled by motor horse box across Europe to The Hague, and from there by sea to England, still with the horse boxes, and drove on to Burghley, where they stayed in quarters especially reserved for them.

'How many horses, and how many men?' I said.

Boris said six horses, and stumbled over the number of people. I suggested that this was because the Russians had paid for only seven 'human' tickets but had actually taken ten or more men ... Make it a joke, I said to Ian Young: not an insult.

He made it enough of a joke for Boris and everyone else almost to laugh, which handily released much tension all round and steadied the temperature.

'They want to know how you know,' Ian said.

'The shipping agent told me. Tickets were bought for six riders and a *chef d'équipe*, but three or four grooms travelled among the legs of the horses. The shipping agents were amused, not angry.'

Ian relayed the answer and got another round of appreciative noises in the throat. Boris gave a more detailed account of the Russian team's performance in the trials than I had memorized, and by the end I had no doubt that he was genuine. He had also recovered his temper and lost his rigidity, and I reckoned we might go carefully back to the minefield.

'Right,' I said. 'Now ask him if he knew Hans Kramer personally. If he ever spoke to him face to face, and if so in what language.'

The question at once stiffened up the sinews, but the reply looked only moderately nervous.

Ian Young translated. 'Yes, he did talk to Hans Kramer. They spoke German, though Boris says he knows only a little German. He had met Hans Kramer before, when they both rode in the same trials, and they were friendly together.'

'Ask him what they talked about,' I said.

The answer came easily, predictably, with shrugs. 'Horses. The trials. The Olympics. The weather.'

'Anything else?'

'No.'

'Anything to do with backgammon, gambling clubs, homosexuals or transvestites?'

I saw by the collective indrawn breaths of disapproval round about that if Boris had been discussing such things he had better not say so. His own positive negative, however, looked real enough.

'Does he know Johnny Farringford?' I said.

It appeared that Boris knew who Johnny was, and had seen him ride, but had not spoken to him.

'Did he see Hans Kramer and Johnny Farringford together?'

Boris had not noticed one way or the other.

'Was he there on the spot when Hans Kramer died?'

Boris's unemotional response told me the answer before Ian translated.

'No, he wasn't. He had finished his cross-country section before Hans Kramer set out. He saw Hans Kramer being *weighed* . . . is that right?' Ian Young looked doubtful.

'Yes,' I said. 'The horses have to carry minimum weights, to make it a fairer test. There is a weighing machine on the course, to weigh the riders with their saddles just before they set off, and also as soon as they come back. The same as in racing.'

Boris, it appeared, had had to wait while Hans Kramer was weighed out, before himself weighing in. He had wished Hans Kramer good luck. '*Alles Gute.*' The irony of it lugubriously pleased the listening friends.

'Please ask Boris why he thinks Hans Kramer was murdered.' I said the words deliberately flatly, and Ian Young relayed them the same way, but they reproduced in Boris the old high alarm.

'Did he hear anyone say so?' I asked decisively, to cut off the emotion.

'Yes.'

'Who said so?'

Boris did not know the man who said so.

'Did he say it to Boris face to face?'

No. Boris had overheard it.

I could see why Ian Young had doubted the whole story.

'Ask in what language this man spoke.'

In Russian, Boris said, but he was not a Russian.

'Does he mean that the man spoke Russian with a foreign accent?'

That was right.

'What accent?' I said patiently. 'From what country?'

Boris didn't know.

'Where was Boris when he overheard this man?'

It seemed a pretty harmless question to me, but it brought an abrupt intense stillness into the room.

Evgeny Sergeevich Titov finally stirred and said something lengthily to Ian.

'They want you to understand that Boris should not have been where he was. That if he tells you, you will hold his future in your power.'

'I see,' I said.

There was a pause.

Ian said, 'I think they're waiting for you to swear you will never reveal where he was.'

'Perhaps he had better just tell me what he heard,' I said.

There was a brief consultation among all of them, but they must have decided before I came that I would have to know.

Evgeny Sergeevich did the talking. Boris, he said, had been on a train, going to London. It was absolutely against orders. If he had been discovered, he would have been sent home immediately in disgrace. He would never be considered for the Olympic team, and he might even have faced imprisonment, as he was carrying letters and other papers to Russians who had defected to the West. The papers were not political, Evgeny said earnestly, but just personal messages and photographs from the defectors' families still in Russia, and a few small writings for publication in literary magazines. Not State secrets, but highly illegal. There would have been much trouble for many people, not just for Boris, if he had been stopped and searched. So that when he heard someone speaking Russian on the train he had been very frightened, and his first urgent priority had been to keep out of sight himself, not to see who had been speaking. He had crept out of the carriage he was in, and walked forward as far as he could through the train. When it reached London, he left it fast, and was met by friends at the barrier.

'I understand all that,' I said, when Ian Young finished translating. 'Tell them I won't tell.'

Encouraged, Boris came to the nub.

'There were two men,' Ian Young relayed. 'Because of the noise of the train, Boris could only hear one of them.'

'Right. Go on.'

Boris spoke into a breath-held attentive silence. Ian

103

Young listened with his former scepticism once again showing.

'He says,' he said, 'that he overheard a man say, "It was a perfect demonstration. You could kill half the Olympic riders the same way, if that's what you want. But it will cost you." Then the other man said something inaudible, and the voice Boris could hear said, "I have another client." The other man spoke, and then the man Boris could hear said, "Kramer took ninety seconds." '

Bloody hell, I thought. Shimmering scarlet *hell*.

Boris crept away at that point, Ian said. Boris was too worried about being discovered himself for the meaning of what he had heard to sink in. And in any case it was not until the next day that he learned of Kramer's death. When he did hear, he was shattered. Before that, he had thought the ninety seconds was something to do with timing on the Event course.

'Ask him to repeat what he heard the man say,' I said.

The exchanges took place.

'Did Boris use exactly the same words as the first time?' I said.

'Yes, exactly.'

'But you don't believe him?'

'He half heard something perfectly innocent and the rest's imagination.'

'But he believes it,' I said. 'He got angry when you argued. He certainly believes that's what he heard.'

I thought it over, all too aware of seven pairs of eyes directed unwaveringly at my face.

'Please ask Mr Titov,' I said, 'why he has persuaded Boris to tell us all this. I might guess, but I would like him to confirm it.'

Evgeny, sitting on a wooden chair in front of a bookcase, answered with responsibility visibly bowing his shoulders. Lines ridged his forehead. His eyes were sombre.

Ian said, 'He has been very worried since Boris came home from England and told him what he had heard. There was the possibility that Boris was mistaken, and also the possibility that he was not. If he did really hear what he thought he heard, there might be another murder at the Olympics. Or more than one. As a good Russian, Evgeny was anxious that nothing should harm his country in the eyes of the world. It wouldn't do for competitors to be murdered on Russian soil. A way had to be found of warning someone who could get an investigation made, but Evgeny knew no one in England or Germany to write to, even if you could entrust such a letter to the mail. He couldn't explain how he had come by such knowledge, because Boris's whole life would be spoiled, and yet he couldn't see anyone believing the story without Boris's own testimony, so he was up a creek without a paddle.'

'Or words to that effect?'

'You got it.'

'Ask if they know anyone called Alyosha who is even remotely concerned with the Russian team, or the trials, or the Olympics, or Hans Kramer, or anything.'

There was a general unhurried discussion, and the answer was no.

'Is Boris related to Evgeny?' I said.

The question was asked and answered.

'No. Boris just values Evgeny's advice ... Evgeny consulted the others.'

I looked thoughtfully at Ian. His face, as always, gave away as much as a slab of granite, and I found it disconcerting to have no clue at all to what he was thinking.

'You yourself knew Mr Titov before this evening, didn't you?' I said. 'And you'd been here before?'

'Yes, two or three times. Olga Ivanovna works in Cultural Relations, and she's a good friend. But I have to be careful. I'm not allowed to be here.'

'Complicated,' I agreed.

'Evgeny rang me this afternoon and said you were in Moscow, and would I bring you here this evening. I said I would if I could, after you'd been to the Embassy.'

The speed of communications had me gasping. 'Just how did Evgeny know I was in Moscow?'

'Nikolai Alexandrovich happened to tell Boris ...'

'*Who?*'

'Nikolai Alexandrovich Kropotkin. The *chef*

d'équipe. You have an appointment with him tomorrow morning.'

'For Christ's sake ...'

'Kropotkin told Boris, Boris told Evgeny, Evgeny rang me, and I had heard from Oliver Waterman that you would be round for a drink.'

'So simple,' I said, shaking my head. 'And if Evgeny knew you, why didn't he tell you all this weeks ago?'

Ian Young gave me a cool stare and relayed the question.

'Evgeny says it was because Boris wouldn't talk to me.'

'Well, go on,' I said, as he stopped. 'Why did Boris decide he *would* talk to *me*?'

Ian shrugged, and asked, and translated Boris's reply.

'Because you are a rider. A man who knows horses. Boris trusts you because you are a comrade.'

CHAPTER SIX

The lifts at the Intourist Hotel did not stop at the lower of the two restaurant floors, which was where the English tourists ate. One could either walk up one storey from the lobby, or stop the lift at the floor above and walk down. I did that, after parking my coat in my room, and walked down the shallow treads of the broad circular staircase, where, through the handrail, I could see the faces in the dining room before they looked up and saw me.

Natasha was on her feet, consulting her watch and looking worried. The Lancashire Wilkinsons were drinking coffee, unaffected: and if I read anxiety and anger into the fidgets of Frank Jones it was probably only because I guessed they were there.

'Evening,' I said, reaching the bottom. 'Am I too late? Is there anything left?'

Natasha sped across with visible relief. 'We thought you were lost.'

I gave her a full and ingenuous story about a friend driving me up to the University to look down on the lights of the city by night. The Wilkinsons listened with interest, and Frank with slowly evaporating tenseness, as they all, like me, had been up at the semi-official look-out spot in the afternoon on the bus tour; and I almost convinced myself. 'Afraid we were a bit longer than I expected,' I said apologetically.

The Wilkinsons and Frank stayed for company while I ate, and kept up a thoroughly touristy flow of chat. I looked at Frank with a great deal more interest than before, trying to see behind the mask, and failing to do so. Outwardly, he was still a raw-boned twenty-eight or so with an undercombed generosity of reddish-brown curls and the pits and scars of long-term acne. His views were still diluted Marx and his manner still based on the belief in his own superiority to the bulk of mankind.

There were four courses to the evening meal, and the only choice was eat it or don't. The meat looked identical to the tasteless rubber of the evening before, and when it arrived I stared at it gloomily.

'Aren't you going to eat that?' Frank demanded, pointing fiercely at my plate.

'Are you still hungry? Would you care for it?' I said.

'Do you mean it?' He took me at my word, slid the plate in front of him, and set to, proving that both his appetite and molars were a lot stronger than mine.

'Did you know,' he said with his mouth full, giving us a by now accustomed lecture, 'that in this country rents are very low, and electricity and transport and telephone calls are cheap? And when I say cheap, I mean cheap.'

Mrs Wilkinson, who had twice the life of Mister, sighed with envy over so perfect a world.

'But then,' I said, 'if you're a retired welder from Novosibirsk, you can't go on a package tour of London, just for a bit of interest.'

'There, Dad,' Mrs Wilkinson said. 'That's true.'

Frank chewed on the meat and made no comment.

'Isn't it term time?' I said to him innocently.

He took his time getting to swallowing-point while he thought of the answer. He was between jobs, he said. Left one school back in July, starting at another in January.

'What do you teach?' I said.

He was vague, 'You know. This and that. Bit of everything. Junior school, of course.'

Mrs Wilkinson told him that her nephew, who had ingrowing toenails, had always wanted to be a teacher. Frank opened his mouth and then decided not to ask what ingrowing toenails had to do with it, and I smothered my laughter in ice cream and blackcurrant jam.

I was glad to laugh. I needed something to laugh about. The intensity and fear that had vibrated among the Russians in Evgeny Titov's flat remained with me as a sort of hovering claustrophobic depression. Even leaving the place had had to be carefully managed. It would never have done, I gathered, for so many people to have left at once. Evgeny and Olga had pressed Ian Young and me to stay for a further ten minutes after Boris had gone, so that if anyone were watching, we should not be connected.

'Is it always like this?' I had asked Ian Young, and he had said prosaically, 'Pretty much.'

Evgeny, having shifted the burden of his knowledge squarely on to me, had shaken hands gravely in farewell, clasping my hands in both of his. He had done his best, I supposed. He had passed on the flaming torch, and if now the Olympics were scorched by it, it would be my fault, not his.

Olga had seen us out with the same prudence as she had let us in. We picked our way through the scaffolding – 'old apartment building being renovated' Ian explained in the car later – and walked back through the garden. There were still only two sets of black footprints in the snow on the path – our own from the outward journey; and no one came after us through the gates. Two dark silent figures, we eased our way into the car, and the noise of the engine starting seemed suddenly too loud for safety. To have to live like that, constantly wary, seemed to me dreadful. Yet the Russians and even Ian Young considered it normal: and perhaps that was most dreadful of all.

'What are you going to do?' Ian asked, driving back towards the city centre. 'About this story of Boris's?'

'Ask around,' I said vaguely. 'What are you?'

'Nothing. It's just his overheated imagination.'

I didn't altogether agree with him, but I didn't argue.

'And I'd be glad if you'd do me a favour, my old son.'

'What's that?' I said, internally amused.

'Don't mention Evgeny or his apartment to anyone from the Embassy. Don't mention our visit. I like our good Oliver to be able to put his hand on his heart among the natives and swear he has no knowledge of any of his staff making private visits to Russian homes.'

'All right.'

He turned into a wide, well-lit dual carriageway which at eight-thirty held as much traffic as four in the morning back home.

'And don't get them into trouble,' he said. 'Evgeny and Boris.'

'Or you'll kill me.'

'Yeah . . .' He laughed awkwardly. 'Well . . . it sounds stupid, out here.'

I didn't ask if he really meant it. It was a question to which there was no answer, and I hadn't any intention of putting him to the test.

With the image of Ian Young in my mind I glanced across the table at Frank Jones: the one who looked Russian and walked carefully on the wrong side of the regulations, and the other who looked English and harmless and could throw you to the spikes.

Natasha brought her marvellous eyebrows to the table and drew up a chair. She wore a neat pink wool

112

dress, which went with the lipstick and displayed curves where they looked best. Her voice had a small disarming lisp, and she was achieving a slightly anxious smile.

'Tomorrow,' she said, 'the Exhibition of Economic Achievements . . .'

'Tomorrow,' I said, providing my best giving-no-offence expression, 'I'm going to see some horses. I'm sure the exhibition is great, but I'm much better at horses, and I have this absolutely wonderful chance to see some of your very best, your really top horses, the ones that are being trained for the Olympics, and that will be such a treat for me that I simply can't miss it.'

The floweriness more or less did the trick, and it was Frank who asked, with natural-looking interest, where the horses were that I was going to see.

'At the racecourse,' I said. 'They are stabled near there, I believe.'

I saw no point in not telling him. It would have looked odd if I hadn't, and in any case he could have found out by following.

Stephen Luce appeared promptly at ten the following morning outside the hotel, his round cheerful face the brightest thing under the grey Moscow sky. I made the passage from hot air to cold through the double entrance to join him, passing at least six men standing around doing nothing.

113

'Metro and bus to the Hippodrome,' Stephen said. 'I've looked up the stops.'

'Taxi,' I said firmly.

'But taxis are expensive, and the metro's cheap.'

'And the far side of the Hippodrome could be two miles' walk from the front entrance.'

We took a taxi. Pale greeny-grey saloon, with a meter. Stephen carefully explained where we wanted to go, but the driver had to stop and ask twice when we reached the area. Passengers, it appeared, very seldom asked to be driven to the back of the racecourse. I resisted two attempts to decant us with vague assurances that the place we wanted was 'just down there', and finally with a scowl or two and some muttering under the breath we drove right into the stable area, with the track itself lying a hundred yards ahead.

'You're very persistent,' Stephen said, as I counted out the fare.

'I don't like wet feet.'

The air temperature must have been about one degree centigrade and the humidity ninety-five per cent: a damp icy near-drizzle. The slushy snow lay around sullenly melting, lying in puddles on the packed clay surface in the centres of the stable roadways, banked up in ruts along the edges.

To left and right a double row of lengthy stable blocks stretched away, built of concrete on the barn principle, with the horses totally enclosed, and not sticking their heads out into the open air. Ahead the stable area led directly out through a wide gap on to the railed racing circuit, which was of the grey sticky consistency of dirt tracks the world over.

In the distance, over on the far side, one could see the line of stands, grey and lifeless at that time of day. All around us, where the morning action lay, horses and men trudged about their business and paid no attention to us at all.

'It's staggering,' Stephen said, looking around. 'You practically can't get into anywhere in the Soviet Union without talking your way past some sort of guard, and we just drove straight in here.'

'People who work with horses are anti-bureaucratic.'

'Are you?' he said.

'Every inch. Stick to essentials, and make your own decisions.'

'And to hell with committees?'

'The question nowadays is whether it's possible.' I watched some horses without saddles being led by on their way from a stable block out towards the track, their feet plopping splashily in the wet. 'You know something? These are not racehorses.'

'It's a racecourse,' he said, as if I were crazy.

'They're trotters.'

'What do you mean?'

'Trotting races. The driver sits on a little chariot thing called a sulky, and the horse pulls it along at a fast trot. Like that,' I added pointing, as a horse and sulky came into view on the track.

It wheeled up speedily to the entrance of the stables, and there the handlers unfastened the harness which held the shafts of the sulky, and led the horse away. The sulky was harnessed to the next horse to be exercised, and the driver took up the reins and got on with his job.

'Don't you think we ought to look for Mr Kropotkin?' Stephen suggested.

'Not really. We're still a few minutes early. If we just stand here, maybe he will come and find us.'

Stephen looked as if life were full of surprises but not altogether bad ones, and several more horses slopped past. The stable hands leading them all seemed to be small weatherbeaten men with unshaven chins and layers of uncoordinated clothes. None of them wore gloves. None of them even looked our way, but shambled on with stolid unsmiling faces.

A new and larger string of horses appeared, coming not from one of the stable blocks, but across the road we had arrived by, and in through the unguarded, ungated entrance. Instead of being led, these were ridden; and the riders were neatly dressed in jodhpurs and quilted jackets. On their heads they wore not leather caps but crash helmets, with the chin-straps meticulously fastened.

'What are those?' Stephen said, as they approached.

'They're not thoroughbreds ... not racehorses. I should think those might be the Eventers.'

'How can you tell they're not racehorses?'

'Thicker bones,' I said. 'The more solid shape of the head. And more hair round the fetlocks.'

Stephen said 'Oh' as if he wasn't much wiser, and we noticed that behind the horses walked a purposeful man in a dark overcoat and a fur hat. His gaze had fallen upon us, and he changed course ten degrees to starboard and came our way.

Stephen went a step to meet him.

'Nikolai Alexandrovich Kropotkin?' he said.

'*Da*,' said the newcomer. 'That is so.'

His voice was as deep as chocolate and the Russian intonation very pronounced. He looked at me closely. 'And you are Randall Drew,' he said, carefully stressing each word separately.

'Mr Kropotkin, I am very pleased to meet you,' I said.

He clasped my outstretched hand and gave it a good pump with both of his own.

'Randall Drew. Pardubice. You are three.'

'Third,' I said, nodding.

Words failed him in English and he rumbled away in his own language.

'He is saying,' Stephen said, his eyes grinning, 'that you are a great horseman with a bold heart and hands of silk, and he is honoured to see you here.'

Mr Kropotkin broke off the exaggerations to shake hands in a perfunctory way with Stephen, giving him the fast head-to-toe inspection of a horseman for a horse. He said something to him abruptly which

Stephen said afterwards was 'Do you ride?' and on receiving a negative treated him henceforth merely as a translating machine, not as a valued friend.

'Please tell Mr Kropotkin that the Russian team rode with great courage and skill at the International Trials, and the fitness of his horses here today does his management great credit.'

Mr Kropotkin's appreciation of the compliments showed in a general aura of pleased complacency. He was a big man of about sixty, carrying a good deal of excess weight but still light on his feet. A heavy greying moustache overhung his upper lip, and he had a habit of smoothing the outer edges downwards with his fore-finger and thumb.

'You watch horses,' he said, his way with English putting the words halfway between a command and an invitation. I would be pleased to, I said, and we walked forward on to the track.

His five charges were circling there, waiting for the instructions which he gave decisively but briefly in his rolling bass. The riders stopped circling and divided into two groups.

'Horses canter,' Kropotkin said, sweeping out an arm. 'Round.'

'Yes,' I said.

He and I stood side by side in the manner of horse-watchers the world over and eyed the training exercises. There was a lot of muscle, I thought, and all five had good free-flowing actions; but it was impossible to tell how good each was at Eventing, because speed alone had little to do with it.

Kropotkin launched into several sentences and waited impatiently for Stephen to translate.

'These are a few of the Olympic possibles. It is too soon to decide yet. There are other horses in the south, where it is warmer. All the flat racehorses from the track have gone south to the Caucasus for the winter. Some horses are training there for the Olympics also, but he will have them back in Moscow next summer.'

'Tell him I am very interested.'

Kropotkin received the news with what I took to be satisfaction. He too had the inexpressive face and unsmiling eyes which were the Moscow norm. Mobility of features, I supposed, was something one did or didn't learn in childhood from the faces all round; and the fact that they didn't show, didn't conclusively prove that admiration and contempt and hate and glee weren't going on inside. It had become, I dared say, imprudent to show them. The unmoving countenance was the first law of survival.

The horses came back from circling the mile-long track without a flutter of the nostril. The riders dismounted and spoke to Kropotkin with respect. They didn't look to me like Olympic material either on horseback or on their feet: nothing of the self-confident presence of Boris: but I asked all the same.

'*Niet*,' Kropotkin said. 'Misha is young. Is good.'

He pointed at a boy of about nineteen who was,

like the others, leading his horse round in a circle under Kropotkin's stony gaze. Kropotkin added more in Russian, and Stephen translated.

'He says they are all grooms, but he is teaching Misha, because he is brave and has good hands and can get horses to jump.'

A dark green horse box drove in through the stable area behind us, its engine making an untuned clatter which stirred up the horses. Kropotkin stolidly watched while it made a bad job of reversing down between the two rows of stable blocks, its old-fashioned wooden sides rattling from the vibration of the engine. The noise abated slightly once it was out of sight on the other side of a concrete barn, and when Kropotkin could once again make himself heard, he said a good deal to Stephen.

'Mr Kropotkin says,' Stephen said, 'that Misha went to the International Trials in September as a groom, and perhaps you would like to talk to him also. Mr Kropotkin said that when a man from the British Embassy came to ask him some questions about Lord Farringford and Hans Kramer, he said he knew nothing, and that was true. But he has remembered since then that Misha does know something about Hans Kramer, but not Lord Farringford, and he arranged for Misha to be riding this morning in case you should wish to see him.'

'Yes,' I said. 'Thank you very much indeed.'

Kropotkin made a small inclination of the head, and addressed himself to the riders.

'He's telling them to lead the horses back to the stable, and to be careful crossing the road outside. He's telling Misha to stay behind.'

Kropotkin turned back to me and stroked his moustache. 'Horse of Misha is good. Go to Olympics,' he said.

I looked at Misha's charge with interest, though there was no way in which it stood out from the others. A hardy chestnut with a white blaze down its nose, and two white socks: a rough coat, which would be normal at that time of year, and a kind eye.

'Good,' Kropotkin said, slapping its rump.

'He looks bold and tough,' I said. Stephen translated and Kropotkin did not demur.

The four other horses were led away, and Kropotkin introduced Misha formally but without flourish.

'Mikhail Alexeevich Tarevsky,' he said, and to the boy added what was clearly an instruction to answer whatever I asked.

'*Da*, Nikolai Alexandrovich,' he said.

I thought there were better places for conducting interviews than in near-freezing semi-drizzle on an open dirt track, but neither Kropotkin nor Misha seemed aware of the weather, and the fact that Stephen and I were shifting from one cold foot to the other evoked no offers of our adjourning to a warm office.

'In England,' said the boy, 'I learn little English.'

His voice and manner were serious, and his accent a great deal lighter than Kropotkin's. His eyes, unexpectedly blue in his weather-tanned face, looked full of unguarded intelligence. I smiled at him involuntarily, but he only stared gravely back.

'Please tell me what you know of Hans Kramer,' I said.

Kropotkin instantly rumbled something positive, and Stephen said, 'He wishes Misha to speak in Russian, so that he may hear. He wishes me to translate what you ask.'

'OK,' I said. 'Ask Misha what he knows of Kramer. And for God's sake let's get on. I'm congealing.'

Misha stood beside his horse, pulling the reins over the chestnut's head to hold them more easily below the mouth for leading, and stroking his neck from time to time to soothe him. I couldn't see that it was doing any good for an Olympic-type horse to stand around getting chilled so soon after exercise, but it wasn't my problem. The chestnut, certainly, didn't seem to mind.

Stephen said, 'Mikhail Alexeevich – that is, Misha – says that he was near Hans Kramer when he died.'

It was amazing how suddenly I no longer felt the cold.

'How near?'

The answer was lengthy. Stephen listened and translated.

'Misha says he was holding the horse of one of the Russian team who was being weighed – is that right?

– and Hans Kramer was there. He had just finished his cross-country, and had done well, and people were there round him, congratulating him. Misha was half watching, and half watching for the rider of the horse.'

'I understand,' I said. 'Go on.'

Misha talked. Stephen said, 'Hans Kramer staggered and fell to the ground. He fell not far from Misha; about three metres. An English girl went to help him and someone else ran off to fetch the doctor. Hans Kramer looked very ill. He could not breathe properly. But he was trying to say something. Trying to tell the English girl something. He was lying flat on the ground. He could hardly breathe. He was saying words as loudly as he could. Like trying to shout.'

Misha waited until Stephen had finished, clearly understanding what Stephen was saying and punctuating the translation with nods.

'Hans Kramer was saying these words in German?' I said.

'*Da*,' said Misha, but Kropotkin interrupted, wanting to be told the question. He made an assenting gesture with his hand to allow Misha to proceed.

'And does Misha speak German?'

Misha, it appeared, had learned German in school, and had been with the team's horses to East Germany, and knew enough to make himself understood.

'All right,' I said. 'What did Hans Kramer say?'

Misha said the words in German, and then in Russian, and one word flared out of both like a beacon.

Alyosha.

Stephen lit up strongly with excitement, and I thought there was probably a good deal to be said for a face that gave nothing away. His enthusiasm seemed to bother Kropotkin, who made uneasy movements as if on the point of retreat.

'Cool it,' I said to Stephen flatly. 'You're frightening the birds.'

He gave me a quick surprised look, but dampened his manner immediately.

'Hans Kramer said,' he reported in a quiet voice, ' "I am dying. It is Alyosha. Moscow." And then he said, "God help me." And then he died.'

'How did he die?' I said.

Misha, via Stephen, said that he turned blue, and seemed to stop breathing, and then there was a sort of small jolt right through his body, and someone said it was his heart stopping; it was a heart attack. The doctor came, and agreed it was a heart attack. He tried to bring Hans Kramer back to life, but it was useless.

The four of us stood in the Russian drizzle thinking about the death of a German in England on a sunny September day.

'Ask him what else he remembers,' I said.

Misha shrugged. 'The English girl and some of the people near had understood what Hans Kramer had said. The English girl was saying to other people that he had said he was dying because of Alyosha who came from Moscow, and other people were agreeing. It was very sad. Then the Russian rider came back from being weighed, and Misha had to attend to him and the horse, and he saw from a little way off that the ambulance people came with a stretcher. They put Hans Kramer on the stretcher and put a rug right over him and over his face, and carried him off.'

'Um,' I said, thinking. 'Ask him again what Hans Kramer said.'

Hans Kramer had said, 'I am dying. It is Alyosha. Moscow. God help me.' He had not had time to say any more, although Misha thought he had been trying to.

'Is Misha sure that Hans Kramer did not say "I am dying because of Alyosha from Moscow"?'

Misha, it seemed, was positive. There had been no 'because', and no 'from'. Only, 'I am dying. It is Alyosha. Moscow. God help me.' Misha remembered very clearly, he said, because Alyosha was his own father's name.

'Is it really?' I said, interested.

Misha said that he himself was Mikhail Alexeevich Tarevsky. Mikhail, son of Alexei. And Alyosha was the affectionate form of Alexei. Misha was certain Hans Kramer had said, 'It is Alyosha. *Es ist* Alyosha.'

I looked unseeingly over the sodden racecourse.

'Ask Misha,' I said slowly, 'if he can describe any of the people who were with Kramer before he staggered and fell down. Ask if he remembers if any of them

125

was carrying anything, or doing anything, which did not fit in to the normal scene. Ask if anyone gave Kramer anything to eat or drink.'

Stephen stared. 'But it was a heart attack.'

'There might have been,' I said mildly, 'contributive factors. A shock. An argument. An accidental blow. An allergy. A sting from a wasp.'

'Oh, I see.' He asked the alarming questions as if they were indeed harmless. Misha answered straight-forwardly, taking them the same way.

'Misha says,' Stephen reported, 'that he did not know any of the people round Hans Kramer, except that he had seen them at the trials that day and the day before. The Russians are not allowed to mix with the other grooms and competitors, so he had not spoken to them. He himself had seen nothing which could have given anybody a heart attack, but, of course, he had not been watching closely. But he couldn't remember any argument, or blow, or wasp. He couldn't remember for certain whether Hans Kramer had eaten or drunk anything, but he didn't think so.'

'Well,' I said, pondering, 'was there anyone there who Misha considers could have been Alyosha?'

The answer to that was that he didn't really think so, because when Hans Kramer was saying that name he was not saying it *to* anyone, except perhaps to the English girl, but *she* couldn't have been Alyosha, because it was a man's name.

The cold was creeping back. If Misha knew any more, I didn't know how to unlock it.

I said, 'Please thank Misha for his very intelligent help, and tell Mr Kropotkin how much I value his assistance in letting me speak to Misha in this way.'

The compliments were received as due, and Kropotkin, Stephen and I began to walk off the track, back towards the main stable area and the road beyond. Misha, leading the horse, followed a few paces behind us.

As we passed the opening between the two rows of stable blocks, the green wooden horse box, whose engine had been grumbling away in the background all the while we had been talking, suddenly revved up into a shattering roar.

Misha's horse reared with fright, and Misha cried out. Automatically, I turned back to help him. Misha, facing me, was tugging downwards on the reins, with the chestnut rearing yet again above him, and the horse's bunched quarters were, so to speak, staring me in the face.

As I came towards him, Misha's gaze slid over me and fastened on something behind my back. His eyes opened wide in fear. He yelled something to me in Russian, and then he simply dropped the reins and ran.

CHAPTER SEVEN

From a purely reflex action I grabbed the reins, which he had left dangling to the ground, and at the same time glanced back over my shoulder.

The time to death looked like three seconds.

The towering top of the green horse box blotted out the sky. The engine accelerated to a scream. I could remember the pattern of the radiator grille for ever after. Six tons unladen weight, I thought. One had time, I found, for the most useless thoughts. Thoughts could be measured in fizzing ten-thousandths of a second. Action took a little longer.

I grabbed the horse's mane with my left hand and the front of the saddle with my right, and half jumped, half hauled myself on to his back.

The horse was terrified already by the noise and the proximity of the horse box, but horses don't altogether understand about the necessity of removing themselves pronto from under the wheels of thundering juggernauts. Frightened horses, on the whole, are more apt to run *into* the paths of vehicles, than away.

Horses, on the other hand, are immensely receptive of human emotions, especially when the human is on their back, and scared out of his wits. The chestnut unerringly got the unadulterated message of fear, and bolted.

From a standing start a fit horse can beat most cars over a hundred yards, but the horse box was a long way from standing. The chestnut's blast-off kept him merely a few yards ahead of the crushing green killer roaring on our heels.

If the horse had had the right sort of sense he would have darted away to left or right down some narrow cranny where the horse box couldn't follow. Instead, he galloped ahead in a straight true line, making disaster easy.

It was of only moderate help that I was still grasping a section of rein. Owing to the fact of Misha having taken the reins over the horse's head to lead him, they were not now neatly to hand, with each rein leading tidily to its own side of the bit: they were both on the left side and came from below the horse's mouth. Since horses are normally steered by pulling the bit upwards against the mouth's sensitive corners, any urgent instructions had little chance of getting through. There were also the difficulties that my feet were not in the stirrups, I was wearing a heavy overcoat, and my fur hat was tipping forward over my spectacles. The chestnut took his own line and burst out on to the open spaces of the track.

He swerved instinctively to the right, which was the way he always trained, and his quarters thrust him onwards with the vigour of a full-blown stampede. His hurtling feet set up clouds of spray behind us, and it was while I was wondering how long he could keep up the pace and hoping it was for ever, that I first thought that perhaps the sound of the motor had diminished.

Too good to be true, I thought. On the straight and level, a horse box could go faster than a horse; perhaps it was in overdrive and simply made less noise that way.

I risked a look over my shoulder, and my spirits went up as swiftly as a helium balloon. The horse box had given up the chase. It was turning on the track, and going back the way it had come.

'Glory be', I thought, and 'Allelujah', and 'Oh noble beast'; jumbled thanks to the horse and his putative maker.

There was still the problem of getting the noble beast to stop. Panic had infected him easily. Non-panic was not getting through.

My hat fell completely off. Speed drove cold air through my hair, and stung my ears. The drizzle misted my glasses. Heavy double-breasted close-buttoned overcoats were definitely bad news on bolters. Flapping trousers never reassured any horse. I thought that if I didn't do something about the pedals and steering I could very well ignominiously fall off: and what would

Mr Kropotkin have to say if I let his Olympic horse go loose?

Little by little, a vestige of control returned to the proceedings. It was, after all, a mile-long, left-hand circuit, and the one way I had a chance of influencing our direction was to the left. Constant pressure on the reins pulled the chestnut's head all the time towards the inner rails, and, once I'd managed to put my feet in the stirrups, pressure from my right knee did the same. Some soothing exhortations like 'Whoa there, boy, whoa there you old beauty' also seemed to help; even if the words were English, the tone and intention were identical.

Somewhere on the home stretch in front of the stands the steam went out of the flight, and in a few strides after that, he was walking. I patted his neck and made further conversation, and after a bit, he stood still.

This time, unlike after his training canter, he showed great signs of exertion, taking in breaths in gusts through his nostrils, and heaving out his ribs to inflate his lungs. I brushed the wet off my glasses, and undid a couple of buttons on my coat.

'There you are, then, chum,' I said. 'You're a good old boy, my old fellow,' and patted his neck some more.

He shifted only a little while I cautiously leaned far forward to his ears, and put my arms right round under his chin, and brought the reins back over his head. It seemed to me that he was almost relieved to have his headgear returned to its normal riding configuration, because he trotted off along the track again at my signal with all the sweetness of a horse well schooled in dressage.

Kropotkin had come a little way out to meet us, but no man walked far on that sticky dirt from choice, and he was back by the stable entrance when the chestnut and I completed the circuit.

Kropotkin showed considerable emotion, which was, not surprisingly, all for his horse. After I had dismounted and handed the reins to a stunned-looking Misha, he rumbled away in basso profundo, anxiously feeling each leg and standing back to assess the overall damage. Finally he spoke at some length to Stephen, and waved an arm in a gesture which was neither anger nor apology, but perhaps somewhere between the two.

'Mr Kropotkin says,' Stephen relayed, 'that he doesn't know what the horse box was doing here today. It is one of the horse boxes which take the Olympic horses, when they travel. Mr Kropotkin had not ordered a box to come to the track. They are always parked beside the stables he is in charge of, across the road. He is sure that none of the drivers would drive so badly in a stable area. He cannot understand how you and the horse came to be in the way when the horse box prepared to leave the stables.' Stephen's eyebrows were rising. 'I say,' he said dubiously, 'you weren't in its way. The bloody thing drove straight at you.'

'Never mind,' I said. 'Tell Mr Kropotkin that I quite understand what he is saying. Tell him I regret having stood in the way of the horse box. Tell him that I am glad the horse is unharmed, and that I see no reason why I should need to mention the morning's happenings to any other person.'

Stephen stared. 'You learn fast.'

'Tell him what I said.'

Stephen obliged. Kropotkin's manner lost so much tension that I only then realized quite the extent of his anxiety. He even went so far as to produce a definite lightening of the features: almost a smile. He also said something about which Stephen seemed less doubtful.

'He says you ride like a Cossack. Is that a compliment?'

'Near enough.'

Kropotkin spoke again, and Stephen translated.

'Mr Kropotkin says he will give you any further help he can, if you ask.'

'Thank you very much,' I said.

'Friend,' the deep voice said in its slow heavy English. 'You ride good.'

I pushed my glasses hard against the bridge of my nose and thought murderous thoughts about the people who had stopped me racing.

Stephen and I trudged about half a mile to where Kropotkin had said there was a taxi rank.

'I thought you'd be one for rushing off to the police,' Stephen said.

'No.' I picked some of the dirt off my fur hat, which someone had retrieved. 'Not this trip.'

'Not this country,' he said. 'If you complain to the fuzz here, you as likely as not surface in clink.'

I gave up cleanliness in favour of a warm head. 'Hughes-Beckett would have a fit.'

'All the same,' Stephen said, 'whatever Kropotkin may say, that horse box was trying to kill you.'

'Or Misha. Or the horse,' I said, untying the ear-flaps.

'Do you really believe that?'

'Did you see the driver?' I asked.

'Yes and no. He had one of those balaclava things on under a fur hat with the ear-flaps down. Everything covered except his eyes.'

'He took a hell of a risk,' I said thoughtfully. 'But then, he darned near succeeded.'

'You take it incredibly calmly,' Stephen said.

'Would you prefer screaming hysterics?'

'I guess not.'

'There's a taxi.' I waved, and the green-grey saloon swerved our way and slowed. We piled aboard.

'I've never seen anyone jump on a horse like you did,' Stephen said, as we set off to the Intourist. 'One second on the ground, the next, galloping.'

'You never know what you can do until Nemesis breathes down your neck.'

'You look,' Stephen said, 'like one of those useless la-di-dahs in the telly ads, and you perform . . .' Words failed him.

'Yeah,' I said. 'Depressing, isn't it?'

He laughed. 'And by the way . . . Misha gave me a telephone number.' He put a hand in a pocket and brought out a crumpled scrap of paper. 'He gave it to me while Kropotkin was chasing after you on the track. He says he wants to tell you something without Kropotkin knowing.'

'Does the taxi driver speak English?' I asked.

Stephen looked only faintly and transiently alarmed. 'They never do,' he said. 'You could tell them they stink like untreated sewage and they wouldn't turn a hair. Just try it.'

I tried it.

The taxi driver didn't turn a hair.

On the principle of turning up where and when expected, I arrived on time for lunch in the Intourist dining room. The soup and the blinis were all right, and the ice cream with blackcurrant jam was fine, but the meat with its attendant teaspoonfuls of chopped carrot, chopped lettuce, and inch-long chips went across the table to Frank.

'You'll fade away,' said Mrs Wilkinson, without too much concern. 'Don't you like meat?'

'I grow it,' I said. 'Beef, that is. On a farm. So I suppose I get too fussy over stuff like this.'

Mrs Wilkinson looked at me doubtfully. 'I would never have guessed you worked on a farm.'

'Er ... well, I do. But it's my own ... passed down from my father.'

'Can you milk a cow?' Frank said, with a hint of challenge.

'Yes,' I said mildly. 'Milk. Plough. The lot.'

He gave me a sharp look from over my chips, but in fact I spoke the truth. I had started learning the practical side of farming from about the age of two, and had emerged from agricultural college twenty years later with the technology. Since then, under Government sponsorship, I'd done some work on the interacting chemistry of land and food, and had set aside some experimental acres for research. After racing, this work had been my chief interest ... and from now on, I supposed, my only one.

Mrs Wilkinson said disapprovingly, 'You don't keep calves in those nasty crate things, do you?'

'No, I don't.'

'I never do like to think of all the poor animals being killed, when I buy the weekend chops.'

'How were the Economic Achievements?'

'We saw a space capsule.' She launched into a grudgingly admiring outline of the exhibition. 'Pity we don't have one in England,' she said. 'Exhibition like that, I mean. Permanent. Blowing our own trumpet for a change, like.'

'Did you go?' I asked Frank.

'No.' He shook his head, munching. 'Been before, of course.'

He didn't say where he had been instead. I hadn't noticed him following Stephen and me, but he might have done. If he had, what had he seen?

'Tomorrow we're going to Zagorsk,' Mrs Wilkinson said.

'Where's that?' I asked, watching Frank chew and learning nothing from his face.

'A lot of churches, I think,' she said vaguely. 'We're going in a bus, with visas, because it's out of Moscow.'

I glanced at her as she sat beside me, divining a note of disappointment in her voice. She was a short woman, solid, late fifties, with the well-intentioned face of the bulk of the English population. An equally typical shrewdness lived inside and poked its nose out occasionally in tellingly direct remarks. The more I saw of Mrs Wilkinson, the more I saw to respect.

Opposite her, next to Frank, Mr Wilkinson ate his lunch and as usual said nothing. I had gathered he had come on the trip to please his wife, and would as soon be at home with a pint and Manchester United.

'Quite a few people are going to the Bolshoi this evening, to the ballet,' said Mrs Wilkinson a little wistfully. 'But Dad doesn't like that sort of thing, do you, Dad?'

Dad shook his head.

Mrs Wilkinson said in a lower voice to me, confidingly, 'He doesn't like those things the men wear. Those tights. You know, showing all the muscles of their behinds . . . and those things in front.'

'Cod-pieces,' I said, straight-faced.

'What?' She looked embarrassed, as if I'd used too strong a swear word for her shock-threshold.

'That's what they're called. Those things which disguise the outlines of nature.'

'Oh.' She was relieved. 'It would be much nicer if they wore *tunics*, that's what I think. Then they wouldn't be so *obvious*. And you could concentrate on the dancing.'

Mr Wilkinson muttered something which might or might not have been 'Poncing about', and filled his mouth with ice cream.

Mrs Wilkinson looked as if she'd heard that before, and instead said to me, 'Did you see your horses?'

Frank's concentration on food skipped a beat.

'They were great,' I said, and enlarged for two minutes on the turn-out and the training exercise. There was nothing else in Frank's reaction to say he knew I was giving an incomplete account, but then I supposed if there had been, he would have been bad at his job.

Natasha drifted up purposefully to complicate my life.

'We have been lucky,' she said earnestly. 'We have

a ticket for you in a box at the Bolshoi tomorrow evening, for the opera.'

I caught Mr Wilkinson's eye, with its message of sardonic sympathy, as I started feebly to thank her.

'It is *The Queen of Spades*,' Natasha said firmly.

'Er . . .' I said.

'Everyone enjoys the opera at the Bolshoi,' she said. 'There is no better opera in the world.'

'How splendid,' I said. 'I will look forward to it.'

She began to look approving and I seized the moment to say I would be going out with friends for the evening, and not to expect me in for dinner. She tried very delicately to lead me into saying exactly where I was going, but as at that moment I didn't actually know, except that it was anywhere for some decent grub, she was out of luck.

'And this afternoon . . .' I said, forestalling her, 'the Lenin museum.'

She brightened a good deal. At last, she was no doubt thinking, I was behaving as a good tourist should.

'Mind if I tag along?' Frank said, shovelling in the last of my lunch. His face looked utterly guileless, and I understood the full beauty of his method of working. If following a person might raise their suspicions, tag along in full sight.

'Pleasure,' I said. 'Meet you in the lobby, in half an hour,' and I vanished as soon as he'd started his specially ordered double portion of ice cream. It would take a good deal to shift him before he had finished it.

I made fast tracks out of the hotel and along to the main Post Office, which was conveniently nearby.

Telephoned to the Embassy. Reached Oliver Waterman.

'This is Randall Drew,' I said.

'Where are you calling from?' he said, interrupting.

'The Post Office.'

'Ah. Right. Carry on, then.'

'Have there been any telex messages for me, from Hughes-Beckett, or anyone in London?'

'Ah, yes,' he said vaguely. 'There was something, I think, my dear chap. Hang on . . .' He put the receiver down and I could hear searching sounds and consulting voices. 'Here we are,' he said, coming back. 'Got a pencil?'

'Yes,' I said patiently.

'Yuri Ivanovich Chulitsky.'

'Please spell it,' I said.

He did so.

'Got it,' I said. 'Go on.'

'There isn't any more.'

'Is that the whole of the message?' I asked incredulously.

His voice sounded dubious. 'The whole message, as received by us from the telex people, is "inform Randall Drew Yuri Ivanovich Chulitsky", and then there are a few numbers, and that's all.'

'Numbers?'

'Could be a telephone number, perhaps. Anyway, here they are: 180–19–16. Got that?'

I read them back, to check.

'That's right, my dear chap. How's it going?'

'Fair,' I said. 'Can you send a telex for me, if I give you the message?'

'Ah,' he said. 'I think I should warn you that there's a spot of trouble brewing on the international scene, and the telex is pretty busy. They told us pretty shirtily just now not to bother them with inessentials like music. Inessentials, I ask you. Anyway, my dear chap, if you want to be sure your message gets off, I should take it along there yourself.'

'Take it where?' I said.

'Oh yes, I was forgetting you wouldn't know. The telex machine is not here in the Embassy, but along with the Commercial section in Kutuzovsky Prospect. That's the continuation of Kalinin Prospect. Do you have a map?'

'I'll find it,' I said.

'Tell them I sent you. They can check with me, if they want. And I should stand over them, my dear chap. Make yourself a bit of a nuisance, so they send it to get rid of you.'

'I'll take your advice,' I said, smiling to myself.

'The British Club is along there in Kutuzovsky Prospect,' he said languidly. 'Full of temporary exiles, wallowing in nostalgia. Sad little place. I don't go there much.'

'If any more messages come for me,' I said, 'please would you ring me at the Intourist Hotel?'

'Certainly,' he said civilly. 'Do give me your number.'

I stifled the urge to tell him I'd given it to him twice already. I repeated it again, and wondered whether, by the time I left, he would find his office scattered with small pieces of paper all bearing the same number, which he would peer at with willowy bewilderment while smoothing back his grey-tinged hair.

I rang off and debated whether or not to lose Frank there and then, and make·tracks for the telex: but the message would keep for an hour or two and wasn't worth the stirring up of trouble. I hurried back to the Intourist, went upstairs, came downstairs, and strolled out of the lift to find Frank waiting.

'Oh there you are,' he said. 'Thought I'd missed you.'

'Off we go, then,' I said fatuously, and we walked out of the hotel, down into the long pedestrian tunnel which led under The Fiftieth Anniversary of the October Revolution Square and up into a cobbled street with the red walls of the Kremlin away to the right.

On the underground way he gave me his thoughts on Comrade Lenin, who was, according to Frank, the only genius of the twentieth century.

'Born, of course, in the nineteenth,' I said.

'He brought freedom to the masses,' Frank declared reverently.

'Freedom to do what?' I said.

Frank ignored me. Somewhere under the wet and woolly sociological guff, which he ladled so unstintingly over the Wilkinsons and me, there had to be a hard-core card-carrying fully indoctrinated Communist. I looked at Frank's angular, pitted face framed in a long striped college scarf, and thought he was marvellous: he was giving a faultless performance as a poorly educated left-wing encumbrance of the National Union of Teachers, so convincing that it was hard to believe he was acting.

It flickered across my mind that perhaps Ian Young was wrong, and Frank was not KGB after all: but then if Ian was what I thought, he would be right. If Frank were not KGB, why should Ian say he was?

I wondered how many lies I had been told since I had arrived in Moscow: and how many more I had yet to hear.

Frank more or less genuflected on the threshold of the Lenin museum, and we went inside to have our ears bent about the clothes, desk, car and so on that the liberator of the masses had personally used. And this was the face, I thought, looking at the prim little bearded visage reproduced without stint on paintings and posters and booklets and cards, who had launched a million murders and left his disciples bloodily empire-building round the world. This was the visionary who had unleashed the holocausts: the man who had meant to do good.

I looked at my watch and told Frank I'd had enough of the place; I needed some fresh air. He ignored the implied insult and followed me out, simply saying that he had visited the museum every time he'd been to Moscow and never tired of it. Easy enough to believe that that, at least, was true.

Stephen, back from lunch and an unmissable tutorial, was waiting, as arranged, outside. He had arranged, that is, to meet only me. Frank was surplus to requirements.

I introduced them without explanations. 'Frank Jones . . . Stephen Luce,' and they disliked each other at once.

Had they been dogs, there would have been some unfriendly sniffing and a menacing show of teeth: as it was, their noses actually wrinkled. I wondered whether Stephen's instinctive response was to the real Frank, or to the cover Frank: to an individual or to a type.

Frank, I supposed, merely guessed that any friend of mine was no friend of his; and if Ian were right about him following me, he had certainly seen Stephen before.

Neither of them wanted to say anything to the other.

'Well, Frank,' I said cheerfully, hiding my amusement, 'thank you for your company. I'm off now with Stephen for the rest of the day. See you at breakfast, I guess.'

'You bet.'

We turned away, but after a step or two Stephen glanced back, frowning. I looked where he did: Frank's back view, walking off.

'Haven't I seen him before?' Stephen said.

'Where?'

'Couldn't say. Yesterday morning, up here in the Square, maybe.'

We were walking along the side of Red Square, towards the GUM department store.

'He's staying at the Intourist,' I said.

Stephen nodded, dismissing it. 'Where to?' he said.

'Phone box.'

We found one and inserted the two kopeks, but there was no answer from the number Misha had given us. Tried again, this time for Yuri Ivanovich Chulitsky. Same result.

'Telex in Kutuzovsky Prospect,' I said. 'Where do we get a taxi?'

'The metro is cheap. Only five kopeks, however far you go.'

He couldn't understand why I should want to spend money when I didn't have to: incredulity halfway to exasperation filled his eyes and voice. I gave in with a shrug and we went by metro, with me battling as usual against the claustrophobic feeling I always got from hurtling through mole-runs far underground. The cathedral-like stations of the Moscow metro seemed to have been built to the greater glory of technology (down with churches) but on the achingly long and boring escalators I found myself quite missing London's vulgar advertisements for bras. Ritzy, jazzy, noisy, dirty, uninhibited old London, greedy and gutsy and grabbing at life. Gold coaches and white horses along the Mall instead of tanks, and garbage collectors on strike.

'Do the dustbin men ever strike here?' I said to Stephen.

'Strikes? Don't be silly. Strikes are not allowed in Russia.'

We finally resurfaced, and after a good deal of asking and walking, arrived at the Commercial section, which was guarded, as before, by a soldier. Again we talked our way in, and, by following Oliver Waterman's advice and making a nuisance of myself, I persuaded the inmates to telex my message, which was:

REQUEST DETAILS OF LIFE AND BACKGROUND OF HANS KRAMER. ALSO WHEREABOUTS OF HIS BODY. ALSO NAME AND TELEPHONE NUMBER OF THE PATHOLOGIST WHO DID THE AUTOPSY.

'Don't expect an answer,' I was told brusquely. 'There's all hell breaking loose in some place in Africa which is chock-a-block with Soviet guns and so-called advisers. The telex is steaming. The diplomats have priority. You'll be way down the list.'

'Thanks very much,' I said, and we trudged our way back to the pavement outside.

'Now what?' Stephen said.

'Try those numbers again.'

We found a glass-walled box nearby and put the kopeks in the slot. No answer, as before.

'Probably not home from work yet,' Stephen said.

I nodded. At four in the afternoon the daylight was fading fast to dusk, the lighted windows shining brighter with every minute.

'What do you want to do now?' Stephen said.

'I don't know.'

'Like to come up to the University, then? We're not all that far away, actually. Nearer than to your hotel.'

'No hope of anything to eat, there, I suppose?' I said.

He looked surprised. 'Yes, if you like. There's a sort of supermarket for students in the basement, and kitchens upstairs. We can buy something and eat in my room, if you like.' He seemed doubtful. 'It won't be as good as the Intourist Hotel, though.'

'I'll risk it.'

'I'll ring up and say you're coming,' he said, turning back to the telephone box.

'Can't we just go?'

He shook his head. 'In Russia, everything has to be arranged first. If it is arranged, it is OK. If it's not arranged, it's irregular, suspicious, or subversive, and what's more, you won't get in.' He fished around for another two-kopek piece and put it to good use.

Coming out of the telephone box and saying my visit was fixed, he began planning a route via the metro, but I was no longer listening. Two men were walking towards us, talking intently. From thinking there was something familiar about one of them I progressed by a series of mental jumps to realizing that I knew them both.

They were Ian Young and Malcolm Herrick.

CHAPTER EIGHT

They were, if anything, more surprised to see me.

'Randall!' Ian said. 'What are you doing here?'

'If it isn't the sleuth!' Malcolm Herrick's English voice boomed confidently into Kutuzovsky Prospect, scorning discretion. 'Found Alyosha yet, sport?'

'Afraid not,' I said. 'This is Stephen Luce. A friend. English.'

'Malcolm Herrick,' said the Moscow correspondent of the *Watch*, introducing himself, shaking hands, and waiting for a reaction. None came. He must have been used to it. 'Moscow correspondent of the *Watch*,' he said.

'Great stuff,' said Stephen vaguely, obviously not having read a word from the Herrick pen.

'Are you going to the British Club?' Ian asked. 'We're just on our way there.'

His watchful eyes waited for a reply. There were some replies I saw no harm in giving, and this was one.

'I came to send a telex,' I said. 'Oliver's suggestion.'

'The snake,' Herrick said unexpectedly, narrowing

his eyes. 'He usually gives messages for the telex to the guy in the hall.'

'And the guy in the hall relays them to you?' I said.

'Sources, sources, sport.' He tapped the side of his nose.

Ian was unmoved. 'If an answer comes,' he said to me, 'I'll see that you get it.'

'I'd be grateful.'

'Where are you going now, sport?' Malcolm said, loud and direct as always.

'To the University, with Stephen, for tea.'

'Tea!' He made a face. 'Look, why don't we meet later for a decent meal? All of us,' he added expansively, including Ian and Stephen. 'The Aragvi do you, Ian?'

Ian, who had not reacted visibly to the original suggestion, seemed to find favour with the choice of place, and nodded silently. Malcolm started giving me directions, but Stephen said he knew the way.

'Great then,' Malcolm said. 'Eight-thirty. Don't be late.'

The faint drizzle which had persisted all day seemed to be intensifying into sleet. It put, anyway, an effective damper on further conversation in the street, and by common consent we split up and went our own ways.

'Who is the man who looks Russian?' Stephen asked, ducking his head down and sideways to avoid the stinging drops. 'The one imitating the Sphinx.'

'Let's get that taxi,' I said, waving to a grey-green

car coming with the green light shining for availability in its windscreen.

'Expensive,' he protested automatically, slithering into the back seat beside me. 'Ve vill have to cure this disgusting bourgeois habit.' He had a rich way of imitating a Russian accent while sardonically putting forward the Russian point of view. 'Vorkers of the Vorld unite . . . and go on the metro.'

'Caviar is immoral,' I said dryly.

'Caviar is not bourgeois. Caviar is for everyone who can scrape up a fortune in roubles.' He considered me, relapsing into ordinary English, 'Why did you say caviar is immoral? It's not like you.'

'Not my idea. A friend's.'

'Girl?'

I nodded.

'Aha,' he said. 'I diagnose a rich middle-class socialist rebelling against Mummy.'

'Not far out,' I said, a touch sadly.

He peered anxiously at my face. 'I haven't offended you?'

'No.'

I got him to ask the taxi driver to stop by a telephone kiosk, and to wait while we tried our numbers again. There was still no answer from Misha, but the second number was answered at the first ring. Stephen, holding the receiver, made a brief thumbs up sign to me, and spoke. Listened, spoke again, and handed the receiver to me. 'It is Yuri Ivanovich Chulitsky himself. He says he speaks English.'

I took the instrument. 'Mr Chulitsky?' I said.

'Yes.'

'I am an Englishman visiting Moscow,' I said. 'My name is Randall Drew. I have been given your name and telephone number by the British Embassy. I wonder if I could talk with you?'

There was a longish pause. Then the voice at the other end, calm and with an accent that was a carbon copy of Stephen's imitation, said, 'Upon what subject?'

Owing to the meagreness of the telex bearing his name, I couldn't entirely answer. I said hopefully, 'Horses?'

'Horses.' He sounded unenthusiastic. 'Always horses. I do not know horses. I am architect.'

'Er,' I said. 'Have you already talked about horses to another Englishman?'

A pause. Then the voice, measured and still calm. 'That is so. In Moscow, yes. And in England, yes. Many times.'

Bits of light began to dawn. 'You were at the International Horse Trials? At Burghley, in September?'

The pause. Then, 'At many horse trials. September . . . and August.'

Bingo, I thought. One of the observers.

'Mr Chulitsky,' I said, persuasively, 'please may I meet you? I've been talking to Nikolai Alexandrovich Kropotkin, and if you want to check up on me, I think

152

he will tell you it would be all right for you to talk to me.'

A very long pause. Then he said, 'Are you writing for newspaper?'

'No,' I said.

'I telephone Nikolai Alexandrovich,' he said. 'I find his number.'

'I have it here,' I said, and read it out slowly.

'You telephone again. One hour.'

The receiver went down at his end with a decisive crash, and Stephen and I went back to the taxi.

Stephen said, 'When we get up to my room, don't say anything you don't want overheard. Or not until I tell you it's OK.'

'Are you serious?'

'I'm a foreigner. I live in the section of the University reserved for foreign students. Every room in Moscow which is used by foreigners should be considered bugged until proved different.'

The University building, of vast blocks of narrow windows punctuated by soaring fluted towers, like an immense grey stone blancmange, looked from its hill to the river and the city centre beyond; and on the far bank lay, spread out, the Lenin Stadium, where the Olympic athletes were scheduled to run and jump and throw things.

'How will they manage with the whole city full of foreigners?' I said.

'Apartheid will prevail.' The Russian accent made it

a wicked joke. 'Segregation will be ruthlessly maintained.'

'Why did you come to Russia?' I said. 'Feeling as you do?'

He gave me a quick, bright glance. 'I love the place and hate the regime, the same as everyone else. And nowhere's a prison when you can get out.'

The taxi shed us at the gate, and we walked to the foreign students' entrance, a door dwarfed by the sheer height of the adjoining walls. Inside, coming down to human scale, there was a dumpy middle-aged woman behind a desk. She looked at Stephen with a lack of reaction which meant she knew him, and then at me; and she was out of her seat and barring my way with the speed of a rattlesnake.

Stephen spoke to her in Russian. She dourly shook her head. Together they consulted a list on her desk; and with severe looks she let me through.

'Dragons like that guard doorways all over Russia,' Stephen said. 'The only way past is to be expected. Short of slaying them, of course.'

We went for a long walk which ended one floor down in a help-yourself foodshop. All the packages were unfamiliar, and owing to the Cyrillic alphabet, which made restaurants look like 'РЕСТОРАН' to Western eyes, I couldn't even guess at the contents. Stephen went round unerringly, choosing what later turned out to be crisp-sided cream cakes and ending with a bottle of milk.

A girl stood at the cash desk before us, paying for her groceries. A pretty girl, with light-brown hair curling on to her shoulders, and the sort of waist Victorian young ladies swooned over. When Stephen greeted her, she turned her head and gave him a flashing smile with a fair view of excellent teeth. The smile, I saw, of at least good friends.

Stephen introduced her as Gudrun, and the unpretty lady behind the cash register pointed to her packages and clearly told her to pick them up and go.

The girl picked up her bottle of milk, and the bottom fell out of it. Milk cascaded on to the floor. Gudrun stood looking bewildered with the whole-looking bottle still in her hand and milk stains all over her legs.

I watched the pantomime that followed. Stephen was saying she should have another bottle. The unpretty lady shook her head and pointed to the cash register. Everyone engaged in battle, and the unpretty lady won.

'She made her *buy* another bottle,' said Stephen, disgusted, as we set off on another interior tramp.

'So I gathered.'

'They make the bottles like tubes here, and just stick a disc in for the bottoms. Anyway,' he finished cheerfully, 'she's coming along to my room for a cup of tea.'

Gudrun was West German, from Bonn. She filled and illuminated Stephen's tiny cell, which was eight feet long by six across, and contained a bed, a table covered with books, a chair, and a glass-fronted book-case. On the bare wooden floor there was one small imitation Brussels rug, and at the tall narrow window, skimpy green curtains.

'The Ritz,' I said ironically.

'I'm lucky,' Stephen said, taking three mugs from the bookcase and making a space for them on the table. 'A lot of the Russian students are two to a room this size.'

'If you had two beds in here you couldn't open the door,' I said.

Gudrun nodded. 'They stand the beds up against the wall in the daytime.'

'No protest marches?' I said. 'No demos for better conditions?'

'They are not allowed,' Gudrun said seriously. 'Anyone who tried would lose his place.'

She spoke English perfectly, with hardly a trace of accent. Her Russian, Stephen said, was just as good. His own German was passable, his French excellent. I sighed, internally, for a skill I'd never acquired.

Stephen went off to make the tea.

'Don't come,' he said. 'The kitchen is filthy. About twenty of us share it, and we're all supposed to clean it, so nobody does.'

Gudrun sat on the bed and asked me how I was enjoying Moscow, and I sat on the chair and said fine. I asked her how she was enjoying her course, and she said fine.

'If the Russians are so keen to keep foreigners at arm's length,' I said, 'why do they allow foreign students in the University?'

She glanced involuntarily round the walls, a revealing glimpse into the way they all lived. The walls had ears; literally.

'We are exchange students,' she said. 'For Stephen, there is a Russian student in London. For me a Russian student in Bonn. Those students are dedicated Communists.'

'Spreading the gospel and recruiting?'

She nodded a shade unhappily, again glancing at the walls and not liking my frankness. I went back to harmless chit-chat, and Stephen presently arrived to distribute the goodies, which, for me at least, nicely filled an aching void.

'Show you something,' he said, stuffing the last of the cake into his mouth and shifting along to the end of the bed, on which he was sitting. 'A little trick.'

He picked up what I saw was a tape-recorder, and switched it on. Then with a theatrical flourish he stood up and pressed it against the wall beside my head.

Nothing happened. He removed it and pressed it to another spot. Again nothing. He took it away, and put it delicately against a spot above his bed. From the tape-recorder came a high-pitched whine.

'Abracadabra,' he said, taking the tape-recorder down and switching it off. 'From ordinary walls, you get nothing. From a live mike inside a wall, you get feedback.'

'Do they know?' I said.

'Of course they do. Like to borrow it?' He pointed to the recorder.

'Very much.'

'Then I'll dash to get a chit to take it out.'

'A chit?'

'Yes. You can't just walk out of here carrying things. They say it's to stop people stealing, but it's just the usual phobia about knowing what goes on.'

I glanced at the wall behind his head. Stephen laughed. 'If you *don't* complain about the whole bloody repressive Soviet system they suspect you're putting on an act.'

In the corridor, from the telephone installed for the students, I called Yuri Ivanovich Chulitsky. The telephone was safe, Stephen said. The only telephones which were tapped were those in the houses of known dissidents: and Yuri Chulitsky would be anything but a dissident, if he had been sent to England as an observer.

He answered at once.

'I talk with Nikolai Alexandrovich,' he said. 'I meet you tomorrow.'

'Thank you very much.'

'I drive car. I come outside National Hotel, ten o'clock, tomorrow morning. Is right?'

'Is right,' I said.

'Ten o'clock.' Down went the receiver with the same crash, before I could ask him how I would know him or his car. I supposed that when I saw him, I would know.

Stephen tried the other number. The bell rang hollowly at the far end, and after ten rings we prepared to give up. Then the ringing stopped and there was suddenly a breathless voice on the line.

'It's Misha,' Stephen said.

'You talk to him. It's easier.'

Stephen listened. 'He wants to see you again, and it must be tonight. He says he is going to Rostov tomorrow with two horses. The snow is coming, and the horses are going south. Nikolai Alexandrovich – that is, Mr Kropotkin – is going next week. It was decided today.'

'All right,' I said. 'When and where?'

Stephen asked, and was told. He wrote it down, and the directions took some time.

'Well,' he said, slowly replacing the receiver and looking at what he had written, 'it is miles out of the centre. I think it must be an apartment block. He says he will wait outside, and when you arrive, don't speak English until he says it's OK.'

'Aren't you coming?'

'You don't really need me. Misha does speak some

English.' He handed me the address, written in Russian script. 'Show that to a taxi driver. He'll find it. And I'll meet you later, at the Aragvi.'

I looked beyond him to the open door of his room. Gudrun half sat, half lay, on the bed, her long legs sprawled in invitation.

I hesitated, but finally I said, 'I wish you could come. Someone did try to kill Misha or me this morning. I expect you'll laugh, but if I'm going off into the wilds to meet him, I would feel safer with a back-up system.'

He didn't laugh. He said goodbye to Gudrun, and came. He also said, 'Ve have vays of postponing our pleasures until tomorrow,' and made a joke of it: and I thought that for plain good nature he would be hard to beat.

'It's very difficult to think of a good meeting place, if you're an ordinary Russian and you want to talk to a foreigner,' Stephen said. 'There are no pubs in Russia. No discreet little cafés. And there are always watchers, with tongues. You'd have to be pretty solid with the hierarchy to be seen anywhere public with a foreigner.'

We flagged a passing taxi, again without much of a wait.

'No shortage of these,' I said, climbing in. Then, as Stephen's mouth opened, I interrupted. 'Don't say it. Taxis are dear, the metro's cheap.'

'And the taxi charges have practically doubled recently.'

'Ask the driver to go via the Intourist Hotel, so that I can drop off the recorder.'

'Right.'

We sped down the Komsomolsky Prospect and I looked two or three times out of the back window. A medium-sized black car followed us faithfully, but we were on a main road where that was likely to happen anyway.

'When we get to the Intourist,' I said, 'I will get out and say goodnight to you unmistakably. I'll then go into the hotel, and you and the taxi will drive off, and go round the corner, and wait for me outside the National Hotel entrance. I'll dump the tape-recorder, and come and meet you there.'

Stephen looked out of the rear window.

'Seriously,' he said. 'Do you think you're being followed?'

'Seriously,' I said. 'Most of the time.'

'But . . . who by?'

'Would you believe, the KGB?'

For all his guided tour to the prying state, he was staggered. 'What makes you think so?'

'The Sphinx told me.'

It reduced him to silence. Ve have vays of making you stop talking, I thought facetiously. We arrived in due course at the Intourist, and went through the act.

I spent some time on the pavement talking to Stephen through the taxi window, and then bade him goodnight in ringing tones, and waved a farewell as I went through the double glass entrance; overdoing it, no doubt. I collected my key from the desk, removed hat and coat, and went up in the lift. Then I parked the tape-recorder in my room, and without hurrying, so as not to alert the old biddy sitting watchfully at her desk by the lifts, walked back, still carrying outdoor clothes, and descended to the ground floor. There were several routes from the lifts to the front door, as it was a very large hotel: I took the most roundabout, putting on hat and coat on the way, and wafted at an ordinary pace out again on to the pavement. No doubt the watchers there took general note, but no one broke away to bob in my wake.

I stopped at the corner and glanced back. No one seemed to be peeling off to look in non-existent shop-windows. I walked on, thinking that if the followers were determined as well as professional, my amateur attempts at evasion would have been useless. But they would have had no reason to suppose I knew they were there, or that I would try to duck them, as I had given no signs so far of wanting to; so perhaps they might think I was still somewhere inside the hotel.

The taxi driver was agitated and grumbling at having had to wait a long time where he was not supposed to. Stephen greeted my arrival with sighs of relief, and we set off again with a jerk.

'Your friend Frank went into the hotel just after you,' Stephen said. 'Did you see him?'

'No,' I said tranquilly.

162

He didn't pursue it. 'The driver says the temperature is dropping. It has been warm for November, he says.'

'It's December, today.'

'He says it will snow.'

We motored a good way northwards, and then north-east, through the wide well-lit mostly empty streets. When the roads became narrower I said, 'Ask the driver to stop for a moment.'

'What now?' Stephen said.

'See if we've a tail.'

No car stopped behind us, however, and when we went on, we found no stationary car waiting ahead. I asked Stephen to get the driver to circle a fairly large block. The driver, thoroughly disillusioned by these junketings, began muttering under his breath.

'Get him to drop us before we reach the address,' I said. 'We don't want him undoing the good work by reporting our exact destination.'

A large tip on top of the big fare cured most of the driver's grumbles, but wouldn't, I guessed, keep his mouth shut. He sped off back to the brighter lights as if glad to be rid of us. But no black cars, or any others, passed or stopped. As far as we could tell, we were on our own.

We stood in an area which was being developed. On each side, end on to the road, were ranks of newly built apartment blocks, all about forty feet thick and nine storeys high, clad in grey-white pebbledash and stretching away into the darkness, with ranks of windows front and back.

'Standard-issue housing,' Stephen said. 'Egg boxes for the masses. Six square metres of floorspace per person; the maximum regulation allowance.'

We walked along the slushy pavement, the only people in sight. The block we were currently passing was unfinished, with its walls in place but empty holes for windows. The one after that, although still unin-habited, had glass. The one after that looked furnished, and the one after that had residents. It proved also to be where we were going.

A last look at the street showed no one taking the slightest notice of us. We wheeled into the broad space between the two blocks and discovered from the numbers that the entrance we wanted was the second door along. We went towards it without haste, and stopped a few paces short.

We waited. A minute ticked past, and another. No Misha. With every lungful the wet freezing air chilled from the inside out. If we had travelled all this way for nothing, I thought, I would be less than amused.

A voice spoke softly, from behind us.

'Come.'

CHAPTER NINE

We turned, startled. We hadn't heard him, but there he stood in his leather coat and his leather cap, young and neat. He made a small beckoning movement with his head, and turned on his heel. We followed him out into the street, along the pavement, and round into the space between the next two blocks. He made steadily for one of the entrances, and in silence we traipsed in his footsteps.

Inside, the brightly lit and warm hall smelled of new paint. There were two lifts, both not working, and a flight of stairs. Misha addressed himself to the stairs. We followed.

On the landing above there were four doors, all closed. Misha continued up the stairs. On the next landing, four identical doors, again all closed. Misha went on climbing. On the fourth floor, we stopped for breath.

Between the fifth and sixth floors we came across two young men struggling to carry upwards an electric cooker. They had ropes and protective wadding around it, and leather straps with carrying handles to help them, but they were both sweating and panting from exertion. They stopped work, with the cooker poised precariously half on and half off a step, to let us pass. Misha said something which sounded consoling, and on we went at a slower and slower pace.

It had to be the ninth floor, I thought. Or the roof.

The ninth floor. Misha produced a key, unlocked one of the uninformative doors, and led us in.

The apartment consisted of kitchen, bathroom, and two meagre rooms, and was almost unfurnished. There were some rather gloomy green tiles in the kitchen, and nothing much else; certainly no cooker. The bare necessities in the bathroom. Bare floors, bare windows and bare walls in the two rooms, with two wooden chairs and a table in one of them, and the frame of a bed in the other. But, like everywhere indoors in Moscow, it was warm.

Misha closed the door behind us, and we took off our hats and coats. Misha swept an arm around, embracing the flat, and Stephen translated what he said.

'It is his sister's flat. When the flats are ready, the people on the list draw lots for them. His sister and her husband drew the ninth floor, and she hates it and is very depressed. They have a baby. Until the lifts are working she will have to carry the baby and her shopping up nine floors all the time. The cooker for the flat is provided, but it has to be carried up, like we saw the others doing. All the furniture has to be carried up, by friends.'

'Why don't the lifts work?' I said.

Misha said (via Stephen) that it was because the caretaker said the interiors of the lifts would be damaged if people used them for taking up cookers and furniture, so the lifts would not be switched on until all the flats were furnished and occupied. It seemed monstrous, but it was quite true.

'Why don't they put an extra, temporary, lining inside the lifts, and remove it later?' I said.

Misha shrugged. It was impossible to argue, he said. The caretaker would not listen, and he was in control. He gestured to us to sit on the chairs, and he himself perched half on and half off the table. He was thin but strong, fit rather than undernourished. The vivid blue eyes in the tanned face looked at us with more friendliness than in the morning and reinforced my belief in his brains.

'Thank you for coming,' he said. 'Tomorrow, I go. I speak again.'

'Tell Stephen in Russian,' I said. 'It will be easier for you. And you can say more.'

He nodded a shade regretfully, but saw the sense of it. He spoke in bursts, waiting for Stephen to catch up, and again nodding as he heard his intentions put into English.

'Later, after we had gone,' Stephen translated, 'Nikolai Alexandrovich, Mr Kropotkin, had more visitors; your friend the English journalist, Malcolm Herrick, and someone who sounds like the Sphinx. They came together. Mr Kropotkin got Misha to repeat to them what he had just told us. Misha thinks that Mr Kropotkin knew the Sphinx quite well . . .'

'His name is Ian,' I said. 'And yes, they had talked together before.'

'Mr Kropotkin thinks you need help,' Stephen went on. 'He sent Misha to fetch his little book with telephone numbers, and he telephoned to several people to ask if they knew anything about Alyosha, and if they did, to tell him, and he would tell you. Boris Dmitrevich Telyatnikov, who is one of the possible Olympic riders, came in the afternoon to see the horses, and Mr Kropotkin asked him also. Boris said he didn't know anything about Alyosha, but Misha thinks Boris was worried.'

'Yes,' I said. 'Carry on.'

'Practically everyone in Moscow who has anything to do with the Olympic equestrian games now seems to be looking for Alyosha.'

'My God,' I said.

Misha looked a little anxious. 'Nikolai Alexandrovich help,' he said. 'You save horse. Nikolai Alexandrovich help.'

'It is kind of him,' I said dazedly.

Stephen listened, and reported. 'The Sphinx . . . Ian . . . told Mr Kropotkin that once you had found Alyosha and talked to him, you could go home. Mr

Kropotkin said, "Then we will find Alyosha for him. He saved our best horse. Nothing is too much."'

'My God,' I said again.

'According to what Mr Kropotkin told everybody, the horse swung unexpectedly in front of the horse box as it approached. The driver had no time to swerve, but you rescued the horse.'

'Is that what Misha thinks?' I said.

'*Niet.*' Misha understood and was positive. 'Driver go . . . boom.' He smashed his fist unmistakably into his hand.

'Did you know him?' I asked.

'*Niet.* No see.'

It was the horse box, Misha told Stephen, in which he and the chestnut and another horse were to travel the next day to Rostov. When he had led the chestnut back to its stable, the horse box had been parked in its usual place. Mr Kropotkin had felt the engine, to make sure it was that horse box which we had seen, and yes, the engine was warm. No one could be found who had driven it. Mr K's view of things was that the driver was ashamed of his carelessness and afraid of being disciplined.

'Well,' Stephen said, standing up, and straightening his spine, 'thank you for telling us.'

Misha hopped off the table and waved him back to his chair, talking earnestly.

'That is not why he asked us to come here,' Stephen relayed.

'No,' I said. 'He gave you his phone number before all this happened.'

'Never miss a trick, do you?'

'I don't really know,' I said.

'That figures.'

'I speak to German,' Misha said.

'What?' I looked at him with quickened interest. 'Do you mean you spoke to Hans Kramer?'

Misha regretfully did not. Misha told Stephen that he had become friends with the boy who had looked after Hans Kramer's horse. He had been unable to tell us that in the morning, because, of course, it was forbidden to talk to the foreigners and he had disobeyed orders.

'Yes,' I said resignedly. 'Go on.'

It appeared that the two young men had formed a pleasant habit of retiring to a disused hay-loft to talk and smoke cigarettes. Smoking in the stables was forbidden also. Misha had enjoyed both talk and smoke, because they were forbidden.

Misha's blue eyes were brightly alive, full of pleasure at his own daring, and totally unsophisticated.

'What did you talk about?' I prompted.

Horses, of course. And Hans Kramer. The German boy disliked Kramer, who was, Stephen translated succinctly, a bastard.

'In what way?'

Misha talked. Stephen translated. 'Kramer was

170

apparently OK with horses, but he liked to play nasty little jokes on people.'

'Yes, I was told of one,' I said, thinking of Johnny and the pink-boa girl-boy. 'Go on.'

'He was also a thief.'

I showed disbelief. Misha nodded vigorously, not just with his head, but from halfway up his back.

'Misha says,' Stephen went on, 'that Kramer stole a case from the veterinary surgeon's car when he called to see the horses of the British team, before the trials began.'

'A case containing drugs?' I said.

'*Da*,' Misha said. 'Drug.'

'People are always stealing cases from doctors and vets,' I said. 'You'd think they would chain them up like bicycles, not leave them around in cars. Well . . . so was Kramer an addict?'

I felt doubtful as I said it, because heavy drug addiction and international-standard riding didn't seem to be happy bedfellows. Misha, however, didn't know. The German boy had told him there was a fuss when the vet discovered his loss, but Kramer had hidden the case.

'How did the German boy know?'

'He found it somewhere in the stable, hidden in Kramer's kit. Four days later, when Kramer died, the German boy took the case to the hay-loft, and he and Misha shared out the contents.'

'For God's sake,' I said.

'It sounds to me,' said Stephen, speaking frankly

after another long tale from Misha, 'that the German boy took the case itself and all the saleable items like barbiturates, and gave Misha the rubbish. Not surprising, really. Our Misha is a proper little innocent at large.'

'What did he do with his share?'

Stephen consulted. 'Brought it back to Moscow with some other stuff . . . souvenirs of the trip, that's all. To remind him of the happy talks in the hay-loft.'

I stared vacantly at the double-glazed window, seeing in my mind not an uncurtained black square, but an old-world cottage in England.

Johnny Farringford, I thought, had not wanted to be thought to be connected too much with Kramer. He had not wanted me to seek or find Alyosha; had wanted the rumours forgotten, and had denied there was any scandal to hush up. Suppose, I thought bleakly, that the Alyosha business was, after all, unimportant, and the thing Johnny desperately did not want uncovered was nothing to do with unorthodox sex but all to do with drugs.

'Has Misha still got the stuff he brought back?' I said.

Misha had.

'Would you let me see it?' I asked him.

Misha was not unwilling, but said he would be going away first thing in the morning.

'Is it important?' Stephen said.

'Only in a negative sort of way.' I sighed. 'If Kramer

172

had the case for four days before he died, he probably took out of it what he wanted. Then the German boy took his share ... whatever Misha still has, it is not what Kramer wanted ... which might tell us something. Besides barbiturates, vets usually carry other things. Pethidine, for example. It's a painkiller, but I believe it is so addictive for humans that you can get hooked by using it a few times. And Butazolidin ... and steroids ...'

'Got you,' Stephen said, and spoke to Misha. Between them they had a long chat which ended in evident agreement.

'Misha says his souvenirs are at his mother's flat, but he himself has a room with the other grooms, near the stable. He has to be back there soon, and tomorrow morning he goes. He can't get to his mother's. But he will telephone, and ask his sister, who lives at home until she moves into this place, to bring the stuff to you tomorrow morning. But she cannot come to the hotel, as it would not do to be seen talking to foreigners, so she will meet you inside the main entrance of GUM. She will wear a red woollen hat with a white pompom, which Misha gave her last week for her birthday, and a long red scarf. She speaks some English, because she learned it in school.'

'Great,' I said. 'Could she make it fairly early? I have to meet Chulitsky outside the National Hotel at ten.'

Misha said he thought she could get there by half-past nine, and on that we agreed.

I thanked Misha for all his trouble and kindness in giving us this information. I enthusiastically shook his hand.

'Is good,' he said, looking pleased. 'You save horse. Nikolai Alexandrovich say help. I help.'

We arrived outside the Aragvi restaurant ten minutes late because of an absence of taxis in the far-flung suburb, and a scarcity of buses. The metro, we had discovered, came to an end three miles short of the flat. Misha travelled towards the city centre with us, but apart, not looking at us, not speaking. He left us on the train, when he reached his interchange station, without a flicker of farewell, his face as stolid as the others ranged about.

'Don't tell Malcolm Herrick what Misha has just told us,' I said, as we hurried the last hundred yards on foot. 'He's a newspaperman. My brief is to hush up what I can, not get it printed in the *Watch*; and we'd get Misha into trouble.'

'Silent as the sepulchre,' Stephen promised, in a voice which spoke of teaching grandmothers something about eggs.

The Aragvi turned out to be less than half a mile from the Intourist Hotel: up Gorky Street, and turn right at the traffic lights. Malcolm and Ian were waiting a short distance short of it and Malcolm grumbled, quietly for him, that we had kept them waiting in the cold.

There was a short queue outside the restaurant, shivering.

'Follow me, and don't talk until we are inside,' Malcolm said. He by-passed the queue and opened the firmly shut door. The by now familiar argument took place, and finally, grudgingly, we were let in.

'I booked,' Malcolm said as we peeled off our coats. 'I come here often. You'd never think it.'

The place was full, and somewhere there was some music. We were led to the one vacant table and a bottle of vodka materialized within five seconds.

'Of the two decent restaurants in Moscow,' Malcolm said, 'I like this the better.'

'Two?' I said.

'That's right. What do you want to eat?' He peered into the large menu. 'The food is Georgian. It is a Georgian restaurant. Most of the customers are from Georgia.'

'For Georgia, USSR, read Texas, USA,' Ian said.

The menu was written exclusively in Russian, and while the other three chose from it, I used my eyes instead on the customers. There were three men at the next table, and beyond them, sitting with their backs to the wall, two more. Very few women. The faces, I realized, were livelier, and varied. The two men over by the wall, for instance, were not Moscow types: they

175

had sallower skins, fierce dark eyes, black curling hair. They ate with concentration, intent on their food.

The three men at the table next to ours were on the other hand intent on their drink. Not much tablecloth showed between full bottles, empty bottles, full and empty glasses. The men, one huge, one medium, one small, were diving into vast tulip-shaped glasses of champagne.

Malcolm looked up from the menu and followed my gaze. 'Georgians,' he said. 'Born with hollow legs.' I watched with fascination while the gold liquid disappeared like beer. The eyes of the smallest were faintly glazed. The huge one looked as sober as his grey flannel suit; and there were three empty vodka bottles on the table.

Ian, Malcolm and Stephen all ordered expertly, and I told Stephen just to double his for me. The food when it came was strange and spicy, and light years away from the grey chunks down the road. The huge man at the next table roared at the waiter, who hurried to bring a second bottle of champagne.

'Well, how's it going, sport?' Malcolm said, forking some chicken in bean sauce into his mouth.

'The smallest one's legs are full,' I said.

'What?' He looked round at the three men. 'No, I meant the Sherlock Holmes bit. What've you come up with so far?'

'The German who died at Burghley called on

Alyosha with his dying breath,' I said. 'And that's about all.'

'And anyway, you knew that,' said Stephen.

I kicked him under the table. He gave me a sharp enquiring look and then realized that except for Misha we wouldn't have been aware that they knew. Neither Malcolm nor Ian commented, however. The four of us ate thoughtfully.

'Not much in that, is there, sport?' Malcolm said.

'Alyosha must exist,' I said. 'Alyosha. Moscow.' I sighed. 'I'll have to go on looking.'

'What'll you do next?' Ian said.

I took off my glasses, and squinted at them, and polished some non-existent smears with my hand-kerchief.

'Er,' I said.

'How bad are your eyes, sport?' Malcolm said, interrupting. 'Let's look through your windows.'

Short of breaking the frames, I couldn't have prevented him. He took the glasses firmly out of my hand and placed them on his own nose.

To me, his face, and all the others in the place, looked a distorted blur. Colours told me roughly where hair, eyes and clothes were, but outlines had vanished.

'Christ,' Malcolm said. 'You must have corkscrew vision.'

'Astigmatism,' I said.

'And some.'

They all had a go at looking at the world through my

eyes, and then handed them back. Everything became nicely sharp again.

'In both eyes?' Ian said.

I nodded. 'And both different. Frightfully handy.'

The small man at the next table was propping his head up with his champagne glass and seemed to be going to sleep. The friends kept up a steady intake and ignored him. The huge one roared at the waiter again and held up three fingers, and with my mouth open I watched three more bottles of vodka arrive at the table.

Coffee was brought for us, but I was glued to the scene in front. The small man's head, still balanced on the glass of champagne, sank lower and lower. The glass came to rest on the table, and the hand holding it dropped away, and the little man sat there with his head on the glass, fast asleep.

'Georgians,' said Malcolm, glancing at them, as if that explained everything.

The huge man paid the bill and stood up, rising to a good seven feet tall. He tucked the three full bottles of vodka under one arm and the sleeping friend under the other, and made the stateliest of exits.

'Bloody marvellous,' I said.

The waiter who had served them came and spoke to us, watching the departure with respect.

Malcolm said, 'The waiter says they started with a whole bottle of vodka each. Then they had two more bottles of vodka between them. Five in all. Then the two bottles of champagne. No one but Georgians could do that.'

I said mildly, 'I thought you didn't speak Russian.'

He gave me a startled glance and a short burst of the flat hard stare of the first evening.

'Yeah, sport. I remember. I told you I don't speak Russian . . . Well, I don't. That doesn't mean I don't know it. It means I don't let the Russkies in general cotton on. Right, sport?'

'Right,' I agreed.

'It's not in your file,' Ian said, conversationally.

'Dead right. The Russkies have my file too, don't forget. I learned the lingo in private from twelve long-playing records and some text books, and you just forget that piece of information pronto.'

'Never misses a trick,' Stephen said.

'Who doesn't?'

'Our friend Randall.'

Ian regarded me with slightly narrowed eyes, and Malcolm called for the bill.

The two sallow men from over by the wall had gone in the wake of the Georgians, and the place was emptying fast. We collected our coats and hats and shuddered out into the saturated air. It seemed colder to me than ever. The other three made off for the metro, and I risked a fine by crossing Gorky Street above ground instead of tunnelling under. After eleven at night there were even fewer cars than usual to mow

179

one down, and not another pedestrian in sight, let alone a policeman.

The Intourist Hotel lay in the distance, down the slight hill, with its large canopy stretching out over the pavement. I turned up my coat collar, wondering, for about the tenth time, why most of the centre of the canopy was an intentional rectangular hole, like a skylight without glass, open to every drop of rain or snow which cared to fall. As a shelter for people arriving and departing, the canopy was a non-starter. Of as much practical use as a bath with no plug.

A mind floating along in neutral is in rotten shape for battle. A black car rolled quietly down the road beside me and came to a halt ten paces ahead. The driver got out of the car, and the front passenger door opened. The front passenger stood up on to the pavement, and as I approached, he sprang at me.

The surprise was absolute. His hand snaked out towards my spectacles, and I hit it violently aside as one would a wasp. When it came to saving my sight, my reflexes were always instantaneous: but for the rest, I was unbalanced.

He crowded after me across the pavement to pin me against the unyielding stone of the flanking building. His friend hustled to help. There was a fierce brutal strength in their manner, and there was also no doubt that, whatever they intended next, their first target was still my eyes.

One wouldn't actually choose to fight while wearing

a thick overcoat and a fur hat, even if the opposition were similarly handicapped. To fight, however, seemed imperative.

I kicked the storming passenger very viciously on the knee, and when his head came forward I grabbed hold of the woolly balaclava he wore under his hat and swung him round so that his head hit the wall.

The driver arrived like a whirlwind and grabbed my arm, his other hand again aiming at my glasses. I ducked. His fingers sank only into fur. My hat, dislodged, fell off. I let go with a kick at him, which connected but not very effectively, and I also opened my mouth and started shouting.

I shouted 'Ya-ya-ya-ya-ya' at the top of my voice, roaring into the empty street, which had no traffic noise to drown the decibels.

They hadn't expected such a racket. I felt the impetus slacken in them fractionally, and I tore myself out of their grasp and ran. Ran downhill, towards the Intourist. Ran with all the power I could bring to every muscle. Ran like the Olympics.

I heard one of the car doors slam. Heard the car coming behind me. Went on running.

There was life and waiting taxis and people outside the Intourist. There were also the watchers, earning their keep. I wondered fleetingly if watchers ever went to the help of people running away from other people in black cars, and supposed not.

Not in Moscow.

I didn't bother to yell for their help. I simply ran. And I made it. Just.

The men in the car must have decided it was too near the Intourist for them to make another attack, especially as I was now running flat out and not walking along with woolly thoughts. In any case, after it had passed me, the car didn't stop, but accelerated away past the hotel, and turned right at the end of the street, and went out of sight.

I slowed to a fast walk for the last hundred yards, heart thumping madly and chest heaving to take in vast lungfuls of cold wet air. I was nothing like as fit, I thought grimly, as I would have been in any other autumn, when I'd been racing.

I covered the last few yards at ordinary walking pace, and attracted no more eyes than usual when I went in through the big double airlock-type glass entrance. The warmth inside seemed suddenly cloying, stoking up the sweat of exertion: I peeled off my coat and collected my room key, and thought that nothing on earth would persuade me to go back up Gorky Street to retrieve my hat.

My room looked calm and sane, as if to reassure me that hotel guests could not be frighteningly attacked in one of the main streets of the city.

It could happen in Piccadilly, I thought. It could happen in Park Avenue and the Champs-Élysées and the Via Veneto. What was so different about Gorky Street?

I threw my coat and room key on to the bed, poured a large reviver from the duty-free Scotch, and sank on to the sofa to drink it.

Two attacks in one day. Too bloody much.

The first had been a definite attempt to cripple or kill. The second had been – perhaps – an attempt at abduction. Without glasses, I would have been a pushover. They could have got me into the car. And after the drive . . . what destination?

Did the Prince expect me to stick to the task until I was dead? Probably not, I thought; but then the Prince hadn't known what he was sending me into.

More than anything, I'd been lucky. I could be lucky again. Failing that, I had better be careful. My heart gradually steadied. My breath quietened to normal. I drank the Scotch, and felt better.

After a while I put down my glass and picked up the tape-recorder. Switched it on. Started methodically beside the window, and made slow comprehensive sweeps of the walls. Top to bottom. Every inch.

There was no whine.

I switched the recorder off and put it down. No whine was inconclusive. It didn't mean no listening probe embedded into the plaster, it meant no listening probe switched on.

I went slowly to bed and lay awake in the dark, thinking about the driver and the passenger in the black car. Apart from general awareness of their age, twenty–thirty, and height, five-nine, they had left me with three clear impressions. The first was that they knew about my eyesight. The second, that the savage quality I had sensed in their attack was a measure of the ferocity in their minds. And third, that they were not Russian.

They had not spoken, so their voices had given me no clue. They had worn only the sober garb of the Russian man-in-the-street. Their faces had been three-quarters covered, with the result that I had seen only their eyes, and even those, very briefly.

So why did I think . . .? I pulled the duvet over my shoulders and turned comfortably on to one side. The Russians, I thought drowsily, didn't behave like that unless they were KGB, and if the KGB had wanted to arrest me they would not have done it in that way, and they would not have failed. Other Russians were tamed by deterrents like labour camps, psychiatric hospitals, and the death sentence. Frank's voice drifted back to me from breakfast. 'There are no muggings in Russia. The crime rate is very low indeed. There are practically no murders.'

'Repression is always the outcome of revolution,' I said.

'Are you sure you've got it the right way round?' Mrs Wilkinson asked me, looking puzzled.

'People don't actually like being purged of their lazy and libertine old ways,' I said. 'So you have to force their mouths open, to give them the medicine. Revolutionaries everywhere are by nature aggressive, oppressive and repressive. It's they who have the power-over-others complex. All for your own good, of course.'

I got no rise out of Frank. He merely repeated that in a perfect Socialist state like Russia there was no need for crime. The State supplied all needs, and gave to the people whatever it was good for them to have.

Sixty years or so on from the October Revolution (now confusingly celebrated in November owing to the up-dating of the calendar) its wind-sown seeds were germinating their bloody crops around the world, but way back where it all started the second and third generation were not given to acts of private violence.

The eyes looking out of the balaclavas had burned with a hunger for a harvest yet to come: sixty years younger than the blank dull look of a people for whom everything was provided.

CHAPTER TEN

Frank followed me to GUM the following morning.

When I had gone in through the main door without once looking back, I stood still in the shadows, and watched, and presently he appeared, hurrying a little.

At breakfast, upon Natasha's insistent enquiry, I had said I was going to see some more horse people, but before that I was going to GUM to buy a new hat, as I had lost my last one.

The tiniest frown crossed Frank's face, and he looked at me with a shade of speculation. I remembered that when he had followed me into the hotel the evening before, after I had ostensibly said goodnight to Stephen, I had been wearing the hat. How careful one had to be, I thought, over the most innocent remarks.

'Where did you lose your hat?' he said, showing only friendly interest.

'Must have dropped it in the foyer or the lift,' I said easily, 'I don't really know.'

Natasha suggested I ask at the desk. I would, I said;

and did. One learned. If not fast enough, one learned in the end.

I turned away from GUM's main door while Frank was still a little way off, and saw the red woollen hat with a white pompom immediately. Below the hat there were two blue-grey eyes in an elfin face, and straight hair in escaping wisps. She looked too young and slight to be married and a mother, and I could see why nine storeys up with no lifts was a crying disaster.

'Elena?' I said, tentatively.

She nodded a fraction, and turned to walk purposefully away. I followed a few paces behind. For talking to a foreigner she would have to pick her own moment, and it suited me well for it to be out of Frank's sight.

She wore a grey coat with a red scarf falling jauntily over her shoulder, and carried a string bag with a paper-wrapped parcel inside it. I shortened the distance between us and said so that she could hear, 'I want to buy a hat.' She gave no sign of understanding, but when she stopped it was, in fact, outside a shop selling hats.

The inside of GUM was not a department store along Western lines but like those in the Far East; a huge collection of small shops all under one roof. A covered market, two storeys high, with intersecting alleys and a glassed roof far above. Drips of melted snow fell through the cracks in the heavens and made small puddles underfoot.

I bought the hat. Elena waited outside in the alley

displaying no interest in me, and set off again when I came out. I looked carefully around for Frank, but couldn't see him. Shoppers blocked every long perspective; and it worked both ways. If I couldn't see him, very likely he couldn't see me.

Elena squeezed through a long queue of stolid people and stopped outside a shop selling folk arts and crafts. She transferred the string bag to my hand with the smallest of movements and no ceremony whatsoever. Her gaze was directed towards the goods in the window, not at me.

'Misha say give you this.' Her accent was light and pretty, but I gathered from the disapproval in her tone that she was on this errand strictly for her brother's sake, and not for mine.

I thanked her for coming.

'Please not bring trouble for him.'

'I promise I won't,' I said.

She nodded briefly, glancing quickly at my face, and away.

'You go now, please,' she said. 'I queue.'

'What is the queue for?'

'Boots. Warm boots, for winter.'

I looked at the queue, which stretched a good way along one of the ground-floor alleys, and up a staircase, and along the gallery above, and away out of sight. It hadn't moved a step forward in five minutes.

'But it will take you all day,' I said.

'Yes. I need boots. When boots come in shop,

everyone come to buy. It is normal. In England, the peasants have no boots. In Soviet Union, we are fortunate.'

She walked away without any more farewell than her brother had given on the metro, and attached herself to the end of the patient line. The only thing that I could think of that England's bootless peasantry would so willingly queue all day for would be Cup Final tickets.

A glance into the tissue-wrapped parcel revealed that what Misha had sent, or what Elena had brought, was a painted wooden doll.

Frank picked me up somewhere between GUM and the pedestrian tunnel under Fiftieth Anniversary et cetera Square. I caught a glimpse of him behind me underground: a split second of unruly curls and college scarf bobbing along in the crowd. If I hadn't been looking, I wouldn't have noticed.

It was already after ten. I lengthened my stride and finished the journey fairly fast, surfacing on the north side of the square and veering left towards the National Hotel.

Parked just beyond the entrance was a small bright yellow car, with, inside it, a large Russian in a high state of fuss.

'Seven minutes late,' he said. 'For seven minutes I sit here illegally. Get in, get in, do not apologize.'

I eased in beside him and he shot off with a crash of gears and a fine disregard for other traffic.

'You have been to GUM,' he said accusingly. 'And therefore you are late.'

I followed the direction of his gaze and began to feel less bewildered by his clairvoyance: he was looking at the printed tissue-paper inside the string bag which Elena had given me. How cautious of her, I thought, to have brought Misha's souvenirs in a wrapping to suit the rendezvous, in a bag any foreign tourist could acquire. A bag, too, I thought contentedly, that friend Frank would not query. The secret of survival in Russia was to be unremarkable.

Yuri Ivanovich Chulitsky revealed himself, during the time I spent with him, as a highly intelligent man with a guilt-ridden love of luxury and a repressed sense of humour. The wrong man for the regime, I thought, but striving to live honourably within its framework. In a country where an out-of-line opinion was a treachery, even if unspoken, he was an unwilling mental traitor. Not to believe what one believes one should believe is a spiritual torment as old as doctrine, and Yuri Chulitsky, I grew to understand, suffered from it dismally.

Physically he was about forty, plumply unfit, with pouches already under his eyes, and a habit of raising the centre of his upper lip to reveal the incisors beneath. He spoke always with deliberation, forming the words carefully and precisely, but that might have been only the effect of using English, and, as on the telephone, he gave the impression that every utterance was double-checked internally before being allowed to escape.

'Cigarette?' he said, offering a packet.

'No . . . thank you.'

'I smoke,' he said, flicking a lighter one-handed with the dexterity of long practice. 'You smoke?'

'Cigars, sometimes.'

He grunted. The fingers on his left hand, resting on the steering-wheel with the cigarette stuck between them, were tanned yellowish brown, but otherwise his fingers were white and flexible, with spatulate tips and short well-tended nails.

'I go see Olympic building,' he said. 'You come?'

'Sure,' I said.

'At Chertanovo.'

'Where?'

'Place for equestrian games. I am architect. I design buildings at Chertanovo.' He pronounced design like dess-in, but his meaning was clear. 'I go today see progress. You understand?'

'Every word,' I said.

'Good. I see in England how equestrian games go. I see need for sort buildings . . .' He stopped and shook his head in frustration.

'You went to see what sort of things happened during international equestrian games, so that you would know what buildings would be needed, and how

191

they should best be designed for dealing with the needs and numbers of the Olympics.'

He smiled lop-sidedly. 'Is right. I go also Montreal. Is not good. Moscow games, we build good.'

The leisurely one-way system in central Moscow meant, it seemed to me, mile-long detours to return to where one started, but facing the other way. Yuri Chulitsky swung his bright little conveyance round the corners without taking his foot noticeably off the accelerator, the bulk of his body making the car's skin seem not much more than a metal overcoat.

At one point, arriving at a junction with a main road, we were stopped dead by a policeman. Yuri Chulitsky shrugged a trifle and switched off the engine.

'What's the matter?' I said.

The main road had, I saw, been totally cleared of traffic. Nothing moved on it. Chulitsky said something under his breath, so I asked again, 'What's the matter? Has there been an accident?'

'No,' he said. 'See lines in road?'

'Do you mean those white ones?'

There were two parallel white lines painted down the centre of the main road, with a space of about six feet between them. I had noticed them on many of the widest streets, but thought of them vaguely as some sort of no-man's-land between the two-way lines of traffic.

'White lines go to Kremlin,' Chulitsky said. 'Politburo people drive to Kremlin in white lines. Every people's car stop.'

I sat and watched. After three or four minutes a long black car appeared, driving fairly fast in lonely state up the centre of the road, between the white lines.

'Chaika,' Chulitsky said, as the limousine slid lengthily past, showing curtains drawn across the rear windows. 'Is official car. Chaika, in English, is seagull.'

He started his engine, and presently the policeman stepped out of the middle of the side road and waved us on our way.

'Was that the Chairman?' I asked.

'No. Many politburo peoples go in Chaika on white lines. All people's cars always stop.'

Democratic, I thought.

The small yellow car sped south of the city, along what he told me was the road to Warsaw, but which to my eyes was plainly labelled M4.

He said, 'Nikolai Alexandrovich Kropotkin say tell you what you ask. You ask. I tell.'

'I'm looking for someone called Alyosha.'

'Alyosha? Many people called Alyosha. Nikolai Alexandrovich say find Alyosha for Randall Drew. Who is this Alyosha?'

'That's the problem,' I said. 'I don't know, and I haven't been able to find out. No one seems to know who he is.' I paused. 'Did you meet Hans Kramer in England?'

193

'*Da*. German. He die.'

'That's right. Well . . . he knew Alyosha. The autopsy said Kramer died of a heart attack, but people near him when he died thought he was saying that Alyosha had caused him to have a heart attack. Er . . . have I said that clearly enough?'

'Yes. Is clear. About Alyosha, I cannot help.'

I supposed I would have been surprised if he had said anything different.

'You have been asked before, about Alyosha?' I said.

'Please?'

'An Englishman came to see you at the Olympic committee building. He saw you and the two colleagues who went with you to England.'

'Is right,' he agreed gruffly. 'Is writing for newspaper.'

'Malcolm Herrick.'

'*Da*.'

'You all said you knew nothing at all about anything.'

A long pause; then he said, 'Herrick is foreigner. Comrades not say things to Herrick.'

He relapsed into silence, and we drove steadily along the Warsaw highway, leaving the city centre behind and making for another lot of egg-box suburbs. Some light powdery snow began to fall, and Yuri switched on the windscreen wipers.

'Today, tomorrow, it snow. This snow not melt. Stay all winter.'

'Do you like the winter?' I said.

'No. Winter is bad for building. Today is last day is possible see progress of buildings at Chertanovo. So I go now.'

I said I would be most interested in the buildings, if he felt like showing me round. He laughed in a small deep throaty rumble, but offered no explanation.

I asked him if he had personally known Hans Kramer, but he had spoken to him only about buildings. 'Well ... Johnny Farringford?' I asked.

'Johnny ... Farringford. Are you saying *Lord* Farringford? Is a man with red hairs? Ride in British team?'

'That's the one,' I said.

'I see him many times. Many places. I talk with him. I ask him about buildings. He is no good about buildings. I ask other peoples. Other peoples is more good.' He stopped, obviously unimpressed by the planning ability of earls, and we drove four or five miles while he seemed to be thinking deeply about anything except my mission: but finally, as if coming to a difficult decision, he said, 'Is not good Lord Farringford come to Olympics.'

I held my breath. Damped down every quick and excited question. Managed in the end to say without even a quaver, 'Why?'

He had relapsed, however, into further deep thought.

'Tell me,' I said, without pressure.

'It is for my country good if he come. It is for your country not good. If I tell you, I speak against the good for my country. It is difficult for me.'

'Yes,' I said.

After a long way he turned abruptly off the M4 to the right, along a lesser but still dual-carriageway road. There was, as usual, very little traffic, and without much ado he swung round in a U-turn across the central reservation to face the way we had come. He pulled in by the roadside and stopped with a jerk.

On our left the road was lined as far as the eye could see with rows of apartment buildings, greyish white. On our right there was a large flat snow-sprinkled space bordered on the far side by a stretch of black-looking forest of spindly young trees packed tightly together. On the side near the road there was a wire fence, and between the fence and the road itself, a wide ditch full of white half-melted slush.

'Is there,' Yuri said, pointing into this far from prom-ising landscape with a gleam of relaxed humour, 'equestrian games.'

'Ye gods,' I said.

We got out of the car into the bitter air. I looked away down the road in the direction we had originally been travelling. There were tall concrete lamp stan-dards, electricity pylons, dense black forest on the left, white unending impersonal apartment blocks on the right, a grey double road with no traffic, and, at the side, wet white snow. Over it all softly fell the powdery forerunners of the winter freeze. It was silent and ugly and as desolate as a desert.

'In summer,' Yuri said, 'forest is green. Is beautiful place for equestrian games. Is grass. Everything beautiful.'

'I'll take your word for it,' I said.

Further along, on the side of the road where we had stopped, there were two large hoardings, one bearing a long announcement about the Olympics, and the other sporting a big picture of the stadium as it was one day going to be. The stands looked most ingenious, shaped like a Z, with the top and bottom ranks of the seats facing one way, and the centre rank facing the other. Events, it appeared, would take place on both sides of the stands.

Yuri gestured to me to return to the car, and he drove us through a gate in the wire, on to the site itself. There were a few men there driving mechanical earth-movers, though how they knew what they were moving was a mystery to me, as the whole place looked a sea of jumbled mud with pools of icy slush amid the usual broken white blanket of half-melted snow.

Yuri reached into the space behind my seat and brought forth a huge pair of thigh-high gumboots. These he put on by planting them firmly outside the opened car door, removing his walking shoes, wrapping his trousers round his legs, and sinking his feet into the depths as he stood up.

'I talk to men,' he said. 'You wait.'

Superfluous advice, I thought. Yuri unfastened his ear-flaps against the chill wind and talked to his men, trudging about and making sweeping gestures with his arms. After a fair while he returned and reversed the gumboot process, tucking the now wet and muddy objects in behind his own driving seat.

'Is good,' he said, lifting the centre of his lip and giving me a gleam of teeth. 'We finish foundations. In spring, when snow melt, we build quickly. Stadium,' he pointed, 'stables,' he pointed again, 'restaurants, buildings for riders, buildings for officials, buildings for television. There,' he waved an arm at a huge slightly undulating area bordered by forest, 'is cross-country for trials, like Badminton and Burghley. In summer, is beautiful.'

'Will everyone who wants to come to the Games get visas?' I said.

'*Da*. All people have visas.'

'It isn't always like that,' I said neutrally, and he replied in the same level tone. 'For Olympics, all peoples have visas. Stay in hotels. Is good.'

'What about the Press?' I said. 'And the television people?'

'We build Press building for foreign Press. Also television building for foreign television peoples, near Moscow television building. Use same . . .' He described a transmitting mast with his hands. 'Foreign peoples go only in these buildings. In England, we ask

Press peoples about Press buildings. We see what Press peoples need. We ask many Press peoples. We ask Herrick.'

'Herrick?' I said. 'Did you ask him in England, or in Moscow?'

'In England. He help us. He come to Burghley. We see him with Lord Farringford. So we ask him. We ask many peoples about buildings. We ask Hans Kramer about buildings. He was . . .' Words failed him but gestures did not. Hans Kramer, I gathered, had given the Russian observers a decisively rude brush-off.

He tied up the ear-flaps of his hat without taking it off. I spent the time scanning the road for anything that looked like a following car, but saw nothing of note. A bus passed, its tyres making a swishing noise on the slushy tarmac. I thought that the low level of traffic on most roads would make a following car conspicuous: but on the other hand there seemed to be very little variety in make, so that one car tended to look exactly like the next. Difficult to spot a tail. Easy, however, to follow a bright yellow box on wheels.

'What sort of car is this?' I said.

'Zhiguli,' he said. 'Is my car.' He seemed proud of it. 'Not many peoples have car. I am architect, have car.'

'Is it expensive?' I asked.

'Car expensive. Petrol cheap. Driving examination, very difficult.'

He finished the bow on his hat, checked that his

boots were inside, slammed the door, and backed briskly out on to the road.

'How is everyone going to get here?' I said. 'Competitors and spectators.'

'We build metro. New station.' He thought. 'Metro on top of ground, not deep. New metro for Chertanovo peoples. Many new buildings here. Chertanovo is new place. I show you.'

We set off back towards the Warsaw highway, but before we reached it he turned off to the right, and drove up another wide road where apartment blocks were springing up like mushrooms. All whitish grey; all nine storeys high, marching away into the distance.

'In Soviet all people have house,' Yuri said. 'Rent is cheap. In England, expensive.' He shot me an amused look as if challenging me to argue with his simplistic statement. In a country where everything was owned by the state, there was no point in charging high rents. To enable people to pay high rents, or high prices for electricity, transport and telephones, for that matter, it would be necessary to pay higher wages. Yuri Chulitsky knew it as well as I did. I would have to be careful, I told myself, not to underestimate the subtlety of his thoughts because of the limitations of the English they were expressed in.

'Can I make a trade with you?' I said. 'A bargain? One piece of information in exchange for another?'

For that I got a quick, sharp, piercing glance, but all he said was, 'Car need petrol.' He pulled off the road into a station with pumps, and removed himself from the car to talk to the attendant.

I found myself taking off my glasses and polishing the already clean lenses. The playing-for-time gesture, which was not at that moment needed. I wondered if it had been intuitively sparked off by Yuri's purchase of petrol, which seemed hardly urgent as the tank was well over half full, according to the gauge.

While I watched, the needle crept round to full. Yuri paid and returned to the car, and we set off towards the city centre.

'What information you exchange?' he said.

'I don't have it all yet.'

A muscle twitched beside his mouth. 'You diplomat?' he said.

'A patriot. Like you.'

'You tell me information.'

I told him a great deal. I told him what had really happened at the Hippodrome, not Kropotkin's watered-down version, and I told him of the attack in Gorky Street. I also told him, though without names or places or details, the gist of what Boris Telyatnikov had overheard, and the inferences one could draw from it. He listened, as any faithful Russian would, with a growing sense of dismay. When I stopped, he drove a good way without speaking, and in the end his comment was oblique.

'You want lunch?' he said.

CHAPTER ELEVEN

He took me to what he called the Architects' Circle and in the big basement restaurant there gave me food I hadn't believed existed in Moscow. Prime smoked salmon, delicious ham off the bone, tender red beef. An apple and some grapes. Vodka to toss off for starters, followed by excellent red wine. Good strong coffee at the end. He himself ate and drank with as much enjoyment as I did.

'Marvellous,' I said appreciatively. 'Superb.'

Yuri leaned back at last and lit a cigarette, and told me that every profession had its Circle. There was a Writers' Circle, for instance, to which all Soviet writers belonged. If they did not belong to the Circle, they did not get published. They could, of course, be expelled from the Circle, if it was considered that what they wrote was not suitable. Yuri's manner dared me to suggest that he didn't entirely agree with this system.

'What about architects?' I asked mildly.

Architects, I gathered, had to be politically sound, if they wished to be members of the Architects' Circle.

Naturally, if one did not belong to the Circle, one was not allotted anything to design.

Naturally.

I drank my coffee and made no remark. Yuri watched me, and smiled with a touch of melancholy.

'I give information,' he said, 'about Lord Farringford.'

'Thank you.'

'You are clever man.' He sighed and shrugged resignedly, and kept his side of the bargain. 'Lord Farringford is foolish man. With Hans Kramer, he go bad places. Sex places.' Distaste showed in his face, and the top lip lifted even further off the incisors. 'In London, is disgusting pictures. In the street. All people can see. Disgusting.' He searched for a word. 'Dirty.'

'Yes,' I said.

'Lord Farringford and Hans Kramer go into these places. Three, four times.'

'Are you sure it was more than once?' I said attentively.

'Sure. We see. We . . . follow.' The confession came out on a downward inflection, drifting off into silence, as if he hadn't quite said what he had.

Wow, I thought: and what I said, without any emphasis of any sort, was, 'Why did you follow?'

He struggled a great deal with his conscience, but he told me what I was sure was the truth.

'Comrade with me, he look in England and in many

country for foolish peoples. When foolish peoples come to Soviet Union, comrade use . . . make . . .'

'Your comrade makes use of them through their liking for pornography?'

He blew out a sharp breath.

'And if Farringford comes to the Olympics, your comrade will make use of him?'

Silence.

'What use could Farringford be? He isn't a diplomat . . .' I stopped, thought, and went on more slowly. 'Do you mean,' I said, 'that in return for not . . . embarrassing the British people, for not exposing a scandalous misdemeanour into which your comrade has lured him, your comrade will demand some concession from the British government?'

'Say again,' he said.

I said it again, more forthrightly. 'Your comrade traps Farringford into a dirty mess. Your comrade says to the British government, give me what I want, or I publish the mess.'

He didn't directly admit it. 'The comrades of my comrade,' he said.

'Yes,' I agreed. 'Those comrades.'

'Farringford is rich man,' Yuri said. 'For rich man, comrade feel . . .' He didn't know the word, but his meaning was unmistakable, and it was contempt.

'For all rich men?' I said.

'Of course. Rich man bad. Poor man good.' He spoke with utter conviction and no suggestion of cynicism, stating, I supposed, one of humanity's most fundamental beliefs. Camels through eyes of needles, and all that. Rich men never got to heaven, and serve them right. Which left absolutely no hope of eternal bliss for Randall Drew, who had an unequal share of this world's goods... If I warned Johnny Farringford, I wondered, putting a stop to my dribbling thoughts, would it be enough? Or would it really be wiser for him to stay at home?

'Yuri,' I said, 'how about another bargain?'

'Explain.'

'If I learn more here, I will exchange it for a promise that your comrade will not try to trap Farringford, if he comes to the Olympics.'

He stared. 'You ask things impossible.'

'A promise in writing,' I said.

'Is impossible. Comrade with me ... impossible.'

'Yeah ... Well, it was just a thought.' I reflected. 'Then if I learn more, I would exchange it for information about Alyosha.'

Yuri studied the tablecloth and I studied Yuri.

'I cannot help,' he said.

He stubbed out his cigarette and raised his eyes to meet mine. I was aware of a fierce intensity of thought going on behind the steady gaze, but upon what subject I couldn't guess.

'I take you,' he said finally, 'to Intourist Hotel.'

*

He dropped me, in fact, around the corner outside the National, where he had picked me up, implying, though not saying, that there was no sense in engaging the attention of the watchers unnecessarily.

It was by that time growing dark, as for various reasons our lunch had been delayed in arrival and leisurely in the eating, not least because of a wedding party going on in the next room. The bride had worn a long white dress and a minuscule veil. Did they get married in church? I asked. Of course not, Yuri said: it was not allowed. Pagan rituals, it seemed, had survived the rise and fall of Christianity.

The powdery snowfall of the morning had thickened into a determined regularity, but by no means into a raging blizzard. The wind, in fact, had dropped, but so had the temperature, and there was a threatening bite to the cold. I walked the short distance from one hotel to the other among a crowd of hurrying pedestrians and no men in black cars attempted to pick me off.

I arrived at the Intourist entrance at the same time as the Wilkinsons and their package tour, fresh back from the coach trip to Zagorsk.

'It was quite interesting,' said Mrs Wilkinson gamely, pushing through into the suddenly crowded foyer. 'I couldn't hear the guide very well, and it seemed wrong somehow, guided tours going in through churches, when there were people in there praying. Did you know that they don't have any chairs in Russian churches? No pews. Everyone has to stand all the time. My feet are fair killing me. There's a lot of snow out in the country. Dad slept most of the way, didn't you, Dad?'

Dad morosely nodded.

Mrs Wilkinson, along with nearly everyone else on the bus tour, carried a white plastic bag with a green-and-orange swirly pattern on it.

'There was a tourist shop there. You know, foreign-currency shop. I bought ever such a pretty matroshka.'

'What's a matroshka?' I said, waiting beside her at the desk, to collect our room keys.

'One of these,' she said, fishing into the white plastic depths and tearing off some tissue-paper. 'These dolls.'

She produced with a small flourish an almost identical double of the fat brightly coloured wooden doll I too carried in the string bag dangling from my left hand.

'I think matroshka means little mother,' she said. 'Anyway, you know, they pull apart and there's another smaller one inside, and you go right down to a tiny one in the middle. There are nine inside here. I'm going to give it to my grandchildren.' She beamed with simple pleasure, and I beamed right back. If only all the world, I thought regretfully, were as wholesome and as harmless as the Wilkinsons.

Wholesome and harmless did, I supposed, describe the outward appearance of my tidy room upstairs, but this time, when I swept the walls with the tape-recorder, I heard the whine. High-pitched, assaulting the ear, and originating from a spot about five feet up from the floor, and about midway along the bed. I switched off the recorder and wondered who, if anyone, was listening.

The matroshka doll which Elena had handed me proved, on a closer look, to be a well-worn specimen with paint scratched off all over her pink-cheeked face and bright blue dress and yellow apron. In shape, she was a very large elongated egg, slightly smaller round the head than lower down, and flat at the bottom, in order to stand. In all, about ten inches high and rotund in circumference.

Pull apart she should, Mrs Wilkinson had said, and pull apart she did, across the middle, though either the two halves were a naturally tight fit, or else Misha or Elena had used some sort of glue. I tugged and wrenched, and the little mother finally gave birth with a reluctant jerk and scattered her close-packed secrets all over the sofa.

I collected Misha's souvenirs of England and laid them out on the dressing-table shelf; a row of valueless bits and pieces brought home by an unsophisticated young rider.

Easily the largest in size was the official programme of the International Event, printed in English but with the results and winners written in, in several places, in Russian script. The programme had been rolled to fit into the matroshka doll, and lay in an opening tube with the pages curling.

There were two picture postcards, unused, with views of London. A brown envelope containing a small bunch of wilted grass. An empty packet of Players cigarettes. A small metal ashtray with a horse's head painted on the front, and 'Made in England' stamped into the back. A flat tin of mentholated cough pastilles. Several pieces of paper and small cards with writing on, and, finally, the things which had come from the vet's stolen case.

Stephen had been right in thinking that Misha's share had not been very much, and I wondered what, in fact, he had made of it, with all the wording on the labels being in English.

There were four flat two-by-two-inch sachets of a powder called Equipalazone, each sachet containing one gram of phenylbutazone B Vet C, otherwise known succinctly in the horse world as 'bute'.

I had used the drug countless times myself, in ten years of training my own horses, as it was the tops at reducing inflammation and pain in strained and injured legs. In Eventing and show jumping one could give it to the horses up to the minute they performed, but in British racing, though not in some other countries, it had to be out of the system before the 'off'. Bute might be the subject of controversy and dope tests, but it was also about as easy to get hold of as aspirins, and one did not have to get it through a vet. The amount that

Misha had brought home was roughly a single day's dose.

There was next a small plastic tub of sulphanilamide powder, which was useful for putting on wounds, to dry and heal them: and a sample-sized round tin of gamma benzine hexachloride, which, as far as I could remember, was anti-louse powder. There was a small, much folded advertisement leaflet extolling a cure for ringworm; and that was all.

No barbiturates. No pethidine. No steroids. Either Kramer, or the German lad, had cleaned out the lot.

Well, I thought, as I began to pack everything back into the doll; so much for that. I went through everything again, more thoroughly, just to make sure. Opened up the sample-sized tin of louse powder, which contained louse powder, and the small plastic tub of sulphanilamide powder, which contained sulphanilamide powder. Or, at least, I supposed they did. If the two white powders were actually LSD or heroin, I wasn't sure that I would know.

The Equipalazone sachets were foil-packed, straight from the manufacturers, and hadn't been tampered with. I stuffed them back into the doll.

There was nothing lodged between the leaves of the programme. I shook it; nothing fell out. The writings on the pieces of card and paper were some in Russian and some in German, and I laid these aside for a translation from Stephen. The empty cigarette packet contained no cigarettes, or anything else, and the small tin of cough lozenges contained ... er ... no cough lozenges. The tin of cough lozenges contained another piece of paper, much handled and wrinkled, and three very small glass phials in a bed of cotton wool.

The phials were of the same size and shape as those I had for adrenalin: tiny glass capsules less than two inches in length, with a much-narrowed neck a third of the way along, which snapped off, so that one could put a hypodermic needle through the resulting opening, and down into the liquid, to draw it up. Each phial in the tin contained one millilitre of colourless liquid, enough for one human-sized injection. Half a teaspoonful. Not enough, to my mind, for a horse.

I held one of the phials up in the light, to see the printing on it, but, as usual with such baby ampoules, it was difficult to see the lettering. Not adrenalin. As far as I could make out, it said 0.4 mg naloxone, which was spectacularly unhelpful, as I'd never heard of the stuff. I unfolded the piece of paper, and that was no better, as whatever was written there was written in Russian script. I put the paper back in the tin and closed it, and set it aside with the other mysteries for Stephen to look at.

Stephen himself had planned to spend the day between lectures and Gudrun, but had said he would be near the telephone from four o'clock onwards, if I should want him. It frankly didn't seem worthwhile for me to traipse up to the University, or for him to come down, to decipher Misha's bits of paper, without first seeing if it could be done by wires; so I rang him.

'How's it going?' he said.

'The walls are whining.'

'Oh cripes.'

'Anyway,' I said, 'if I spell some German words out to you, can you tell me what they mean?'

'If you think it's wise.'

'Stop me if you don't think so,' I said.

'OK.'

'Right. Here goes with the first.' I read out, letter by letter, as far as I could judge, the three lines of German handwriting on one of the cards.

Stephen was laughing by the end. 'It says "With all good wishes for today and the future, Volker Springer." That's a man's name.'

'Good God.'

I looked at the other cards more attentively, and saw something I had entirely missed. At the bottom of one of them, signed with a flourish, was a name I knew.

I read out that card too, letter by letter.

'It says,' Stephen said, ' "Best memories of a very good time in England. Your friend . . ." Your friend who?'

'Hans Kramer,' I said.

'Bull's eye.' Stephen's voice crackled in my ear. 'Are those by any chance Misha's souvenirs?'

'Yes.'

'Autographs, no less. Anything else?'

'One or two things in Russian. They'll have to wait until tomorrow morning.'

'I'll be with you at ten, then. Gudrun sends her love.'

I put the receiver down, and almost immediately the bell rang again. A female English voice, calm, cultured, and on the verge of boredom.

'Is that Randall Drew?'

'Yes,' I said.

'Polly Paget here,' she said. 'Cultural attaché's office, at the Embassy.'

'How nice to speak to you.'

I had a vivid picture of her; short hair, long cardigan, flat shoes and common sense.

'A telex has just come for you. Ian Young asked me to phone and tell you, in case you were waiting for it.'

'Yes, please,' I said. 'Could you read it to me?'

'Actually, it is complicated, and very long. It really would be better, I think, if you came to collect it. It would take a good half hour for me to dictate it while you write it down, and to be honest I don't want to waste the time. I've a lot still to do, and it's Friday evening, and we're shutting down soon for the weekend.'

'Is Ian there?' I asked.

'No, he left a few minutes ago. And Oliver is out on official business. There's just me holding the fort. If you want your message before Monday, I'm afraid it means coming to get it.'

'How does it start?'

With an audible sigh and a rustle of paper, she began, 'Hans Wilhelm Kramer, born July 3rd, 1941, in Dusseldorf, Germany, only child of Heinrich Johannes Kramer, industrialist . . .'

'Yes, all right,' I said, interrupting. 'I'll come. How long will you be there?' I had visions of uncooperative taxis, of having to walk.

'An hour or so. If you're definitely coming, I'll wait for you.'

'You're on,' I said. 'Warm the Scotch.'

Having grown a little wilier, I engaged a taxi to drive me to the far side of the bridge, pointing to a street map to show where I meant. The road over the bridge, I had found, extended into the Warsaw highway and was the road we had taken to Chertanovo. In another couple of days I would have Moscow's geography in my head for ever.

I paid off the driver and stepped out into the falling snow, which had increased to the point of flakes as big as rose petals and as clinging as love. They settled on my sleeve as I shut the taxi's door, and on my shoulders, and on every flat surface within sight. I found I had stupidly forgotten my gloves. I thrust my hands in my pockets, and turned down the steps to the lower road, to turn there along to the Embassy.

It had seemed to me that I was unfollowed and safe;

but I was wrong. The tigers were waiting under the bridge.

They had learned a few lessons from the abortive mission in Gorky Street.

For a start, they had chosen a less public place. The only sanctuary within running distance was now not the big bustling well-lit mouth of the Intourist Hotel, but the heavily closed front door of the Embassy, with an obstructive guard outside at the gate.

They had learned that my reflexes weren't the slowest on record, and also that I had no inhibitions about kicking them back.

There were still only two of them, but this time they were armed. Not with guns, but with riot sticks. Nasty hard things like baseball bats, swinging from a loop of leather round the wrist.

The first I knew of it was when one chunk of timber connected shatteringly with the side of my head. The fur ear-flaps perhaps saved my skull from being cracked right open, but I reeled dizzily, bewildered, not realizing what had happened, spinning under the weight of the blow.

I had a second's clear view of them, like a snapshot. Two figures in the streetlights against the dark shadows under the bridge. The snow falling more sparsely in the bridge's shelter. The arms raised, with the heavy truncheons swinging.

They were the same men: no doubt of it. The same brutal quality, the same quick ferocity, the same unmerciful eyes looking out of the same balaclavas. The same message that human rights were a laugh.

I stumbled, and my hat fell off, and I tried to protect myself with my arms, but it wasn't much good. There's a limit to the damage even a riot stick can do through thick layers of jacket and overcoat, so that to an extent the onslaught was disorientating more than lethal, but bash numbers three or four by-passed my feeble barriers and knocked off my glasses. I stretched for them, tried to catch them, got hit on the hand, and lost them entirely in the falling snow.

It seemed to be all they were waiting for. The battering stopped, and they grabbed me instead. I kicked and punched at targets I could no longer properly see, and did too little damage to stop the rot.

It felt as though they were trying to lift me up, and for a fraction of time I couldn't think why. Then I remembered where we were. On the road beside the river . . . which flowed along uncaringly on the other side of the breast-high wall.

Desperation kept me struggling when there was absolutely no reasonable hope.

I had seen the Moscow River from several bridges, and everywhere its banks were the same. Not sloping grassy affairs shading gently into the water, but grey perpendicular walls rising straight from the river bed to about eight feet above the surface of the water.

They looked like defences against flooding more than tourist attractions: designed to keep everything between them from getting out.

I clung grimly to whatever I could reach. I tore at their faces. At their hands. I raised from one of them a grunt and from the other a muttered word in a language I didn't recognize.

I didn't rationally think that anyone would come along the road and beat them off. I fought only because while I was still on the road I was alive, but if I hit the water I would be as good as dead. Instinct and anger, and nothing else.

It was hopeless, really. They had me off my feet, and I was being bundled over. I carried on with the limpet act. I pulled the knitted balaclava clean off one of them, but whatever he might have feared, I still couldn't have sworn to a positive identification. One of the streetlights was shining full on his face and I saw him as if he'd been drawn by Picasso.

In my racing days, I had kept my glasses anchored by a double headstrap of elastic, a handy gadget now gathering dust with my five-pound saddle. It had never crossed my mind that it might mean the difference between life or death in Moscow.

They pushed and shoved, and more and more of my weight was transferred over the wall. It all seemed both agonizingly fast and painfully endless: a few seconds of physical flurry that stretched in my mind like eternity.

I was hanging on to the parapet and life with one hand, the rest of me dangling over the water.

They swung, as I had time to realize, one of the riot sticks. There was an excruciating slam on my fingers. I stopped being able to use them, and dropped off the wall like a leech detached.

CHAPTER TWELVE

Winter had already penetrated the Moscow River. I went down under the surface, and the sudden incredible cold was the sort of numbing punching shock which Arctic Ocean bathers don't survive.

I kicked my way up into the air, but I knew in my heart that the battle was lost. I felt weak and half blind, and it was dark, and thickly snowing. The temperature made me breathless, and my right hand had no feeling. My clothes got heavier as they saturated. Soon they would drag me under. The current carried me down river, under the bridge and out the other side, away from the Embassy; and even while I tried to shout for help, I thought that the only people who would hear me would be the two who wouldn't give it.

The yell, in any case, turned into a mouthful of icy water; and that seemed the final reality.

Lethargy began slowing my attempts to swim and dulling my brain. Resolution ebbed away. Coherent thought was ending. I was anaesthetized by cold: a lump of already mindless matter with all other bodily systems freezing fast to a halt, sinking without will or means to struggle.

I began, in fact, to die.

I dimly heard a voice calling.

'Randall . . . Randall . . .'

A bright light shone on my face.

'Randall, this way. Hold on . . .'

I couldn't hold on. My legs had given their last feeble kick. The only direction left was downwards into a deep numbing death.

Something fluffy fell on my face. Fluffier and of more substance than snow. I was past using a hand to grab it, past even thinking that I should. But somewhere in the last vestiges of consciousness an instinct must still have been working, because I opened my mouth to whatever had fallen across it, and bit it.

I held a lot of soft stuff between my teeth. There was a tug on it, as if something was pulling. I gripped it tighter.

Another tug. My head, which had been almost under water, came up again a few inches.

A sluggish thought crept back along the old mental pathways. If I held on to the line I might be pulled out on to the bank, like a fish.

I should hold on, I vaguely thought, with more than my teeth.

Hands.

There was a problem about hands.

Couldn't feel them.

'Randall, hold on. There's a ladder along here.'

I heard the words, and they sounded silly. How could I climb a ladder when I couldn't feel my hands?

All the same, I was awake enough to know that I had been given one last tiny chance, and I clenched my jaws over the soft lifeline with a grip that only total blackout might loosen.

The line pulled me against the wall.

'Hold on,' yelled the voice. 'It's along here. Not far. Just hold on.'

I was bumping along the wall. Not far might be too far. Not far was as far as the sun.

'Here it is,' shouted the voice. 'Can you see it? Just beside you. I'll shine the torch on it. There. Grab hold, can't you?'

Grab hold. Of what?

I lay there like a log.

'Jesus Christ,' said the voice. The light came on my face again, and then went off. I heard sounds coming nearer, coming down the river side of the wall.

'Give me your hands.'

I couldn't.

I felt someone lift up my right arm, pulling it by the sleeve out of the water.

'Jesus Christ,' he said again; and dropped it back.

He pulled my left arm out.

'Hold on with that,' he commanded, and I felt him

221

trying to curl my fingers round some sort of horizontal bar.

'Look,' he said. 'You've got to climb out of the bloody river. You're bloody nearly dead, do you know that? You've been in there too bloody long. And if you don't get out within a minute, bloody nothing will save you. Do you hear that? For Christ's sake ... *climb*.'

I couldn't see what I was supposed to climb, even if I had the strength. I felt him put my right arm up again out of the water, and I thought he was trying to thread my right hand behind the horizontal bar until I had the bar against my wrist.

'Put your feet on one of the steps under the water,' he said. 'Feel for them. The ladder goes down a long way.'

I began vaguely to understand. Tried to lodge a foot on an underwater horizontal bar, and by some miracle found one. He felt the faint support to my weight.

'Right. The bars are only a foot apart. I'll pull your left hand up to the next one. And whatever you do, don't let your right hand slip out.'

I dredged up the last remnants of refrigerated strength and pushed, and rose twelve inches up the wall.

'That's right,' said the voice above me, sounding heartily relieved. 'Now keep bloody going, and don't fall off.'

I kept bloody going and I didn't fall off, though it

seemed like Mount Everest and the Matterhorn rolled into one. At some point when half of me was out of the water I opened my mouth and let the fluffy but now sodden thing full out: and there was an exclamation from above, and presently the line was tied round my left wrist instead.

He went up the ladder above me, still cursing, still instructing, still yelling at me to hurry up.

Step by slow step, we ascended. When I reached the top he was standing on the far side, grabbing hold of me to roll me over on to the flat solid land. My legs buckled helplessly as they touched down, and I ended in a dripping heap on the snow-covered ground.

'Take your coat and jacket off,' he commanded. 'Don't you realize cold kills as fast as bloody bullets?'

I could crookedly see him in the streetlights, but it was his voice I, at last, conclusively recognized, though I supposed that at some point up the wall I had subconsciously known.

'Frank,' I said.

'Yes. Get on with it. Look, let me unbutton this.' His fingers were strong and quick. 'Take them off.' He tugged fiercely and stripped off the clinging wet sleeves. 'Shirt too.' He ripped it off, so that the snow fell on to my bare skin. 'Now put this on.' He guided my arms into something dry and warm, and he buttoned up the front.

'Right,' he said. 'Now you'll bloody well have to

walk back to the bridge. It's only about a hundred yards. Get up, Randall, and *come on.*'

There was a sharp edge to his voice, and it struck me that it was because he too was feeling cold, because whatever it was that was sheltering me had come off him. I stumbled along with him on rubbery knees and kept wanting to laugh weakly at the irony of things in general. Didn't have enough breath, however, for such frivolities.

When I nearly walked into a lamppost he said irritably, 'Can't you see?'

'Lost my g-glasses,' I said.

'Do you mean,' he said incredulously, 'that you can't even see a bloody big lamp standard without them?'

'Not . . . reliably.'

'Jesus Christ.'

Inside his coat my whole body was shuddering, chilled deep into the realms of hypothermia. Although they were apparently functioning, my legs didn't feel as if they belonged to me, and there was still a pervading wuzziness in the thinking department.

We arrived at a flight of steps and toiled upwards to the main road. A black car rolled up and stopped beside us with amazing promptness. Frank threw my wet coats into the back of the car and shovelled me in after them. He himself sat in the front, instructing the driver briefly in Russian, with the result that we went round the by now familiar and lengthy one-way system and arrived in due course outside the Intourist Hotel.

Frank took my coats and escorted me through the front doors into the embrace of the central heating. He collected my room key without asking me the number. Shovelled me into the lift, pressed the button for the eighth floor, and saw me to my door. He fitted the key, and turned it, and steered me inside.

'What are you going to do, if you can't see?' he said.

'G . . . got a s . . . spare pair.'

'Where?'

'T . . . top drawer.'

'Sit down,' he said, practically pushing me on to the sofa; and only the tiniest push was necessary. I heard him opening the drawer, and presently he put the reserves into my hands. I fumbled them on to my nose and again the world took on its proper shape.

He was looking at me with unexpected concern, his face firm and intelligent: but even while I watched, the hawk-like quality dissolved, and the features slackened into the mediocrity we saw at meals.

He was wearing, I saw, only a sweater over his shirt, and, wound round his neck, his long striped college scarf. My life-line.

I said, 'I'd b . . . better give you your coat,' and tried to undo the buttons. The fingers of my right hand seemed both feeble and painful, so I did them with the left.

'You'd better have a hot bath,' he said diffidently. No decision, no swearing, no immense effectiveness in sight.

'Yes,' I said. 'Thanks.'

His eyes flickered. 'Lucky I happened along.'

'Luckiest thing in my life.'

'I was just out for a walk,' he said. 'I saw you get out of a taxi ahead and go down those steps. Then I heard a shout and a splash, and I thought it couldn't possibly be you, of course, but anyway I thought I'd better see. So I went down after you, and luckily I had my torch with me, and well . . . there you are.'

He had omitted to ask how I could have fallen accidentally over a breast-high wall.

I said obligingly, 'It's all a bit of a blank, actually,' and it undoubtedly pleased him.

He helped me out of his coat and into my dressing gown.

'Will you be all right, then?' he said.

'Fine.'

He seemed to want to go, and I made no move to stop him. He picked up his torch and his hat, from where they were lying on the sofa, and his coat, and, murmuring something about me getting the hotel to dry my clothes, he extricated himself from what must have been to him a slightly embarrassing proximity.

I felt very odd indeed. Hot and cold at the same time, and a little light-headed. I took off the rest of my clammy clothes and left them in a damp heap on the bathroom floor.

The fingers on my right hand were in dead trouble. They hadn't bled much because of their immersion in ice water, but there were nasty tears in the skin of three of them from nails to knuckles, and no strength anywhere at all.

I looked at my watch, but it had stopped.

I really had to get a grip on things, I thought. I really had to start functioning. It was imperative.

I went over to the telephone and dialled the number of the University, foreign students department. Stephen was fetched, sounding amiable.

'Something else?' he said.

'What time is it? My watch has stopped.'

'You didn't ring just to ask me that? It's five-past-six, actually.'

Five-past-six ... it seemed incredible. It was only three-quarters of an hour since I had set off to the Embassy. Seemed more like three-quarters of a century.

'Look,' I said. 'Will you do me a great favour? Will you go ...' I stopped. A wave of malaise travelled dizzily around my outraged nervous system. My breath came out in a weird groaning cough.

Stephen said slowly, 'Are you all right?'

'No,' I said. 'Look ... will you go to the British Embassy, and pick up a telex which is waiting there for me, and bring it to the Intourist? I wouldn't ask, but ... if I don't get it tonight I can't have it until Monday ... and be careful ... because we have rough friends ... At the Embassy, ask for Polly Paget in the cultural attaché's office.'

'Have the rough friends had another go with a horse box?' he said anxiously. 'Is that why you can't go yourself?'

'Sort of.'

'All right,' he said. 'I'm on my way.'

I put the receiver back in its cradle and wasted a few minutes feeling sorry for myself. Then I decided to ring Polly Paget, and couldn't remember the number.

The number was on a sheet of paper in my wallet. My wallet was or had been in the inside pocket of my jacket. My jacket was wet, and in the bathroom, where Frank had put it. I screwed up the energy, and went to look.

One wallet, still in the pocket, but, not surprisingly, comprehensively damp. I fished out and unfolded the list of telephone numbers and was relieved to see they could still be read.

Polly Paget sounded annoyed that I had not even started out.

'I've finished my jobs,' she said crossly. 'I want to leave now.'

'A friend is coming instead of me,' I said. 'Stephen Luce. He'll be there soon. Please do wait.'

'Oh, very well.'

'And could you give me Ian Young's phone number? Where he lives, I mean.'

'Hang on.' She went away, and came back, and read out the number. 'That's his flat here in the Embassy grounds. As far as I know, he'll be home most of the weekend. Like all of us. Nothing much ever happens in Moscow.'

Lady, I thought, you're a hundred per cent wrong.

Stephen came, and brought Gudrun.

I had spent the interval putting on dry pants, trousers and socks, and lying on the bed. I disregarded Frank's advice about hot baths, on the Ophelia principle that I'd had too much of water already. It would be just too damned silly to pass out and drown surrounded by white tiles.

Stephen's cheerful grin faded rapidly.

'You look like death. Whatever's happened?'

'Did you bring the telex?'

'Yes, we did. Reams of it. Sit down before you fall down.'

Gudrun folded her elegant slimness on to the sofa and Stephen dispensed my Scotch into toothmugs. I went back to sitting on the bed, and pointed to the sensitive spot on the wall. Stephen, nodding, picked up the tape-recorder, switched it on, and applied it to the plaster.

No whine.

'Off duty,' he said. 'So tell us what's happened.'

I shook my head slightly. 'A dust-up.' I didn't particularly want to include Gudrun. 'Let's just say . . . I'm still here.'

'And we have vays of not making a fuss?'

I more or less smiled. 'Reasons.'

'They'd better be good. Anyway, here's your hot

news from home.' He pulled an envelope out of his pocket and threw it to me. I made the mistake of trying to catch it naturally with my right hand, and dropped it.

'You've hurt your fingers,' Gudrun said, showing concern.

'Squashed them a bit.' I took the telex message out of the envelope and, as reported, there was reams of it: Hughes-Beckett busy proving, I thought sardonically, that my poor opinion of his staff work was unjustified.

'While I read all this,' I said, 'would you cast your peepers over that stuff there?' I pointed to the cough-lozenge tin and Misha's pieces of paper. 'Translate them for me, would you?'

They picked up the little bunch of papers and shuffled through them, murmuring. I read the first section of the telex, which dealt exhaustively with Hans Kramer's life history, and included far more details than I'd expected or asked for. He had won prizes on ponies from the age of three. He had been to eight different schools. He appeared to have been ill on and off during his teens and twenties, as there were several references to doctors and clinics, but he seemed to have grown out of it at about twenty-eight. His earlier interest in horses had from that time intensified, and he had begun to win horse trials at top level. For two years, until his death, he had travelled extensively on the international scene, sometimes as an individual, and sometimes as part of the West German team.

Then came a paragraph headed 'CHARACTER ASSESS-
MENT', which uninhibitedly spoke ill of the dead.
'TOLERATED BUT NOT MUCH LIKED BY FELLOW MEMBERS
OF EVENT TEAM. UNUSUAL PERSONALITY, COLD, UNABLE TO
MAKE FRIENDS. ATTRACTED BY PORNOGRAPHY, HETERO AND
HOMO, BUT HAD NO KNOWN SEXUAL RELATIONSHIP OF ANY
LENGTH. LATENT VIOLENCE SUSPECTED, BUT BEHAVIOUR IN
GENERAL SELF-CONTROLLED.'

Then a bald, brief statement. 'BODY RETURNED TO
PARENTS, STILL LIVING IN DUSSELDORF. BODY CREMATED.'

There was a good deal more to read on other sub-
jects, but I looked up from the typed sheets to see how
Stephen and Gudrun were doing.

'What've you got?' I said.

'Four autographs of Germans. A list in Russian of
brushes and things to do with looking after horses.
Another list in Russian of times and places, which I
should think refer to the horse trials, as they say things
like "cross-country start two-forty remember weight-
cloth". Both of those must have been written by Misha,
because there is also a sort of diary, in which he lists
what he did for his horses, and what feed he gave
them, and so on, and that's all.'

'What about the paper in the cough-lozenge tin?' I
said.

'Ah. Yes. Well. To be frantically honest, we can't be
much help with that.'

'Why not?'

'It doesn't make sense.' He raised his eyebrows at

231

me comically. 'Or do ve have vays of sorting out gibberish?'

'You never know.'

'Well, right then. We are of the opinion that the letters on the paper probably say the same thing twice over, once in Russian and once in German. But they aren't ordinary words in either language, and they're all strung together anyway, without a break.'

'Could you write them in English?'

'Anything to oblige.'

He picked up the envelope which had contained the telex and wrote a long series of letters, one by one.

'There are some letters which come near the end, which do make an actual English word . . .' He finished writing, and handed me the envelope. 'There you are. Crystal as mud.'

I read: Etorphinehydrochloride245mgacepromazinemaleate lomgchlorocresolo1-dimethylsulphoxide90-antagonistnaloxone.

'Does it mean anything?' Stephen said. 'A chemical formula?'

'God knows.' My brains felt like scrambled eggs. 'Maybe it's what's in these ampoules: they're stamped with something about naloxone.'

Stephen held one of the baby phials up to the light, to read the lettering. 'So they are. Massive chemical name for a minute little product.' He put the phial back in the tin, and the original paper on top of it. 'There you are, then. That's the lot.' He closed the tin and put it down. 'What a dingy-looking matroshka.' He picked up the doll. 'Where did you get it?'

'It contains the rest of Misha's souvenirs.'

'Does it? Can I look?'

He had almost as much difficulty in pulling it apart as I had had the first time, and everything scattered in a shower out of it, as before. Stephen and Gudrun crawled about on the floor, picking up the pieces.

'Hm,' he said, reading the veterinary labels. 'More of the same gobbledegook. Anything of any use?'

'Not unless you have bed bugs.'

He put everything back in the doll, and also the tin and the autographs.

'Do you want me to take this out to Elena's new flat some time, after she's settled in?' he said.

'That would be great, if you have the time.'

'Better to give Misha his bits back again.'

'Yes.'

Stephen looked at me closely. 'Gudrun and I are on our way out to supper with some friends, and I think you'd better come with us.' I opened my mouth to say I didn't feel like it and he gave me no chance to get the words out. 'Gudrun, be a lamb and go and wait for us in those armchairs by the lifts, while I get our friend here into some clothes and do his buttons up.' He waved at my non-functioning fingers. 'Go on, Gudrun, love, we won't be long.'

Good-temperedly, she departed, long-legged and liberal.

'Right, then,' Stephen said, as the door shut behind her. 'How bad is your hand? Come on, do come with us. You can't just sit there all evening looking dazed.'

I remembered dimly that I was supposed to be going to the opera. Natasha's earnest ticket to fantasy seemed as irrelevant as dust: yet if I stayed alone in my room I should feel worse than I did already, and if I slept there would be visions of death in balaclavas . . . and hotel bedrooms were not in themselves fortresses.

Frank had not mentioned seeing my attackers, and very likely when he ran to the rescue they had kept out of his sight. But that didn't mean that they hadn't hung around for a bit . . . and they might know that he had fished me out.

'Randall!' Stephen said sharply.

'Sorry . . .' I coughed convulsively, and shivered. 'Wouldn't your friends mind, if I came?'

'Of course not.' He slid open the wardrobe door and pulled out my spare jacket. 'Where's your coat . . . and hat?'

'Shirt first,' I said. 'That checked one . . .'

I stood up stiffly and took off the dressing gown. There were beginnings of bruise marks on my arms, where the riot sticks had landed, but otherwise, I was glad to see, my skin had returned from an interesting pale turquoise to its more normal faded tan. Stephen helped me speechlessly to the point where he went into the bathroom for something and came out looking incredulous.

'All your clothes are wet!'

'Er, yes. I got shoved in the river.'

He pointed to my hand. 'With that sort of shove?'

'I fear so.'

He opened and closed his mouth like a goldfish. 'Do you realize that the temperature tonight has dropped way below zero?'

'You don't say.'

'And the Moscow River will freeze to solid ice any day now?'

'Too late.'

'Are you delirious?'

'Shouldn't be surprised.' I struggled into a couple of sweaters, and felt lousy. 'Look,' I said weakly, 'I don't think I can manage the friends . . . but I also don't want to stay in this room. Would there be any chance, do you think, of me booking into a different hotel?'

'Not the faintest. An absolute non-starter. No other hotel would be allowed to take you without a fortnight's advance booking and a lot of paperwork, and probably not even then.' He looked around. 'What's wrong with this room, though? It looks fine to me.'

I rubbed my hand over my forehead, which was sweating. The two sweaters, I thought, were aptly named.

I said, 'Three times in two days, someone's tried to kill me. I'm here through luck . . . but I've a feeling the luck's running out. I just don't want to . . . to stand up in the butts.'

'*Three* times?'

I told him about Gorky Street. 'All I want is a safe place to sleep.' I pondered. 'I think I'll ring Ian Young... he might help.'

I dialled the number Polly Paget had given me for Ian's flat in the Embassy grounds. The bell rang and rang there, but the Sphinx was out on the town.

'Damn,' I said, with feeling, putting down the receiver.

Stephen's brown eyes were full of troubled thought. 'We could slip you into the University,' he said. 'But my bed's so narrow.'

'Lend me the floor.'

'You're serious?'

'Mm.'

'Well... all right.' He looked at his watch. 'It's too late to get you in through the proper channels, so to speak. They'll have knocked off for the day... We'll have to work the three-card trick.'

He took his student pass out of his pocket and gave it to me.

'Show it to the dragon when you go in, and keep on going, straight up the stairs. They don't know all the students by sight, and she won't know you aren't me. Just go on up to my room. OK?'

I took the pass and stowed it in a pocket in my jacket. 'How will you get in, though?' I said.

'I'll ring a friend who has a room in the block,' he

said. 'He'll collect my pass from you, and bring it out to me, when Gudrun and I get back.'

He held my jacket for me to put on, and then picked up the sheets of telex and folded them back into the envelope. I put the envelope in my jacket and thought about black cars.

'I'd awfully like to make sure I'm not followed,' I said.

Stephen raised his eyes to heaven. 'All in the service,' he said. 'What do you want me to do?'

What we did, in the event, was for me to travel in one taxi to the University Prospect, the tourist stopping place for the view down over the stadium to the city, and for him and Gudrun to follow in another. We all got out of the cars there in the thickly falling snow and exchanged vehicles.

'I'll swear nothing followed you,' Stephen said. 'If anyone did, they used about six different cars, in relays.'

'Thanks a lot.'

'Any time.'

He told the taxi driver where to take me, and disappeared with Gudrun into the night.

CHAPTER THIRTEEN

The dragon on the door was arguing with someone else when I went in. I shoved Stephen's pass under her nose closely enough for her to see that it *was* a pass, and kept it moving. Her eyes hardly slid my way as her tongue lashed into some unfortunate offender, and I went on up the stairs as if I lived there.

Stephen's cell-like room felt a proper sanctuary. I struggled out of my jacket and one sweater and collapsed gratefully on to his bed.

For quite a long time I simply lay there, waiting for what one might call the life force to flow back. What with illness and the inevitable knocks of life on the land, not to mention the crunches involved in jump racing, I was fairly experienced in the way one's body dealt with misfortunes. I was accustomed to the lassitude that damped it down while it put itself to rights, and to the way that this would eventually lift it into a new feeling of vigour. I knew that the fierce soreness of my fingers would get worse for at least another twelve hours, and would then get better. I'd been concussed enough times to know that the sponginess in my mind would go away slowly, like fog clearing, leaving only an externally tender area of bruised scalp.

All that, in fact, would be the way of it if I gave it rest and time: but rest and time were two commodities I was likely to lack. Better to make the most of what I had. Better, I dared say, to sleep: but one factor I was not used to, and had never had to deal with before, was keeping me thoroughly awake. The sharp threat of death.

There wouldn't be any more lucky escapes. The fourth close encounter would be the last. For if my attackers had learned one thing conclusively during the past two days, it must have been that it was necessary to kill at once, and fast. No fooling around with horse boxes, kidnappings, or icy rivers. Next time ... if there was a next time ... I should be dead before I realized what had happened. It was enough, I thought, to send one scurrying to the airport ... to leave the battle to be fought by someone else.

After a while, I sat up and took the long telex out of my pocket.

Read again the pages about Hans Kramer.

Eight schools. Doctors, hospitals, and clinics. Ill-health, like mine. And, like me, success on ponies, and on horses. Like me, a spot of foreign travel to equestrian events: I to the awesome Pardubice in Czechoslovakia and the Maryland Hunt Cup over fixed timber fences in America, and he to top-rank horse trials around Europe: Italy, France, Holland and England.

Died at Burghley in September of a heart attack, aged thirty-six. Body shipped home, and cremated.

End of story.

I took off my glasses and tiredly rubbed my eyes. If there was anything useful to be gleaned from all the unasked detail it was totally invisible to my current mental sight.

I tried to clear my mind by shaking it, which was about as useful as stirring old port with a teaspoon. Bits of sediment clogged my thoughts and little green spots slid around behind my eyes.

I read the rest of the telex twice and by the end had taken in hardly a word.

Start again.

YURI IVANOVICH CHULITSKY, ARCHITECT. PHONE NUMBER SUPPLIED EARLIER BUT NOW REPEATED . . . ONE OF THE RUSSIAN OBSERVERS IN ENGLAND DURING AUGUST AND SEPTEMBER LAST. FORMERLY WENT TO OLYMPICS AT MONTREAL. ADVISER ON BUILDINGS NECESSARY FOR EQUESTRIAN GAMES AT MOSCOW.

Yes, I knew all that.

IGOR NAUMOVICH TELYATIN, COORDINATOR OF BROADCASTING. NO TELEPHONE NUMBER

AVAILABLE. RUSSIAN OBSERVER, IN ENGLAND
DURING AUGUST AND SEPTEMBER. HIS BRIEF:
TO LEARN THE BEST GENERAL POSITIONING FOR
TV COVERAGE; TO SEE WHAT OTHER FACILITIES
WERE ESSENTIAL AND WHICH MERELY DESIR-
ABLE; TO SEE HOW BEST TO GIVE THE WORLD
A GOOD VIEW OF SOVIET SHOWMANSHIP AND
EFFICIENCY.

SERGEI ANDREEVICH GORSHKOV. NO TELEPHONE
NUMBER AVAILABLE. RUSSIAN OBSERVER,
STATED TO BE STUDYING CROWD CONTROL
AT BIG EQUESTRIAN EVENTS, WHERE THE
MOBILITY OF SPECTATORS WAS A PROBLEM.
RELIABLY REPORTED TO BE A FULL COLONEL OF
KGB, AN EXTREME HARD-LINER, WITH A DEEP
CONTEMPT FOR WESTERN STANDARDS. SINCE
HIS VISIT, INFORMATION HAS COME TO HAND
THAT HE HAS IN THE PAST ATTEMPTED TO
COMPROMISE MEMBERS OF THE EMBASSY STAFF,
AND THEIR VISITORS, FAMILY, AND FRIENDS.
STRONGLY ADVISE AGAINST CONTACT.

I put the sheets down. Hughes-Beckett, if it was
indeed he who had sent the telex, which was unsigned
and had no indication of origin, was up to his old tricks
of seeming to help while encouraging failure. Flooding
me with useless-looking information while warning me
away from the one who really might pose a threat to
Johnny Farringford.

Hughes-Beckett, I thought a shade irritably, had not the slightest idea of what was actually going on.

To be fair to him, how could he know if I didn't tell him?

The mechanics of telling him were not that easy. Anything sent from the Embassy via the telex ran the gauntlet of Malcolm Herrick's inside informer: and since Malcolm had learned of Oliver telling me to send a message directly from Kutuzovsky Prospect, he had probably made his arrangements there as well. The one place I did not want my adventures turning up was on the front page of the *Watch*.

There was the telephone, to which someone at either end might listen. There was the mail, which was slow, and might be intercepted.

There was Ian, who, if I read it right, probably had his own secure hot-line to the ears back home, but might not have the authority to lend it to any odd private citizen who applied.

In the back of my mind, also, there hovered an undefined question mark about the soundness of Ian as an ally.

Stephen's friend duly came to collect Stephen's pass, at shortly after eleven: and Stephen and Gudrun returned, full of bonhomie and onions.

'Onions!' Gudrun said. 'Back in the shops today

after four months without them. No eggs, of course. It's always something.'

'Want some tea?' Stephen suggested, and went to make it.

There floated about both of them the glow of an evening well spent, and perversely their warmth depressed my already low spirits to sinking point; like Scrooge at Christmas.

'What you need,' Stephen said, coming back and making an accurate diagnosis with a glance, 'is half a pint of vodka and some good news.'

'Supply them,' I said.

'Have a biscuit.'

He unearthed a packet from the recesses of the bookcase and cleared a space on the table for the mugs. Then, seeming to be struck by a thought, he began rigging up a contraption of drawing-pins and string, and upon the string he threaded his bedside alarm clock, so that it hung there loudly ticking on the wall. It was only towards the end of this seemingly senseless procedure that I remembered that that exact spot was the lair of the bug.

'Better interference than nothing, if they're listening,' he said cheerfully. 'And they get a right earful when the alarm goes off.'

The tea probably did more good than the unavailable vodka. A certain amount of comfort began to creep along the nerves.

'All visitors have to be gone by ten-thirty,' Stephen nonchalantly said.

'Will they check?'

'I've never known it.'

Halfway down the mug, a modicum of order returned to my thoughts. Very welcome: like a friend much missed.

'Gudrun,' I said lazily, 'would you cast your peepers over something for me?'

'Sorry?'

I put down the mug and picked up the telex, and she noticed the up-to-date state of the hand I hadn't used.

'Oh!' she said. 'That must really hurt.'

Stephen looked from my fingers to my face. 'Are they broken?' he said.

'Can't tell.'

I could scarcely move them, which proved nothing one way or the other. They had swelled like sausages, and gone dark, and it was a fair certainty the nails would go black, if they didn't actually come off. It was no worse, really, than if one had been galloped on by a horse, and injuries of that order had been all in the day's work. I smiled lop-sidedly at their horrified faces and handed Gudrun the telex.

'Would you read all the stuff about Hans Kramer, and see if it means anything to you which it doesn't to me? He was German, and you are a German, and you might see a significance I've missed.'

'All right.' She looked doubtful, but compliantly read right to the end.

'What strikes you?' I said.

She shook her head. 'Nothing very much.'

'He went to eight different schools,' I said. 'Would that be usual?'

'No.' She frowned. 'Not unless his family moved a lot.'

'His father was and is a big industrialist in Dusseldorf.'

She read through the schools again, and finally said, 'I think one of these places specializes in children who are ... different. Perhaps they have troubles like epilepsy, or perhaps they are ...' She made tumbling motions with her hands, at a loss for the word.

'Mixed-up?'

'That's right. But they also take people who have a special talent and need special schooling. Like athletes. Perhaps Hans Kramer went there because he was exceptionally good at riding.'

'Or because seven other schools slung him out?'

'Perhaps, yes.'

'What about the doctors and hospitals?'

She read through the list again with her mouth negatively pursed, and finally shook her head.

'Would they be, for instance,' I said, 'anything to do with orthopaedics?'

'Bones and things?'

'Yes.'

Her eyes went back to the list, but the no's had it.

'Anything to do with heart troubles? Are any of those people or places specialists in chest surgery?'

'I honestly don't know.'

I thought. 'Well,' I said, 'anything to do with psychiatry?'

'I'm awfully sorry, but I don't know much about . . .' Her eyes widened suddenly and she looked rather wildly down at the list. 'Oh my goodness . . .'

'What is it?'

'The Heidelberg University Clinic.'

'What about it?'

'Don't you know?' She saw from my face that I didn't. 'Hans Kramer attended it, it says here, for about three months in nineteen seventy.'

'Yes,' I said. 'Why is that important?'

'Nineteen seventy . . . There was a doctor called Wolfgang Huber working there. He was supposed to be great at straightening out . . . mixed-up . . . children from rich families. Not *little* children . . . teenagers and young adults, our age. People who were violently rebellious against their parents.'

'He seems to have managed it all right with Hans Kramer, then,' I said. 'Because isn't that clinic the last on the list?'

'Yes,' Gudrun said. 'But you don't understand.'

'Tell me.'

She could hardly frame the sentences, so intense were her thoughts.

'Dr Huber taught them that to cure themselves they had to destroy the system which was making them feel the way they did. He told them they would have to destroy the world of their parents . . . He called it terrorism therapy.'

'My God.'

'And . . . and . . .' Gudrun practically gasped for breath. 'I don't know what effect it had on Hans Kramer . . . but . . . Dr Huber was deliberately teaching his patients . . . to follow in the footsteps of Andreas Baader and Ulrike Meinhof.'

Time, as they say, stood still.

'You've seen a ghost,' Stephen said.

'I've seen a pattern . . . and a plan.'

The teachings of Dr Wolfgang Huber, I supposed, had been a sort of extreme extension of the theories behind the Communist revolution. Destroy the corrupt capitalist system and you will emerge into a clean healthy society run by the workers. A seductive, idealistic dream which seemed always to appeal most to intellectuals of the middle class, who had both the brains and the means to pursue it.

Even in the hands of visionaries, the doctrine had led to widespread killing. People like Dr Huber, however, had preached their gospel not to reasoning adults, but to already disturbed youth, and the result, in widening ripples, had been the Baader–Meinhof followers, the Palestinian Black September, the Irish Republican Army, the Argentinian ERP and the Japanese Red Army, with endless virulent offshoots among small groups like Croatians, South Moluccans, and Basques.

The place most free from terrorism was the land which still encouraged and nurtured it, the land where the seedling had raised its attractive head.

At the Munich Olympics, the world had awakened in a state of shock to the existence of the growing crop.

Eight years later, at the Moscow Olympics, someone was planning to carry the fruit home.

CHAPTER FOURTEEN

Stephen lent me his bed and went to share Gudrun's, which seemed to please them both well, and was certainly all right by me. Foreign students were positively encouraged to lie together, he said sardonically, so that they didn't go out and pursue the natives.

I shivered a good deal, and at the same time felt feverish, which boded ill.

I didn't sleep much, though that didn't matter. My hand throbbed like a pile-driver but my head was clear, and I much preferred it that way round. I spent most of the time thinking and wondering and guessing, and coming back to the problem of the next day. I had somehow got to take some positive steps towards staying permanently alive.

In the morning, Stephen fetched some tea, lent me his razor, and bounced cheerfully off to a student breakfast.

He returned with some things like empty hamburger buns from the basement supermarket, and found me studying the long string of letters on the envelope which had held the telex.

'Deciphering the chemical junk?' he said.

'Trying.'

'How's it coming?'

'I don't know enough,' I said. 'Look . . . when all this was written in Russian and German, was it *translated*? I mean . . . are you sure that this is what was meant?'

'It wasn't translated,' Stephen said. 'It was those letters in that order, but written in formal German script . . . the sort you see in books. The Russian script version was more or less phonetically the same, but there are more letters in the Russian alphabet, so we adjusted the Russian letters to be the equivalent of the German . . . was that all right?'

'Yes,' I said. 'You see here where it reads "antagonist"?'

'Uh huh.'

'Was that word translated into Russian or German? Or were the letters a n t a et cetera written in German script?'

'It wasn't translated, as such, because antagonist is much the same word in all three languages.'

'Thanks.'

'Is that of any help?'

'Yes, in a way,' I said.

'You amaze me.'

We buttered and shared the hamburger buns and

drank some more tea, and I coughed on and off with an ominous hollowness.

After that, I cadged a sheet of paper and wrote the long row of letters into sensible words, adding a few reasonable-looking decimal points. The revised effort read:

> etorphine hydrochloride 2.45 mg
> acepromazine maleate 1.0 mg
> chlorocresol 0.1 –
> dimethyl sulphoxide 90
> antagonist naloxone.

Stephen looked over my shoulder. 'That, of course,' he said, 'makes a world of difference.'

'Um,' I said thoughtfully. 'Would you do me a favour?'

'Fire away.'

'Lend me an empty tape for your recorder, and another one with music on it. Or rather, two empty tapes, if you have them.'

'Is that all?' He sounded disappointed.

'That's for starters.'

He rustled around and produced three tapes in plastic boxes.

'They've all got music on,' he said. 'But you can record on top, if you like.'

'Great.' I hesitated, because what I wanted him to do besides sounded melodramatic; but facts had to be faced. I folded the list of chemicals in half and gave it to him. 'Would you mind keeping that?' I made my voice as matter-of-fact as possible. 'Keep it until after I've got home. I'll send you a postcard to say it's OK to tear it up.'

He looked puzzled. 'I don't see . . .'

'If I don't get home, or you don't get a postcard from me, will you send it to Hughes-Beckett at the Foreign Office. I've put the address on the back. Tell him that Hans Kramer had it, and ask him to show it to a vet.'

'A *vet*?'

'That's right.'

'Yes, but . . .' He realized exactly what I'd said. 'If you don't get home . . .'

'Yeah . . . well . . . fourth time unlucky, and all that.'

'For heaven's sake.'

'Do you have lectures on Saturdays?' I said.

His eyebrows vanished upwards under his hair. 'Is that a general invitation to put my head in the trap alongside yours?'

'Probably just to make phone calls and tell taxis where to go.'

He gave an exaggerated shrug and a large gesture of surrender, and put on an expression of ''ve have vays of not believing a vord you say'. 'What first?'

'Ring Mr Kropotkin,' I said. 'And if he's in, ask if I can come to see him this morning.'

Kropotkin, it seemed, was not only in but anxious.

'He says he's been trying to get you at the hotel. He says to arrive at ten o'clock, and we can find him inside the first stable block on the left, on the racecourse.'

'Fine . . .' I blew a cooling breath on to my hot, swollen fingers. 'I think I'll also try Ian Young.'

Ian Young was back on British soil and seemed to take a while to realize who he was talking to. He was feeling fragile, and no one, he said eventually, with a mixture of misery and admiration, could drink like the Russians; and please would I not talk so loudly.

Sorry, I said, pianissimo. Could he please tell me how best to make a telephone call to England. Try from the main Post Office just round the corner from my hotel, he said. Ask for the International operator. He was discouraging, however, about my prospects.

'Sometimes you can get through in ten minutes, but it's usually more like two hours, and with the new flap going on this morning you'll be lucky if you get through at all.'

'Newer than the dust-up in Africa?' I said.

'Oh sure. Some high-up guy has defected. In Birmingham, of all places. Shock, horror, drama, and all that. Is it important?'

'I want to ring my vet . . . about my horses,' I said. 'Could I get through from the Embassy?'

'I doubt if you'd do any better. There's no one like the Russians for blank obstruction. Brick-wall specialists, the Russians.' He yawned. 'Did you get your telex last night?'

'Yes, thanks.'

'Make the most of it, I should.' He yawned again. 'Do you feel like swilling the hair of the dog with me? Round about noon?'

'Don't see why not.'

'Good . . . Go past Oliver's office, and past the tennis court . . . and my flat's in the row at the back of the grounds, second door from the left.' He put down the receiver with all the gentleness of the badly hungover.

The snow had temporarily stopped, though the sky was a threatening oily yellow-grey and the air cold enough to freeze the nose's mucous lining in its tracks. I started coughing and gasping for breath before we'd gone a hundred steps, and Stephen thought it extraordinary.

'What's the matter?' he said, his own lungs chugging easily away like an electric bellows.

'Taxi . . .'

We caught one without much difficulty, and immediately, within its comparative warmth and with the help of the pocket bronchidilator inhaler I kept in my pocket like loose change, my chest stopped its infuriating heaving.

'Are you always like this when it's cold?' Stephen said.

'It depends. The river didn't help.'

He looked mildly anxious. 'You caught a chill? Come to think . . . it's not surprising.'

We stopped twice on the way. The first time, to buy two bottles of vodka; one to give to Kropotkin and one to keep. The second time, to buy me yet another hat to top off my assorted clothing, which now consisted, from the skin outwards, of a singlet, shirt, two sweaters, jacket, and Stephen's spare coat, which was a size too small and left my forearms sticking out like an orphan.

The main roads had already been cleared of the overnight snow, but the Hippodrome itself was white. There were horses there all the same, exercising on the track, and even one or two trotters pulling sulkies. We paid off the taxi practically at the stable door, and went inside to enquire for Kropotkin.

He was waiting for us in a small dark office used by one of the trainers of the trotters. There were heaps of tyres everywhere, which seemed stunningly incongruous in a stable until one remembered the sulkies' wheels, and apart from that only a desk with a great deal of scattered paperwork, and a chair, and large numbers of photographs pinned to the walls.

Nikolai Alexandrovich cordially grasped my hastily offered left hand and pumped it up and down with both of his own.

'Friend,' he said, the heavy bass voice reverberating in the small space. 'Good friend.'

He accepted the gift of vodka as the courtesy it

represented. Then he set the chair ceremoniously for me to sit on, and himself lodged comfortably with his backside half on the desk. Stephen, it seemed, could stand on his own two feet; and, via Stephen, Kropotkin and I exchanged further suitable opening compliments.

We arrived in due course at the meat inside the pastry.

'Mr Kropotkin says,' Stephen said, 'that he asked everyone in the world of horses to give any help they could in the matter of Alyosha.'

I expressed my warmest appreciations and felt the faintest quickening of the pulse.

'No one, however,' Stephen continued, 'knows who Alyosha is. No one knows anything about him.'

My pulse returned to normal with depressing speed.

'Kind of him to try,' I said, sighing slightly.

Kropotkin stroked his moustache downwards with his thumb and forefinger and then set off again into a deep rumble.

Stephen did a dead-pan translation although with more interest in his eyes.

'Mr Kropotkin says that although no one knows who Alyosha is, someone has sent him a piece of paper with the name Alyosha on it, and the piece of paper originally came from England.'

It hardly sounded the ultimate solution, but definitely better than nothing.

'May I see it?' I said.

It appeared, though, that Nikolai Alexandrovich was not to be rushed. Bread and butter first; sweeties after.

'Mr Kropotkin says,' Stephen translated, 'that you should understand one or two things about the Soviet system.' His eyebrows went upwards and his nostrils twitched with the effort of keeping a straight face. 'He says it is not always possible for Soviet citizens to speak with total freedom.'

'Tell him I've noticed. Er ... tell him I understand.'

Kropotkin looked at me broodingly and stroked his moustache.

'He would like it,' Stephen said, relaying the next wedge of rumble, 'if you could use everything you have learned here at the Hippodrome without explaining where you heard it.'

'Give him my most solemn assurance,' I said sincerely, and I think Kropotkin was probably convinced more by my tone than the actual words. After a suitable pause, he continued.

'Mr Kropotkin says,' Stephen faithfully reported, 'that he doesn't know who sent him the paper. It was delivered to his flat by hand yesterday evening, with a brief note of explanation, and a hope that it would be handed on to you.'

'Does he sound as if he really doesn't know who sent it, or do you think he's just not telling?'

'Impossible to know,' Stephen said.

Nikolai Alexandrovich showed signs at last of producing the goods. With great deliberation he drew a large black wallet from an inside pocket and opened it wide. His blunt fingers carefully sank into a deep section at the back, and he slowly drew out a white envelope. He accompanied the hand-over ceremony with a small speech.

'He says,' Stephen said, 'that to himself this paper does not seem to be of much significance. He wishes it were. He would like it to be of some use to you, because of his earnest desire to express his thanks for your speed in saving the Olympic horse.'

'Tell him that if it should not turn out to be a significant paper, I will always remember and appreciate the trouble he has taken to help.'

Kropotkin received the compliment graciously, and slowly parted with the envelope. I took it from him at the same unhurried pace, and drew out the two smallish sheets of paper which were to be found inside.

They were fastened to each other with a small paper-clip. The top one, white and unremarkable, bore a short paragraph written in Russian.

The lower, also white but torn from a notebook and ruled with feint blue lines, was chiefly covered with a variety of geometric doodles, done in pencil. Near the top there were two words: *For Alyosha*, and about an inch lower down, surrounded by doodled stars, *J. Farringford*. Underneath that, one below the other, as in a list, were the words Americans, Germans, French, and below that a row of question marks. That seemed to be more or less all, though near the bottom of the page, in their own individual doodled boxes, were four sets of letters and numbers, which were DEP PET, 1855, K's C, and 1950.

On top of all the scribbles, across the whole page from top to bottom, there was the wide flowing S-shaped scrawl of someone crossing out what they had written.

I turned the small page over. The reverse side bore about fifteen lines of what must have been handwriting, written in ballpoint, but this had been meticulously scribbled over, line by line, also in ballpoint but in a slightly different colour.

Kropotkin was watching me expectantly. I said, 'I am very pleased. This is most interesting.' He understood the words, and looked heavily satisfied.

The business at that point seemed to be over, and after a few more compliments on both sides we stepped from the office into the central corridor of the stable block. Kropotkin invited me to see the horses, and we walked side by side along to where each side of the corridor was lined with loose boxes.

Stephen made choking noises behind me as he reached them, which I guessed was because of the smell. My own nose twitched a bit over the unusually piercing stink of ammonia, but the trotters seemed none the worse for it. They would be racing that evening, Kropotkin said, because the snow was not yet too deep. Stephen manfully translated to the end, but gulped at the eventual fresh air as if it were a fountain in the desert.

There were still several horses exercising on the track, and to my eyes they came from lower down the equine class system than racehorses or Eventers.

'All the riding clubs are here,' Kropotkin explained through Stephen. 'All stables for horses in Moscow are in this district, and all exercising is done at the Hippodrome. All the horses are owned by the State. The best horses go for racing and breeding, and the Olympics; then the clubs share what is left. Most horses stay in Moscow all winter, because they are very hardy. And I wonder,' added Stephen on his own account, 'what it smells like in these barns come March!'

Kropotkin said a solemn goodbye at the still unattended main entrance. He was a great old guy, I thought, and through him and Misha I had learned a good deal.

'Friend,' I said. 'I wish you well.'

He pumped my hand with emotion in both of his, and then gave me the accolade of a hug.

'My God,' said Stephen as we walked away. 'Talk about schmaltzy sob-stuff . . .'

'A little sentiment does no harm.'

'Ah . . . but did it do any good?'

I handed him the envelope and coughed all the way to the taxi rank.

'To Nikolai Alexandrovich, by hand,' said Stephen, reading the envelope. 'So whoever sent it, knew Kropotkin fairly well. You'd only use that form of someone's name – the patronymic Alexandrovich without the last name Kropotkin – if you knew him.'

'It would be more surprising if they *didn't* know each other.'

'I guess so.' He picked out the two small clipped-together pages. 'This paragraph on the front says, "*Note paper*" ... sort of jotting paper, that is ... "*used at International Horse Trials. Please give it to Randall Drew.*" '

'Is that all?'

'That's the lot.'

He peered at the second page, and I waved uninhibitedly at a taxi cruising with its windscreen light on. Once more on our way, Stephen handed back the treasure trove.

'Not much cop,' he said. 'A case of the lion straining to produce a gnat.'

The taxi driver spoke into my thoughtful silence.

'He wants to know where we're going,' Stephen said.

'Back to the hotel.'

We stopped, however, on the way, at a shop he identified as a chemist. The Russian letters on the shopfront, when approximated into English, read Apotek. Apothecary ... what else? I went inside with him, seeking dampeners for the troubles in fingers and chest, but ended only with the equivalent of aspirins. For his own purchase, he leaned across a counter and spoke low to the ear of a buxom battleaxe.

She replied very loudly, and all the nearby customers turned to stare at him. His face was a scarlet study of embarrassment, but all the same he stood his ground and brought the transaction to the desired conclusion.

'What did she say?' I asked, as we left.

'She said "This foreigner wants ... preservativy ..."' And don't bloody laugh.'

My chuckle anyway ended in a cough. 'Preservativy being contraceptives?'

'Gudrun insists.'

'I should darned well think so.'

At the hotel we went straight through the foyer to the lifts, as I had taken my room key with me to the University so as not to advertise my absence to the reception desk.

Up to the eighth floor, past the watchful lady at the desk, and along the corridor ... and the door of my room was open.

Cleaners?

Not cleaners. The person who was standing inside was Frank.

He had his back to the door and was over by the dressing shelf under the window, head bent, looking down at something in his hands.

'Hello, Frank,' I said.

He turned round quickly, looking very startled: and what he was holding was the matroshka. Intact, I saw, with all her secrets still inside. His fingers were still tight with the effort of trying to open her.

'Er . . .' he said. 'You didn't come to breakfast. I . . . er . . . came to see if you were all right. After last night. I mean, falling in the river . . .'

Not bad, I thought, as a spot of thinking on the feet.

'I went to the Hippodrome to see the horses work,' I said, playing the game that anyone could play if they had a lying tongue.

Frank relaxed his grip and put the painted doll slowly down on the shelf, giving his best weak-schoolteacher laugh.

'Right on, then,' he said. 'Natasha was worried about you not coming to breakfast. Shall I tell her you'll be in for lunch?'

Lunch . . . the prosaically normal in the middle of a minefield.

'Why not?' I said. 'And I'll have a guest.'

Frank looked at Stephen with sustained dislike, and took himself off; and I descended a bit feebly on to the sofa.

'Let's have a drink,' I said.

'Scotch or vodka?' He pulled the morning's newly bought bottle out of his overcoat pocket and stood it on the shelf.

'Scotch.'

I took two of the Apotek's pills with it, without noticeable results.

Looked at my watch, now miraculously ticking again

despite immersion. Eleven-thirty. Picked up the telephone.

'Ian?' I said. 'How's the hangover?'

From the sound of it, on the mend. The hair of the dog had bitten an hour ago, no doubt. I said I couldn't make it after all before lunch, and how about him tottering along to my room at the hotel at about six?

Totter, he said, might just about describe it, by then: but he would come.

Stephen was sweeping the walls with the tape-recorder, trying to find the tender spot. I pointed to it, but again there was no whine. And then, just as he was about to give up, the whine suddenly began.

'Switched on, by God,' he said under his breath.

'Let's have some music.'

He pulled the three tapes from his obliging overcoat and slotted in an energetic rendering of *Prince Igor*.

'What next?'

'I brought some paperbacks ... which would you like?'

'And you?' he said, looking at the titles.

'Drink and think.'

So the bug listened for an hour to Stephen turning the pages of *The Small Back Room* against the urgencies of Borodin, and I listened inside my head to everything I'd been told, both in England and Moscow, and tried to see a path through the maze.

*

Lunch seemed unreal.

The Wilkinsons were there, and Frank was there. Frank hadn't told the Wilkinsons he'd saved my life the evening before, and behaved throughout as if nothing of the sort had ever happened. What he thought of my silence on the subject was a mystery.

Natasha and Anna tried by a mixture of scolding and persuasion to make me promise to stop disappearing without telling them where I was going, and I helpfully said I would do my best, without meaning a word of it.

Frank ate my meat.

Mrs Wilkinson talked. 'We've always voted Labour, Dad and me, but isn't it funny, in England it's always the far-left people who want more and more immigrants, but here, where it's about as far left as you can get, there aren't any. You don't see black people walking around in Moscow, do you?'

Frank took no notice.

'It just strikes me as funny that's all,' Mrs Wilkinson said. 'Still, I don't suppose there's much of a queue in India for wanting to live in Moscow, come to think.'

Mr Wilkinson muttered to his small-sized chips, 'They've got more sense.' He wouldn't say much else for the rest of the day.

Frank came to life with a routine damnation of the anti-black policies of the National Front.

Mrs Wilkinson gave me a comical look of

bewilderment and despair at never being able to get through to Frank.

'Front,' I said mildly, 'is an overworked word. A cliché. We have Fronts for this and Fronts for that . . . One should always ask what . . . if anything . . . is *behind* a Front.'

It was again ice cream with blackcurrant jam. I quite liked it.

Stephen ate like Frank and told me afterwards that the Intourist Hotel food was high-class luxury compared with the students' grub.

Apart from all that, which seemed to be going on in a separate life, I was more positively hearing the voices of Boris and Evgeny, and Ian, and Malcolm, and Oliver, and Kropotkin, and Misha and Yuri Chulitsky, and Gudrun, and the Prince and Hughes-Beckett and Johnny Farringford . . . and the dead voice of Hans Kramer: I could hear them all clearly.

But where, oh where, was Alyosha?

CHAPTER FIFTEEN

Upstairs in my room Stephen balanced the chair on my bed, my suitcase on the chair, and the tape-recorder on the suitcase: and switched on. The whine came forth, alive and healthy.

He switched off the 'record' button and pressed the 'play', and the listeners got a close earful of a tape of Stravinsky which seemed to be suffering from wow if not flutter.

I spent the time pondering the pieces of paper Kropotkin had given me; the back as much as the front.

'You don't happen to have any blue glass handy, I suppose?' I said. 'Of a certain particular shade?'

'Blue *glass*?'

'Yes . . . a blue filter. You see all this handwriting which has been scribbled out? It was written in a darker colour of blue than the scribble . . . you can see the dark loops underneath.'

'Well . . . so what?'

'So if you looked at the page through some blue glass which was the same colour as the lighter scribble, you might be able to see the darker blue writing. The colour of the glass, so to speak, would cancel out the colour of the scribble, and you could read what was left.'

'For crying out loud . . .' he said. 'I suppose you could. And where would that get you?'

'I might guess who sent this to Kropotkin, but I'd like to be certain.'

'But it could be *anybody*.'

I shook my head. 'I'll show you something.'

I opened the drawer which contained my private pharmacy and brought out the folded piece of paper which lay beneath it. Opening it, and smoothing out the crease, I laid it on the dressing shelf, and put Kropotkin's paper beside it.

'They're the same!' Stephen said.

'That's right. Torn from the same type of notebook: white paper, feint blue lines, spiral binding.'

The two notebook pages lay side by side with their ragged torn-off fringes at the top. On one, 'For Alyosha', 'J. Farringford', and all the rest. And on the other, the name Malcolm Herrick, and a telephone number.

'He gave that to me the first night I was in Moscow,' I said. 'In the bar of the National Hotel.'

'Yes . . . but . . . Those notebooks are universal. You can buy them everywhere. Students . . . typists . . . Aren't they especially printed to take shorthand?'

'And constantly used by newspaper reporters,' I said.

'Who have a great habit of crossing out pages when they've finished with them. I've seen them over and over, at the races, talking to me maybe when I've won a race. They flick over the pages to find a fresh one . . . they go all through the pad one way, and then they turn it over and start on the backs. And to save themselves looking through endless pages afterwards to find just the bits they want, they put a scribble or a cross over the whole page when they've finished with it . . . just like this one, which we got from Kropotkin.'

I turned over the sheet Malcolm had given me with his telephone number on, and there, on the back, were some notes about a visiting puppet theatre, sprawlingly crossed through with a wide flowing S.

'*Malcolm*,' said Stephen, looking bewildered. 'Why should Malcolm send this to Kropotkin?'

'I shouldn't think he did. Maybe he just gave it to whoever did that writing on the back.'

'But why should he?' Stephen said frustratedly. 'And what does it matter? It's all *crazy*.'

'It's unlikely that he'll remember who he gave an odd piece of paper to nearly three months ago,' I said. 'But I think . . . we might ask him.'

I dialled the number on the paper, and he was at home. His big voice positively crackled through the receiver.

'Where've you been, sport? Been trying to reach you. Moscow at weekends is like Epsom when they're racing at Ascot.'

'Out to the Hippodrome,' I said obligingly.

'Zat so? How's it going? Found Alyosha yet?'

'Not yet.'

'Told you it was a bum steer, sport. I looked. I told you. If I couldn't find a story, there is no story. Right?'

'You're an old hand, and I'm not,' I said. 'But Kropotkin at the Hippodrome has called on all the horse people in Moscow to work on it. So we've an army of allies.'

He grunted, not sounding very pleased. 'Has the army come up with anything?'

'Only with something pretty small, so far. In fact,' I said, half making a joke of it, 'a page which looks as if it came from one of your notebooks.'

'A what?'

'Page . . . with the name Alyosha on it. And Johnny Farringford's name, ringed with stars. And a lot of doodling. I'm sure you wouldn't remember writing it. But the thing is . . . do you remember lending or giving a piece of scrap paper to anyone at Burghley who could now be here in Moscow?'

'Christ, sport, you ask damn silly questions.'

'Yeah . . .' I said, coughing on a sigh. 'Um . . . if you're dead bored, care to come to the Intourist Hotel for a drink in my room, around six? I'm going out for a bit, but I'll be back by then.'

'Sure,' he said easily. 'Bloody good idea. Saturday night's made for drinking. What's the room number?'

I told him and he said fine, and disconnected. I put

the receiver down slowly and reflected that I'd done some silly things in my time but that that probably topped the lot.

'I thought you didn't much like him,' Stephen said.

I made a face and shrugged. 'Maybe I owe him for the dinner in the Aragvi.'

I sat on the sofa and gingerly explored my right-hand fingers with those of the left. The worst of the soreness was beginning to wear off, and I could bend and unbend them a bit. It seemed probable that a couple of bones were cracked, though one often couldn't tell for sure without X-rays. I supposed I should count myself lucky they weren't splintered.

'When do you doodle?' I said.

'Doodle?'

'Like that.' I nodded towards the page of Malcolm's notebook.

'Oh . . . during lectures, mostly. I do zigzags, and triangles, not boxes, stars and question marks. Any time when I'm listening with a pencil in my hand, I suppose. On the telephone, for instance. Or listening to the radio.'

'Mm . . . Well . . .' I stopped unsuccessfully doctoring my fingers and got through on the telephone to the International operator. Calls to England, I was told, would entail a long delay. How long was a long delay? Calls to England were not at present being connected. Did that mean hours or days? The International operator couldn't or wouldn't say. Frustratedly, I stood up. 'Let's go out.'

'Where to?'

'Anywhere. Round and round Moscow in a taxi.'

'Out of thugs' reach?'

'Sometimes,' I said with mock disparagement, 'you're quite bright.'

We took with us the matroshka in its string bag, and also (in my pocket along with the telex) the two pages from Malcolm's notebook, on the basis that as these four treasures were the only tangible results of my efforts, they should not be carelessly left around to be pinched by Frank or anyone else who could open my bedroom door.

Even though he'd stopped saying it was cheaper on the metro, Stephen boggled a bit at the expense of that afternoon. The Prince was paying, I said, dealing out roubles in hefty instalments at half-hour intervals to a taxi driver who thought I was mad. Stephen suggested the University, for which in the morning he had got me a visitor's pass in order to avoid the juggling of the day before: but for some reason I always thought best on wheels, and had planned many a campaign while driving continually up and down on a tractor. There was something about a moving background that triggered shifts of mind, and left new ideas standing sharp and clear where they hadn't existed before. I was an outdoor man, after all.

We saw a lot of Moscow, old parts and new. Old

elegance and new functionalism, historically at odds but united in the silent white freezing slide into hibernation. Thick white caps on the golden domes. Shops with more space than goods. Huge advertisements saying 'Glory to the Communist Party' over the rooftops. On me, the cumulative effect was a powerful pervading melancholy, a sadness for so great a city entangled in such suffocating bureaucracy, such denial of liberty, such a need to look over its shoulder before it spoke.

When darkness closed in we stopped once, to buy a couple of glasses and some reinforcements in the booze line, and a souvenir for me to take home to Emma: and I chose a bright new matroshka with all its little matroshkas nestling inside, because it seemed to me that what I had been doing in Moscow had been in effect like opening that sort of doll. When one pulled off one layer, there was another layer underneath. Remove that, and another layer was revealed. Under that, another: and under that, another. And, in the centre, not a tiny wooden mama with rosy cheeks, but a germinating seed of terror.

When we finally returned to my room it looked uninvaded, undisturbed.

Perhaps we could have stayed there safely; but wasted precautions were never to be regretted. 'If only' were the saddest words in the language.

The tape-recorder still stood silently on its precarious tower, and, when Stephen pressed the 'record' button, it told us mutely that the listeners slept.

It was five to six. We left the recorder switched on, and went along to the armchairs by the lifts to await the guests.

Ian came first, by no means drunk but slightly rocking. It made no difference to his face, which was as white, calm and expressionless as ever, or to his speech, which had no fuzzy edges. He told us with great lucidity that on Friday evenings and Saturdays, when there was no flap on, he embraced the great Russian leisure-time activity with the fervour of the converted. And where, he asked, did I keep the bottle?

We retracked down the corridor to my room. Ian chose vodka and had tossed off his first before I had finished pouring Stephen's. I refilled his glass, and got myself some Scotch.

Without visible emotion he regarded the tape-recorder.

'If you play that up there much, my old son,' he said, 'you'll want to look around for a sticky stranger. If they think you've got something to hide, they'll plant another ear.'

Stephen silently reached for the recorder and took it on a thorough journey round the room. Ian watched, absentmindedly downed his drink, and poured himself a replacement with an almost steady hand.

The search results were fortunately nil. Back on its

perch, still no whine. Stephen left the recorder there on sentry duty, and he and Ian sat down on the sofa.

Ian spent five minutes describing the extreme boredom of the diplomatic life as lived by the British in Moscow, and left me fervently wishing he were stone cold sober.

Malcolm arrived like a gale blowing in from the desert, hard, noisy and dry.

'Extra,' he said boisterously, picking up the vodka bottle and reading the label. 'The Rolls-Royce of the domestic distilleries. I see you cotton on to the best pretty damn quick, sport.'

'Stephen's choice,' I said. 'Help yourself.'

For him, too, it appeared, Saturday night was to-hell-with-inhibitions night. He poured and tossed back in one draught enough to put an abstainer asleep for a month. 'You didn't tell me it was a party, sport,' he said.

'Only the four of us.'

'Could have brought a bottle.'

At the present rate of consumption, we might need it. Stephen was looking as if that sort of party was low in his list of favourite hobbies, and I guessed that he was only staying out of a vague sense of not leaving the sinking ship before the rats.

'What've you got, then, sport?' Malcolm said, with half a toothmugful in his grasp. 'What's all this about a page from my notebook?'

I fished it out of my pocket and gave it to him. He

buried his nose in his glass and looked at the small page sideways, over the rim. Some loose drops of vodka trickled down his chin.

'Christ, sport,' he said, removing the glass and wiping himself up with the back of his hand, 'it's just a lot of doodles.' He turned it over. 'What's all this writing?'

'I don't know.'

He looked at his watch and seemed to be coming to a fast decision. A fresh gulp brought him near to the bottom of the glass, and he put it down on the dressing shelf with a snap.

'Look, mate, got to run.' He folded the page of notebook and began to put it in his jacket pocket.

'I'd like to keep that for a bit,' I said mildly. 'If you wouldn't mind.'

'What on earth for?' He tucked it firmly away out of sight.

'To see if I can decipher the writing on the other side.'

'But what's the point?'

'I'd just like to know who you gave it to in England . . . to see what he wrote on it.'

Malcolm still hesitated. Ian clawed his way to his feet and helped himself to Extra.

'Oh give it to him, Malcolm,' he said irritably. 'What the hell does it matter?'

Malcolm collected observant stares from three pairs of eyes and reluctantly put his hand in his pocket.

'It won't do you any bloody good, sport.' His voice was sharp with the beginnings of malice.

'All the same,' I said, taking back the note and stowing it away, 'it's interesting, don't you think? You wrote that page at Burghley . . . but you didn't tell me you were at that meeting. I was surprised that you didn't mention being there. I was surprised you *were* there, actually.'

'So what? I went to write it up.'

'For the *Watch*? I thought you were a foreign correspondent, not a sportswriter.'

'Look, sport,' he said, the muscles setting like rock in his solid neck. 'Just what is the point of all this crap?'

'The point is,' I said, 'that you know . . . you've known all along . . . what I came here to find out, and you've been trying all along to make sure I ended up in a fog . . . if not in a mortuary.'

Stephen and Ian had their mouths open.

'Balls,' Malcolm said.

'Can you drive a horse box?'

His only reply was a stare of intense animosity reinforced by some sort of inner decision.

'Dinner at the Aragvi,' I said. 'Your invitation, your dinner. There were two men there, sitting near us. They in my sight . . . I in theirs. Face to face, for a couple of hours. After that, they would always know me again. You took my glasses away . . . and everyone could see I was lost without them. When we left the restaurant I was attacked in Gorky Street . . . by two men who tried first to knock my glasses off, and then to bundle me into a car. They wore balaclavas, but I saw their dark un-Russian eyes very clearly. And I asked myself . . . who knew that I would be walking alone down Gorky Street at precisely that moment?'

'This is a load of horse shit. Look, sport, you'll end up in a psychiatric hospital at the wrong end of a needle if you go on like this.'

Malcolm was deeply angry, but his basic confidence was unshaken. He was still certain that I would not hit the absolute bull's-eye.

'The telex,' I said, 'and your little informer. I've no doubt that when a very long telex came for me, you were told. So I set off to the Embassy by the shortest route, and on the way I was jumped on by the same two men, who were *waiting for me*. That time I was saved only by a sort of ironic miracle . . . but when I got my senses back I asked myself, who could possibly have known I would make that journey?'

'Half of Moscow,' Malcolm said roughly.

'I knew,' Ian said, sounding studiedly impartial.

'Of course,' Malcolm said forcefully. 'And Ian knew we were dining at the Aragvi. And Ian knew you were going to see Kropotkin at the Hippodrome, because you told us both in Oliver's office . . . So why the hell aren't you accusing Ian of all this? You're off your bloody rocker, sport, and I'll have you for slander if you don't back down and apologize this immediate bloody instant.' He looked at his watch again and revised his ultimatum. 'I'm not staying here to listen to any more of this bloody junk.'

'Ian helped me. You just told me to go home,' I said.

'All for your own bloody good.'

'It isn't enough,' Ian said uneasily. 'Randall . . . all this might be *possible*, but you've surely got it all wrong.'

'I haven't got to prove anything to any court of law,' I said. 'All I do have to do is to let Malcolm know what I think. That's enough. If a prying neighbour knew you were planning to rob a bank, you'd be a fool to go on with the plan. So call me a prying neighbour . . . but what Malcolm was planning was far worse than robbing banks.'

'What, then?' Ian said.

'Killing people at the Olympics.'

Malcolm's reaction went a long way to convincing Ian and Stephen. The shock turned his skin as white as the walls, leaving odd blotchy patches of broken thread veins on cheeks and nose. He literally lost his breath: his mouth opened, and no sound came out. There was sick disbelief in his eyes; and this time I really had chopped into the self-confidence with a lethal axe.

'So you may never get to court,' I told him. 'But if any of the Olympic riders die the same way Hans Kramer died, the world will know where to look.'

He was, in effect, stunned: almost as if losing consciousness on his feet. The room was still, with a silent intensity you could almost touch. Ian and Stephen and I all watched him almost without breathing: and at this impossibly fraught moment, someone knocked briskly on the door.

It was Ian's bad luck that it was he who moved first and went to open it.

Malcolm's friends attacked with their usual brutal speed, bursting in through the opening door like bulls and hitting out at whatever stood in their way. The sheer animal fury swept into the room like an emotional volcano, and the half-concealing balaclavas only seemed to intensify the horrendous impact.

The swinging riot stick wielded by the one in front crunched solidly into Ian's head. He fell without a sound and lay unmoving by the bathroom door.

The one behind kicked shut the door to the corridor and strode forward purposefully, holding a small screw-topped glass jar. On his hands, he wore rubber gloves. In the little jar, a pale golden liquid, like champagne.

Everything happened exceedingly fast.

Malcolm came to life with wide-staring eyes and shouted, 'Alyosha.' Then he said, 'No, no.' Then, as he saw the riot stick swinging at Stephen he said, 'No, no, that one,' and pointed at me.

I leapt on to the bed and picked up the tape-recorder, and threw it at the man who was attacking Stephen. It hit him in the face and hurt him, and he turned my way even more murderously than before.

The man with the little jar unscrewed its cap.

'That one,' Malcolm screamed, pointing at me. 'That one.'

The man with the jar stared with appalling ferocity at Malcolm, and drew back his arm.

Malcolm screamed.

Screamed.

'No. No. No.'

I picked up the chair and lashed out at the man with the jar, but the one with the riot stick stood in the way.

The man with the jar threw the contents into Malcolm's face. Malcolm gave a high wailing cry like a seagull.

I crashed the chair down again and hit the wrist of the jar-carrier with a blow like chopping wood. He dropped the jar and jerked with agony. I jumped off the sofa and laid into both of them with the chair with a fury fed by theirs, and Stephen picked up one of the vodka bottles and slammed it at one of the eye-slits of the balaclavas.

I had never in my life felt such a rage. I hated those men. Shook with hate. I swung the chair not to preserve my life, but to smash theirs. Sheer primitive blood-lusting vengeful hatred, not only for what they were doing in this city and this room, but for all their counterparts round the world. For all the helpless hostages, for all the ransom victims, I was bashing back.

It may have been reprehensible and uncivilized, but it was certainly effective. Stephen smashed his bottle against the wall and crowded into them with the broken ends thrusting forward sharply, and I simply belted them with chair and feet and fury, and we beat them back into the narrow passage by the bathroom, where Ian still lay unmoving.

With what looked like a joint and instantaneous decision they suddenly turned their backs on us, dragged open the door to the corridor and fled.

I turned back into the room, panting.

'After them,' Stephen said, gasping.

'No ... come back ...' I heaved for breath. 'Shut the door ... Got to see to Malcolm.'

'Malcolm? ...'

'Dying,' I said. 'Ninety seconds ... Jesus Christ.'

Malcolm had collapsed, half on the floor, half on the bed, and was whimpering.

'Open the matroshka,' I said urgently. 'Misha's matroshka. Quick. Quick ... Get that tin with the naloxone.'

I yanked open the drawer which contained my breathing things and snatched out the plastic box. My fingers wouldn't work properly. Serve him bloody right, I thought violently, if I couldn't save his life because they'd smashed my hand when he tried to have me killed.

Couldn't tear the strong plastic cover off the hypo-dermic syringe. Hurry. For God's sake hurry ... Did it with my teeth.

'This?' Stephen said, holding out the cough-lozenge tin. I opened it and put it on the dressing shelf.

'Yes ... Get his trousers down.'

Ninety seconds. Jesus Christ.

My hands were trembling.

Malcolm was gasping audibly for air.

'He's turning blue,' Stephen said with horror.

The needle was packed inside the syringe. I got it out and fitted it in place.

'He's hardly breathing,' Stephen said. 'And he's unconscious.'

I snapped the neck of one of the ampoules of naloxone. Stood it with shaking hands upright on the shelf. Mustn't ... mustn't knock it over. Needed two good hands, two hands working properly and not shaking.

I picked up the syringe in my right hand and the ampoule in my left. I was right-handed ... I couldn't do it at all the other way round, though I would have done, if I could. Lowered the needle into the precious teaspoonful of liquid. Hauled up the plunger of the syringe, sucking it in. My fingers hurt. So what, so what. Ninety seconds ... all but gone.

I turned to Malcolm. Stephen had pulled the trousers down to expose a bit of rump. I shoved the needle into the muscle, and pressed the plunger: and God, I thought, could do the rest.

We lifted him on to the bed, which was no mean task, taking off his jacket and tie and ripping open the front of his shirt. His colour and breathing were still dreadful, but no worse. He was conscious again, and terrified, and he said, 'Bastards,' between his teeth.

Along by the bathroom, Ian began groaning. Stephen went over to him, and found him rapidly regaining consciousness and trying to rise to his feet. He helped him up and supported him, and got him as far as the sofa.

The little glass jar lay near the sofa on the carpet, and Stephen almost automatically bent down to pick it up.

'Don't touch it,' I said, my voice going high with alarm. 'Don't touch it, Stephen. It'll kill you.'

'But it's empty.'

'I doubt it,' I said. 'And I think a few drops would be enough.' I picked up the fallen chair and planted it over the jar. 'That'll have to do for now ... Don't let Ian touch it.'

I turned back to Malcolm. His breathing seemed to be slightly stronger, but not by much.

'How do we get a doctor?' I said.

Stephen gave me a despairing look which I interpreted as dismay at getting ourselves enmeshed in any form of Soviet officialdom, but he picked up the telephone and dialled through to the reception desk.

'Tell them the doctor should bring naloxone.'

He repeated the request twice and spelled it out once, but looked troubled as he replaced the receiver. 'She said she would call a doctor, but about the naloxone . . . she said the doctor would know what to bring. Unhelpful. Obstructive. The more you insist, the more they just stick their toes in.'

'Randall . . .'

Malcolm's lusty voice came out as a weak croak.

'Yes?' I bent over him, to hear better.

'Get . . . the . . . bastards.'

I took a deep breath. 'Why did they throw the stuff at you, and not at me?'

He seemed to hear and understand, but he didn't answer. Sweat stood out suddenly in great beads all over his face, and he began gasping again for air.

I filled the syringe from the second ampoule of naloxone, and pushed the needle into his haunch. The reaction came again, sluggish but definite, taking the laboured edge off the breathing but leaving him in a dangerous state of exhaustion.

'The bastards . . . said . . . I . . . robbed them.'

'How do you mean?'

'I sold them . . . the stuff. They said . . . it wasn't worth . . . the money.'

'How much did they pay you?' I said.

285

'Fifty ... thousand ...'

'Pounds?'

'Christ ... sport ... of course. They said ... this afternoon ... I'd robbed ... them. I told them ... to come here ... finish you ... too clever ... by half. Didn't know Ian ... would ... be here.'

I reflected that when he had found Ian and Stephen with me he had attempted to leave and intercept his friends before they reached my room. No one could tell whether the outcome would have been much different if he'd succeeded. The friends were about as predictable as forked lightning.

I took a toothmug to the bathroom, half filled it with water, and brought it back to hold to Malcolm's mouth. It did little more than wet his lips, but that seemed to be all he wanted.

Looked at my watch. It was two minutes since I'd given him the second injection: four since the first. It seemed a lifetime.

Ian was recovering fast and beginning to ask questions. It was extraordinary, I thought, that no one at all had heard the fracas and come running. No one had heard ... or reacted ... to Malcolm's scream, and I would have thought they would have heard Malcolm's scream in the Kremlin. When the bugs were switched off, the walls were deaf.

Malcolm went into another sudden and devastating collapse. I grimly filled the syringe from the last ampoule and injected the teaspoonful into his muscles.

There was no more naloxone: no safety margin for any of us.

CHAPTER SIXTEEN

The upswing came again. He breathed a little more positively and regained consciousness, although his skin was still greyish blue and his pupils remained pinpoints.

'I feel ... dizzy,' he said.

I gave him a few sips of water and said casually, 'Was it you or your friends who poured the stuff on Hans Kramer?'

'Christ, sport ... not me. I'm no killer ...'

'What about the horse box?'

'Only meant ... to hurt you ... frighten ... send you home.' He took another sip. 'Reckoned you wouldn't stay ...'

'But your friends weren't fooling,' I said. 'Not in Gorky Street, and not by the river.'

'They said ... not safe ... with Kropotkin helping ... you might ... find out ... things.'

'Mm,' I said. 'And that was after you told them that I knew what Hans Kramer had said when he was dying?'

'Bloody boy ... Misha ...'

'Was this deadly liquid your idea, or Hans Kramer's?' I said.

'I learned of it ... by chance. Got Hans ... to steal it.' He achieved a faint sneer. 'Stupid bastard ... conned him ... he did it for nothing ... for his ideals ...'

'He went to the Heidelberg Clinic,' I said.

'Christ ...' Even in his cooperative state, he was unpleasantly surprised. 'In the telex ... didn't think you'd spot that, but it was ... risky. They wanted to prevent ... you from seeing it.'

'So why did they kill Hans? Why Hans, who had helped you?'

He was tiring visibly. His voice was faint, and his breathing was still slow and shallow.

'Cover ... all ... tracks ...'

Ian stood up restlessly and came over to the bed. It was the first close view he'd had of Malcolm since the attack, and the shock penetrated the inscrutability of his face.

'Look, Randall,' he said, horrified, 'leave all these questions until he's better. Whatever he's done, it will keep.'

He had no idea, I thought, of the sort of thing we were dealing with, and it was hardly the moment to tell him.

I gave Malcolm some more water, and because of Ian's intervention he began to reflect and regret that he had so willingly answered. Reactivated hostility sharpened visibly in his pin-point eyes, and when I took the glass from his lips his whole face settled into the old stubborn mould.

'What are their names?' I said. 'And their nationality?'

'Sod off . . .'

'Randall!' Ian protested. 'Not yet.'

'One of them is Alyosha,' Stephen said, steering a careful path round the chair, and crossing to join us. 'Didn't you hear? Malcolm called one of them Alyosha.'

There was almost a laugh from the bed. A large sardonic sneer twisted his mouth. His voice, although almost a whisper, came out loaded with spite.

'Alyosha, sport,' he said, 'will kill you yet.'

Stephen looked at him incredulously. 'But your *friends* tried to kill you . . . It's Randall who saved you.'

'Balls.'

'He's confused,' I said. 'Just leave it.'

'Christ . . .' Malcolm said. 'I feel sick.'

Stephen looked rapidly around for a suitable receptacle, but there wasn't one, and it wasn't needed.

Malcolm's shallow breathing perceptibly lessened. I picked up his wrist, and could feel no pulse. His eyes slowly closed.

'Do something,' Ian said urgently.

'We can try artificial respiration,' I said. 'But not mouth to mouth.'

'Why not?'

'That stuff was thrown at his face ... You can't trust it.'

'Do you mean he's dying?' Stephen said. 'After all?'

Ian energetically began pulling Malcolm's arms up and backwards in the old method of artificial respiration, refusing to let him go without having done everything possible.

Malcolm's neck and hands and bare chest turned from bluish grey to dark indigo. Only his face stayed pale.

Ian persevered, hauling the rib cage up and down, trying to get air into the lungs mechanically. Stephen and I watched in silence for what seemed a very long time.

I didn't try to stop him. Stopping had to be his own decision. And I suppose some quality in Malcolm's total lack of response finally convinced him, because he reluctantly laid the arms down to rest, and turned to us a blank and Sphinx-like face.

'He's dead,' he said flatly.

'Yes.'

There was a long pause while no one could quite bring themselves to say what was in all of our minds, but Ian, at length, put it into words.

'The doctor's on his way. What do we tell him?'

'Heart attack?' I suggested.

The others nodded.

'Let's tidy up, then,' I said, looking round at the

aftermath of battle. 'What we desperately need is some rubber gloves.'

The small glass jar still lay on its side under the guarding chair. I reckoned it would have to be shovelled somehow into a toothmug, and was looking around for a suitable long spoon for supping with the devil when Stephen brought out his packet from the chemist.

'What about these?' he said. 'They're supposed to be impermeable.'

On any other occasion we'd have laughed too much to make it possible. Instead, I quite seriously dressed the thumb and fingers of my left hand in preservativy, keeping them in place with an elastic band round my knuckles.

Stephen had protested that as they were his preservativy, it should be he who used them, especially as I was proposing a left-handed operation. Shut up, I said, and let's get on. It was my job, I thought. It was where the buck stopped. A matter of the beginning and the end of responsibility.

He removed the chair. I knelt on the floor, and, summoning up an act of faith in the baggy and improvised rubber glove, picked up the little jar and stood it upright in the toothglass.

My mouth, to be honest, was dry.

The jar had looked more or less empty when it lay on its side, but this had been deceptive. There was now clearly about a dessertspoonful of pale golden liquid lying in the bottom. Pale gold ... a pretty shade of death.

'The cap of the jar must be somewhere,' I said. 'But don't touch it.'

Ian found it under the sofa. He shifted the end of the sofa, and I picked up the small screw-top and put it in the glass alongside the jar.

'What will you do with it?' Stephen said, looking at the remnants with understandable awe.

'Dilute it.'

I took the toothmug into the bathroom and stood it in the centre of the bath. Then I put in the plug, and turned on the taps. The water poured in in a tumbling cascade and the level quite soon rose to cover the glass. The little jar floated out like a bathtime toy, still holding its fearsome cargo. I pushed it, with my covered fingertips, into the depths.

Turned off the taps. Stirred the jar around in the water briskly with the handle of my toothbrush, and then pulled out the plug to let the water run away. When it had gone, the washed jar, the cap, and the toothglass lay in harmless wet heaps on the clear white enamel. I picked them out of the bath and put them into the wash basin, and immersed them once again, to make doubly certain.

Then I stripped off the preservativy and flushed them appropriately down the loo: and took a great deep breath of relief.

In the room, Stephen and Ian had straightened and

restored everything to order. The syringe and the empty ampoules were out of sight. The matroshka stood with her two halves joined. The broken bottle and its scattered fragments had vanished. The chair stood quietly by the dressing shelf. The tape-recorder stood upon it harmlessly. My suitcase was back in the wardrobe. All tidy. All calm. All innocent.

And Malcolm . . . Malcolm lay in his permanent silence with his trousers up and fastened, and his shirt buttoned to near the top. His jacket and tie lay on the sofa, but folded neatly, not in the heap into which we'd thrown them. Malcolm dead looked a deal more peaceful than Malcolm dying.

The Russian doctor came with an expressionless face and unemotionally began to roll out the red tape. Stephen and Ian gathered that he took a poor view of foreigners who keeled over on Saturday evenings when all services were at a low ebb.

We drifted around as we were told, waiting mostly in the chairs by the lifts and not speaking much. The stumpy lady at the desk came and went several times, and Stephen asked her if she found her work boring.

She said stolidly that nothing much ever happened, but her job was her job. Stephen translated question and answer, and we nodded sympathetically and guessed she'd been away from her desk when Malcolm's friends called.

The doctor was unsuspicious. In England, Hans Kramer's death had been adjudged a heart attack even after an autopsy, and with luck it would happen again. The doctor had not mentioned having been asked to bring naloxone, and it appeared that the reception desk had not, in fact, passed on Stephen's request: fortunately, as it turned out.

Ian developed a thundering headache from the effects of vodka and concussion and sat moaning gently with his eyes shut.

Stephen bit a couple of fingernails.

I coughed.

There were a good many unsmiling faces coming and going, some of which finally said we could return to my room, for Stephen and Ian to retrieve their hats and coats, and me to pack to remove to another room in the hotel.

Ian groaned off home at that point, but Stephen helped to carry my belongings up in the lift to the fifteenth floor. The new room was identical in lay-out; slightly different in colour: and there was no stiff shape lying under a white sheet on the bed.

Stephen cast his gaze round the walls and put two fingers to his mouth. I nodded. It didn't seem worthwhile fiddling about with the tape-recorder. We made one or two suitable and shocked remarks about heart attacks, just in case, and left it at that.

I had found that in his fast tidying he had rolled all the broken glass and ampoules and the syringe in my dressing gown and stowed it in the suitcase. We had judged it sensible, in discussion while walking along the corridor, to get rid of them altogether, so we put them all in the outermost shell of the new matroshka, leaving a smaller little mother beaming upon the shelf. We put the rubbish-filled doll into the string bag, and picked up the tape-recorder, and very quietly let ourselves out of the room.

The lady at the fifteenth-floor desk gave us an uninterested stare. We smiled at her as we waited for the lifts, but smiling back wasn't her habit.

Made it to the ground floor. No trouble. Strolled unhurriedly around the longer route to the door, unaccosted. Walked outside under the watching eyes, which did nothing more than watch.

Climbed into a taxi. Travelled trustfully, and arrived safely at the University.

There was nowhere private to suffer from reaction. Stephen and I were both shaking after we'd taken off our hats and coats in his room, and we felt a great compulsive need to talk. I had seldom found anything so difficult as making asinine conversation with a mind stuffed with the evening's horrors, but the recorder had proved definitely again that we were not alone. The unreleased tension made us both uncomfortable to the point of not being able to meet each other's eyes. In the end he said a shade violently that he would brew tea and empty the matroshka into the students' communal rubbish bin: and I went into the passage and made a long telephone call to Yuri Chulitsky.

CHAPTER SEVENTEEN

Yuri picked me up in the wan December light of nine o'clock on a Sunday morning from outside the National Hotel.

There had been a fresh fall of snow during the night, and the roads had not yet been cleared, so that everything lay like Malcolm under a white shroud, and my spirits were as low as the air temperature.

The bright yellow car zoomed up like a golden cube, and I slid into the passenger seat beside him, coughing violently.

'You have illness?' he said, letting in the clutch as if the cogs were made of titanium.

Death warmed up, I thought: but it wasn't the best of similes.

'You say,' Yuri said, 'you want very important comrade.' The familiar accent rose above the engine noise. The bags under his eyes looked heavier and there was a slumped quality in his body. The upper lip rose convulsively two or three times, giving me the gleams of teeth. He lit a cigarette, one-handed, expertly, dragging the smoke urgently into his lungs. There was a fine dampness on his forehead.

He had come dressed, as I had, in his neatest and most formal suit, with clean shirt, and tie. He was nervous, I thought: which made two of us.

'I get Major-General,' he said. 'Is very high comrade.'

I was impressed. I had asked him for a comrade of sufficient rank to be able to make decisions: although from what I'd known before and seen since I'd arrived, it had seemed that there was no one at all of that stature. The Soviet method seemed to be 'action only after consultation', or 'until the committee's met, just keep saying *Niet*'. No official would make a decision on his own, for fear of it being wrong.

'Where are we going?' I said.

'Architects' Circle.'

So even the Major-General wasn't sure enough to meet me upon official ground.

'He say,' Yuri said, 'you call him Major-General. He not say his name.'

'Very well.'

We drove a little without speaking. I coughed a bit and thought of the night gone past, much of which I had spent writing. It had been a laborious process physically, as I couldn't hold the pen properly. In the heat of battle I'd picked up a chair and gripped it hard to cut and thrust; but the anaesthesia of hot blood was definitely missing in the cold hours after midnight. In the morning, when he had returned from Gudrun, I had given Stephen the explanatory sheets to read, while I put the telex, the formula, and the two pages of Malcolm's notebook into a large envelope.

He had read to the end, and looked at me speechlessly.

I smiled lop-sidedly. 'Ve have vays of taking out insurance.'

I put the hand-written sheets into the envelope, and addressed it to the Prince, which raised his mobile eyebrows another notch. Then I looked at the walls and by common consent we went out and strolled down the passage.

'If the comrades should be so inhospitable as to cast me in the clink,' I said, 'you just beetle round to the Embassy tomorrow morning and insist on seeing Oliver Waterman personally. Tell him the mountains will fall on his head if he doesn't send that envelope off pronto in the diplomatic bag.'

Stephen said, 'I know of a letter which was supposed to come to Moscow by diplomatic bag but ended up in Ulan Bator.'

'So helpful.'

'They say the Lubianka goes down seven floors underground.'

'Thanks very much.'

'Don't go,' he said.

'Come to lunch in the Intourist Hotel,' I said. 'They have pretty good ice cream.'

Yuri drove round a white corner at speed and corrected the resultant skid with a practised flick.

'Yuri,' I said, 'did you deliver a page of Malcolm's notebook to Mr Kropotkin?'

The ash fell off his cigarette. His upper lip did a positive jig.

'I thought it must be you,' I said. 'You said you talked to him at Burghley, about buildings. If one could disentangle the writing on the back of that piece of paper with the help of blue filters, would it be notes about buildings?'

He was silent.

'I'll not speak of it,' I said diffidently. 'But I would like to know.'

There was another of the long, familiar pauses, and in the end he said, 'I think paper not help,' as if it excused his action in delivering it.

'It helped very much.'

He moved his head in a way that I took to mean satisfaction, though I guessed that he still felt uneasy about allying himself with a foreigner. I wondered how I would feel if I were helping a Russian investigator and was not sure that anything he discovered might not be to the detriment of my own country. It made Yuri's dilemma most human, most understandable. And he was another, I thought, to whom I must do no harm.

*

Even at that hour on that day, there was a dragon on guard inside the door: short, dumpy, female, and stolid. She showed no pleasure at all in letting us through.

We shed our coats and hats. Everywhere in reception areas in Moscow there were acres of rails and hangers, and to every acre, a man in charge. We took our numbered discs and went through into the lofty ground-floor hall. Hall as in large meeting area, not as in entrance passage.

I had seen it two days earlier, passing through to the restaurant. Yellowish parquet floor, lightweight metal and plastic armchairs, and upright boards in loose groups, which divided the space like random screens. Pinned upon these with colour-headed drawing pins were large matt-surfaced blown-up photographs of recent architectural activity.

Yuri led the way round one set of screens and arrived at an open central spot.

There were three of the light armchairs grouped round a low table there; and on one of the chairs, a man.

He stood up as we approached.

He was of about my own height. Solid of body. Immensely well groomed. Dark hair sprinkled with grey, smoothly brushed back. About fifty, perhaps. Chin freshly shaved, everything immaculate. He wore understated spectacles and an elegantly cut business suit. The impression of power was instant and lasting.

'Major-General,' Yuri said deferentially, 'this is Randall Drew.'

We exchanged a few preliminary courtesies. He spoke perfect English with only the ghost of an accent; and his voice was markedly urbane. Rupert Hughes-Beckett, Soviet version, I thought.

'I would have asked you to come to my office,' he said, 'except that on Sundays it is not fully staffed, and perhaps here also we will be less interrupted.'

He waved me to one of the chairs, and sat down again himself. Yuri delicately hovered. The Major-General suggested pleasantly, in English, that he should go and organize some coffee, and wait for it to be made.

He watched Yuri's obediently departing backview, and then turned to me.

'Please begin,' he said.

'I was sent to Moscow,' I said for openers, 'by the British Foreign Office, and by the Prince.' I gave the Prince his full title, because I guessed that even to a good son of the revolution the fact that I was on an errand for the monarch's cousin might pull some weight.

The Major-General gave me a placid stare from uninformative grey eyes.

'Please continue.'

'My brief was to find out if John Farringford – Lord Farringford, the Prince's brother-in-law – would be likely to be involved in a damaging scandal if he should come to ride in the Olympic Equestrian Games. There was some mention of a certain Alyosha. I was to find and interview this Alyosha, and see how the land lay ... Er ... am I making myself clear?'

'Perfectly,' he said courteously. 'Please go on.'

'John Farringford had indiscreetly visited several rather perverted sexual entertainments in London with a German rider, Hans Kramer. This German subsequently died at the International Horse Trials, and people near him said that in his last few breaths he istinctly said, "It is Alyosha." ' I paused. 'For some reason that I cannot understand, a rumour arose that if Farringford came to Moscow, Alyosha would be waiting. The implication was clear that Alyosha would cause trouble. It was this rumour which led the Prince to ask me to look into things.'

'I follow,' he said slowly.

'Well ... I came,' I said. A couple of coughs convulsively squeezed my chest. There was a well-known slow fever stoking up in there, but for that day at least it would be manageable. The next day, and the next and the next, would be a matter of luck. I girded up at least the mental loins.

I said, 'I found I was not investigating a minor muckheap, but something a great deal different. I asked to see you today because what I discovered was a terrorist plot to disrupt the Olympic Games.'

He was not surprised, and Yuri, of course, must

have told him that much in order to persuade him to meet me. Not surprised, but unconvinced.

'Not in the Soviet Socialist Republics,' he said with flat disavowal. 'We have no terrorists here. Terrorists would not come here.'

'I'm afraid they have.'

'It is impossible.'

I said, 'If you encourage a plague, you must expect to catch it.'

His reaction to this unwise statement was an ominous stiffening of the spine and a raising of the chin, but at least we advanced into a territory in which he was prepared to face the possibility of pus on his own doorstep.

'I am telling you this so that you can avert a disaster in your capital,' I said neutrally. 'If you don't wish to hear me, I'll leave now.'

I didn't move, however, and nor did he.

After a pause he said, 'Please proceed.'

'The terrorists aren't Russians, I'll grant you that,' I said. 'And, so far as I know, you only have two here at present. But I think they live here all the time ... and no doubt at the Games they would be reinforced.'

'Who are they?'

I took off my glasses, and squinted at them, and put them on again.

'If you keep a check on every foreigner who lives here in your city,' I said, 'you should seek out two men of between twenty and thirty years old, one of whom has today a badly bruised or broken wrist, and the other a damaged face. They may, in addition, have other bruises and cuts. They have sallow skins, dark eyes, and dark curling hair. I could, if necessary, identify them.'

'Their names?'

I shook my head. 'I don't know.'

'And what could they hope to achieve?' he said, as if the whole idea was ridiculous. 'It would be impossible for them to take hostages in this country.'

'I don't think they mean to,' I said. 'The trouble with taking hostages is that it involves so much time. Time while the demands are delivered and discussed. Time, which means feeding the captors and the hostages, and sewage, and absolutely mundane things like that. The longer it goes on, the less chance there is of success. And the world has grown tired of these threats, and a great deal tougher. It's no longer seen as sense to release imprisoned terrorists to save innocent lives, when the released terrorists simply go out and kill a different lot of innocents. And I agree with you that a mass kidnapping here would be smartly stepped on by your comrades. But these men didn't mean to kidnap, they meant to kill.'

He showed no emotion at all. 'And how would they do this? And how would it help them?'

'Suppose,' I said, 'that they killed, for instance, Lord Farringford. Suppose they then said, if such and such a demand of ours is not met, a member of the French riding team will die, and a member of the Germans, and a member of the Americans. Or all the American team. Suppose they moved terrorism to a different level, where the hostages had no chance at all. No one would know who the hostages were until they were dead, and the supply of potential hostages would be the number of people at the Games.'

He briefly thought it over and was not convinced.

'The theory is possible,' he said. 'But there is no suitable weapon. The murderers would quickly be caught.'

'Their weapon is a liquid,' I said. 'A spoonful per person would be enough. It doesn't have to be drunk. It is deadly if it's just poured on the skin. And that's what makes the equestrian part of the Games so vulnerable, because it is there that the performers and the spectators mingle most freely.'

A longer pause. I couldn't tell what he was thinking. I took a breath to go on, but he interrupted.

'Such liquids are extremely top secret and are kept in places of the utmost security,' he said. 'Are your supposed terrorists going to break into highly guarded laboratories to steal it?' The urbanity in his voice said that he thought this unlikely.

I pulled out of my pocket a copy I had made of the formula, and handed it to him.

'That liquid is neither top secret nor difficult to obtain,' I said. 'And it kills within ninety seconds. One of my supposed terrorists could tip a spoonful on to

307

your bare hand without you thinking anything of it, and he'd be lost in the crowd before you could say you felt ill.'

He unfolded the paper with the slightest of frowns, and read the list of words.

'What is it?' he said. 'I am no chemist.'

'Etorphine,' I said. 'That, I think, is a morphine derivative. Etorphine, acepromazine and chlorocresol, those first three ingredients, would be an anaesthetic. I am absolutely certain, though I haven't been able to check it in Moscow, as I could at home, that they make up a particularly useful anaesthetic for use on animals.'

'Anaesthetic?' he said dubiously.

'It anaesthetizes horses and farm animals,' I said. 'But it is fatal for humans, in the tiniest amounts.'

'Why should anyone wish to use such a dangerous anaesthetic?' he said.

'Because it is the best for the animals,' I said. 'I've seen it used twice. Once on one of my horses, and once on a bull. Both animals recovered quickly, with none of the complications we used to get.'

'You've seen it . . .'

'Yes. And each time, the vet prepared a syringe of a neutralizing agent for use on himself, if he should be so unfortunate as to scratch himself with the needle of the syringeful of anaesthetic. He filled the neutralizing syringe before he even touched the phial with the anaesthetic, and he wore rubber gloves. He told me

308

that the excellence of the anaesthetic for the animal's welfare was worth the precautions.'

'But is this ... rare?'

I shook my head. 'More or less routine.'

'You said ...' He thought briefly. 'You said "scratch himself". Does that mean this mixture would have to enter through a cut ... a break in the skin? But you said it would be enough just to pour it ...'

'Yes,' I said. 'Well ... most liquids don't penetrate the skin, and that doesn't either. Normally, all a vet does have to worry about is getting it into him through a cut or a scratch, except that if they do get a drop on them accidentally, even if there's no cut involved, they sluice it off again with a bucket or so of water.'

'Did your vet have the water ready also?'

'He did indeed.'

'Please go on,' he said.

'If you look at the formula again,' I said, 'you'll see that the next ingredient is dimethyl sulphoxide, and I actually do know what that is, because I've used it myself countless times on my horses.'

'Another sort of anaesthetic?'

'No. One uses it on sprains, bruises, sore shins ... on practically everything. It's a general-purpose embrocation.'

'But ...'

'Well,' I said, 'it's chief property is that it's a liquid which *does* penetrate the skin. It carries its active ingredients through to the tissues beneath.'

309

He gave me a grave comprehending stare.

I nodded. 'So if one mixes the embrocation with the anaesthetic, it will go clean through the skin into the blood stream.'

He took a visibly deep breath, and said, 'What happens exactly if this mixture invades the body?'

'Depressed breathing and cardiac arrest,' I said. 'Very quick. It looks like a heart attack.'

He looked pensively down at the paper.

'What does this last line mean?' he said. 'Antagonist naloxone.'

'An antagonist is a drug which works against another drug.'

'So naloxone is . . . an antidote?'

'I don't think it's the stuff they give animals to bring them back to consciousness,' I said. 'I think it's what the vet prepares as a precaution for himself.'

'Do you mean . . . you have to give the animal a second injection? The anaesthetic does not simply wear off?'

'I don't know if it would in the end,' I said. 'But it's always reversed as soon as possible, as far as I know.'

'So naloxone is for humans.'

'Even terrorists wouldn't handle that stuff without protecting themselves,' I said. 'And I think,' I went on tentatively, 'that the amount of naloxone needed would depend on the amount of liquid one had absorbed. With animals, you see, the vet uses equal quantities of anaesthetic and reviving agent. And sometimes a further injection of reviver is needed.'

For Malcolm, I thought, it had simply been a matter of quantities. Too much killing liquid: not enough naloxone. His bad luck.

'All right,' the Major-General said, tucking the formula away into an inner pocket. 'Now please will you tell me what led you to these conclusions.'

I coughed because I couldn't help it, and took off my glasses and put them on again because the outcome of telling him might be not what I hoped.

'It started,' I said, 'at the International Horse Trials, which were held in England in September. At that event, a British journalist, Malcolm Herrick, who worked here in Moscow as a correspondent for the *Watch*, persuaded Hans Kramer to steal a vet's case of drugs when the vet came to attend some of the horses. Malcolm Herrick received the anaesthetic from Kramer. He then mixed it with the embrocation, which is easy to come by. And he then sold it to the terrorists for fifty thousand pounds.'

'For *what*?' The Major-General showed the first sign of uncontrolled surprise.

'Yes . . . It was not a matter of ideology, but of hard cash. Someone, after all, sells weapons to the terrorists. They don't actually manufacture their own guns. Fifty thousand, you are no doubt thinking, was a great deal too much for an easily accessible commodity. The thing was, of course, that Herrick didn't tell them what it was.

I dare say he made out that it was, in fact, one of your top-secret things from maximum-security laboratories. Anyway, they paid for it, but not without a demonstration . . . A sort of trial run.'

I waited for the Major-General to comment, but nothing came.

'They used a little of it on Hans Kramer,' I said. 'Herrick no doubt suggested he should be the test victim because if he was dead he couldn't tell anyone he had given the stuff to Herrick.'

'Given . . .? Didn't he *sell* it to Herrick?'

'No. Kramer sympathized with terrorists. He did it for the cause.'

The Major-General slightly compressed his lips.

'Go on.'

'Kramer's death was adjudged a heart attack. Herrick returned to Moscow, and so did the two terrorists. I think this may mean that he knew them here . . . met them here, perhaps . . . and that *because* he knew them, he thought up the scheme to sell them a compound he had at one time heard of by chance. And that is where everything would have stood until the Olympics; a nice little time-bomb ticking away in the dark. Except that people started asking questions about Alyosha.'

'At which point you came to Moscow.'

I nodded. Coughed. Wished the coffee would come. Swallowed with a dry mouth, and continued with the dicey bits.

'Since then, Herrick has tried to persuade me to go home, both with words and trying to knock me over with a motor horse box. The two terrorists have also had a go, and I'm only still here because I've been lucky. But sometime yesterday they discovered that they'd paid a great deal of money for a very cheap product, and they became extremely angry.'

I took a much needed deep breath. 'Herrick had told them to come to my room at the Intourist Hotel and finish me off properly. I think he meant them to do it by mechanical means . . . bashing my head in, and so forth. But when they came, they brought a good deal of the liquid in a small jar, perhaps all they had, and whether they meant any of it for me or not, they threw nearly all of it at Herrick.'

His mouth slowly opened and shut again.

I ploughed on. 'I had two friends with me, besides Herrick. We fought off the terrorists, which is why one of them has a damaged wrist and the other a damaged face, as well as other minor injuries, and they ran away.'

'Malcolm Herrick . . . is dead?'

'We called a doctor,' I said. 'The doctor believes it was a heart attack. Unless someone does an extremely thorough autopsy, that's how it will stand.'

The very faintest of smiles crossed his pale face. He rubbed a hand slowly round his jawline, and watched me with assessing eyes.

'How have you learned all this?' he said.

'I've listened.'

'To Russian people? Or all to foreigners?'

'Everyone who has spoken to me has been concerned that Russia should not be shamed by terrorism at the Games.'

'You speak like a diplomat,' he said.

The chin-rubbing went on for a bit. Then he said, 'And Alyosha. Did you, in the end, find this Alyosha?'

'Mm,' I said. 'Hans Kramer and Malcolm Herrick both said "Alyosha" in horror before they died. They both knew what they were dying of ... and I think they had given it that name. A sort of code name, so that they could talk of it conveniently. I couldn't find Alyosha, because Alyosha is not a person. It's the liquid. Alyosha is the way of death.'

CHATER EIGHTEEN

Yuri Chulitsky drove me back to the Intourist and actually dropped me outside the door. He shook my left hand emotionally, and gave me several pats on the shoulder. And then, with a great air of having a burden well shed, he drove away.

He had been visibly pleased when the Major-General had shaken his hand on parting, and on the way back to the hotel he had stopped the car abruptly by the kerb and put the handbrake on with a jerk.

'He said is good I ask him to meet you,' he said. 'Was correct decision.'

'Great,' I said, and meant it.

'Now, I keep bargain.'

I looked at him in surprise.

'You help my country. I tell you about Alyosha.'

I was puzzled. 'Tell me what?'

'I tell peoples, many peoples, is not good Lord Far-ringford come to Moscow. I say, in Moscow, Alyosha is waiting. Alyosha is not good peoples.'

'You told people . . . people in England?'

'*Da*. Peoples tell me, Hans Kramer die, it is Alyosha, Hans Kramer is bad man, is friend of Lord Farringford. Is bad Lord Farringford come to Moscow. So I say to peoples . . . Alyosha is bad peoples. Alyosha is trouble if Lord Farringford come.'

I shook my head slowly in amazement.

'But why, Yuri? Why didn't you want Lord Farringford to come to Moscow?'

He took a long time to answer. The longest pause of all. The lip went up and down six times. He lit a cigarette and took several deep drags. And at last he gave birth to his treason.

'Is not good . . . comrades use Lord Farringford . . . not good we follow him . . . use him in bad things . . . I feel shame for comrades who do this. I feel shame . . . for my country.'

Stephen and Ian were both sitting in the foyer, waiting and looking glum.

'My God,' Stephen said, seeing me standing before them. 'They've let him go!' His face lit into instant good spirits. 'Where are the handcuffs?'

'Being debated, I should think.'

There was still nowhere private to talk, since we couldn't trust my new room, so we simply transferred to the end of the line of seats along the foyer wall, and fell silent if anyone came close.

'What's happening?' Ian said.

'With luck, nothing much. I don't think they'll want to advertise terrorist activity in Moscow, not if they can help it. From your knowledge of this place, would you think the comrades would hush up a murder? Would they be allowed to? I had to tell the big noise that Malcolm was bumped off.'

Ian said, 'Easier here than anywhere else, my old son. If it suits them to say our pal died of a heart attack, they'll say it.'

'Let's hope it suits,' I said fervently.

'Look,' Ian said, 'Stephen has told me all you wrote last night. You must think me a poor dumb cluck not to have put all this together myself. But when I looked into it, I got nowhere.'

'But then I had the password,' I said, slightly smiling.

'Alyosha?' he said, puzzled.

'No . . . Horse.'

'The brotherhood of the saddle,' Stephen said sardonically. 'It opens the most private doors all round the world.'

'And don't you scoff,' I said. 'Because you're right.'

'There's just one thing we want to know,' Ian said, his calm unchanging face showing no sign of the previous day's ravages. 'And that is, why were you so utterly certain that Malcolm was at the heart of things? I mean . . . it was all so circumstantial . . . but you were quite sure.'

'Um . . .' I said. 'It was nothing conclusive in itself. It was really just one more circumstance . . . and there were already so many. It was the page from his note-book, which Yuri Chulitsky sent to Kropotkin. You remember what it looked like? All doodles. So when do you doodle? When you're listening, or waiting. When you're waiting for an answer on the telephone. If you remember, near the bottom of the page there were some letters and numbers, DEP PET 1855 and K's C 1950. Well ... they meant nothing much to me at first sight, but yesterday afternoon, while we were rolling around Moscow, I thought ... suppose Malcolm doodled because he was *waiting* for those numbers ... and then we passed a metro station and I thought of trains ... And there it damn well was, staring me in the face. DEP PET 1855 meant Depart Peterborough 18.55 hours, and K's C 1950 meant arrive King's Cross at 19.50. He had been ringing up the time-table enquiries to find out.'

'But what's so blinding about that?' Stephen said.

'Peterborough is the mainline station for Burghley.'

'So,' Ian said slowly, seeing the point, 'when Boris overheard what he did on the train from Burghley to London, he was listening to Malcolm ... who was selling his goods to his friends.'

'It seemed possible,' I said. 'In fact, it seemed extremely likely. And on that same sheet of paper, probably while still waiting for the time-table people to answer, because they take ages sometimes, Malcolm pencilled in Johnny Farringford as a star possibility for

Alyosha. I don't know how well he knew Johnny, but he didn't like him. He referred to him as a shit.'

'But why on earth should he give such an incriminating piece of paper to anyone else?' Stephen said. 'He was really stupid.'

I shook my head. 'It was only by the merest chance that it reached me and meant anything. To him, it was only a doodle. He scrawled over it. It was just a piece of rubbish to be thrown away ... or given to someone who wanted some scrap paper for making notes.'

'How's your cough?' Stephen said.

'Bloody awful. Let's have some lunch.'

Because there were three of us, we sat at a different table, the next one along from the Wilkinsons and Frank.

Ian eyed Frank benignly and asked me quietly if the *status* in that area was still *quo*.

'Does he know I know?' I said. 'No, he doesn't. Does he know you know? Who can tell?'

'Does he know I know you know they know she knows you know?' Stephen said.

Mrs Wilkinson leaned across the gap. 'Are you going home on Tuesday, like us?' she said. 'Dad and I won't be sorry to be back, will we, Dad?'

Dad looked as if he couldn't wait.

'I hope so,' I said.

Natasha brought the soaring eyebrows and a fixed

319

smile and said I hadn't kept my promise to tell her where I was going.

Nothing, it seemed, had changed; except that it was Stephen who ate my meat.

After lunch the three of us went up to my room for Ian and Stephen to collect the coats and hats they had left there just before, and while we were debating when next to telephone and next to meet, there was a sharp knock on the door.

'Christ, not again,' Ian said, instinctively putting a hand to his bruised head.

I went to the door and said, 'Who is it?'

No reply.

Stephen came and said, 'Who is it?' in Russian.

There was this time an answer, but to Stephen it seemed unwelcome.

'He said the Major-General sent him.'

I let down the drawbridge. Outside in the corridor stood two large men with stolid faces, flat uniformed caps, and long greatcoats. From the look on Stephen's face, I guessed that the posse had come for the outlaw.

One of them handed me a stuck-down envelope addressed to Randall Drew. Inside there was an extremely brief hand-written note, saying simply, 'Accompany my officers', and below that, 'Major-General'.

Stephen, looking round-eyed and a little pale, said, 'I'll wait here. We'll both wait here.'

'No ... You'd better go. I'll telephone.'

'If you don't,' he said, 'first thing in the morning, I take the goods to Oliver Waterman. Is that right?'

'Uhuh.'

I pulled hat and coat from the wardrobe and put them on. The two large unsmiling men unsmilingly waited. We all walked along in a cluster of five, and went down in the lift without saying very much.

During our progress through the foyer there was a certain amount of drawing aside of skirts, and several frightened glances. The bulk and intent of my two escorts was unmistakable. No one wanted to be involved in my disaster.

They had come in a large black official car, with a uniformed driver. They gestured to me to sit in the back. I had a parting view of Ian and Stephen's strained-looking faces as they stood side by side on the pavement, and then the car set off and made unerringly for Derzhinsky Square.

The long façade of the Lubianka loomed along one side of it, looking like a friendly insurance-company building if one didn't know better. The car, however, swept past its huge sides and pulled up in front of the big building next door, which was pale blue with white-painted scrolls, and would on any other day have looked rather pretty.

My escorts opened the car door for me to get out,

and walked beside me into the building. Inside, Lubianka or not, it was clearly no jolly children's home. We marched at a sturdy pace down wide institutional corridors, and came to a halt outside an unmarked door. One of my escorts knocked, opened the door, and stood aside for me to go in. With a dry mouth and galloping pulse, I went.

It was a comfortable, old-fashioned office, with a lot of dark polished wood and glass-fronted cupboards. A desk. A table. Three or four chairs. And by the window, holding back a dark curtain to look out at the snowy street, the Major-General.

He turned, and walked towards me, and held out his hand. I was so relieved that I automatically gave him my right one in return, and tried not to wince when he grasped it. I wondered if he knew he'd just given me one of the most shaking half hours of my life.

'Come,' he said. 'I have something to show you.'

He led me through a second door in the back wall of the office, into a narrower secondary corridor. After a few yards we came to a door which opened on to a staircase, leading down. We descended to the next floor, and went along another, grittier corridor.

We stopped at a totally smooth metal door. The Major-General pressed a button in the wall beside it, and the door swung open. He went into the room in front of me, and beckoned to me to follow.

I stepped into a square, bare room, brightly lit.

There were two armed policemen standing guard in there, and two other men, sitting on stools, with their arms fastened behind their backs.

If I was surprised to see them, it was nothing to their reaction on seeing me. One of them spat, and the other said something which seemed to shake even the KGB.

'These are the men?' the Major-General said.

'Yes.'

I looked into the faces remembered from the Aragvi restaurant. Into the eyes remembered from Gorky Street and under the bridge. Into the souls that had killed Hans Kramer and Malcolm Herrick.

One seemed slightly older, and had a drooping moustache. His lips were a little retracted, showing a gleam of teeth clenched in a travesty of a grin; and even in this place he exuded a bitter hostility.

The other had taut skin over sharp bones, and the large eye-sockets of so many fanatics. Across the eyebrow and down the side of his face there was a scarlet cut, and there was a split swelling on his lower lip.

'Which of them killed Herrick?' said the Major-General.

'The one with the moustache.'

'He says his wrist is broken,' the Major-General remarked conversationally. 'They were waiting at the airport. We had no trouble finding them. They speak very little English, by the way.'

'Who are they?' I said.

'They are journalists.' He sounded surprised at this discovery. 'Tarek Zanetti,' pointing to the man with the moustache, 'and Mehmet Sarai, with the cut.'

Their names meant nothing to me, even if they were the ones they were born with, which might be doubtful.

'They have been living in the same compound as Herrick,' the Major-General said. 'He could have seen them easily every day.'

'Do they belong to something like the Red Brigades?' I asked.

'Something new, we think,' he said. 'A breakaway group. But we have yet to make more than the most preliminary interrogation. Immediately they arrived here, I sent for you. However, I will show you something. When we searched the bags they were attempting to leave with, we found this.' He took a letter out of his pocket, and gave it to me. I unfolded it, but it was typewritten in a language I didn't know even by sight.

I shook my head and began to hand it back.

'Read lower down.'

I did as he said, and came across the familiar words, etorphine ... acepromazine ... chlorocresol ... dimethyl sulphoxide.

'It's a copy of a report from a chemical company,' he said, 'sending an analysis asked for by your friend with the moustache. It seems to have been delivered to him yesterday.'

'So they wanted to find out what they'd bought.'

'It would seem so.' He took back the letter and restored it to his pocket. 'That is all,' he said. 'Your positive identification of these men was required, but nothing more. You are at liberty to go back to England when you wish.' He hesitated slightly, then continued, 'It is believed that you will be discreet.'

'I will,' I said, and hesitated in my turn. 'But . . . these two will have colleagues . . . and that liquid does exist.'

'It may be necessary,' he said heavily, 'to search every spectator at the entrances.'

'There's a quicker way.'

'What is that?'

'It will be summer . . . Watch for anyone wearing gloves. If they have rubber gloves underneath, arrest them.'

He gazed at me from behind his glasses and rubbed his chin, and slowly said, 'I see why they sent you.'

'And gallons of naloxone at every turn . . .'

'We will work out many precautions.'

I looked across for the last time at the naked hate-filled faces of international terrorism, and thought about alienation and the destructive steps which led there.

The intensifying to anger of the natural scorn of youth for the mess their elders had made of the world. The desire to punish violently the objects of scorn. The death of love for parents. The permanent sneer for all forms of authority. The frustration of not being able to scourge the despised majority. And after that, the deeper, malignant distortions . . . The self-delusion that one's feelings of inadequacy were the fault of society, and that it was necessary to destroy society in order to feel adequate. The infliction of pain and fear, to feed the hungry ego. The total surrender of reason to raw emotion, in the illusion of being moved by a sort of divine rage. The choice of an unattainable end, so that the violent means could go on and on. The addictive orgasm of the act of laying waste.

'What are you thinking?' the Major-General said.

'That they are self-indulgent.' I turned away from them with a sense of release. 'It is easier to smash than to build.'

'They are pigs,' he said, with disdain.

'What will you do with them?'

But that was one question he had no intention of answering directly. He simply said, with polished blandness, 'Their newspapers must find other writers.'

The *Watch*, I thought, would be facing the same problem: and an old irrelevant piece of information floated to the surface.

'Ulrike Meinhof was a journalist,' I said.

326

CHAPTER NINETEEN

The flight home was met at Heathrow at four in the afternoon by one of Hughes-Beckett's minions, who whisked me off to what he called a debriefing and I called a bloody nuisance.

I coughed my way into the mandarin's office and protested. I got an insincere apology and a small glass of sherry, when the only thing likely to bring me back to animation was a quadruple Scotch.

'Can't it wait until tomorrow?' I said, feeling feverish.

'The Prince wants you to meet him at Fontwell Park races in the morning.'

'I thought of staying in bed.'

'What's wrong with your arm?' he said, disregarding this frivolous statement and eyeing Stephen and Gudrun's farewell attempt at a restful sling for the journey.

'Fingers got hammered. But not sickled.' I must be lightheaded, I thought. Lightheaded from the upsurge of relief at being back where liberty still poked up a few persistent tendrils. Lightheaded at the sight of people smiling in the street. At Christmas trees, and bright lights and cornucopias of shops. One could spurn the affluent society and seek the simple life if one wanted to: the luxury lay in being able to choose.

Hughes-Beckett eased himself in his comfortable office chair and studied the back of his hand.

'And how . . . ah . . . did it go?' he said.

I told him more or less exactly what I had told the Major-General. He stopped looking at his hands and came to mental life in a very positive and alert way, quite different from his habitual air of boredom.

I talked and coughed, and coughed and talked, and he gave me another and slightly larger sherry.

'So there you are,' I said finally. 'As far as I could tell there will be a great deal of hush over the whole scene. And as for Johnny Farringford . . . well, I got no definite assurances, but I doubt if after this the comrades would consider him a suitable prospect. So from that point of view I think it would be safe for him to go . . . but it's, of course, up to you and the Prince.'

I stood up. I really felt most unwell. Nothing new, however. The story of my life.

He came with me all the way to the front door and saw me off in an official car, which represented a radical rethink on his part of the usefulness of horses.

*

I found that meeting the Prince at Fontwell Park races involved lunch with him, the Princess, Johnny Farringford, the Chairman of the racecourse, sundry Stewards and assorted ladies, all in the glass-walled corner box at the top of the stands, looking down over the green turf.

There was a lot of champagne and civilized chat, which on other days would have pleased me well enough: but the shadows of Moscow still sat close at my shoulder, and I thought of the fear of Boris and Evgeny and the doubts and caution of Yuri and Misha and Kropotkin. I should be glad to hear in time from Ian and Stephen that none of them had come to harm.

I had spent a toss-and-turn night in a hotel and hired a car and driver to take me to the races. Practically every remedy in the plastic box had been pressed into service, to only moderate avail. It was a bore to drag around with lungs filling up like sumps and every breath an effort, but I'd ridden in races in that state once or twice in my foolish life, so why fret at some gentle spectating. Bits of lines of the Scottish ballad of the dying Lord Randall, with whom I'd identified heavily as a child, ran from long habit in my mind, more as a sort of background music than organized thought, but now with an added new meaning . . .

> . . . *make my bed soon,*
> *For I'm weary wi' hunting, and fain would lie doon.*

'Randall,' the Prince said, 'we must talk.'

We talked in short snatches through the afternoon, standing alone on the Stewards' balcony between the races, using the times when everyone else went down to look at the horses in the parade ring.

Make my bed soon . . .

'There were two plots involving Johnny,' I said.

'*Two?*'

'Mm . . . Being who he is, he's a natural target. He always will be. It's something that needs to be faced.'

I told him bit by bit about the terrorists, and about the identity of Alyosha. It all shocked him a great deal more deeply than it had those two wily gamesplayers, Hughes-Beckett and the Major-General.

'Dreadful. Dreadful,' he said.

'There was also,' I said eventually, 'some question of the KGB setting him up.'

'How do you mean?'

I explained about the pornography.

'Johnny?' The Prince looked surprised and most displeased. 'The bloody fool . . . doesn't he realize that is just what the Press are always looking for?'

'If he was warned, sir . . .'

'Warned?' He looked grim. 'You can safely leave that to me.'

I'd like to be a fly on the wall, I thought.

330

A memory struck him. 'But look here, Randall,' he said. 'What about those two men who attacked Johnny on the day he came to my house? The day he crashed into your car. Where did they come from? Were they . . . the terrorists?'

'No . . . um . . . as a matter of fact . . . they didn't exist.'

He gave me a right Royal stare. 'Are you meaning to say that Johnny was *lying*?'

Yes, I was. I said, however, more temperately, 'I think he invented them, certainly.'

'But he couldn't have done! He was badly beaten up.'

I shook my head. 'He was injured from crashing into my car.'

'There you are, Randall,' the Prince said with exasperation. 'He only crashed because he was already hurt.'

'Er . . .' I said. 'I think, sir, that he crashed because he fainted at the sight of blood. I think . . . he cut his finger to make it bleed . . . to put some blood on his face to back up his story of being attacked . . . and when he got to the front of your house he simply passed out. He had his foot on the accelerator, and his car kept on going.'

'You can't be right!'

'You could ask him, sir.'

Make my bed soon . . .

'But why, Randall? Why ever should he invent such a story?'

'He passionately wants to go to the Olympics. He didn't want people poking into his relationship with Hans Kramer, which was a little less innocent than he would have us believe, but not really so terrible. I would guess he was afraid all the same that if you found out you might not buy him the new horse ... so he invented two men and a beating up to persuade you not to send me to look for Alyosha. I quite believe that Johnny himself knew of no scandal, but he didn't know what I might find out about Hans. He didn't want me to look, that was all.'

'But,' he said, looking bewildered, 'it had the opposite effect. After that I was more sure than ever that the rumours must be looked into.'

I watched Johnny and the Princess weaving their way through the crowds returning to the stands for the next race, his crisp red curls gleaming like copper in the December air.

I sighed. 'He's a great rider, sir.'

The Prince slid me a sideways glance. 'We all do dumb things from time to time, Randall. Is that it?'

'Yes, sir.'

... and fain would lie doon.

'Why are you so sure they weren't your terrorists?'

'Because from Johnny's account they weren't at all

the same sort of people. Johnny said they spoke English and were ordinary British men . . . which the terrorists were not.'

Johnny and the Princess climbed the steps and came up on to the balcony. The Princess was untroubled, but Johnny had been uncomfortable with me all day.

I said mildly, 'Johnny, how well did you know Malcolm Herrick?'

'Who?'

'Herrick. Journalist. Wrote for the *Watch*.'

'Oh, him.' Johnny's face said it was an unwelcome memory. 'He was at Burghley. Always hanging around Hans. Er . . . Hans Kramer.' He hesitated, shrugged, and went on. 'I didn't like the fellow. Why? What's he done? He called me "sport" all the time. Can't say I liked it, what? I told him to piss off. Haven't seen him since.'

It seemed a bit much to put a man at the top of the death list for saying piss off, but Malcolm had done it. 'Sport' and 'piss off' . . . next stop, Alyosha.

For I'm weary wi' hunting, and fain . . .

'Cards on the table, Johnny,' the Prince said. 'Were you beaten up by those two chaps, or weren't you?'

The Farringford expression went through a lot of motions in very quick time. He started to nod and say yes, and then switched his gaze suddenly to my face. Correctly read my scepticism; realized I had told the

Prince; changed his plea instantaneously to guilty, and finished with a sheepish little-boy grin.

The Prince compressed his lips and shook his head. 'Grow up, Johnny,' he said.

Emma came for the weekend, two days later, silver and brittle and a-jangle with tensions.

'How boring of you to be in bed,' she said. 'I'm lousy at mopping fevered brows.'

She moved restlessly round the room, getting rid of electric energy in purposeless fidgeting.

'You're wheezing like an old granny,' she said. 'And spitting ... That's a really disgusting disease.'

'I thought you liked facing life's nitty-gritties.'

'Why did you want me to come?' she said, rearranging the brushes on my dressing chest. 'You usually tell me to stay away, when you're ill.'

'I wanted your company.'

'Oh.' She seemed disconcerted, gave me a quick sharp glance like a startled bird, and went out of the room. Friday night, I thought ruefully, was too soon for truth.

She returned in an hour, bringing a tray; bringing supper. Soup, bread, fruit, cheese, and a bottle of wine.

'They seemed to be lying around,' she said defensively, 'so I thought I might as well lug them up here.'

'Great.'

We ate in reasonable peace, and she asked about Moscow.

'You might like it there,' I said, peeling a tangerine. 'Mind you, over there the life you choose to lead here wouldn't be an act of rebellion, but a necessity forced upon you.'

'I hate you sometimes.'

'If you ever get tired of your shop,' I said, 'I could give you another job here.'

'What as?'

'Domestic servant. Nanny. Cook. Laundry-maid. General all-purpose dogsbody. Farmhand. Wife.'

'It wouldn't work.'

I looked at the shining fall of platinum hair and at the finality in the delicate well-loved determined face. The patterns of youth couldn't be changed. One became a rebel, a romantic, a puritan, a bigot, a hypocrite, a saint, a crusader, a terrorist . . . One became it young and stayed it for ever. She could never return to the well-off, well-ordered country life she had kicked her way out of. She would revisit it uneasily for weekends as long as I pleased her, but one Monday morning she would drive off and not come back.

I might regret, might feel lost and lonely without her, but she was depressingly right.

As a long-term prospect, it wouldn't work.

*

In the New Year edition of the *Horse and Hound* I read that the Germans had sold one of their best young horses to Lord Farringford, who would be training it in the hope of being considered for the Olympic Games.